Firefly

THE ARAB LIST

JABBOUR DOUAIHY

Firefly

TRANSLATED BY
PAULA HAYDAR AND NADINE SINNO

LONDON NEW YORK CALCUTTA

The Arab List
SERIES EDITOR: Hosam Aboul-Ela

Seagull Books, 2022

First published in Arabic as *Shared Al-Manazel*
by Jabbour Douaihy, 2011
© Dar Al Saqi, Beirut, Lebanon
Represented by Yasmina Jraissati, Raya Agency, Paris, France
In collaboration with Rocking Chair Books Ltd, London, UK

First published in English translation by Seagull Books, 2022
English translation © Paula Haydar and Nadine Sinno, 2022

ISBN   978 0 8574 2 981 0

British Library Cataloguing-in-Publication Data
A catalogue record for this book is available from the British Library.

Typeset by Seagull Books, Calcutta, India
Printed and bound in the USA by Integrated Books International

For
Jad, Unsi, Bushra,
Gabrielle and Emma

CONTENTS

PART ONE

Lavender and Other Things • 1

PART TWO

Beirut? There's Beirut for You • 73

PART THREE

Are You Ahmad? • 179

PART FOUR

Firefly • 285

PART ONE

Lavender and Other Things

Suddenly, summer vacationing in Hawra became contagious.

Hawra, with its red-tiled roofs, perched uneasily between a rocky mountain they call 'The Breezeway' and the monastery of St Yaqoub al-Habashi, of whom no accurate biography is known.

Echoes of laughter from the freestyle-wrestling match between 'Masked Eagle' and 'Nile Boy', being played out on the porch of the Palace Hotel up in Hawra, reverberated in the Brazilian café down in Tripoli near the Ottoman clock tower. Those were catchy names for a couple of amateurs who liked to drag out the bout as long as they could to maximize the profits they split with each other.

News also reached Tripoli about the movie *The Lost Heart* being filmed in the verdant apple orchards on the mountaintops of Hawra, where farmers, bearing tools on their backs, abandoned their watering duties to devour the beautiful actress with their eyes, as they watched her put on her makeup before the director demanded silence and yelled, 'Action!'

Eyewitnesses spread stories about hasty bets between two rich men from Aleppo gambling with each other—just the two of them—over a classic Roulette table. There was no end to the winking and whispering about women from well-known families seen playing Baccarat, flaunting their bare backs while gripping glasses of scotch on the rocks that never parted from their hands. Hawra did not truly become an attraction in the eyes of regular summer vacationers and others, like merchants from Bazerkan Souq or municipality and port employees, until the day the news spread that the brother of the Mufti of Tripoli had bought a house surrounded by cherry trees there.

'*Bought* it?'

Yes, bought the house. And paid for it in cash.

That summer, there wasn't a single room left to rent, and many villagers even slept in tents up on their rooftops so vacationers could stay in their homes. It happened to be the month of Ramadan, so the mayor handed the lemonade street vendor a drum—which he beat at dawn in the neighbourhoods where Muslim families were staying—after someone whispered in his ears to call out, 'Get up for your *suhur* meal, the prophet is coming to visit you . . . '

He managed to wake everyone up, Muslims and Christians alike. Some of them would come out onto the balconies in their pajamas, irritated. But as soon as they found what was causing all the commotion, they would back down and try their best to go back to sleep so as not to 'ruin the summer vacation', as they said.

The summer vacation did almost get ruined that year when the treasurer of the municipality emptied the bullets from his gun into the belly of an army officer after he confirmed that the latter was meeting up secretly with his stunningly beautiful but dimwitted wife. The man escaped to the pine forests high up on the mountain, so the army received orders to arrest all the adult male villagers, and a few soldiers even rounded up some of the summer vacationers they encountered, barking sharp orders while forcing them into their truck. The vacationers tried to protest by insisting they were strangers to the area, just there for the summer, but the sergeant who was a Druze from the Shouf region thought they were lying. He told the truck driver to start moving, but one of the townspeople intervened and explained to the sergeant that he might have the right to arrest the people of Hawra, but the summer vacationers had nothing to do with the issue and should be released. The sergeant would not back down until it occurred to one of the detainees to identify himself by name, as Abd al-Majeed, son of Ahmad. He also identified a friend of his sitting nearby, Mohammad Ali. It was then that the sergeant recognized his mistake. He demanded to see their identity cards and then released all the Muslims midway, forcing them to have to wait for someone to give them a ride back to their families. The killer, unable to find anyone in the remote mountains to provide him shelter, grew weary. He feared that if night fell upon him in the wilderness, he might die of a heart attack. So he surrendered, and it was all over.

The following May, Mahmoud Yasser al-Alami decided that the heat in Tripoli was no longer bearable.

Every day at nightfall, upon returning from work at the travel agency, he would claim that he was suffocating there in the living room. Half-naked, he would go to the porch and ask his wife Sabah to serve him his *akkoub* stew with rice and yogurt outside. Sometimes, he tolerated the sting of the cold night air just to prove that it was not possible to spend the summer on the port road near al-Bahr Mosque, across from Pâtisserie Moderne.

He had lucked out with a summer house in Hawra, thanks to the agent he'd had to wait for at the town's café while he sobered up after a night of drinking before he could show him the vacant houses whose keys he had in his possession. The agent had to try out every single key in every lock, as he slurred and blabbered, before Mahmoud finally settled for a spacious house with a red-tiled roof owned by an elderly couple. They had not been blessed with children because, according to the wobbling agent, the wife, Rakheema, was 'just like her aunt. The same trembling voice and can't get pregnant.' The couple owned and lived in another house nearby.

Vacation fever gripped Mahmoud after a second successful year of booking flights and organizing trips for the Hajj pilgrimage. He made sure to secure visas for his clients and to accompany them to the holy city of Mecca and then to Medina to visit the prophet's grave. He was preparing for what would be the first semblance of luxury in his life, ever since marrying the daughter of a cattle merchant from the city of Homs, a man who used to come by his uncle's shop in the Attareen Souq, the fragrance market. That was when protests erupted in Tripoli during the commemoration of the resolution to partition Palestine. An impromptu crowd of angry young men gathered, with some carrying the Arab flag. They chanted and marched from the direction of the Mansouri Great Mosque in the old souqs towards the government Sérail. The protestors almost broke down the door to Mahmoud's travel agency just because he had named it 'Orient Tours', written in the Latin script. Had he not confronted them, climbing up on a chair he had put out on the pavement, and screamed at them that he was the son of Haj Yasser al-Alami, who led the strike in 1936, they would not have left him alone to go find a less dubious target. This unrest became a perfect excuse for Mahmoud to speed up the process of transporting his family to the new summer destination in his Citroën DS19.

The road leading to Hawra wrapped around the hills and overlooked deep valleys dotted with monasteries, causing Mahmoud al-Alami's only son to squeeze his eyes shut in fear while his sister, on the other hand, gazed at the slopes without blinking. The furnished house they rented had a beautiful façade. It had high ceilings and an outside terrace where one could put chairs in the afternoon, drink coffee with cardamom and watch the summer headquarters of the Maronite Patriarchate gradually drown in the evening splendor.

Life changed for them in a single day. Being 1,200 metres above sea level, they could not sleep well on the first night. That night was also hotter and more oppressive than the nights at the port, where the sea breeze lightened up the evenings. They tossed and turned in their beds until a late hour, listening to the sounds of the squeaky metal bed frames, before finally surrendering to sleep shortly after two o'clock in the morning.

The boy Nizam got up from his bed before dawn. He was crying, carrying the model aeroplane that British Airways had given his father as a decorative office gift in support of his efforts. The little one had clutched it during one of the surprise visits his mother made to his father's office, and now he could not sleep without it. He would contemplate its details and read its markings before falling asleep, while also making sure that he was surrounded by the small Jaguar, and the three cotton-stuffed 'see no evil, hear no evil, speak no evil' monkeys and a set of prayer beads that he had snatched from the hands of his maternal aunt Zayneddar the day she was reciting God's names over it.

He opened his eyes as if a scream had jolted him awake. He left his room and went to the porch sobbing. His older sister Maysaloun was awakened by his screams and followed him barefooted, worried that he might hurt himself while sleepwalking. They would fight at least once a day, but whenever he needed her, she would appear out of nowhere. She put her hands on his head, muttering a Quranic verse she had heard from her aunt but did not memorize very well. Then she sat down next to him to calm him down a bit, but he remained burdened by the dream.

He whispered, 'Why doesn't my mother come to my rescue when I call her?'

'Where?'

'On Port Said Street.'

'What are you doing on Port Said Street?'

'I am trying to escape. It's raining, and people at the port are making fun of me. But she won't answer me. She can't hear me . . .'

He waved around the model aeroplane from British Airways as he spoke and almost scratched Maysloun's face with it. She did not know what to tell him, so she held him in her arms, and he slept with his head on her chest. She, too, fell asleep until sunrise, when Mahmoud—who was surprised to find them on his way outside in search of the fresh air and the enjoyable mornings that the mountain promised—woke them up.

The next day, before straightening up the house, Sabah tried to compensate for the homesickness that struck them as a result of the sudden move. She inquired about the city women who were spending the summer in the neighbourhood so she could invite them for a morning gathering at her place, with the hope that this would become habitual and she would regain some of the flavour of the life she knew.

After the chaos typical of new beginnings, the days went on monotonously. Mahmoud would go down to the city every morning. It was said that his persistence in making the long commute stemmed from his inability to be away from Madame Jeanette, one of the two employees who ran his business in the city. As soon as Mahmoud would leave the summer home and go to his office at the New Orient Travel Agency—which now succumbed to an Arabic-only sign—the city-women vacationers would arrive in swarms. They would make the rounds among the houses, most likely ending up at the al-Alami house, which was soon pervaded with the smell of coal and Persian tobacco, amid the morning gossip that generally revolved around the women who were not present at these morning gatherings. Nizam and Maysaloun would withdraw to the porch, where the only thing the bored little boy could do to entertain himself was to count out loud all the cars headed up to the Cedars Forest. There he would stand, clutching his aeroplane, monitoring everything that passed along the road winding up into the mountains, while Maysaloun wrote dreamily in her little notebook, in her own world. She made no attempt to branch out and find some friends for herself among the village girls, but unlike Nizam, she didn't suffer from boredom and was content with whatever she was given. She was born grown up, her mother would say, and sometimes add for no clear reason, 'Maysaloun will suffer in her life.'

Maysaloun, Nizam. These were two names the al-Alamis' neighbours snickered about for quite some time at first, before they finally got used to them. Mahmoud, whose first business venture had been to open a bookshop on Izzeddine Street, spent long hours—after the back-to-school season and the bustling sales that came with it died down—reading books that were popular at the time. He perused titles like *Nushou' al-Umam* (The Genesis of Nations), *Fee Sabeel al-Ba'ath* (For the Sake of the Ba'ath Party), and even delved into *Das Kapital*, which some of his acquaintances scoffed about, saying he was only trying to read Karl Marx out of obstinacy. They told everyone that he would sit for hours reading, turning page after page, without understanding a single thing. They were probably right because Mahmoud al-Alami was never able to grasp ideas, despite constantly grappling with them. None of his old friends ever remembered hearing him make a comment of any significance during the low season when his bookshop turned into a meeting place for public school teachers and employees of the water department or other municipal agencies. There were never enough chairs for everyone, so they would just stand, leaning against the bookshelves, smoking and arguing loudly about the nationalization of the Suez Canal or the influence of language and religion on the unity of peoples. Barricaded behind his desk, Mahmoud tried in vain to participate in heated debates over the obligation to educate women or the Free Officers Revolt in Egypt. Occasionally, he would succeed in getting the attention of the debaters by pounding on his desk, and they would give him a chance to put his two cents in. Having broken through the barriers, he would jump up from his chair in an unexpected fury, just to put forth his feeble-minded idea and say, 'The Jews are the enemy of our religion and our homeland,' no matter what the topic of conversation was. This only impelled the others to interrupt him straightaway and pick up where they had left off, debating ideas he hadn't been able to follow in the first place.

Mahmoud would get distracted from the discussion whenever any of his acquaintances happened to show up at the bookshop, like the real estate agent or the nightclub owner with bloodshot eyes from all the late nights at the bar. These were friends he was too ashamed to introduce to those eloquent ones crowded around him, so he preferred to greet them in the back room, where all the dictionaries and archives of local newspapers were kept. There, they would have lively whispered discussions on obscure topics. Muflih al-Haj Hassan, however, was a source of pride for Mahmoud. A rather large man, he would enter through the doorway sideways, sporting his agal and Baalbek-style keffiyeh, as he greeted everyone in a brash Beqaa accent. Mahmoud would get up immediately and offer him his chair, promising all the bookshop patrons that the man who had just arrived was going to teach them a lesson in politics and history. They would listen to the tribesman and American University of Beirut graduate—who stuck stubbornly to his traditional clothing and thick accent—go on at length with his appeal to morality and adherence to Greater Syrian identity, until the gathering was eventually broken up by the approach of lunch time. Then Muflih would be left alone with Mahmoud to discuss matters whose true nature would only be understood with the passing of time.

There was only one other person Mahmoud would give his chair to: Sheikh Bassim al-Khatib. Every time he stopped by the 'Bookshop for Heathens', as he mockingly labelled them, he would let out his boisterous laugh and go on about the futility of trying to step outside of religion. He insisted that there was going to be major unrest because the poor were not going to wait for those in charge to do something, and that Israel was the greatest threat of all. He was in the process of expounding upon his theory in a book they could soon find on the shelves of this very bookshop, which would have the title *Justice in Islam*. He would pronounce the words menacingly, emphasizing the preposition, in order to imply that there is no justice except *in* Islam.

When his daughter was born, Mahmoud asked his bookshop patrons to weigh in on a name for her, specifically asking them to stay away from names like those of his sisters Najeeha and Zayneddar. The suggestions came pouring in, and between Gamal—after the valiant Egyptian president—and Syria—out of deference for Greater Syria—he chose the name Maysaloun, despite the fact that the famous battle ended in the death of Yusuf al-Azma and the collapse of the fledgling Arab army in their fight against the French forces.

By the time his son was born, the New Culture Bookstore had started to decline, its proprietor having fallen victim to loan sharks, one in particular who wore a western-style hat and stammered to the point that Mahmoud would take the money and sign the promissory notes without grasping more than a few blurts of what he said. The interest doubled as did the loan shark's stammering and his threats to take him to court, while Mahmoud pleaded for settlements and delays and couldn't make sense of his objections. Finally, they agreed the loan shark would bring someone along who could explain what he was saying. What cut into Mahmoud's soul most of all was that every time the loan shark accepted a delay or agreed to an extension on one of Mahmoud's debts, he would choose a title from his display. One time it was *Churchill's Memoirs*, another time it was *War and Peace*—a two-volume set. He'd just pick them up and walk out the door without even a look in the direction of the person they belonged to—his way of saying they were the price for accepting a late payment.

Mahmoud al-Alami decided to depend upon himself in choosing a name for his son, especially since his eloquent friends had deserted him during the period of his mounting financial worries. He had been deeply touched by something in a novel he had most recently read—the fate of the reformist Persian vizier Nizam al-Mulk, and how the Hashashin sent an ignorant boy to stab him to death. At first Mahmoud wanted to give his son the full name Nizam al-Mulk and surprise his former bookshop friends with his broad reading knowledge. Sabah was against it in the beginning, afraid the little boy's name would become a source of mockery. But then she thought about it some more, remembering one of her mother's friends in Hama called Umm Nizam, who used to bring her cotton candy, and she agreed to Nizam, without al-Mulk. Her only regret—it would be hard to come up with an endearing nickname for him.

The son was born, and the gates of freedom flew open for his father who, despairing as work opportunities dwindled before his eyes, decided to take the advice of the loan shark. Every time he came by to collect on one of those cursed promissory notes, he would chide Mahmoud as he brushed the dust off his jacket and pointed to all the books, insisting they brought him nothing but moths. His face would light up as he flapped his arms like a bird and told Mahmoud that he should take up travel sales instead. The bookshop was transformed into a travel agency, and all of

Mahmoud's old friends stopped coming around, except for Muflih al-Haj Hassan, who would come by in the winter, wrapped in a camel-hair abaya, with a long set of prayer beads dangling from his hand, to carry on his conversations with Mahmoud al-Alami.

The travel agency finally brought Mahmoud enough income to pay off his debts. He even started saving some money in an account he opened at the bank one street over from his office. Every time he came back from the Palace Hotel in Hawra, where he played a game of backgammon one of his textile merchant buddies from the city had challenged him to, he would sit on the porch of his summer home watching the sunset and feeling for the first time in his life a tinge of relief and satisfaction. He treated Maysaloun to a playful side of himself she hadn't been used to, and then he would ask about Nizam, who, unable to find a space for himself inside the house before noon, had gone out to the backyard to play. He could not be seen from the porch, so his sister had to walk over to the bedroom window to check on him whenever his voice went quiet or she couldn't hear his usual clamour. It wasn't long before Nizam discovered this watchtower, though, and moved his games to where she couldn't find him.

The neighbours liked to tease and poke at him at the nearby shop or on the road. They would stare at him for a long time, and some of the women would grab him by the chin to get a good look at his face and gaze at his features and blue eyes, wishing for a child just like him. He would back away, raising his shoulders as they muttered, 'May the Holy Cross protect you!'

Secretly they wondered how a Muslim boy could have such blond features and assumed that his family must have Kurdish origins. They would make whispering sounds to draw his attention as if they were calling a cat, or shout out his name when they came out onto their porches, or pat his wavy hair or steal a quick caress as they passed through the yard before he managed to get away from them and return to where he had been playing with the ball against the wall with untiring enthusiasm.

He would toss it, and it would bounce back. Then he'd throw it harder and it would bounce back harder. And so on until one day when Maysaloun was checking to make sure he was OK, she discovered that the wall was covered with black charcoal drawings of women's faces, each with two pigtails. Below each drawing he had written a woman's name—his mother, his sister, some of his mother's morning visitors—Umm Ahmad, Fatima al-Hilwani, or Haji Iftikhar. He would back up, kick the ball and howl in delight if he made a direct hit on one of his targets. Maysaloun chuckled to herself and didn't tell anyone. Neither did she rush to tell her mother when she saw Nizam playing with a couple of neighbourhood boys she heard blaspheming and blurting out all sorts of curses and swears on Almighty God and the dead while Nizam delighted in it all, laughing on and on, adding some of his own and testing them out in turn upon everything that moved in his vicinity—a bird fluttering its wings, or a tractor making too much noise. He rattled off a string of obscenities and laughed, while his buddies never got tired of making fun of his Tripoli accent. They mimicked his words and took their turn bursting into fits of laughter as he joined in their mischief, chasing cats and dogs and finding sparrow nests. When the ladies' morning gathering broke up, he would spend as much time as he could playing his games until he heard the sound of his father's car horn. Then he would throw the ball to his two pals who had disappeared into the background so they could continue playing in his absence, and he'd rush home to eat lunch with the family, gobbling up everything within reach after having forgotten to eat anything all morning. After that, he would be forced to silence, because Mahmoud would have just finished telling Sabah about the murder of one of the tough guys in the gold souqs in the city, for example, at the hands of some young guy who didn't like some insult the former had slung at him. Then Mahmoud would plop down on the living-room sofa, refusing to go into the bedroom instead because, as he claimed every time, he didn't want to nap long. This prohibited the rest of the family from listening to the radio and even talking among themselves for fear of waking him up. After all, he was exhausted from his daily trip up and down the mountain to the city and back.

Once again, Nizam would slip outside to resume kicking his ball at the women's heads on the wall. He started bringing his two friends over to join him, and one day, one of them managed to kick the ball way up into the air and it landed far off in the distance. Nizam got very upset and ran around the wall, panting and making threats against the perpetrator. When he reached the end, he found the iron gate open.

2

He took a few stealthy steps inside the orchard and then stopped to listen to a voice, to some human presence, before cautiously continuing on his way. It was as if he was treading into a world of unexpected secrets. He forgot what he was looking for as he contemplated the massive walnut tree. The way the sun penetrated it, its green leaves appeared translucent as they drowned in the dust of fine sunlight that extended like ropes, illuminating the entire orchard. As he approached a huge red rose plant, in whose shade one could sit, he heard the whistling of a man who suddenly appeared, carrying a pair of clippers in one hand and Nizam's lost ball in the other. The man was of a medium build and had broad shoulders. He looked like he belonged to a more noble profession because of his elegant outfit: trousers with suspenders, a clean button-down shirt and a white Panama hat. The only thing that betrayed him as someone who did gardening work was a pair of muddy, rubber boots.

That is how Nizam first met Touma Abu-Shaheen, who greeted Nizam by name. Nizam grabbed the ball but did not head for the gate because he remained engrossed in contemplating the possibilities of the orchard. His eyes kept inquiring about the small square boxes with all the bees hovering around them. They lurked over the black-and-white hunting dog that wiggled his ears as he followed Touma. A few minutes earlier, Nizam al-Alami couldn't have imagined the existence of all these things behind that filthy wall.

Touma disappeared once again behind the brush, which gave Nizam the opportunity to meow like a cat in defiance of the dog that suddenly barked in his face. Touma came back with his hands full of delightful pink cherries that he poured into Nizam's little hands, which could only hold a few of them. He accompanied Nizam to the door and watched as he gobbled up the cherries, his half-closed eyes sparkling as he relished their exquisite flavour.

The following day, as soon as Nizam went down to play, he rushed to the door of the orchard and found it locked. He banged on it loudly, first with his hand and then with a stone. But it was in vain. He paused for a moment and then grabbed the ball and kicked it high and far. It was as if the ball's landing amid the orchard was the secret key to entering it. And so it was. A little while later, he heard the door creak. Breathless, he ran happily towards it. Touma greeted him by peeling a mukh al-baghil—'mule's brain'—pear for him. The juice from the pear trickled down his face and clothes. He kept eating, laughing, until he polished off three pears. Touma was peeling the pears so quickly he almost injured his hand. Nizam ate but remained cautious of the dog that stood beside him panting, his tongue hanging out. Touma started teaching Nizam how to get closer to the dog so he'd get used to him.

'Rex, close the door.'

Rex rushed to do what he was told. Touma told Nizam that at first the dog used to slam the iron door shut, but then he trained him to close it slowly. He told Nizam to pet him and put his hands around his jaws. Eventually, the dog started running to him as soon as he entered and would walk him to the door on his way out, which was always later than the curfew set by his parents.

One time, Maysaloun lost track of him, so she called his name. He went outside the orchard to the area where she could see him. His clothes were stained with fruit of all colours. He asked for more time, saying that he was busy preparing a special glue for catching birds, but Mahmoud personally intervened to bring him back home before sunset.

When he returned the next day, Touma taught him how to catch a green- and black-backed Japanese beetle. He would tie a fine string around its head and trap it in an empty match box filled with rose petals. And when Nizam wanted to take it out of the box and let it fly on the end of the string like a kite, Touma taught him how to sing to it so it would not get too sad about being in the box for so long: 'If you're a girl, sleep, sleep. And if you're a boy, get up, get up.'

On the second attempt, Nizam let go of the string on purpose, so the beetle flew off, the string dangling from it, only to get stuck again in the branches of the rose bush. Intent on setting the beetle free, Nizam endured the thorns until he released it, and then demanded another beetle and another matchbox to trap it in.

'Why, so you can release it again?'

Touma put his hands on Nizam's shoulders as he roamed the orchard with him. He gave him his hat to wear. He showed him how the neighbours neglected their land such that it became overgrown, inviting snakes. He warned him not to touch the yellow plum tree even if one of its branches crossed the borders into Touma's orchard.

'This isn't ours.'

Nizam stood next to the mountain apple tree. He petted its trunk and asked, 'Is *this* ours?'

Touma smiled. He felt a great warmth and offered him a taste of the apple's small green fruit, still tart.

Nizam's parents felt reassured that he was spending a lot of time in Touma's orchard. They were relieved of his constant whining during the first few days of their stay, of his putting a damper on the summer they had craved, and of his frequent waking up in the night as he cried from the horror he saw in his nightmares. Maysaloun noticed that the nightmares did not visit him when he was allowed to spend as much time as he pleased in Touma's orchard. If they deprived him of that, he would find himself running about in the middle of the night, panting all over again on Port Said Street in Mina, in the rain . . . They had memorised the details of his recurrent dream, so they started overlooking his late stays at the orchard, sometimes until nightfall. Touma would take the opportunity to show him a firefly that lit up, as it flew at arm's length. He would challenge him to catch one. Nizam would try, but it was in vain. Touma laughed and explained to him that by the time he closed his hand on a firefly— thinking it had nowhere to go—it would have stopped glowing and found another place. He would try again until he got upset and started pouting and crying. He almost banged his head on the trunk of the walnut tree. Touma would console Nizam. Swiftly, he would catch a firefly, trapping it in the palm of his hand, and give it to him. But Nizam always insisted on catching them himself. Time would fly by, until his family would call for him again from the window. He would go back to his parents, the palms of his hands clasped against one another, thinking that he was holding that glowing creature. He would delay unclasping his palms . . . until he had to wash his hands before dinner, only to discover that all this while after leaving the orchard, he had been holding onto nothing but air.

During the first few days of Nizam's visits, and thanks to the boy's curious nature that made him impatient, Touma showed him how to use his hunting rifle to shoot the harmful moles that hid in the dirt. If Nizam volunteered to insert his hand in search of the moles, Touma would not allow him because they could bite him. He introduced him to everything—from hornworms that attacked tomatoes, and worms that gnawed at the trunks of cherry trees causing them to shrivel up and die, to the honeydew that covered the walnut leaves. The orchard was transformed into an ongoing battlefield against enemies for whom Touma was always on the lookout. For each one of them, he had just the right remedy and weapon.

When Touma would leave for a little while to redirect the irrigation flow, he would come back to find that Nizam had fed his clothes, face and hands the juicy Damascus mulberries he had climbed the tree to pick. He would go home dirty and get punished, prohibited from going to the orchard the following day. Whenever Nizam would come back, his face all lit up, Touma would spare him the trouble of climbing trees by carrying him on his back. Nizam would soil Touma's shirts, pull his suspenders and then let them snap back, hurting him. Touma would raise him up so he could reach the top of the Raincloud plum tree with his little hand. Nizam would look down from atop Touma's shoulders and ask, 'Who's this?' pointing to the icon of St Mama, the Roman soldier who embraced Christianity. In Hawra, he was the patron saint of newlyweds. No wedding procession passed by without stopping to let the bridal couple light a candle to him. He had been martyred on his wedding day. A picture of him had been placed in Touma's orchard inside a small shrine carved into the rock that was kept locked with an iron door, which also had a lit candle in front of it. Nizam chuckled at the saint's name and was captivated by his story.

'Rakheema loves St Mama. She says he wards off the evil eye from us and the orchard, too,' Touma said, grinning as if he didn't give much credence to the things his wife believed.

Rakheema Abu-Shaheen. He heard her voice before seeing her for the first time.

'Touma!' she cried in her soft trembling voice. She had rosy red cheeks, as if she had blushed from embarrassment at some point and the redness never faded from her cheeks.

Rakheema was delicate. She wore polka dot dresses and had an embroidered black veil that she folded and unfolded with great care and reverence. She only put it on when entering St Joseph's Church.

Her hair was always so shiny it seemed wet, as if just washed. And her smell was the fragrance of lavender and other things.

So many people loved to hug Nizam close to their chests, from his mother to his paternal aunts and even his father—his father rarely, and only after Nizam returned from accompanying travel agency customers on one of the agency's organized two-week tours. Sabah could not understand why Nizam joined them. They were always showering him with kisses or clutching him with their chubby hands, especially the ones who tugged coquettishly at his fat cheeks. They suffocated him. They made him lose his patience, and so he would let out a long whine of complaint and break free of them, using his hands and his feet to get away.

Except from Rakheema.

Sometimes, when she wrapped her arms around his head, he wished her embrace would last a long time. If only he could keep his face buried in her bosom forever. He could not get enough of her smell, like on the day she asked him to shut his eyes so she could clasp a necklace around his neck with a blue bead dangling from it. She had asked Touma to buy the necklace from the gold souq in Tripoli where he went to shop for fertilizer and insecticide and traps for field mice. She requested this of Touma the very first time he called her to the window to point out Nizam to her while he was learning to head the ball, aiming at the drawings of his mother and her friends in the backyard.

'There are hungry eyes out there!'

Nizam did not understand what she was trying to impress upon him as she clasped the necklace on him and kissed him on the cheeks without squeezing his face between her hands as she usually did. He felt as though she were trying to defend him against others who coveted him. She did not ask him to conceal the matter from anyone, but he preferred to hide the blue bead from his parents and from Maysaloun, so she would not poke fun at him. His mother discovered it two days later while helping him bathe. She refrained from removing it so as not to tempt fate. She did not ask him who put it on him, for she liked to believe it had been sent to her son by some secret divine will that watched over him.

Rakheema always tucked lavender flowers into the pockets of the apron she wore over her dress. Nizam liked to steal little branches of it from her, pluck off the purple buds and sprinkle them into the air. Rakheema took care to smell good, with that refreshing fragrance of hers. His mother, Sabah, was always dressed to the hilt. She never showed herself to people without looking her best, always stylish and not to be messed with. Nizam could not go near her without her putting up her defences and snapping, 'Hands off!'

He could never seem to touch her without messing something up—her hair, her nails, her makeup, the creases she spent such a long time ironing into her dress. Rakheema was easy-going, gave herself over to him, allowed him to do whatever he liked, mess up whatever he liked. He could sit in her lap an entire hour, trace her face and hands with his fingers, make ponytails in her hair, wipe his mulberry-covered mouth on her apron.

During his first summer in Hawra, he spent most of his time in Touma's company. But one day Nizam begged to go inside the house during a brief retreat from the garden, so Rakheema took him into the kitchen and started pointing out the jars of jam and pickles she had placed on the high shelf out of reach. Rakheema canned all sorts of things she fancied. Nizam insisted on reaching them, so she would stand him up on a chair and he would ask her about the little green tomatoes, or she would open the pickled eggplant stuffed with walnuts and almonds, or give him a taste of the apricots and grapes soaked in syrup.

'These are all yours, like the mountain apple tree . . . ' she said.

As the start of the new school year approached, Rakheema volunteered to help Nizam with his reading and writing. She would sit down beside Nizam on the stone bench in the garden, after Touma threatened not to put him up on his shoulders to pick up the baby bird hatchling and place it back in the nest out of kindness to its mother, unless he worked on his lessons with Rakheema for at least half an hour each day. That was the extent of the torture he could bear from arithmetic exercises. After that, he would lose his focus and get distracted by a line of ants marching by, or he would start whistling to a passing sparrow, or he would send Rex on some sort of mission.

She would bring an old notepad and take hold of his hand. Her beautiful fingers would guide his, making sure he wrote between the lines. She would wipe away his sweat if the sun beat down on him, bring him a glass of water before he even asked, and promise him that if he improved his writing she would take him to town for a ride on the white donkey. There was a local villager who, dressed in his sherwal trousers and red tarbush, would bring his white donkey into town so the children of summer vacationers could ride on it for a small fee. And their delight would not be complete if they didn't also get one of the colourful paper pinwheels they waved at each other during the ride.

Day by day, Sabah's friends began to miss Nizam. His mother would tell them, while serving them plates of cheese kanafeh, how sweet and loving the neighbours were, praying for 'Almighty God to bless them with children, bless all people with children.' Nizam's trips to the orchard next door were the best way to appease his mother's worries about him getting in with a bad crowd. She would lower her voice to say, 'People around here,' and she would draw a big circle around the house with her hand, 'blaspheme a lot. If he had continued hanging around with the local kids he had fallen in with when we first arrived in Hawra, he would have learnt all sorts of bad behaviours. They make fun of the priest and mock his voice when they run into him on the road.'

'It takes all kinds to make a world,' Sabah would say, with eyebrows raised and hands open in surrender. But she would not go on with her criticisms for long, out of shyness, even if the women she was addressing there in her living room were all Muslims. She was quick to make up for it by saying that despite all that, she found them to be 'good people who love their guests and who everybody praises even behind their backs'. If she felt she had gone too far in her criticism, she would repeat in front of the women who didn't already know, the fact that her mother was a Christian who did not convert to Islam when she got married and continued to swear by the Virgin Mary and pray to her for help in front of her children. She recalled one time when her mother took her and her sisters to visit the monastery of St Simeon Stylites and how she knelt down and prayed before him.

'Do you know the Church of St Simeon Stylites?' she would ask to change the subject, in the Syrian accent she never lost despite living among the people of Tripoli. Maysaloun, who inherited that accent from her mother, surprised her one time after the morning gathering had broken up and they had finished airing out the smell of tobacco. When Sabah asked if she had seen her brother, Maysaloun responded with a prophetic statement to which Sabah turned a deaf ear: 'They are going to take Nizam!'

3

Finally, the autumn equinox brought with it the rain that signalled the end of summer. And so, the al-Alami family packed up their things and said farewell to their neighbours. Touma and Rakheema stood for a long time waving goodbye to Nizam, who would not leave without putting up a good fight first, complete with kicking and screaming. His parents listed off the names of his friends back in Mina, reminded him of the nearby amusement park, but none of that did any good. It was only when they threatened him with a spanking that he gave in, and only on condition they let him take some grapes and walnuts and the embroidered cushion Rakheema sat him on so he wouldn't 'catch a cold' while doing his summer lessons. He stuck his head out the car window at first, and then, when they yelled at him, he drew himself inside and pressed his face against the rear window, his eyes glued to Touma and Rakheema, watching as they faded into the dust. He didn't exactly know what was happening to him. His heavy breaths against the glass created a fog that prevented him from seeing anything through the window. He was holding tightly to the matchbox filled with rose petals in which Touma had secretly imprisoned another beetle for him—a small gift to take back to the city and show off to his friends. But he could not restrain himself for more than two days after their return to Tripoli before slyly setting the beetle free inside al-Bahr Mosque where he and a few of his buddies had gone to play. They were enjoying themselves with their shoes off, watching the worshippers, some of whom took notice of the strange insect that intruded on the noon prayer. They waved their hands above their heads, trying to shoo it away, while Nizam delighted in his little deed, which he kept secret even from his friends.

Back in Hawra, the day after the al-Alamis' departure, the sun glowed hot in the sky, and Touma did not hear the squeak of the iron gate announcing Nizam's entrance into the orchard. He sat in silence on the edge of the rock, his hands folded, struck with a feeling of frailty. He spent the entire day in the shade of the walnut tree without the least desire to pick up the shovel or his pruning clippers.

Noon passed and Rakheema had not brought Touma his lunch.

'I don't have any appetite today.'

Each one avoided contact with the other. Rakheema kept to herself in the kitchen. She sifted through the dry lentils, then had to do the same a second time, because she had been so lost in thought she let the grains sift through her fingers without checking for the little stones and chaff that needed to be removed. Touma stayed out in the garden until late in the evening, for Rakheema had failed to call him as she usually did at sunset. They did not feel hungry that day, and at the end of it, Rakheema stayed up tossing and turning in bed.

The days followed routinely—Touma's gardening work became a sort of delusion as he tried to work the fields and sow crops now that the weather had grown cold and the first snowfall blanketed the top of Mount al-Makmal. The couple managed to restore a bit of their vitality. They did not voice their longing for Nizam; each one kept the feeling of emptiness to him or herself. Instead, they rivaled each other with praise for the al-Alami family, without mentioning Nizam, as though talking about him might make things worse. Even two years into their marriage, when she dreamt most fervently of having children, Rakheema never

imagined a son for herself 'more beautiful' or 'more perfect' than
he was. That was something she said to herself silently, for fear
of hurting Touma's feelings. Indeed, her love for Touma had
only grown stronger after they resigned themselves to a life without
children.

They barely made it to All Saints' Day before Touma suggested
to Rakheema that they go visit the al-Alamis at their home at the
entrance to Mina. As it turned out, when the al-Alamis left the
house in Hawra, they took the keys with them, which undoubtedly
meant they would come back the following summer. It occurred
to Rakheema that the boy might be at school if they went during
the week, so she recommended they visit on a Sunday. They filled
the trunk of the taxi with the last grapes of the season and containers of tomato paste and vinegar. The al-Alamis gave them a
warm welcome. Touma held tightly to Nizam while Rakheema
invited Maysaloun to come sit with them, but Maysaloun kept her
distance. Sabah filled them in on Nizam's news and his devilish
behaviour—how he waited for the opportunity to climb onto her
shoulders when she would kneel down to recite her prayers, knowing that in order to preserve the sanctity of her prayers, she would
not be able to rebuke him, and then, as soon as he heard her start
the last prayer, he would skedaddle. They laughed and laughed,
and it was nightfall by the time the couple headed back to Hawra.

The gifts they sent, even if once a week, were their way of
avoiding the embarrassment of visiting too frequently. But they
did not hesitate to go visit again in Mina when they found out
that Sabah was pregnant. Rakheema heaped on the advice, because
a woman over forty should heed every warning. Sometimes
she went by herself. The taxi would take her to Mina and then
come back for her at the end of the day. She spent the time
at Sabah's side, lovingly patting her belly, and undertaking all the
necessary duties for her, such as opening the door for guests and

making coffee for them, and even buying baby clothes and toys from the city market. When the girl at the cash register would ask if the baby was a boy or a girl, Rakheema would reply without hesitation, 'A boy.' If Touma happened to be with her, he would coil in embarrassment and go wait for his wife out on the pavement.

Sabah wanted to reciprocate Rakheema's kindness, so she invited them to Nizam's circumcision, where they met relatives on Mahmoud's side of the family. When they entered the crowded living room, they eagerly attempted to greet everyone, but, much to the surprise of their brother Mahmoud, Nizam's paternal aunts suddenly pretended they did not shake hands with men. They limited their greetings to quick handshakes with Rakheema only, with fake smiles on their faces. The couple sat beside each other in a cramped corner of the living room, bombarded with strange looks and whispers, while they searched every inch of the place for Nizam. He appeared a little while later. He came out from one of the bedrooms, his voice ringing out, dressed in the special gown for the occasion. Liberated from his underwear, he ran between the guests, having a grand time while they pulled him back and forth and showered him with kisses. He was focused on the thing between his legs. When the circumciser sat down to ostentatiously open his little tool case and pull out his forceps and surgical scissors before taking hold of Nizam's penis and snipping the foreskin, a clamour arose from among the celebrants to drown out the boy's pain. He was crying but not screaming, as if he ought to cry, because some of the dark-red blood had dripped onto his pure white gown. Rakheema's eyes welled up with tears upon seeing Nizam so scared and distraught. The circumcision was actually easier for him than putting up with the women's attempts to calm him with words or hugs or kisses after the circumciser left, having advised Nizam to hold onto the edge of his gown and keep it pulled away from his penis, so it wouldn't cause more pain. Touma and Rakheema could not fathom the bliss his relatives were revelling in at the occasion of this circumcision. Both were overcome with an obscure feeling that they were strangers and had stayed too long at a celebration they had no business attending. They said goodbye to the group without shaking hands this time and escaped through the door, while Mahmoud al-Alami, who sensed their embarrassment, apologized repeatedly from the top of the stairs. But they did not back off. They inquired about Nizam's school, The American School in al-Zahiriyyeh quarter, and visited him there several times. They braved the snow and made their way down the mountain where bad weather conditions caused many road closures. They walked the streets of Tripoli dressed in their heavy winter clothes, carrying sweets for Nizam and some pocket money for him to spend at the school's little shop.

They went down to Tripoli on a day that happened to coincide with the flare up of an armed uprising wherein a political movement that had given itself the name 'The Downtrodden in our Good Land' announced the establishment of a 'government' for itself inside the old souqs. They distributed pamphlets to passersby. It was said that the person who had penned those revolutionary formulations was a high school philosophy teacher who joined the rebels after shooting his wife, who was more than twenty years his junior, after confirming she was cheating on him. He had killed her and fled to hide out where other wanted criminals congregated. Pandemonium started to set in with the first sounds of gunfire. Touma and Rakheema quickened their pace towards the school, where the confusion was at its most extreme. Anyone who read the rebels' pamphlets that had been distributed at night, filled with accusations against the Zionist-backing American colonialists, might have worried the school could be vulnerable to attack, being a prime target. The slogans that had been written on the walls surrounding the school attacked the school system and threatened

President Johnson with dire consequences. When they arrived at the school, the administration didn't know how to ensure the students' safety. The roads were not safe for school buses and one could clearly hear the sounds of explosions in the distance, along with all sorts of crazy news.

'They robbed the gold souqs!'

Someone came to inform them that they had freed the prisoners from the old Sérail, all of whom had been convicted of murder or theft. They were carrying the philosophy teacher up on their shoulders.

'You're leaving the small prison only to enter the big prison!' he shouted into the crowd.

Touma and Rakheema asked for Nizam. The school employees had grown familiar with them, despite the unclear nature of their relation to the al-Alami boy. Nizam came out laughing, his eyes sparkling. It seemed he was enjoying the chaos that had found its way into the school and disrupted classes. His classmates, who were all shoving their way through the narrow doorway, noticed the strange man wearing the fur hat and heavy coat who had lifted Nizam up from the crowd. Touma and Rakheema got Nizam to his parents' house before anyone from his family had made a move to go fetch him, for communication between them had been cut off due to the uprising that ended when the army entered the inner souqs. There were five casualties from among the wanted criminals and the rest surrendered after an attempt to barricade themselves inside one of the mosques. Two soldiers who had gotten lost in the souq alleyways were also killed. They had been fired at from some location no one was ever able to identify, inside the maze of entranceways and exits.

The following season, the al-Alamis moved to Hawra early, but this time for different reasons; Sabah was seven-months pregnant, and the doctor asked her to refrain from any strenuous activity.

'So I should just lie down?'

'You may sit and stand, but only when necessary.'

Now the morning gatherings took place in her house every day, liberating the other women from the burden of hosting. On top of that, Maysaloun came down with whooping cough, and the coughing fits exhausted her so much she had to retreat to the bedroom so her parents wouldn't hear her sob. The doctors prescribed fresh mountain air and cautioned her against transmitting the illness to her little brother who moved in next door in order to be under Rakheema's and Touma's care, per his parents' request. Nizam had gotten stronger, so Touma taught him how to hold the clippers and prune the fine rose stems and how to lift the big tree branches in order to expose the smaller ones to sunlight. When Touma dressed him in a beekeeping suit, Nizam stole a honeycomb from the beehive and started sucking at its tip, an action that he paid for by receiving a sting on the side of his nose, its effects lasting for over a week. He taught him the names of different types of grapes, and whenever he sensed Nizam's eagerness to taste them, Touma would stress that he should not pick them prematurely. He helped him ride on the donkey and taught him how to lead the donkey by the reins and how to give him orders to stop or to go. As soon as the fruit that the birds liked had ripened, they made a scarecrow together, and he taught him to expect rain if thunder came from the direction of Latakia and hot weather if the breeze came from the east. Touma kept Nizam at a distance when he was chopping wood with the axe to avoid getting splinters in his eyes, and together they breathed in the smell of the earth after the first September rain.

At the end of August, Sabah gave birth to twins. Upon Sabah's return from the hospital, Rahkeema threw her a party where she let out joyful ululations, distributed sweets and pomegranate juice, and volunteered to help. She brought the al-Alamis' clothes to her own house where she ironed them, and she sang with joy as she waited by herself at the stove before bringing them a warm, home-cooked meal, ready to eat. It was as if she was celebrating her own wedding. She told Touma about the twins and wasn't at all stingy in praising them, but she didn't compare them to Nizam. She would repeat the twins' names, trying to make them resonate in her heart, but she was so used to saying Nizam's name that it was hard to break in the names 'Khaled' and 'Bilal'. Mahmoud gave the twins these names since he was no longer under the influence of his all-knowing friends, and perhaps as compensation for the strange names he'd given Maysaloun and Nizam.

With the birth of his brothers, Nizam disappeared from the orchard for over ten days, remaining by Sabah's side and watching the twins breastfeed together. He was afflicted with sharp pangs of jealousy and demanded, all at once, all the rights he had forfeited during his long absences at Touma and Rakheema's. He was stricken with a fever that the town doctor could not attribute to any health condition such as a cold or tonsillitis.

Three days later, Nizam got up, turned his back, and returned to the orchard where he spent several nights, staying up until dawn and preventing Touma from getting any sleep. Touma would fight his sleepiness for the boy's sake, and the most beautiful times they spent together were those hot nights in August when they stayed in the treehouse that Touma built for Nizam. Nizam asked questions about everything he saw, and Touma showed him the Great Bear and the Little Bear and promised to show him the Morning Star if he stayed up. But Touma would get drowsy and fall asleep while Nizam stayed up by himself for a long time, gazing at the clear sky, lit up like a chandelier, unconcerned by Touma's snoring and the croaking of frogs and the other night sounds in the orchard.

He savoured the farm eggs Rakheema prepared for him, sprinkled with red sumac and dried mint, gobbled up tabbouleh salad with his hands or with lettuce leaves—oil trickling down his arms as he laughed from the bottom of his heart—and drank goat milk from her hands as he snorted loudly without a care in the world. She started to anticipate his big appetite and would prepare lunch and sometimes dinner as if she had been charged with feeding an entire family. And when Touma had to go down to the city to buy some pesticide, she would take him with her to St Joseph's Church now that Maysaloun's vigilance over his whereabouts had waned.

She brought him in with her through the women's entrance. They all opened their eyes wide as they gazed at Touma Abu-Shaheen's wife and her little companion. The first thing Nizam noticed in the dimly lit church was how the worshippers dipped their fingers in the holy water font before making the sign of the cross. The sight of that surprised him so much he clung to Rakheema during his first visit to the church, as his attention remained fixed on the altar and the priest in his embroidered robe, who lifted a chalice and intoned the consecration prayers. He watched as the hands touched each other, from one seat to another, not forgetting anyone, until the blessing reached Rakheema who passed it on to the woman standing to her left and then gave it to Nizaam, as she cupped his face in her hands.

The second time he entered the church, Nizam familiarised himself with the space by getting away from Rakheema and wandering around, as he contemplated the pictures of saints with bowed heads and the Stations of the Cross engraved in wood and plated in gold that a rich man from the town had vowed to provide for the church in return for his sick daughter's recovery.

His constant running around captured the attention of the worshippers who would sometimes look in Rakheema's direction, so that she might restrain him, especially since such running around wasn't expected from a boy who didn't make the sign of the cross when he walked in front of the altar and whose behaviour resembled that of some foreign tourists who entered the Church of St Joseph as if they were entering a house or an art exhibit.

He grew familiar with the church and figured out when worshippers were supposed to stand up or bow their heads in reverence of Jesus' name while the Bible was being read. But he wouldn't settle down, 'like a fish in the sea', as the neighbours would say. He messed around with the confession chair, watched the women go behind the curtain in front of the place where the priest would disappear, and sneaked in between two confessors until the priest kicked him out. Soon all the churchgoers knew who the little blond child with the pretty face was, and Rakheema was pleased that he wanted to accompany her to St Joseph's Church. Not once did she deter him from stepping forward in the long line of worshippers in order to receive communion on Sunday, until he suddenly came face to face with the priest who refrained from giving him a wafer and shot a dirty look at Rakheema, who had to call to Nizam out loud and ask him to step back. But he remained standing there with his mouth open and his eyes shut. And when the priest pulled him out of the line of communicants, he turned towards the altar in an attempt to examine the hanging censer and then entered into the sacristy, so he could explore the place from which the priest and his assistants came in and out.

During the Feast of Transfiguration, they bought him fireworks which he threw in every direction and almost started a fire in the neglected lot near Touma's orchard. Rakheema took advantage of Mahmoud al-Alami's absence on an overseas trip—on which it was rumoured he'd brought his favourite female employee, leaving his wife to struggle with the twins on her own—and didn't ask for permission to take Nizam with her to a four-hour procession to the Church of Our Lady during the Feast of Assumption. Rakheema and Nizam accompanied a group of young men from the Maronite brotherhood who carried flags, chanted, and prayed the entire way. Soon, Nizam noticed that some of them were walking barefoot, so he insisted on taking his shoes off and draping them over his neck so he could too, despite the objections of Rakheema who explained to him that the bare-footed men had vowed to the Virgin Mary to do that in return for healing a sick relative dear to them. He kept his distance from her and walked for so long that his feet started bleeding, and Rakheema worried that the al-Alamis would find out what happened and get upset. He wouldn't stop walking on his bloody feet until Rakheema begged a young man who was accompanying the procession on his bicycle to give Nizam a ride on the back of his bike. And when they arrived at the church and the mass started, Nizam surrendered to a deep sleep from exhaustion, as he sat in Rakheema's lap, who could not get her fill of gazing at him and the paintings of the winged angels that embellished the ceiling of the church.

4

The end of the summer saw a spate of incidents, one of which led to a warrant for the arrest of Mahmoud al-Alami and had to do with a gunfight that had broken out in Tripoli near a nightclub known for employing foreign women. Mahmoud was accused of being involved in the skirmish, so he stayed out of sight. His wife was forced to leave Hawra and go back home to Mina with two barely one-month-old infants in tow. Powerless to look after her family, she agreed to leave Nizam in the care of Touma and Rakheema. That is, until Mahmoud went down to the Tripoli police station, turned himself in, and spent three nights in jail before getting out on bail—which he didn't have the money for and had to send Sabah to get from the same old loan shark with the hat. Mahmoud came home from jail, and the story of his arrest remained a bewildering mystery. It was said that he worked hard to prevent it from becoming public knowledge in order to protect his reputation, but Sabah found out about everything.

'Give me a divorce and let me go back to Homs!'

That was the nicest plan she had come up with for him during those three days she spent feeling that her friendships and good name had been completely and suddenly ruined and that behind every smile in her direction were tinges of pity and vengeful satisfaction she could not bear.

'The son of Haj Yasser al-Alami is getting drunk and hanging out with prostitutes?'

Mahmoud demanded the return of Nizam, who refused to go down to Mina and started bawling and sobbing and barricading himself in every corner, as if the impending attack to grab him and cart him back to Tripoli could happen any minute. Touma and Rakheema pleaded with him to go back to his parents. An atmosphere of obvious tension reigned over the al-Alami household. Mahmoud wanted to stay out of sight because he would not have been able to get out of jail without posting bail. He was afraid of being sent back to jail, so Sabah was forced to manage the travel agency in his place. She gave a good tongue-lashing to Madame Jeannette, who had feigned illness for more than two weeks, trying to avoid a confrontation with her.

One night, upon returning home exhausted and regretting out loud having ever come to Lebanon, Sabah found Nizam moping about, not playing, not smiling. Maysaloun complained that he had been grumbling all day, letting out hopeless sighs and flailing his arms. He couldn't find anything better to do with himself after school than to go with his friends to al-Bahr mosque where one of the sheikhs sat them down around him in a circle to memorize the Quran. Nizam delighted in the competition and pursued it diligently. As soon as he got home, he would recite what he had memorised to Maysaloun until he finally got fed up with repeating all those verses without understanding what they meant. The sheikh inquired about Nizam's absences later on, saying the boy was a fast learner and had already finished memorizing the Juz Amma section and had started on Juz Tabarak when he quit coming for lessons, which was a shame.

After detours and evasions and a promise to take him on a boat ride to Rabbit Island as soon as the weather cleared and the sea was calm, which Nizam shrugged off and refused with hands raised in resistance, Maysaloun finally exclaimed, 'He just wants to go up to Hawra!'

He did not deny it.

Maysaloun told her mother that Aunt Najeeha had dropped by the house the day Sabah took the twins to the doctor's office for their second round of immunizations. She had arrived suddenly with a gold necklace in her hand that had a small pendant with 'Ayat al-Kursi' engraved on it. She clasped it around Nizam's neck herself. 'We are Muslims, my dear nephew,' she warned. 'Don't forget that, Nizam!'

His mother asked him to show her the necklace, but he was firm in his anger and kept dodging her until she gave up in despair and asked him point blank if he wanted to go back to Touma and Rakheema. He hesitated before saying yes in a soft voice, his eyes gleaming as if he'd won the bout. That was the first time he openly asserted this wish of his.

'OK,' Sabah agreed. 'Goodbye, then. This is what Mahmoud wants, so let it be!'

Life crept back into Nizam. He started playing with his two little brothers, coddling them in their cribs, the moment the promise to send him to Hawra at the start of the break for Christmas and New Year's was confirmed.

Nizam found a snowman waiting for him up in Hawra, in the area where he usually played in the summer. The neighbours had been winking at each other quite a bit while Touma was shovelling the snow into a pile. He formed it into a snow man, giving him two walnuts for eyes and sticking an old broom in his hand. When it was finished, he topped it off with one of his hats. The moment he arrived, Nizam immediately began making snowballs and throwing them at the snowman, wearing the pair of woolen mittens Rakheema had made him put on to protect him from the cold. He squealed in delight. He didn't stop pelting the snowman until he'd turned him into a deformed and scattered mess. For the first time since their marriage, Touma and Rakheema set up a nativity scene for baby Jesus. Touma made water run through it via a network of interlocking tubes and lit up the colourful card-board houses that he had patiently constructed. He also picked out large figurines of St Joseph and Virgin Mary and three bearded wise men with crowns on their heads, a donkey, two cows, an entire flock of sheep of different sizes, and two guardian angels with their trumpets to protect the entrance. Rakheema contributed to the decorations, too, with empty tuna and sardine cans in which she had planted some wheat. All of that to have Nizam jump around them in excitement as he discovered all the details, insisting on carefully examining each figurine one at a time and placing them here and there with his own hands. He noticed that baby Jesus wasn't there, and so he asked for him, but Rakheema explained that it wasn't right to place him there before midnight, the hour of his birth. He consented but begged to have him so he could keep him hidden under his pillow.

Sleep overcame Touma and Rakheema, so when the bells rang at midnight from St Joseph's Church, they woke up to find Nizam in front of the nativity scene placing the baby Jesus in the manger. Rakheema guided him back into bed, and before he fell asleep, he asked her how Jesus could be born again after dying on the cross and being pierced in his side with a spear, as he had seen in one of the Stations of the Cross at St Joseph's. Nizam woke up another time, frightened by the sound of gunfire from automatic weapons ringing in the New Year. Whenever gunshots rang out nearby, reverberating through the house, Nizam would tremble as though he'd had an electric shock, so Rakheema would wrap him up in a wool abaya while Touma cursed that new trend. Nizam would not calm down until they got him fully awake with a glass of water. The new year did not start before his having discovered—when one of the Magi fell to the floor and broke—that the nativity scene figurines were made of plaster that closely resembled the chalk at school. So, he broke the shepherd with the baby lamb draped over his shoulders and started writing with it all over everything within his reach, and with the remnants of St Joseph or the crèche animals that were breathing warmly on Baby Jesus who had been born out in the cold, making a mess of the walls and furniture.

In the end, Mahmoud al-Alami was acquitted. There was talk afterwards that the investigations uncovered other details about him smuggling contraband through the airport with passengers travelling on his travel agency tours. He would ask one of them to check an extra bag as a favour to him, claiming his own bags were over the weight limit, so the passenger would pass through customs while Mahmoud watched from behind with his hand over his heart. He was merely an agent for merchants from the Beqaa Valley who'd found in those organized tours a new way to skirt customs inspections. It was also said that his friend Muflih al-Haj Hassan was the middleman between him and the hashish merchants as well as the mastermind behind this new smuggling scheme, and that when the examining magistrate set Mahmoud free, he warned him that the case was not closed.

After much stalling and resisting and dilly-dallying from Nizam—who knew very well that going down to Tripoli meant going back to the American School—Touma and Rakheema dropped Nizam off at his parents' house, promising that they'd be back for a visit. But Mahmoud's drama was far from over. One morning, Touma and Rakheema came knocking at the al-Alamis' door, but no one answered. The neighbours told them that the al-Alamis had left for Syria, where Sabah had family, and that it all happened so suddenly. Just like that, they pulled the kids out of school, loaded them up into the car, and took off without telling their neighbours when they'd be back.

Touma and Rakheema came back to Hawra, disappointed. The next day, they both became bedridden and spiked a fever, and Rakheema even struggled to drag her body out of bed and into the kitchen to make some tea. And tea was all she needed the entire day. When news of their illness spread, Touma's cousin Aziz dropped in for a visit. Aziz was a famous tailor in Tripoli, where he had moved several years earlier. It was rumoured that as he headed down to Tripoli, he pointed in the direction of Hawra and kept repeating, 'No one can live in these barren mountains except the native monkeys.'

Aziz was one of the few remaining tailors who was good at custom-making vestments for the Maronite clergy, so when Father Gabriel, Hawra's priest, was in the city visiting the Maronite Archdiocese, he took the opportunity to stop by Aziz's shop to put in an order for two vestments. The tailor initiated the conversation by hinting mysteriously that the church should be paying attention to what was happening around it. He made that comment while causally mending a shirt that he spread across his knees, and he didn't clarify what he really meant until the priest pressed him for more information. It was only after the priest grew frustrated with him and decided to head out that Aziz started telling him about how Muslims had been buying houses in Hawra for the past two years. He counted the houses on his fingers, exaggerating the numbers, but he could only name three Muslim households. He warned, without mincing words, that they weren't going to be satisfied with just the houses but that they were now looking to inherit some land. Then he stopped talking, leaving Father Gabriel with some riddles that he now had no difficulty solving on his own. All the while, Aziz swore up and down, on his honour on one hand and on his dead parents' souls on the other, that he had no interest and no right whatsoever to butt into his cousin Touma Abu-Shaheen's business, but that he was just alerting him about what might happen if Touma decided to leave all his assets and houses for the Muslim boy to inherit. They agreed that it was possible that the boy's parents were intentionally pushing him on

Touma and Rakheema, knowing that the couple was rich. As they speculated about the situation, Father Gabriel insisted that while 'adoption is not allowed in Islam,' Touma was free to 'write any of his assets in the boy's name' while he was still alive. In a nutshell, that was Aziz's main concern. So the priest advised him by saying, 'Best to keep an eye on him.'

Aziz closed his shop and took his wife along to visit the Abu-Shaheens. Touma pulled himself together in front of them and denied that he was sick. He wondered how news of their illness had reached his cousin, and within a few minutes of the guests' arrival, he asked Rakheema to make them some coffee so they could send them on their way as soon as possible. The family's strange behaviour was enough proof that there was something fishy about every compliment that any of the relatives gave Touma and Rakheema—ever since news had spread that they had lost all hope of conceiving a child. Rakheema was always talking about how every offer for help that came from their relatives felt like a 'stab' in her heart, and how she had to politely decline it; she talked about how every lunch invitation felt like a setup, forcing them to fake smiles as they made up excuses for not being able to accept. Every meal that was delivered to their door caused them so much embarrassment that they rudely sent it back or—if Rakheema wasn't able to flat out refuse the meal—forced Rakheema to return the favour by sending back an even better one. But she made sure to send them enough hints to indicate that she wasn't interested in continuing such exchanges.

In the end, Mahmoud al-Alami and his family returned to Mina. Two days later, Mahmoud got up early to leave for the travel agency only to find Touma and Rakheema sitting at the building's main entrance, which was now equipped with a new iron gate that was kept locked in the evening after the recent surge in looting incidents and even armed robberies in the middle of the day.

There were also rumours about a gang that was in the business of kidnapping and selling children.

'Did you spend the night out here?'

They were too embarrassed to answer his question since they hadn't been able to find a way to get in, and they couldn't find a taxi that would take them back to Hawra. All the drivers they tried to negotiate with used the excuse that the roads would be covered with ice by night-time, putting them at risk of skidding dangerously or crashing. Mahmoud invited them to come in, and as soon as Nizam, who was still in his pajamas, heard Rakheema's voice, he rushed and threw himself in her lap. In the meantime, Mahmoud and Sabah talked privately in the other room. She rehashed all the rumours surrounding him, from his political wheeling and dealing to his seeing other women and smuggling hashish. On top of all that, she said, some folks who knew what was going on, including relatives, were talking about how he was willing to give up his eldest son to a Christian couple and how his sisters Najeeha and Zayneddar were so upset, calling her heartless and heaping accusations on her because she was Syrian, all the while insisting that Mahmoud was innocent—simply because he was their brother.

After a long argument during which Mahmoud insisted that he had done nothing wrong and promised to silence his sisters, they reached an agreement that would have Nizam spend his weekends and school vacations at Touma and Rakheema's. They informed them of their decision, and the couple said they would be ready to receive Nizam every Friday night and bring him back on Sunday. Then Touma and Rakheema later suggested bringing him back on Monday morning instead of Sunday night, and Nizam's parents gave in to their wishes on condition that they would drop him off at school directly since he'd already missed a lot of classes.

Before the following summer season began, Touma got the impression that the al-Alamis were having second thoughts about going up to Hawra, so he decided not to charge them any rent for the house. Touma and Rakheema started deliberating between each other on how to tell Mahmoud's family about their gesture without it sounding like charity. To their surprise, however, Mahmoud ended up pulling Touma to the side and asking him if he could loan him some money just until he got out of his predicament, which had worsened during his long absence from the travel agency. Touma agreed, and after he told Rakheema the news about the loan, they decided to send Mahmoud the money the very next day. Touma refused to even let him sign a promissory note. But the money Mahmoud borrowed from Touma didn't make much of a difference in the family's wretched situation. Sabah still suffered the burden of raising the twins singlehandedly, so Nizam spent his days at Touma and Rakheema's. When he got the measles, Sabah worried about her other children contracting the illness this time, so she didn't ask to retrieve him for about a month. Touma and Rakheema took turns watching him day and night to ensure that his fever didn't spike up. Mahmoud would disappear for three to four days at a time, while Sabah remained alone with the children. When he appeared again, he seemed very tired and slept for a long time. As soon as he regained his strength, he would leave again. His good old days playing backgammon and spending time at the Palace Hotel were behind him now. He'd take a quick look at his children and then mechanically ask about the ones who were missing. He now barely planted a kiss on the forehead of one of the twins, whom Sabah creatively dressed in different colours so people could differentiate between Khaled and Bilal. Maysaloun's favourite game was to look for distinctive markers separating the two, but their faces were completely identical, and all she could find was a crooked toe in Bilal's foot, which didn't help much with telling them apart. So they put a necklace with pendant engraved with the name 'Muhammad' around Bilal's neck since Bilal was the prophet's muezzin, and they opted for a pendant in the shape of a gold sword for Khaled.

The end of September came, and saying goodbye was hard not only on Touma and Rakheema but also on Nizam. Feeling more self-confident, he clutched Rakheema's dress and refused to go down to the city, so his parents left him behind, hoping he would follow them later as he usually did. Sabah wasn't in the best shape since Mahmoud had been gone the entire previous week; dread and anticipation were written all over her face. Touma had hired a taxi to take them to Mina along with some provisions that he provided. Rakheema repeatedly offered to help Sabah with anything she needed during Mahmoud's absence, and Sabah was forced to take her up on her offer. She thanked her and promised to pay back everything they owed the couple very soon, but Rakheema assured her that she and her husband were blessed, thanks to their presence in their lives, and that she shouldn't preoccupy herself with such nonsense. The most important thing, Rakheema said, was for Sabah to take care of her family and keep an eye on her husband.

5

The days passed without any word from Nizam's family asking for his return, so Touma went down to the city to investigate. He found the travel agency closed. When he asked one of the shop owners nearby what was going on, the man told him that Mahmoud al-Alami was wanted again by the authorities and that he had fled to Syria, and the rest of his family joined him later. He advised him not to ask too many questions about Mahmoud, or he himself might be taken in for questioning by the Lebanese Deuxième Bureau. Touma got the impression that the tall man who'd given him this information wasn't sorry about his neighbour's plight.

Touma seemed excited when he returned to town. He stopped by the grocery shop and bought some provisions and ordered many more as he thought about all the necessities for Nizam's long-term stay at their house. There was a spring in his step as he walked, effortlessly carrying the groceries. He found the chilly air refreshing and started whistling to himself in the dark as he headed down towards the house. He waited until Nizam had gone to bed to tell Rakheema the news. He pretended to be sorry as he told her what he found out about the al-Alamis, and she commiserated with him and warned him not to tell anyone about those matters to protect the family's reputation. They lamented their friends' situation, but the next morning, they took Nizam to get him enrolled at the long-established Lazarus Nuns' School that teemed with children from the neighbouring villages. When the principal first asked them about his name, they just said 'Nizam'. In the meantime, Nizam found a piece of coloured chalk and started scribbling all over the chairs in the principal's office. When she asked them for his last name—knowing exactly what she was asking about—they hesitated before Touma said, 'Is it not enough to just put down Nizam?'

The nun seemed displeased with his answer, so Rakheema intervened and told her to write down whatever name she wanted, all the while looking at her pleadingly, as if beseeching her to be more understanding of their situation. The nun insisted on writing down his real name in full since the school had to supply the Ministry of Education with a list of student names. She wrote down 'Nizam al-Alami' on the form and then paused again before noting the middle name 'Mahmoud'. By then, Nizam was scribbling over the picture of Pope John XXIII with the chalk, and kept asking Rakheema, 'Who's this?'

The nun asked Touma and Rakheema about Nizam's religion but didn't get an answer from either of them. She smiled slyly as she pondered the situation before yelling at Nizam to settle down and snatching the picture of Pope John from his hands. She tapped her pen on the desk, hesitating to make a decision on the matter.

'Officially, his name will be Nizam al-Alami.'

Nizam looked at her when she said his name out loud as if she was calling roll.

For the first few days, Rakheema rode the bus with Nizam since the school was far, and she worried about him going by himself. She would sit beside him—he always insisted on taking the window seat—as the other children gave her strange looks. The driver assured her that he was capable of taking care of Nizam and that she didn't need to accompany him, but she would insist on dropping him off at the nuns' doorstep. On the way back, she would sit by herself in the front row behind the driver's seat and would turn her face away every time the bus passed the main street, so she could avoid making eye contact with the morning café-goers or the church ladies on their way to the eight o'clock Mass. When it wasn't raining, she would walk to school and take the bus back with Nizam, always sitting by his side. Once he got used to his classmates and to being on the bus, he started joking along with his friends. Some of them would make fun of him, and one of the notoriously mischievous boys once called him 'Nizam de Rakheema!'

The teacher scolded them as children laughed here and there. The next day, Nizam asked to ride the bus by himself, but he refused to wear the school uniform like the girls. When he was forced to wear it, he would come back in the evening with his uniform completely soiled—the pockets filled with ink and choco-late—and Rakheema would toss it in the laundry right away, until they finally gave in and purchased a dozen school uniforms for him.

The teachers loved him so much he couldn't walk past any of them without having his neck stroked or his hair tousled. The receptionist wouldn't miss an opportunity to kiss him before he snarled at her or pushed her away from him. Even Sister Francesca would let her hand linger on his hands every time she gave him personal feedback. She claimed she belonged to a group of progressive clergy who followed the recommendations of Vatican II, and she found in Nizam a lost soul who could be turned into a textbook example of a Muslim student who converted to Christianity of his own accord. She encouraged Nizam to attend the morning Mass at school, but he disappointed her when it came to his religious education for which a young priest—a heavy smoker who liked to discuss hazy themes like the Holy Spirit or salvation of the soul—volunteered to take charge. The priest's words would fall upon the children like lashes, and they'd soon get distracted in side conversations. Every time the priest would drop his cigarette butt and stamp it out with the sole of his shoe, he would ask the students to remind him of the last thing he said, and when he didn't get an answer, he would resume talking to himself about the importance of Incarnation and about how Jesus was both man and God at the same time. Nizam noticed two girls who sat on the same bench leave the classroom as soon as the priest came in for religious instruction. The girls would get up and head to the door at the same time, without asking for permission; and if they took too long to leave, the priest would just stand there silently and wait for them to shut the door behind them—while envious looks followed them—before starting his lesson. Nizam inquired about why they left, and one of the girls divulged to him that they were Muslim. Their family usually spent their summers in Hawra, like some of the other well-off families from the city, but this year they also spent the winter because the doctors suggested that the dry weather might help heal their youngest daughter from asthma, a disease that had preyed on her since she was five years old. One sunny day, when birds filled the almost bare poplar trees in the playground, Nizam waited for the two girls to get up and leave the classroom before following them towards the door.

The priest called after him, 'Where are you going?'

He was ready with an answer: 'To the playground.'

The priest thought he was joking or just being cocky, so he scolded him and told him to return to his seat.

'I'm Muslim too.'

The priest scowled, and pandemonium broke out in the classroom. He let the girls leave, then closed the door and asked one of the students to go get the principal.

'He's saying that he's Muslim and doesn't want to attend religious instruction.'

Sister Francesca blushed. By now, the students had stood up and were watching intently, as if some accident had just occurred in the front of the classroom. As usual, the principal hesitated. Nizam seemed too determined not to miss the opportunity of being saved from the priest, so she gestured to him to go out to the playground.

'You're free . . . ' she said, trying to hide her shock behind the sharp features of her face. And so, twice a week, Nizam would wander around the playground with the two girls, who were inseparable, but who wouldn't talk to him at all. Afflicted with a different kind of boredom, he tried to kiss the younger one, catching her off guard, so the older one started screaming. Her screams were heard all the way in the principal's office where people thought that something dangerous and deadly was about to befall her sister.

'She's sick!'

Nizam stayed away from the sisters, and whenever he felt he had nowhere to go during the break that he so craved, he would just go and linger in the bathroom, since it was cool in there.

In the meantime, the al-Alamis rented a house in Homs and enrolled Maysaloun in a free public school, but Sabah couldn't afford to hire some help. Every time she came to Lebanon for a brief visit, where she made the rounds to assure relatives that Mahmoud was fine, she had to put up with the same old chit-chat, where one of her in-laws would start asking about the children, one by one. Sabah knew where that conversation was headed and would make up answers as she went along. She would flatter Najeeha by saying that Maysaloun was strong 'just like her aunty', as Mahmoud had said, but flattery wasn't enough to extract a smile from Najeeha. They would talk extensively about the twins Khaled and Bilal and their simultaneous illnesses.

'What about Nizam? How's *he* doing?'

They saved the best for last. The sister asking the questions would feign ignorance, pretending that she was asking about Nizam as if he was also staying with the family in Homs, just so she could relish Sabah's stuttering. Sabah would always find her way out of this test by resorting to some double entendre or another.

'He's in your neck of the woods . . . '

She would then justify what she said by talking about the 'poor level of education' at the Syrian schools and about Mahmoud's insistence on Nizam getting an education at a private school in Lebanon, but they would shake their heads, unconvinced. After a long silence, one of them warned Sabah that the nuns had changed his name, adding, 'in case you didn't know.' Sabah wasn't sure how to respond and said she highly doubted that the nuns would do something like that. Nizam's news was reaching his aunts through the Muslim family who spent the winter in Hawra. The girls, or rather the older girl—since the younger one who had asthma had taken a liking to Nizam ever since he tried to kiss her and would move over to make room for him to sit next to her on the bench, despite the loud protests of her sister who wouldn't budge an inch from the spot allotted to her—would tell her mother in the evening:

'You know, the blond boy Nizam, the one the nun loves so much? His last name isn't al-Alami any more.'

The joke started when one of the girls from the upper-level classes called him Nizam Abu-Shaheen. His classmates liked the new name and started calling him by it, as they pointed accusatory fingers at him. Instead of standing up for himself, Nizam would get in on the fun and participate as they conjugated his name with all the possessive pronoun suffixes just as they had learnt in grammar lesson. Waving their hands, they sang aloud in the playground, 'Alam-*i*, Alamu-*ka*, Alamu-*hu*, Alamu-*hum* . . . '

Sabah went up to Hawra. She hugged Nizam for a long time, sat him by her side, and asked him how he was getting along in school. She then asked him to write his name for her in French. Meanwhile, Rakheema followed their conversation anxiously. But Nizam was anything but naïve. He started out by writing his first name on the palm of his hand, and when his mother protested that he was getting blue ink all over his hand, he consoled her by writing 'al-Alami' on the other, without the slightest hesitation, so Sabah planted a kiss on his cheek.

She could stop worrying about one little thing, at least—she who had no choice but to keep going back and forth, spending long hours on the road and worrying every time she crossed the borders that Lebanese General Security agents would recognize her. She went on at length about her family's situation, so Touma sent Nizam out to the nearby shop to buy coffee, even though they were still fully stocked. He did not want Nizam to hear about the al-Alami family's inability to pay the rent for the travel agency office, which the owner of the building had reclaimed. Sabah tried to assure them that their financial situation was likely to improve, though she herself was unconvinced. Mahmoud had bought a fully equipped movie theatre in Homs and had been running it for the past two months. Touma and Rakheema exchanged a look that meant this new 'business venture' of his was not likely to be very profitable either. He told Sabah the next time she came to Lebanon to go talk to the American film agents in Beirut. Maybe she could convince them to send to Mahmoud some films that weren't available in Syria, like *The Crimson Pirate* or *The Lone Ranger*. He wrote the titles down for her on a piece of paper, including some old ones starring Gloria Swanson. Sabah told them how much Maysaloun enjoyed the cinema and how they really couldn't forbid her from watching so many movies since she was at the top of her class. She got completely absorbed in them and even after leaving the theatre, she remained taken by them for a long time. Everyone smiled, and then the worries came flooding back. She complained that Mahmoud was constantly worried the Syrian police were going to arrest him and turn him in to the Lebanese authorities, and that his fate depended on the two countries staying at odds with one another, as he always said. They insisted that she should stay the night, saying lightheartedly that the summer house was still waiting for them and she should consider herself at home here or there. She left the same day, much to the relief of Touma and Rakheema who were afraid she might ask to take Nizam with her, and they insisted she take a gift they had carefully prepared for her—some cash in an envelope that they said was a sweet letter from Nizam to his father and mother that she shouldn't open until she was halfway home.

The next day, Touma headed to the school to ask the Sister to adhere to their original agreement and call the boy 'Nizam al-Alami', because his parents 'won't put up' with such a name change. And that's exactly what happened. Just like that, Sister Francesca entered the classroom, called Nizam to stand by her side at the front of the class while she ran her fingers through his wavy hair, and warned his classmates not to call him by anything but his own name.

'What is Nizam's name?' she asked the entire class, whose answer came in the form of a chorus of conflicting voices. A small constituency went along with Sister Francesca and said, 'Nizam al-Alami', while the larger faction, most of whom were girls, stubbornly shouted 'Nizam Abu-Shaheen!' while waving their arms in the air, forcing the principal to silence them by hitting the teacher's desk with the wooden ruler—the one she never parted with—and breaking it. Overjoyed by the commotion Sister Francesca was causing, Nizam chimed in, shouting along with both sides. He even climbed up on the desk so his voice could be heard. Sister Francesca put a decisive end to the matter by declaring that any student who called him Nizam Abu-Shaheen would be duly punished. And they didn't stop at teasing him about his family name. They sweetened his first name, too, sometimes affectionately and other times derisively, until he ended up with the nickname 'Nano' which one of the teachers had given him one morning when she happened not to be in the sour mood she was in most days of the week.

At the start of the following school year, Rakheema was given the surprise of her life. She was helping Nizam put protective covers on his new textbooks and notebooks when she found that on one of them, just one—his math workbook—he had written his name: Nizam Touma Abu-Shaheen. Just like that, out of the blue, not prompted by anyone. Rakheema couldn't believe her eyes. She got all worked up and shouted to Touma who came running as if the house was on fire. She showed him what Nizam had written, and they both started hugging him without stopping until he couldn't take it any more and fled from them to his room. They had given him his own bedroom that they would go into to check on him—until he reached age fourteen—whenever he woke up in the middle of the night. In the beginning, they couldn't decide what to do about the cross hanging on the wall over his bed. Rakheema's mother had taught her to always place a cross over the head of whoever slept in any bed. As a compromise, they decided to remove it from where it was and hang it on the opposite wall. Touma knew the schedule of the calls to prayer that were broadcast from Cairo every day. He rarely missed Sheikh Abd al-Basit Abd al-Samad's recitation. Lying down in the living room whenever he was taking a break from his work, he listened with his eyes closed. Nizam surprised him one day while he was listening to the *adhan*.

Nizam stopped, surprised by what he was seeing, so Touma turned down the radio, embarrassed, as if he had been caught red-handed. Nizam told him that he too liked waking up to the sound of the *adhan* coming from al-Bahr Mosque near their house in Mina.

Nizam went back to visit Mina once during the last week of Ramadan. He stayed as a guest of his Aunt Zayneddar who asked for him to come so he would know 'he has relatives in this world'. He strolled through the streets with his cousins. They mocked some of the mountain vocabulary he'd picked up. They passed by the open fish market, which was empty that day—no people and no fish, nothing but a line of poetry:

Spend not your life with a broken heart for the Good Lord will provide.

The fishermen were on strike because the government was going to award exclusive rights to fish with modernised fishing boats to one of the companies. Some leftist political parties had joined the demonstrations. Nizam and his cousins stood watching as the fishermen closed off the sea with their fishing boats and blocked the roads, and one could see weapons in the hands of some of the party members. In the evening, there were sounds of gunfire and the streets of Mina were deserted early.

When Nizam arrived on the first day, he was surprised when his aunt and her family did not make any lunch, so they reminded him that it was the month of fasting. He had forgotten, which they realized was understandable considering his new living situation, but he in his turn refrained from eating. They told him it was not required since he wasn't old enough yet. But he insisted and would not eat a thing until he heard the canon fired from the city's crusader castle signalling the evening *iftar*, by which time he was nearly about to faint. He was sprawled out on the sofa, so they splashed some water on his face. He had prohibited himself from drinking as well amid that very hot weather. On the first days of Ramadan, they had given him a bouquet of flowers to carry on their visit to the cemetery while he cast scrutinizing glances at the tombstones and the crowds of visitors as though the cemetery had been transformed into a public park. When they got home, Aunt Najeeha took him aside and asked him if they baptised him up in the village. He told her about going to church and confessing his sins to the priest, and how he started making up sins and the priest didn't know he was Muslim because he couldn't see him well from behind the wooden barrier with the narrow holes.

Najeeha's whole face lit up. 'We don't have to worry about you, Nizam al-Alami!'

Her delight did not last long, though, because Nizam went on to tell her that his friends had baptised him in the waters at the spring. Her face tensed up again. 'At the spring? How did that happen?'

She called her sister Zayneddar to come listen before asking for more information. Rather, she started slapping her head with her hands and wailing first, saying that there were going to be major consequences, but Zayneddar told her to hold on until they heard the truth of the matter. Nizam clammed up when he saw his aunt at her wit's end, so they spent some time cajoling him until he resumed his story. His friends led him to Mar Abda Spring, as it was called. Hawra was famous for this spring that gushed forth every May and boomed like thunder in the wintertime. Nizam's friends knew that it was close to the time for the spurting to happen because they always heard the loud roar of the spring before seeing the water flow out. The boys took off their clothes and went in for a swim in its unbearably cold water. Nizam did not go in with them. Not because he was afraid of the water, but 'for another reason', which he stated while staring directly at his aunts, feeling certain that they would understand. His friends asked him to step into the water at least, and there was an older boy among them who had no qualms impersonating John the Baptist standing in the River Jordan, as he had seen him doing in a picture in the religion book. The boy raised his pant legs above his knees, scooped up some water in his hands and poured it over Nizam's head while chanting what sounded like a prayer and laughing until Nizam could no longer bear the cold water over his head and hit him on the hand. The baptism celebration ended with the group dividing into two sides. They threw rocks at one another, splashed water back and forth, got mad and made up, as was the usual sequence of events.

His circle of friends became rougher after he was forced to transfer to May Ziadeh Public School because the nuns did not accept boys past middle school. Sister Francesca had been transferred to another convent in the Beqaa district, so the new principal thought it best to distance Nizam from the girls due to the excessive complaints she'd received about his flirtatious behaviour with them in the classroom or out in the playground, behind the trees. They accepted his advances and then complained about it afterwards.

There, too, his name followed him, and when the Arabic teacher would pound his hand on the table and shout, '*Nizam!*' (the Arabic word for Order) to silence and sow fear into the troublemakers, Nizam's friends would goad him to stand up and say, 'Present!' as if the teacher had been calling roll, which only doubled the racket and their pounding on whatever their hands could reach.

It was during that phase that Nizam called Rakheema 'Mom' for the first time. As he was going up the stairs to the house from the street, he almost slipped, and 'Mom!' just shot out of his mouth, inadvertently. Rakheema's heart swelled upon hearing that from inside the house, but she restrained her emotions. The second time it happened, there was no room for doubt when he called to her. Roughly up until that year, he had guarded against calling out to Touma and Rakheema by name, always speaking to them directly when making his requests. When one of the girls at the nuns' school asked him how he was related to Touma and Rakheema, he shrugged his shoulders as though the question were being raised just to irritate him. This time, he called Rakheema 'Mom' as he pointed out the aeroplanes circling in the clear sky over the Cedars mountain at the onset of summertime. There were two planes high up in the sky that were inaudible, circling together, leaving two parallel lines of white smoke behind them before disappearing behind the peaks. On that day, Touma had been taking a break from his busy springtime gardening work and was resting at home, in the living room, in front of the radio—his wintertime companion that broadcast successive news reports and stirring songs. It was the Arab–Israeli war.

There was no doubt about it this time. He called Rakheema 'Mom' just before calling Touma 'Dad' and took off to start taping blue paper over all the windows of the house so the lights could not be seen by the Israeli planes circling in the sky, per the government's advice to citizens.

6

Nizam entered his teenage years. Acne invaded his face and his voice changed, but he soon came out of his awkward stage. He rarely saw his family. On the other hand, he spent more money on his friends without expecting any favours in return. He'd automatically pick up the tab at restaurants for the entire group to the point that no one even bothered to pretend offering to pay instead. If he ever ran out of money, he'd borrow some so he could pay and refused to allow any of his friends to contribute. Even the owners of shops and cafés refused to take money from the guys he ran around with, and some of them would charge Touma double the amount that Nizam owed when he came to pay Nizam's bills; and when the wife of the grocery shop owner secretly reprimanded her husband for doing that, he explained to her that the people of Hawra were more entitled to Touma Abu-Shaheen's money and his assets than that 'foundling' who would most certainly get it all in the end.

Nizam determined the group's itineraries and activities, and he would easily come up with ideas for having fun in places that the children of Hawra thought they knew too well and were ready to move on from. Just like that, they would head down as a group to the sacred valley, where Nizam would grab hold of the rope of the big church bell, with the help of one of his fat friends who came along on the trip, and start yanking it. They wouldn't let go until they'd succeeded in letting out at least one ill-timed ring, leading one of the monks to chastise them. They would blame the entire thing on Nizam. As soon as the monk asked him his name and he said 'Nizam', the entire choir of young men would add in unison, 'Abu-Shaheen'. Nizam would stubbornly correct them by saying 'al-Alami', and the monk would kick them out of the monastery. Outside, they would squat on the ground and start eating. Nizam would pick pomegranates or pears from the trees of the monastery, indifferent to what his friends kept saying about 'St Anthony being such a cheapskate' that he might retaliate and strike him down with some tragic fate. As if that wasn't enough for him, he would sneak again into the church and inspect the offerings the worshippers had left at the altar. Without him, excursions would have been dull. His friends didn't just love him for his money but rather because he never held a grudge. He was a young man of a rare breed in a village where folks were known for being difficult. It was impossible to make him angry—although there was no shortage of mean kids at that age—because he would try to alleviate the anger of the person attacking him instead of defending himself. He was their peaceful refuge during petty fights, and he 'washed away their sins', as they said. He cultivated their positive self-image, made them reconcile, and bribed them into hugging it out and putting their differences behind them.

And so the years passed. There were days when Mahmoud al-Alami didn't have the cash to pay for some meat and rice—only to be swimming in money the next day. Sabah failed to persuade Maysaloun to marry a young man who came from a rich family that had managed to smuggle their money into Lebanese banks and who still owned a lot of assets, despite the nationalization laws that led to the expropriation of some of their properties. Maysaloun resisted stubbornly, but she didn't cry. She didn't know the man, had only seen him maybe one time, but didn't like the way he looked at her. Everyday, Maysaloun exhorted her family to return to Lebanon—she goaded the twins to side with her, saying that if they did, Nizam would return to them. But there was no one to hear her, since Mahmoud was entangled in a mess—

fighting on several fronts and making promises he couldn't keep. Sabah still came to Lebanon. Carrying boxes of films, she'd stop by the house in Mina, where she spent the day cleaning and straightening things out. She often teared up about her long exile, despite the fact that she was exiled in her own hometown and living near her family. In Lebanon, she would return the films to the distributor and pick up new ones before stopping by al-Haj Hassan's house in the capital. There, he would host her generously, dismiss the taxi that had dropped her off, and pledge to give her a ride to the Lebanese–Syrian border. He would ensure that Sabah made a quick stop in Hawra, so she could give Nizam a series of historical novels by Jurji Zaydan, as Mahmoud had requested, before safely dropping her off at the border. The novels were among the remnants of the New Culture Bookstore, and Mahmoud wanted his son to have them so he could learn about the glorious past of the Arab Ummah. One time, the pile of round, steel reels that sat in the trunk of the taxi caught the attention of a new employee of the Syrian General Security forces. Upon removing and searching them, he discovered drugs tucked inside the reel of *The Prisoner of Zenda*. Sabah was led to the temporary jail at the border, which caused a lot of confusion for the General Security officers who were not used to arresting women. She spent the night there before the news reached Homs and one of her nephews—an officer in the Air Force Intelligence, as it was called—intervened to get her out. But she had already made a full confession. She cried and beat herself up so hard while telling her story that the investigators were convinced it was professional smugglers who had used her as a mule. Mahmoud disappeared again, leaving the twins under the care of Maysaloun and one of their aunts. Sabah left the jail, upset and humiliated. She looked for her husband to tell him she knew that every job he ever worked in his life was just a cover for smuggling—or rather smuggling and womanizing—and she swore that she would get him thrown in jail because she now believed all the whispered allegations that reached her about him opening a bookshop in Tripoli so he could use the books as a means of smuggling hashish. He even had the nerve to tuck the hashish in the Holy Quran and the thick Islamic Hadith collections. When she returned to Homs, she didn't find Maysaloun, who had in turn fled to Tripoli by bus and came knocking at her aunt Najeeha's door, out of nowhere, asking to stay with her because her parents were planning to marry her off against her will.

Sabah struggled to hang on to her family, which sometimes unraveled beyond her control, while Nizam was at the peak of his adolescence, leading the same gang of friends. Once, the friends headed down to the valley, preying on the almond trees on their way, and as soon as they arrived, Nizam's buddies winked at each other before jumping him and pinning him down to the ground. They pulled down his trousers and underwear before he finally realized what they were up to. Laughing, he surrendered and decided to satisfy their curiosity by pulling out his penis—running around in all directions and showing it off to all those who were eager to see what a circumcised Muslim boy looked like. Some of them moved closer to inspect the difference, and one even took out his penis and started comparing it with Nizam's, while another divulged that his younger brother got circumcised at the hospital—drawing boos from some of the friends. All the while, Nizam went on with his show. He climbed over a small hill and started peeing in the air while his friends argued about whether or not it was easier for circumcised men to penetrate a woman and how the first time a Christian man has sex with a woman can be painful. Nizam promised to let them know the verdict on circumcised men as soon as he went down to Beirut and found out for himself. Some of them had become acquainted with masturbation, but they were too shy to make any insinuations about that for fear of being exposed. They bragged about going on dates with girls—although those dates never went beyond holding hands or the occasional kiss—and accused the loser among them of only being capable of pleasuring himself.

In the middle of their quarrelling, they heard someone count with a firm, loud voice, 'one, two . . . ' and bark orders, like 'stop' or 'present arms', in the same stern tone. The sound of hands slapping the butt stocks of rifles ensued. The classmates listened attentively and walked stealthily towards the direction from which the sound was coming.

'The guys are training . . . '

They spied on a row of young men who looked a little older than them, led by a man with a handlebar moustache who wore a military jacket and plain grey trousers in wool broadcloth. His disciples were similarly dressed, sporting military hats and badges in a haphazard fashion, as if whoever provided them with military gear—for acclimatizing to a war-like situation—didn't secure sufficient uniforms for everybody, so they distributed the sundry items among them in a way that seemed fair.

The trainer spotted the teenagers and called for them to come out of hiding and join their comrades since they too must learn how to fight to make sure the Palestinians didn't take over their village. Nizam volunteered to march with some of his friends behind the trainees, imitating their movements until the session ended, before gathering around the trainer who resumed his sermon.

Suddenly, one of the boys pointed to Nizam and addressed the others yelling, 'He's a Muslim!'

A feeling of embarrassment and hesitation filled the air, but the situation was soon diffused by the trainer who—after recovering from his initial shock—started reprimanding the boy who divulged Nizam's religion.

'Muslim or Christian . . . it doesn't matter. We're all Lebanese!'

Nizam wasn't feeling nervous about any of this. He was busy looking at the crosses that the trainees had sewn on the sleeves of their uniforms, the badges of the Lebanese flag with the green cedar, and the caption 'The Homeland Is Ours' on their hats.

Nizam's ongoing mischievous adventures kept him so busy he brought home a failing report card the first semester. It was said that some teachers intentionally lowered his grades, knowing they would soon be invited to give him private lessons at home. Nizam even managed to convince his French teacher to help him write love letters to the girls on whom he was casting his net. He was the first among his classmates to succeed at getting girls to meet him on a deserted road, where he would steal some kisses, before luring them into a far-off field, as they laughed nervously out of fear and a budding desire to explore more. The letters that the teacher helped write—full of innuendos about the importance of 'smelling the roses before they wilted', and 'riding life's train at full speed'—were met with enthusiasm on the part of the Hawra girls. In the meantime, Nizam complemented his seductive moves by showing an interest in their looks and giving them primping advice regarding their clothes and haircuts. He advised them on everything, from how to strut around and what shoes to pick, all the way to choosing the right perfume. But as soon as he succeeded at teaching a girl the basics of elegance and started to see her transform and show off Nizam's infatuation with her to her friends, he would lose interest and ask the teacher to help him write a letter to another girl. He loved to chase girls on his own. He would shower every day and smoke cigarettes secretly. But he was getting unexpected help in these successful pursuits of his, for it was said that the mothers themselves were encouraging their daughters to get closer to him, as they offered the girls old-fashioned advice on how to seduce a man. The possibility of Nizam marrying one of the town girls was seen by Hawra's residents as somewhat of a compromise that would 'keep Touma Abu-Shaheen's assets inside the town.'

As June approached, Nizam and his classmates got busy preparing for the official Baccalaureate exam, scribbling the answers to anticipated questions on small cheat sheets they planned to consult during the exam. Nizam was at least two years behind the rest of his classmates since he had changed schools and missed a lot of school days from time to time.

They all passed, thanks to the Examining Committee's decision to lower the minimum passing score. This was done in accordance with a directive from the Minister of Education, because the exams in some districts had been conducted under abnormal security conditions. Some bloody battles had taken place in the South, and in Beirut, there had been violent demonstrations protesting layoffs at the iron factory that were permeated by gunfire and resulted in a number of protestors being wounded. The Hawra students—Nizam among them—passed the experimental sciences exams, opening the doors to university studies, and presenting Touma and Rakheema with a new dilemma.

During that phase, Sabah resumed her visits to Tripoli, since the storm had settled down a bit. She wanted to go back to Lebanon for good, but Maysaloun worried her. They wanted her to get married, but she was being stubborn. And they were also waiting for a general amnesty, so Mahmoud could return with them from Homs. Sabah would bring Bilal along—her constant companion—and would spend two or three days at the house in Mina. She would hose the floors down and give them a good mopping, open the windows, let the sun in, call the neighbours over for coffee and arguileh, do her best to repair relationships that distance and bad news had broken, air out whatever clothes they had left behind, and remove the books left over from the book-shop days that Mahmoud hadn't been able to sell—in bulk or individually. One time, she came across some old photographs—her wedding album and baby pictures of Maysaloun and Nizam. She sat Bilal down beside her, and they turned the pages one by one. Her eyes filled with tears; she choked up, starting with the first picture—of her and Mahmoud, with his arm around her, standing by her side, as she's holding Maysaloun the day they bought her her first pair of shoes. After that Mahmoud is out of the picture, leaving her alone with her morning girlfriends stand-ing on the porch, with Maysaloun as she took her first steps, with Nizam . . . Bilal was the first to notice something strange. He pointed at the hole in a picture of them taken next to the fountain at the public park. She thought the photo must have torn, worn out over time, causing Nizam's face to blur. But there was the empty spot in the next picture—Nizam again, with no head, in front of the American School with his buddies. She flipped quickly through the pages of the photo album, searching for Nizam, to no avail. There was no trace of him. Someone had torn out his head. She didn't know how to explain the situation to Bilal, who seemed amused and surprised. She called to Maysaloun and asked her about it. She denied it, but Sabah was not convinced. Maysaloun had done it, patiently, with a razor. She had collected Nizam's heads and while sitting in the shade of the jujube tree, stuck them between the pages of a book, after she'd grown tired of writing his name dozens of times on a sheet of paper: 'Nizam Mahmoud Touma al-Alami Abu-Shaheen'. Sometimes straight, sometimes crooked. In blue, in red, in ink, in pencil.

Just like that . . . after he'd spent an entire winter in Hawra fre-quenting the same cafés, and one of the girls whispered in his ear that if she had met him in a faraway place—over 'there', she unabashedly said while pointing southward towards the capital—then she would have let him taste pleasures he could never forget . . . and after he discovered that two of his buddies had enrolled at the university in Beirut, and would come back on the weekends—one of them with his hair grown long in tune with the latest styles and the other addicted to smoking strong brown French cigarettes—talking about singers Nizam had never heard of and films that would not make their way to the cold little theatre in the village for several years, stealing a bit of the superiority Nizam enjoyed in the eyes of others who'd stayed behind in Hawra like him—young men ready to inherit their fathers' professions or think about emigrating to distant countries that would open up the doors of good fortune to them . . . and after signs of another depressing season started to show . . . Just like that, Nizam stood at the door to the sitting room and declared to Touma and Rakheema: 'I'm leaving for Beirut next month . . .'

Rakheema pretended not to hear what he said, whereas Touma asked him if there was something specific he planned to do in the capital.

'I'm going to Beirut. I'm registering in the School of Law, at the Jesuit University . . .

They had been putting off hearing such a thing.

'What are you lacking here? Everything we own is yours. Pass your driver's test and we will buy you a car . . .'

He could go to Beirut, 'have some fun' with his buddies, and come back.

He didn't know anyone there . . . No one knew anyone there.

'Who's going to feed you?' Rakheema asked, her voice trembling even more than usual.

Who's going to wash his clothes and iron them?

'How will you be able to sleep all alone?'

Protests . . . Fedayeen . . .

'Haven't you been listening to the news?'

Shaytan, 'The Devil', was saying the world is in shambles. Shaytan was the owner of the Mercedes that shuttled passengers from Hawra to Beirut. That was the nickname he was known by. Out of all the taxi drivers, he was the only one who specialized in daily trips to the capital. He would find out who his passengers were the night before, and then pick them up in the morning, right from their homes. He sang verses of zajal and ataba poetry for them on the way there, and anyone who wanted to go back the same day, could return with him and be back in Hawra before nightfall.

Nizam wasn't going to have an easy time persuading them. He would pout, stew in silence, and then let it go. He was good-hearted, but he wasn't going to give in. He threatened to go to the capital by himself, by his own personal means. They would go nuts, and he would calm down for a few days. One time, he tried to make the trip on his own, but only got halfway before turning back. Nizam would tell them he wanted to become a lawyer, and Touma would relent, only to go back to resisting again. Nizam nearly cried out of frustration. He would stay in his room, lock his door from the inside, and refuse to eat. Finally, with the first signs of summer beginning to appear, Rakheema started to concede, and so did Nizam.

They'd stood their ground for two years, but Rakheema realized they wouldn't be able to hold him back forever. It occurred to her to get something from him in return. She whispered the idea in his ear, using Touma as a pretext.

'If you get baptised, he'll send you to Beirut . . . '

On a cold, rainy day in March, Nizam set out on his own for the village of Maydoun, which was said to have tumbled seven times before landing at the bottom of the slope. He didn't want any witnesses. He found the priest's house, beautiful with all the pine trees around it. The priest's wife answered the door and saw him standing there, wet and determined. She invited him in and called to her husband. The priest, suffering from a chest cold, was wearing his pajamas and had a crimson scarf wrapped around his neck. He was drinking herbal tea and spoke with a nasally voice. Nizam was in a hurry. He introduced himself and explained his situation to the priest.

'I know who you are, my son . . . ' He knew Touma and Rakheema and all the inhabitants of Hawra.

Nizam told him that he wanted to be baptised, but only on condition that the matter be kept secret, and that he was in a hurry and might change his mind any moment if the priest didn't fulfil his request immediately.

The priest was forced to improvise. He sat up straight, pulled his legs together. He made the sign of the cross and asked Nizam in a formal tone if he wished to embrace Christianity and if he believed in the Holy Trinity, the Virgin Mary, the Holy Catholic and Apostolic Church, and in the Authority of Patriarch St Boutros Boulos al-Maouchi. Nizam nodded his head in agreement with each question before hearing the whole thing. When the priest asked him to recite the Profession of Faith in confirmation of his previous statements, Nizam rattled off the opening so quickly, he swallowed half the words. But the priest quickly stopped him, accepting his profession, and asked him if he would like to change his name. Nizam declined. The priest suggested he might like to do as many others did and adopt a Christian baptismal name—the name of a patron saint that would be recorded in the Baptismal Register but not used in daily life.

He gave him some examples. Nizam hesitated, as if the idea had appealed to him for one fleeting moment. The priest encouraged him by saying that St Anthony's day was the following Sunday, which made it an appropriate name and an appropriate day.

'Today!' Nizam shouted adamantly.

The priest gazed into Nizam's face for a long time, then out the window at the rain hitting the glass. After suffering through a coughing fit, he made his decision. He excused himself for a few minutes and came back wearing his cassock, clerical collar and a black stole. He asked Nizam who he wanted as his sponsors. Nizam responded that it didn't matter, anyone was fine. So, the priest suggested his wife for a godmother, and that they would try to find him a godfather on their way to the church, which they set out for in the pouring rain, sharing one umbrella. The church was completely empty because of the storm, so Nizam grabbed the priest's umbrella and went out in search of a godfather while the priest put on his vestments over his cassock with the help of the church steward, who, the moment he'd seen the priest entering through the back door, had rushed into the church and started lighting candles to get things ready. The steward opened the service book to the Baptism section and remembered there wasn't any water in the church. He was going to come down with a chest cold, too, if he had to go outside with no umbrella, so the priest told him to hold the bowl outside the door and let it fill up with rain water—he would bless it afterwards.

The only person Nizam could find was the shopkeeper. After talking it over with him, the man agreed—mostly out of curiosity—and locked up his shop by propping a chair against the door.

In church, everyone was wet, but Nizam was completely soaked. So was the priest's wife, probably because her husband had held the umbrella directly over his own head as they walked beneath the incessant rain. The priest sped through the various stages of the Baptism ceremony, and when he tried to intone 'Kyrie eleison' in a high pitch, he completely lost his voice, bringing the ceremony to a halt. He summoned the steward to the altar to read with him. The priest moved his lips and mumbled along while the steward chanted the prayers in a loud voice. The shop-keeper helped out by humming the last few words. The first segment of the prayers ended with jarring dissonance. The priest poured the bowl of water over Nizam's head, who stood there persevering through the ceremony, wishing with a burning desire for it to be over. The priest signalled to the steward to turn the pages of the prayer book. As the cold water dripped down Nizam's back, he forced himself not to shiver, held his candle, and started circling through the church. His godparents followed behind him, and the steward, too. He didn't complete a full tour of the church, but turned back halfway, cutting it short to end the ceremony quickly. He tried to hand some money to the priest, who passed it along to the steward. Nizam's godfather left, so the priest sent Nizam immediately after him in the rain to bring him back so he could sign the certificate the priest had written in beautiful script stating that so-and-so appeared before me to proclaim his acceptance of the religion of Our Lord Jesus Christ, according to the faith of the Maronite Church of Antioch . . . Nizam stuffed the paper into the inner pocket of his jacket to protect it from the rain and took it directly to Hawra where he placed it on the table for Touma and Rakheema to see. He asked them not to announce it publicly, not for fear of his mother and father, but his aunts Najeeha and Zayneddar. Then he declared he was leaving for Beirut the next day—by his own personal means. It was as if he was clearing his conscience before obtaining his freedom.

Touma and Rakheema were defeated. They made an agreement with him to finish out the summer in Hawra and leave at the beginning of autumn. Perhaps some important matter would crop up to delay his departure from them.

PART TWO

Beirut? There's Beirut for You

1

Touma and Rakheema suggested that Nizam take the village taxi to Beirut, but he insisted on going by bus.

'Just like everyone else . . . ' he said.

They accompanied him as far as Tripoli, cautioning him the whole way to stay away from bad boys.

'And bad girls!' Rakheema added, shaking her head as she slipped a small pendant into his hand—'The Immaculate Conception'. He put it in his pocket but Rakheema insisted that he wear it around his neck. He, too, would not dare remove it. It was number three on his necklace now after the blue bead and Ayat al-Kursi.

'Don't go out without it . . . '

He was on his way to Beirut fully armed with amulets.

Touma and Rakheema were convinced he was incapable of looking after himself and that he would end up as the victim in everything he attempted to do.

They got out of the car in Tull Square and walked towards the stop for the Beirut-bound buses.

Some soldiers whose leave had come to an end gathered in front of the falafel stand, waiting their turn and watching the cook's every move as he turned the falafel patties over in the vat of hot oil and dripped with sweat.

Nizam walked hurriedly while the two of them tagged along trying to keep up with him and stick by his side until he took off.

'Don't worry,' Touma assured him. 'There's a bus every half hour.'

Nizam slowed his pace out of diffidence.

There were heaps of trash the municipality workers hadn't picked up yet that were getting scattered all over the road by the passing cars. The workers' pay checks were overdue, so they were on strike. The communist party was spurring them on, writing statements for them about higher wages, health insurance, the oppressive ruling class.

A roaming photographer stationed at the entrance gate to the public park started pestering them. He was very tall and had to lean down with his camera and its round flashcube to talk to the passers-by.

'Get your Polaroid picture! Ready in just one minute . . . '

Nizam stood between the two of them, worried that the bus would leave without him. The three of them smiled for the camera.

The cassette tape vendors filled the square with their shouts. The only voice louder than theirs was that of the announcer calling out to passengers at the bus stop, 'Beirut!'

The bus' motor was running, and the driver was seated behind the wheel. Written elegantly on both sides of the bus were two lines of poetry:

If you see the dog rise to power,
make a coat of mail for your legs.
It's shameful to wear it for fear of a dog bite,
but not the bite of a lion.

Touma climbed onto the bus through the front door and leaned over the driver to whisper something in his ear. Maybe it was to ask him to drive carefully and drop Nizam off at his hotel or give him directions to it.

Zahrat al-Shamal Hotel. 'Flower of the North'. Touma knew Raffoul the owner and hoped he would keep a watchful eye over Nizam.

Raffoul left for Beirut early on. He had no living relatives left in the village. He worked as a server in one of the restaurants in Bab Idriss until his parents died. After that he sold the house that he inherited from them in Hawra, sold a piece of land and everything else he owned in order to buy the little hotel.

Nizam picked up his belongings and climbed onto the bus. He was in such a rush that he was the first one on board. He didn't seem bothered by the smell of frying oil and reeking trash that inundated the bus. He made a point to sit on the side with a view of the sea. Rakheema reminded him for the thousandth time to come back at the end of the week and wished him safe travels from behind the glass.

He watched them for a few minutes as they walked down the long public park pavement. Touma was listing to the right and dragging his feet. Rakheema was walking straight with her blue polka-dot kerchief tied around her head. She turned one last time in the direction of the bus. A barefooted young beggar was pestering them. He grabbed Touma's hand but Touma slapped him on the wrist, shooing him away. They proceeded slowly, as though they no longer had any purpose now that Nizam had gone, as though their whole life was behind them. They faded into the commotion of the public square while Nizam could still identify them by Touma's leaning to the right with every step he took towards the parking lot where the taxi that would take them back up the mountain was parked.

All the bus seats filled up.

The faces of Monday riders . . . silent passengers returning to the capital where a week of work was waiting for them.

Nizam took note of everything, tried everything. He bought a lottery ticket from the seller who came down the bus' narrow walkway, waving lottery tickets at the passengers before takeoff. He had wanted to buy a falafel sandwich, too, but he didn't want to suffer hearing Rakheema's warning against consuming fried oil, which she considered poisonous.

He looked again in case he might catch sight of them one last time.

He thought about getting off the bus and chasing after them. He could send that pestering beggar away and wrap his arms around them with a big smile. Together they could gaze at the sweet picture Touma was holding—the Polaroid that he knew they would buy a nice frame for and find the perfect place to hang it in the house. Then he would intertwine his hands with theirs and they would stroll over to the Arabic pastry shop and watch him eat halawat al-jibn all by himself with their hearts bursting with joy. The doctor had warned Touma to stay away from sugar, and Rakheema would not indulge in sweets without him. But they disappeared down Izzeddine Street where Mahmoud al-Alami's travel agency had been located.

A man in his fifties, wearing a suit and a brightly coloured necktie, who appeared, from his dark-brown hair, to be wearing a wig, took the seat beside him. He smiled at Nizam and sat down. The man took Nizam's mind off Touma and Rakheema—with his hair and his smell: wild pine. All the seats filled up but there wasn't any chatter.

The bus set off, so the man beside him made the sign of the cross for safety's sake—using all five fingers. Nizam watched him for a long time. The sea appeared parallel to the road. He shut his eyes, imagining Touma and Rakheema still walking beside the clock tower near the public lavatories.

He checked the numbers on his lottery ticket and discovered it was for the lottery that had been drawn the week before. Young ticket sellers did that to travelers as they were leaving, in the hope that they would never run into them again. He tossed the ticket out the window, and then sharp cries suddenly arose from passengers in the front seats.

The bus slowed down before coming to a stop near a back-up of cars that was blocking the road. Nizam was the first to get off the bus to go see what was happening with the rest of the crowd. A motorcyclist had fallen into one of the salt mine pools. A red stain was colouring the water and growing wider. The sun was still at high noon. A truck loaded with bags of cement exiting the national cement factory was stopped in the middle of the road. It must have collided with the motorcyclist and sent him flying into the salt mine pool. The motorcycle also got thrown to the side of the road. A black Harley-Davidson. The handlebar had been ripped off. People said the policeman had flown off and landed in the middle of the salty pool. His blood was dyeing the saltwater red. He was floating, his hand behind his back, his face looking up at the sky. They said he was dead, and they weren't allowed to move his body before the ambulance arrived. A bearded man with a dark circle on the middle of his forehead was muttering some verses from the Quran with his eyes closed. Traffic came to a halt on both sides of the highway. Women covered the children's eyes with their hands so the image of the dead policeman would not be burned into their memories—his hand moving slightly, making it seem like he was napping in the breeze, his head propped on his elbow as if on a pillow, while the stream of blood stretched to the left in a nearly straight line. Maybe it was the windmills scattered there that were making ripples in the salt mine pool and causing his body to move a little. As soon as Nizam realized what was happening, he ran towards the drowned policeman and shooed away some of the bystanders standing in his path. He insisted on getting closer to him because he wasn't convinced the man was dead, even though they had all been standing there—watching him bleed to death.

He heard objections from the people behind him, but didn't care, advancing from one pool to another until he reached him. The man was peaceful. His eyes, the same colour as the water and the sky, were wide open. Nizam held him by the shoulders and tried to lift him up, his blue eyesfixed on the sky. As he stood in the water mixed with blood and salt, Nizam—who was almost twenty-three—now understood why it was so important to shut the eyes of the dead before anything else.

The paramedics, who arrived after Nizam, carried the dead man. Nizam went back to the road, and a middle-aged woman asked him about the biker's name. He didn't pay her any attention, so she started asking others. She said she had a nephew who worked with the traffic police. And when they passed in front of her, carrying the dead man on a stretcher, she gasped as she admired his handsome face. She tried to touch him, as if seeking his blessing, and she kept asking the paramedics about his name, but they told her that they didn't know. The look on her face showed she was quite moved, but she didn't cry. She kept talking.

The pocket watch stopped. It was an old-fashioned model, and it wasn't waterproof. It was Touma's watch—the one he had given Nizam before going down to Beirut. Rakheema had given him the Virgin Mary and Touma the pocket watch. He loved hearing the clicking sound every time he closed the gold-plated cover.

The water on Nizam's trousers dried out, but the blood remained. When the road was reopened, the bus took off again, and so he entered Beirut up to his knees in blood, as they say.

The trip resumed in silence until they entered the tunnel past the town of Chekka. It was a long tunnel, and once they exited it, they looked out upon the sprawling blueness of the sea. Chatting ensued among the passengers as if the darkness had erased the sight of the biker drowned in his own blood. A business negotiation started in a nearby seat.

The person seated sea-side was trying to persuade the one sitting mountain-side to buy some socks from him, swearing repeatedly in the name of the Prophet Muhammad that they were pure cotton. He was carrying two boxes of them. With some difficulty, he raised his leg to the level of his head so he could expose his socks. The fact that he was wearing the brand he was selling was supposed to be enough proof to persuade his neighbour to buy some. He read the words 'pure cotton', printed in English, and negotiated as if he was guaranteeing the customer a privilege that distinguished him from everybody else.

The woman who had been asking about the dead policeman took out some yarn and two knitting needles from her bag and asked her neighbour to open the window since it was hot. Then she started to knit, all the while mumbling, as if she was counting stitches.

There were only a few swimmers on the beach, but they were right by the highway. Among them were some women in skimpy beach clothes, so those sitting sea-side kept their faces plastered to the windows.

The man sitting next to Nizam looked at his bloody trousers and then at his face. He kept making the sign of the cross. Nizam counted—the man did it more than ten times. He did it when the bus passed a church built of white stone on the main road. The other times he did it, Nizam didn't see any churches. The man looked at Nizam, smiling. He said he knew the locations of the churches inside the villages that weren't visible from the main road, so he made the sign of the cross whenever the bus passed the streets parallel to these villages. And then there were the small shrines whose locations he knew by heart. Nizam became certain that the man was wearing a wig. The man added that it wasn't right to pass a church and not make the sign of the cross.

Nizam took a book out from his bag—a remnant of the New Culture Bookstore—but he didn't get past the first few lines. It returned to him—pressing upon him—the image of the policeman in the water. The view outside captured his attention.

They passed near the Casino du Liban. On the wall by the road next to the Casino, the words 'God', 'Nation' and 'Family' were engraved in stone in several colours. They were in the shape of an equilateral triangle, with 'God', at the top and 'Nation' and 'Family' at each corner of the base.

Nizam asked the man with the wig if he knew why the woman wanted someone to tell her the name of the dead policeman.

'She's lying,' the man asserted. 'She doesn't have a relative in the police force. She just wants to check whether he was Muslim or Christian.'

'What about her? Is she Muslim or Christian?'

The man smiled again. 'Look at her. You'll be able to tell.'

She was sitting in the third row in the front. She sat up straight, without resting her back on the seat, criss-crossing her knitting needles quickly and smoothly as she mumbled. Nizam looked at her, but he couldn't tell.

The bus reached the Dawra area in front of the Almaza beer factory, and from there entered a straight road shaded by eucalyptus trees. The branches that met up high from both sides of the road, like victory arches, were Nizam's oldest memory of Beirut. Back then, they had rushed him to Hôtel-Dieu hospital to be treated for tonsillitis because Rakheema only trusted the doctors in the capital.

The passengers started to fidget. Nizam's neighbour made the sign of the cross one last time as he pointed with his hand to a neighbourhood on the left side and whispered, 'That's St Vartan's Church. He's Armenian, but I love him . . . '

The knitting lady smiled at the passengers sitting beside her. 'Hamdillah as-salameh, Thank God, we made it safely.'

She probably assumed that now that the bus was going through narrow, busy streets, it was no longer at risk of crashing before the final stop.

The driver's assistant opened the door of the bus, expecting that some of the passengers might request to get off before the bus reached its final destination in Burj Square.

A boy latched onto the back of the bus. His red-headed friend chased after him.

'Kurds,' one of the passengers said as he glanced towards the back of the bus.

The red-headed boy was sticking his tongue out at the passengers.

'Kurds, gypsies . . . God knows what,' another added as he pointed towards the vast area between the road and the sea.

Karantina.

The man selling socks pointed out to his neighbour the forest of antennas that sat on top of all the wood and tin huts. A television in every house.

'*We* are the poor ones', he told him, sighing.

Nizam stuck his tongue out at the red-headed boy. The boy responded by giving Nizam the middle finger from behind the window.

The bus stopped in traffic.

A man standing on the pavement, smoking a cigarette, read the poem written on the side of the bus and then asked the driver's assistant jokingly, 'Who's the dog?'

'You'll have to ask the driver,' the assistant said, as he tugged at his shirt, gesturing that he had nothing to do with it.

In turn, as he stood there, the man partially concealed a slogan that was written on the wall behind him. The slogan was written in a crooked handwriting that went downwards as if someone had scribbled it in a rush, under the cover of darkness.

'Feudalism and Capitalism are on their way out!'

Ever since they entered the city, Nizam couldn't help but read everything that could be read. He devoured the signs and the names of shops and small hotels.

The bus passed over the Nahr Beirut Bridge. The assistant closed the door since the odour from the sewers was intolerable.

They reached the port and entered Burj Square. In the centre of the square stood a billboard by the ministry of public health that read, 'Vaccinate your children against polio before it is too late.' Someone had crossed out the word 'polio' and written over it 'a peaceful solution'. A peaceful solution with Israel, that is.

Nizam picked up his bag and walked towards the rear door that the assistant had reopened as the trip was nearing its end. He wanted to be the first one to get off, so he jumped off the bus before it came to a stop; he twisted his ankle and screamed from pain impulsively as he fell and then stood up with some difficulty. The passengers in the back yelled, which prompted the driver to hit the brakes and bring the bus to a halt. Once he looked in the rear-view mirror and saw him manage to get up, albeit on one foot, he addressed the passengers angrily, asking them to be patient and telling them that they were not permitted to get off the bus before he turned the engine off. Nizam tried to stand on the other foot but it was too painful, and so, a slew of recommendations from his friends on the bus descended upon him.

'Soak your foot in warm water so it doesn't swell up,' the driver's assistant advised him.

'No, no. Put it in cold water,' said one of the passengers who seemed more confident.

2

And that's how, one Monday morning, Nizam made his way to Beirut by himself for the first time. He arrived at Zahrat al-Shamal hotel limping, the blood on his trousers now dried out.

He found Raffoul sitting in the lobby. He was wiping his thick glasses with a white handkerchief. Raffoul spent his whole day behind a tall desk with a notebook sitting on it in which he had quit writing the names of guests a long time ago. He heard heavy footsteps on the wooden staircase, whose corners were dark, even in the middle of the day. He lifted his head, waiting to scrutinize the person entering the hotel as if he was seeing him for the first time in his life, even if the person who crossed the threshold was a regular customer Raffoul knew inside and out.

He wasn't surprised by Nizam's arrival, as if he had been expecting him to walk through that door all along.

'How's Touma doing?'

It was the only question he asked, and he didn't wait for an answer.

He showed Nizam to his room, cautioning him not to leave any money or valuables that could be stuffed into pockets whenever he left his room, day or night.

'Robberies are on the rise' he said, but he didn't clarify whether these things were happening just at the hotel or in the country in general.

The room he showed him had two beds and overlooked Burj Square, but he didn't give him a key. In any case, there were no keys to be found at Zahrat al-Shamal. They were lost a long time ago; perhaps some of the guests had forgotten them in their pockets upon departing.

'You'll be spending a few days with Abu Ali al-Simsmani.'

'Who?'

'Metuali . . . '

He didn't know many Metualis.

'He's Shiite?'

'He's a good guy. You won't even know he's there.'

Nizam had thought the smell that filled the staircase wouldn't follow him all the way up to the rooms upstairs. He almost asked Raffoul how he was able to sit there all day with that smell keeping him company. Raffoul remained standing at the door of the room watching as he emptied the few items of clothing he'd brought from his bag.

'Yasmeen will be here every Tuesday and Friday to change the sheets and do some laundry.'

'Don't fool around with her,' he warned. 'You might catch something . . . '

He didn't finish his sentence. Perhaps he knew she was easy and would never turn down money.

Nizam lay down and put the foot with the twisted ankle up on the edge of the bed. It all came to him, from below, from Burj Square, every single sound, every engine roar, every driver's shout about the direction he was headed. A room in the midst of the city's hustle and bustle, in the middle of the main road.

You wanted Beirut? There's Beirut for you.

Nizam had his head propped up on two pillows. He could now see the iron hand holding a torch, its flame also made of iron, waving backwards as if the sculptor wanted to suggest that the wind blew on the Martyrs' Statue from west to east. The wind blew on the flame, but it didn't extinguish it. If Nizam had raised his head up from the pillow a bit, he would have been able to see the whole statue—with its four people—in the middle of the square, including the man rolling on the ground, his arm reaching out as if asking for help from above, and his friend looking at the life-sized model of Anita Ekberg raised above the Rivoli Cinema. The blonde stood there, at a height of three stories of the adjacent building. Most likely, they put the mannequin up in order to advertise for the film *La Dolce Vita*. The film played in the theatre for about a week at most, but the wooden Anita Ekberg remained standing with her bare shoulders, her colours now faded.

The odour was constant, never subsiding or going away all together.

First, there was the stench from the lavatories, which he had yet to use, mixed with the smell of the Dettol detergent which they dumped in there to get rid of the odour. Then there was the smell of exhaust from the taxis, the hundreds of old Mercedes that crossed and roamed Burj Square. Every now and then, the smell of barbecued kafta wafted from the east side, nourishing the stench.

There was one more stubborn ingredient that contributed to that odour, which he couldn't put his finger on.

After a while, he asked one of his friends about the odour at Raffoul's hotel. Smiling, the friend asserted, 'It's the smell of the public souq!'

Only the room in which Raffoul slept had a window that over-looked al-Mutanabbi Street from the east. Raffoul had bought the hotel from its Aleppan owner who had called it 'Nazl al-Udaba', the Writers' Inn. He tried bargaining for a lower price because of the neighbouring public souq but the Aleppan argued that the hotel's proximity to that area attracts—rather than turns off—

customers, and he gave all sorts of examples and numbers to prove his point. Raffoul lived at the hotel in Beirut all by himself, with no children or anything else to his name. The hotel had six rooms, including his own that he gave up whenever the hotel got too crowded. He would settle for the sofa in the lobby, where he'd lie down and sleep in his clothes. Raffoul said he loved Hawra and would reassure those who chastised him for forgetting it that he was certainly planning on returning there one day—to the cemetery.

Even though he rarely left Burj Square and its immediate surroundings, Raffoul served as a guide for the people of Hawra and its surrounding areas—and their mandatory stop. Those who came to the capital and were dropped off by their taxi or bus in Burj Square started their day by stopping by Raffoul's hotel. For example, he would show them how to get to the clinic of Dr Merhej, who had developed quite the reputation for being able to treat every conceivable stomach disease. Sometimes, if Raffoul was able to find someone to take his place behind the desk, he would accompany them to the official government offices nearby. They would store their things and leave each other messages at the hotel. If they needed to use the restroom while they were in Al-Nouriyya Souq, they knew that their best option was to rush over to Zahrat al-Shamal. He neither complained about them nor welcomed them, and he simply alerted them about incidents that might happen during the day they spent in Beirut. For instance, he would caution them against going to al-Bashoura area on a day when the funeral of three Palestinian leaders who were killed in a military operation was going to take place, since he believed that there would be a shooting or that the mourners might clash with the army because 'hearts were full', as he always said when commenting on the slightest incident.

Nizam tried standing up on the foot with the twisted ankle as he headed from the room to the lobby, and Raffoul warned him not to wander too far, gesturing towards the west with his hand.

Nizam went outside to the clamour that never stopped and was repulsed by the smell. He walked slowly, exploring; he went around Zahrat al-Shamal in a semi-circle towards the south-east.

He stood next to a few men who were watching the deft three-card player who spread out his cards, face down, on a chair that he hunched over: two red queens and a black king. One of the men who hovered over the card player first bet on the king of spades and won five liras and then bet ten liras and won again. Nizam saw the king of spades, certain that it was in the middle. Everybody watched as if anticipating something would happen as Nizam bet on the king of spades. He won five liras and saw where the man put the king of spades the second time around, but he missed. He missed and had to pay up. He'd gotten it right only once and kept on missing it every other time. He persisted stubbornly and lost a hundred liras. Nizam looked like he wanted to keep going all the way to the end, but one of the bystanders who was in charge of keeping watch warned them as he whispered, 'John, John, the police are here!'

The three-card player folded his chair and ran in the direction of an inside street while the rest of the people ran in the other direction. It all happened so astonishingly quickly that Nizam found himself standing alone on the pavement, not knowing what to do. There was only one man—whom he hadn't paid any attention to as he was busy betting—left standing beside him. The man told him that the first winner was the dealer's partner and that he let Nizam win the first time around, so he could lure him into playing and that the man who said that the cops were coming was also a partner. He also told him that the card player's name was not John and that no officers were coming. He said the players weren't running away from the police but from Nizam. They had taken off with his money and were now splitting it among themselves in the back alley. He added that they were all brothers or cousins who belonged to the tribes of Arab al-Maslakh—the Arabs of the slaughterhouse.

Nizam laughed, amused.

The man asked him, 'Where are you from?'

Nizam had started wondering a little earlier just how to answer that question and others like it. He usually avoided answering them. He looked at the man talking to him and couldn't decide.

The man saved him from answering by asking, 'You have a northern accent, right?'

'Watch out for yourself,' the man said.

Nizam didn't know him. It was the first time he'd ever talked to him, so he told the man to take care as well. But Nizam didn't really take care. He forgot about his losses as soon as he took a few steps, resuming his stroll uphill.

A man who was setting a trap in front of the cigarette and alcohol shop started pestering him. The man moved his limbs as if he was about to start walking, about to cross or join the rest of the pedestrians downhill in the direction of the vegetable market, but he wouldn't budge, for even one metre. He tried to suggest that he was ready to leave, but he wouldn't move. His eyes were lined with kohl, and his voice was soft and feminine. Nizam smiled at him. The man followed Nizam, staring sharply at him. He complimented Nizam's eyes and hair and gestured with his arms as if wanting to caress his shoulders and neck. Nizam laughed and didn't get mad at him. He looked around to see if there were any witnesses who saw what was happening to him, but didn't see anyone. So he just gave the man the remaining money he had in his hands that he had been planning to bet on the king of spades before the game was broken up. The man snatched the money in disbelief, turned his back and walked away. He returned to his location in front of the cigarette shop. He moved his body all over again in all directions, suggesting that he was about to start walking.

Nizam glanced back and saw him pestering another young man. He had the same look of yearning as someone who had just found his long-awaited lover.

Nizam trembled upon arriving to al-Dabbas Square. A parrot called for him in a piercing voice from the pet shop across the street.

'Are you Ahmad?'

He looked around, sensing that the question was directed at him only, although there were a lot of people exiting the nearby movie theatre which specialized in Indian films.

'Are you Ahmad?' the parrot repeated. Nizam trembled again before stopping at the end of the pavement to look at the parrot sitting in his cage. The taxis started stopping parallel to him because the drivers thought that he was looking for a ride. He didn't want to lose sight of the parrot for fear that he might take him by surprise again with his question. The bird went silent.

At the red light at the top of the square, a man with a red-and-white checkered keffiyeh wrapped around his neck handed him a flyer. On top of the page, two rifles hugged one another over a map of Palestine. The three women who were slowly climbing up the stairs of the white-stone church and chatting together refused to take one of the flyers that the friend of the man in the keffiyeh tried to hand them. The women gestured with their hands towards the door of the church, as if indicating that the sanctity of prayer wasn't compatible with the things that the flyer talked about. Nizam read the entire flyer and then made it into a paper boat.

A man selling used books started to gather his merchandise quickly from the pavement, perhaps because night-time had fallen or because he feared the uninterrupted hail of bullets that sounded like it was coming from the direction of the vegetable market and that made pedestrians pick up their pace without even looking at the man standing in front of the Radio City movie theatre inviting them to watch an X-rated double feature.

A police jeep pulled up. Four officers stepped out of it and stood next to the Martyr Statue as if they were there to protect the man carrying the iron torch and his friends from an imminent attack.

Nizam asked the officer standing with his rifle ready beside the bronze man rolling on the ground what was going on. He answered, trembling slightly, with the demeanour of someone who could use some company. It was an old story that had started in al-Hermel. Feuding clans. Now they'd moved to Beirut. Someone from the Dandash clan had killed three men in the vegetable market to avenge his brother. He was still there, waiting for the police to arrive so he could turn himself and his weapons in. They considered prison safer than staying out on the run . . . Nizam got the feeling the policeman wanted to keep talking, but the assisting officer gruffly ordered Nizam to move along.

He went back to Zahrat al-Shamal. The stench was still there in the stairway and was now in fact enriched with some new, night-time odours.

'Good thing you came back,' said the ever-watchful Raffoul. 'You had me worried. Don't go back out tonight.'

Abu Ali al-Simsmani had returned to the room ahead of him. He was in bed with the blanket pulled up over his head to cover his ears. When he asked Nizam about the gunshots, he told him three people from the Nassereddine family had been killed.

Al-Simsmani cursed the situation without looking at Nizam. A few minutes later he asked from under the covers, 'Are you from the same village as Raffoul?'

'Yes.'

Nizam tried to scrutinize the Metuali face-to-face but was forced to make do with just his voice.

'How are we going to sleep with all this noise?' Nizam asked.

Al-Simsmani lifted the blanket off his head and said, without looking at Nizam, 'The adhan at dawn is the most aggravating of all. The sheikh's voice stabs you like a knife.'

Nizam tried to sleep, but nothing outside was sleeping. Al-Simsmani managed to fall asleep. Nizam tossed and turned until one o'clock in the morning when he finally got out of bed. He put on some clothes and left the hotel through the door that was left open day and night. Raffoul was asleep in his room. Nizam went outside to all the sounds and stood on the pavement, surrendering himself to the hubbub of the night. Then he turned down the narrow road leading to al-Mutanabbi Street.

A woman in her fifties who was all decked out called to him from the doorstep of one of the houses, so he went inside. She didn't try to stop him. Her whole reason for dolling herself up was to lure customers inside. The two women sitting in the salon were much younger than her. They didn't budge, not believing he was actually a customer. He didn't look anything like their usual customers.

A man with such freshness hadn't come their way in years. The decked-out woman followed him inside where she found him talking to the other two. The brunette was talkative, and had an Egyptian accent, while the other one—white-skinned with a scowl on her face—didn't speak at all. Didn't listen either.

'She's Greek . . . ' her companion explained, introducing her before anyone asked.

The decked-out woman brought a bottle of Johnny Walker, two glasses, and a bucket of ice.

Nizam poured whiskey into the glasses and took a sip. The silent Greek woman grabbed his hand, and he accompanied her to the room. She unzipped his trousers and knelt in front of him. She tickled him, and he nearly laughed but managed to control himself with some difficulty. He ran his fingers through her hair as she tried to pleasure him. She stopped briefly to move his hand away, so he wouldn't mess up her sad hairdo. She exerted her best effort and finished him off quickly. He didn't put up much of a fight.

He paid her—a much more generous amount than she was used to—and went back to the salon. They sent him off with the bottle of whiskey. As he headed for the door, the woman who had received him advised him not to pay any heed to the man sprawled on the stairway. He was always passed out drunk. They'd kicked him out of all the Zaytouni area and Phoenicia Street bars, so he'd started hanging around their place every night.

'We get all the rejects . . . '

Nizam sat down beside him on the stairs. The man asked for a sip of whiskey which he took directly from the bottle in one long swig. He cursed the women in a mixture of French and Arabic. Nizam understood from him that the Greek one was not really Greek; she was just faking it because she thought it raised her status in the eyes of customers. All of a sudden, he stopped talking and got up onto his feet to shake Nizam's hand.

'I'm Cyril,' he said, introducing himself. 'I love women and I love men . . . ' he added in French, completing his introduction before flopping back down on the steps.

Something inside Nizam tightened up.

A few customers entered without looking at them. They stepped over them like some sort of obstacle in their path.

The night got cold. Nizam returned to Zahrat al-Shamal at dawn. Abu Ali al-Simsmani was tossing and turning and cursing the muezzin from beneath the pillow he'd put over his head.

Nizam slept a little and then started to get a heavy feeling in his gut. He vomited near Raffoul's desk on his way to the bathroom. Abu Ali woke up. He awakened Raffoul and inspected the whiskey bottle.

'Those Armenians in Burj Hammoud make imitation whiskey. They make imitations of everything!'

That was the first day of the three months Nizam spent in Burj Square.

He stayed under their watchful eyes—Raffoul from behind his glasses and the Hawra taxi driver who showed up on a daily basis.

One day it was to deliver a bag or a box from Rakheema, another day it was words of advice. The driver would pass by her in the morning after picking up his passengers from their homes. Before he even beeped his horn, Rakheema would be standing at the door ready for him. She would divide up, package, and tightly wrap up Nizam's meals, as if he were still living at home with them. Raffoul showed his disapproval every time but weakened before the plates of kibbeh stuffed with meat and pine nuts. Sometimes he'd ask for a small helping for Yasmeen which he'd save to give to her when she came to clean. Abu Ali dined with Nizam; he especially liked the labniyyeh. Nizam set the fruits Rakheema sent aside, saving them for Cyril after everyone had fallen asleep and there was no one else around. If a day passed when she didn't send food, Rakheema would dictate orders to the driver instead.

If, for example, she heard something on the radio about an attack carried out by some masked gunmen on the al-Nahr police station to free one of the detainees, she'd tell him to pick Nizam up and take him to Hawra—even if he had to force him.

At the end of the first week after arriving in Beirut Nizam returned to Hawra, but he only stayed for one night. He didn't go the following week, so they came to him on Monday morning. Touma gave him some fresh new bills sharp enough to cause paper-cuts. They complimented the hotel despite its state of decline and didn't flinch at the stench. Rakheema didn't inspect the room and the bed, for she knew it would be disgusting and completely filthy. Still, she'd rather he stayed at Zahrat al-Shamal than anywhere else.

Sometimes Sundays in Beirut made him sad, so he'd go see them. They kept the doors and windows locked shut, as if no one was home. They'd give him kisses, feed him, gaze at him, talk with him and counsel him, even if jokingly, on the necessity of getting married sooner or later. If he slipped from their hands, at least they could grab onto his children.

He'd head back to Beirut Monday morning with enthusiasm, as though he'd been missing out on big happenings there.

He roamed around during the day and came back at night to find Abu Ali asleep with the pillow over his head. When Nizam woke up late the next morning, Abu Ali would be gone.

'He bets on the horses' Raffoul said, offering an explanation for this behaviour of his.

Nizam went to the university by foot, passing the parrot on his way. He chose a seat in class where he could leave without disturbing anyone. He would remain a first-year law student his entire life. He wrote random words in his notebook and never really acclimated with the academic environment. He never made a single friend at the university. He would tip-toe out and go have some foule—seasoned fava beans—for lunch. He turned his nose up at Rakheema's cooking for the most part. He knew it by heart and yearned for something different. He'd always get up halfway through his lunch to take his plate of foule to the counter to ask for more olive oil and lemon juice. He wandered through the gold souq, stopping to look in at the window displays and read the headlines on all the news-stands. He flipped through the pages of some used books displayed on the pavement but didn't buy any. He tried an arguileh at Palestine Café and billiards at Jumhuriyya Café. He played with men much older than him. One wore a tarbush and played astonishingly well. Nizam paid when he lost and paid when he won, too. He'd get back to Zahrat al-Shamal at ten o'clock at night to find Raffoul and Abu Ali al-Simsmani both fast asleep. Abu Ali would doze off listening to his transistor radio turned down low broadcasting Umm Kulthoum's voice, and whenever one song came to an end, he'd search half-asleep for another station. He'd settle for Abdel Halim Hafez or Warda and then go back to sleep. Nizam usually got sleepy around eleven, but a new sound came along—a blaring car horn—so he opened his eyes. He roamed around the movie theatres and entered one that was still showing movies after midnight. There were a few audience members scattered around the theatre. He bumped into the three-card players and flashed them a smile, so they invited him to play. They hadn't given up hope on him. He continued on his way, always turning in the direction of al-Mutanabbi Street and heading, in fact, for Cyril—not the ladies. Cyril kept him entertained. First, he'd stop in shyly to see the girls and give them money for sex or no sex, out of kindness. Those flabby ladies loved him. He gave them joy. He taught them to call him 'Nano, Nano'. They would call to him from the window when he went outside to Cyril, to the place he met him the very first time, on the steps to Nadia's house, first one on the right—his headquarters. On clear nights at least. Cyril would fill him with sermons and the smell of imitation whiskey. They would be alone, not a soul around, but Cyril always orated as if addressing a crowd. He made Nizam laugh, scorning the new bourgeoisie—those war profiteers. He refuted the notion that people voiced their opinions via general elections, because they didn't know what was good for them. Nizam agreed with him without giving the topic any thought. Cyril would affirm once more, as if bragging, that his sexual preferences were distributed equally among women and men. Every time he mentioned sex, Nizam would back away from him, suddenly realizing Cyril was rubbing up against him. Cyril believed Lebanon was the most beautiful country in the world. His father was Lebanese, his mother was French, and his grandmother had worked with the resistance against the Nazis—believe what you like. Cyril told him how in his capacity as a choreographer he had participated in the Casino du Liban's Paris–Beirut show, but the girls—those dancing harlots—complained to the director that Cyril was pushing them to smoke joints during the breaks. He was just helping them improve their performance, dilating their blood vessels. The administration ended up firing him and also putting his name on the list posted on the door of people banned from entering the game room inside the casino. He got tired of talking about himself one of those nights, so he asked his drinking buddy where he was staying. He raised his eyebrows when he heard Zahrat al-Shamal. And he turned his nose up, too, perhaps remembering the stench. He cursed Raffoul.

'That low-life. One time he made me sleep on the pavement . . .'

He seemed to want to punish Raffoul and rob him of his customer. He told Nizam that a woman friend of his—which he said with a wink—who was a little crazy, was looking for a trustworthy person to rent her place in Ras Beirut.

The next day Cyril reminded him again.

'It's a really nice flat overlooking the sea . . . Olga's dying to rent it out, so she can leave the country for a while.'

He told him about having tried to give her a spot on the Paris–Beirut Dance Troupe, but she refused.

Nizam was still hesitant. Cyril suggested he go see it the next day and make a decision after that. He didn't go, so the next day Cyril pressed him saying, 'She's expecting you tomorrow before she leaves. Bring a whole year's rent with you. Just in case you like the place . . . '

He winked at him and finished his sentence, '. . . and the lady who owns it.'

3

Olga Filipovna.

'A white Russian,' explained Cyril. 'Rousse blanche.'

She lived in the Manara neighbourhood on the top floor of a building overlooking the sea.

Nizam arrived there by bus.

She inspected him from head to toe then took him by the hand on a tour of the house, repeating, 'You're so adorable,' for no apparent reason.

She pointed out the samovar and advised him to take good care of it. It was real silver, she said. He didn't know what a samovar was.

'It was a wedding gift from my husband . . . But I don't believe anything he says any more. Maybe it's not silver.'

She turned the stove burner on for him. It worked. She opened the refrigerator and shut it again. The light didn't come on, but it was cooling well.

She took him outside to the spacious balcony overlooking the sea of Beirut. The sea could read the stars.

'Rain is on the way.' Nizam guessed it right every time. He knew because he lived by the sea.

She huffed and puffed without being tired, panting in anticipation of the excitement and the fatigue of the pending flight to Los Angeles. She surrendered to the reality of the situation.

'There's no time for me to move my things, and I don't have anywhere to move them to, anyway.' She had a very strong lisp on the 'r'.

She instructed him about the potted flowers before looking at him to say, 'I might come back, and I might not. I hope not.'

She caressed his hand lovingly.

She could sense his excitement. She welcomed it.

He stood before the sea, contemplating the anchored ships approaching the port. He pulled some bills out of his pocket and paid her a whole year's rent.

'Cyril tells me you're a student at the university . . . '

It suddenly occurred to her to warn him, 'Don't bring him here . . . I beg you.'

She needed the rent money because James Coburn had sent for her but hadn't sent her any money. He'd met her the year before in Beirut in one of the nightclubs. He fell in love with her, and she fell in love with him. He sent her a telegram. She pulled it out of her purse and read it to Nizam, her voice full of emotion.

'I've made a reservation for us . . . '

She closed her eyes dreamily as she said 'us'.

' . . . at the Marriott, thirtieth floor. I'm waiting for you with bated breath.'

She continued uttering intermittent phrases, warning him of various dangers.

'They won't leave you in peace!'

Nizam didn't ask her who 'they' were or who 'you' were either.

They went back into the living room. She glanced at the clock. She had placed her bags by the door.

He asked her about the picture of the man with a heavy beard and moustache wearing a black fur cap, with a piercing black look in his eyes.

'That's the Grand Duke Nicholas Nikolaevich, uncle of Tsar Nicholas II, dressed in the Circassian uniform . . . '

She wanted to add something but hesitated, smiling apologetically. 'Remind me your name again?' she asked.

He gave only his first name: Nizam. She got lost in the forest of Lebanese names.

She lowered her voice some as she told Nizam about how the Grand Duke was very tall and was married to the Princess Militza of Montenegro, a paragon of beauty. But the important thing was that he took vengeance for them on the Jews, in Kiev and other cities . . .

She hesitated a little.

'If you don't like him, I can hide him in the closet.'

She looked at the icon and then took him by the hand again. He wrapped his arm around her from behind. She didn't try to stop him, but suddenly blurted, 'I forgot to tell you the most important thing! The icon! St George! It's been in our family for generations. My mother carried it all the way here from St Petersburg. She abandoned the fur coat she wore to the reception for poor Tsar Nicholas II at the winter palace, but not the icon.'

The saint's face showed no emotion but rather a childlike innocence that seemed to have appeared on his countenance the moment he thrusted his lance into the dragon's mouth. A small angel was fluttering its wings like a bird and holding a crown of laurel over his head. The king's daughter was standing in a corner of the painting, at the door of her father's palace perhaps. The white horse assumed a prominent position in the scene. The saint's head was capped with a Roman helmet.

She moved his hand away politely and turned to face him. 'Please don't be offended by the question . . . Are you Muslim or Christian?'

He smiled. 'If we meet again,' he promised her, 'I will tell you my whole life story.'

He'd embarrassed her. He held her hand again.

'It doesn't matter. They told me Muslims believe in St George too.'

Then she warned him, 'Whatever religion you are, don't take the icon down from the wall. It protects me when I travel. Keep it positioned there, looking out at the sea . . . '

He corrected her while caressing her neck, 'But St George is looking at the beast!'

'No,' she corrected him, backing away a little. 'The icon is looking out at the sea, not St George!'

He didn't understand, but she seemed certain about it.

He squeezed into the lift with her, insisting on helping her with her luggage. He pressed the down button, and she wrapped her arms around him this time and gave him a long kiss on the lips. She told him he was going to get a good taste of her lipstick. He pressed the emergency stop button, trying to extend their embrace by bringing the lift to a halt. They were unable to get the lift going again after that, so they banged on the door for the concierge to come and get them out. It was the kiss of long-time lovers whose flavour Nizam would never forget.

She got into the taxi while still running her fingers through his hair.

'You will tell me your story someday. Wish me luck.'

'Goodbye,' he said, then paused before adding, 'I'm waiting for you. Come back.'

'I'll be back, at the very least for my mother's sake. She lives with her cats and her memories, over there on the coastal highway in Jounieh. In a beautiful old house.'

She grabbed him by his shirt and started shaking him.

'They're going to burn Beirut very soon. They sent you the Fedayeen and now they've come to kill them. They dressed up as women, put on colourful wigs like hookers. They had some spies here who helped them get in . . .'

He would leave her name as it was on the door and next to the doorbell at the entrance to the building. Olga Filipovna. And if she received any mail, he would keep it for her.

As the taxi sped off, she blew him a kiss, and he waved goodbye.

The taxi stopped suddenly. She forgot something.

She craned her head out the back window to say, 'What's your name? I can't remember it. Forgive me . . .'

'Nizam', he answered once again.

Then she added, 'Take care of the icon, Nizam . . .'

And her final words of advice, 'Get out of Beirut. They're going to destroy it, shake it from its foundations.'

He didn't run, and he didn't bring Cyril over, but he did bring many others instead.

First there was Moussa.

He brought him over the same day he met him, lost and confused at Zahrat al-Shamal.

He'd just come from Hawra, bringing with him a thick blue worsted-wool sweater for Nizam that Rakheema paid one of the women to knit for him because her hands could no longer stay still enough to hold the knitting needles and work with them. Now her hands trembled just like her voice.

'She's worried about you in the cold,' he said, just like that—no 'Rakheema', no 'your mother'.

Nizam invited Moussa to the new flat. He slept in the room Olga had set up for her anticipated children, while Nizam slept in the spacious bed where her squabbles with her husband had undoubtedly taken place. Throughout the two days they spent in Manara and its suburbs, Moussa was in a semi-permanent state of shock. Nizam couldn't leave him alone for even one hour roaming in the nearby hotel district without Moussa hurrying back, grabbing him by the shirt, and leading him outside to point out the dark green camouflage-painted Jeep, splattered with mud, that had the words 'al-Kifah al-Musallah'—'Armed Struggle'—written on it. It was always parked near the Beirut Theatre. The exhausted driver would be fast asleep over the wheel, as if he'd just returned from a night-time battle on some unknown war front. Or Moussa would whisper a question about the man and woman who lived on the first floor of the building. They had smiled at him and offered him a free copy of the New Testament. When he took it, they offered him some other pamphlets. Nizam told him they taught at the American University and tried to scare him by saying they were Jehovah's Witnesses or something of that nature. Moussa got upset all of a sudden and threw the Bible and other pamphlets from his hands as though they'd given him an electric shock or tainted him somehow. Nizam let out a long laugh. When Moussa asked him about the women, 'the hareem of Beirut', as he said, Nizam told him about the beautiful Olga who left for Hollywood to meet up with James Coburn.

'With who? James Coburn the actor?'

He had recently seen Coburn in *The Magnificent Seven* at the movie theatre in Hawra and couldn't believe his ears. He was completely stunned now.

When Nizam said goodbye to Moussa, he recommended that he drop by the public souq before going up to Hawra. He instructed Moussa to be nice to his acquaintances there and cautioned him not to fall prey to the three-card hustlers. But Moussa had stopped listening because he was overwhelmed with all of the horrors he'd seen and just wanted to get away from there. He decided to stay at the hotel and wait for the village taxi driver. When he got back to Hawra, he filled everyone's ears with Nizam's news.

He said that Nizam was tossing money out the window, smoking hashish, gambling on everything from billiards to horse racing, that he lived in the most beautiful flat in Beirut, and that he was in love with a movie star, James Coburn's girlfriend. He spent money on her and others without thinking twice. He said Nizam was going to force Touma into selling land so he could pay for his needs—Touma, who spent his entire life buying land and refusing to buy houses, since there was something sacred about houses. Nizam was going to be the death of Touma—Nizam and diabetes, that is.

Ali Soueidan showed up at the flat uninvited.

He knocked at the door at eleven o'clock at night and asked for Olga's husband whom he said he knew. He knew everything about everyone.

He said he had no other option but to spend the night there.

Nizam thought about the proposition. He found the young man to be pleasant and enjoyed his company, so he decided to let him stay.

Ali considered himself a guest of Olga's husband, so he wore the man's nightrobe and strutted around the house in it. He made coffee—he knew where the sugar and coffee were—fixed an electrical problem, lit a joint and passed it to Nizam who soon broke into a fit of laughter.

Nizam slept happily. In the morning, he found Ali washing and ironing his shirts. He pressed the creases meticulously. He preferred white linen shirts with no collar. He would either buy collarless shirts or take the shirts to a tailor who removed the collars for him.

He said he was from al-Bazouriyyeh in the south, but that he was born where his family was now living in the al-Lija neighbourhood of Beirut, and there was no room for him to sleep at home. They were six brothers, but only one of them had left. He went to Africa where he made money in the diamond business and forgot about al-Lija and its people. There was no news of him, and no letters. There were three sisters in the house as well and only two bedrooms—and the smell of feet. He said he hadn't slept in al-Lija or spent even one night at a hotel in over two years. He hopped from one friend to another.

He took interest in the icon of St George. He approached the picture, pointed to the city in its bottom-right corner and paused at the king's palace, where women watched the battle of the dragon from the palace's balconies. He asked if that city was in fact Beirut. Once, his eyes scanned the walls of the salon, and he suggested moving the picture. But Nizam refused to do that because Olga had advised him to keep St George across from the open door, looking out towards the sea, perhaps in the direction of Los Angeles.

'Los Angeles?'

Ali often belittled Olga and her ideas and her trip, with the certainty of someone who knew her very well.

They went out to the streets together. Ali greeted street vendors and restaurant servers and told Nizam about the Hussein suicide forces that he had once joined and whose members were scattered between al-Lija and Masbagha Street in al-Shiyyah. Soon after the group was founded, the members started having more and more dreams of Fatima al-Zahraa and Al-Hussein. He was disappointed that all the members did was scratch the Jaguars and Cadillacs parked on the streets with sharp instruments that they carried just for that purpose. He had met with them a few times in Hurj al-Qateel and then ran away from them and was still on the run.

Ali Soueidan disappeared as quickly as he had appeared, and with him Olga's husband's shirts disappeared too. He also took the man's robe and his underwear. They were fancy and daintily embroidered, and they looked more like women's clothing. The soft underwear and shirts were monogrammed with Olga's husband's initials.

Ali Soueidan's departure left Nizam lonely. He couldn't muster up enough motivation to go to the university and would sometimes sit on the porch listening to the girl on the fourth floor practicing her opera songs that were often interrupted by the sound of a door slamming shut. He didn't know if that came from a brother who was fed up with her piercing voice or one of the neighbours annoyed by her singing.

He would get bored, leave, and wander around the neighbourhood, hoping to find something that would entertain him in the hours between evening and bedtime. There were some young men who congregated around the statue of Gamal Abdel Nasser at the intersection, chatting in a Beiruti accent. Every time he passed by there at any time of day—or even late at night—he would find them standing on the pavement, constantly monitoring the area in front of the shop that sold orange and carrot juice. They tried to outdo one another speaking in an exaggerated Beiruti accent.

'Where are you going? Shu fee ma fee? What's up?' they would ask, not expecting an answer.

Whenever young women walked down the pavement on the other side of the street, the young men would start talking in code, comparing the pretty pedestrians to Cadillacs or race horses.

They took turns talking and flaunting their dialect, drawing out the vowels at the end of every word. Their normal conversations didn't sound that boorish, but they intentionally spoke in an exaggerated accent whenever someone walked by, as if asserting the local identity of the area they guarded, or so they thought. As Nizam started passing by more frequently, he noticed that as soon as they saw him, they would start talking about Achrafiyeh and the sons of Achrafiyeh. They said they were on the lookout for them and that no one could overtake the sons of Ain Mreiseh, that is, no one could overtake them. They would say things like 'We don't care about Saifi and Mdawwar . . . ' in reference to the Christian areas.

They assumed Nizam was Christian. Amused, he would smile at them and shake his head before continuing on his way up towards the Beirut Theatre where a few people had gathered, each arriving on his own, waiting for the doors to open. He would enter with them without taking a good look at the black-and-white posters. The actors walked in, silent. The auditorium was small, but it had a wide stage. Their calm demeanour was ceremonious in the semi-darkness where the few audience members transformed into ghosts, casting their shadows rather than slouching down in their seats. It was as if the show started in the lobby before moving onto the stage, where a dim beam of light shone over a guard wearing a shabby military uniform and declaring the entrance of a frail king who wore a colourful cardboard crown on his head.

'The king is dying.'

Nizam laughed out loud, and some of the audience members gave him a dirty look.

There were two queens. The first one—black, edgy, and rigid—was trying to help the king die peacefully. The second one—fat, cheerful, and gluttonous—wanted the king to hang on to life. The stumbling king reverted to being a child and spoke with a loud voice.

Nizam restrained himself from laughing. He was having a lot of fun. He was smitten by the voices of the actors, especially the king's clanging voice and the voice of the icy queen as she said, 'We need to inform your majesty that you are going to die . . . '

Nizam came back the next day.

He was the only person who laughed at the king's response, 'You're boring me to death! Yes, I'm going to die. In forty years, fifty years, three hundred years . . . whenever I want, when I've got plenty of time, when I decide . . . ' or when the king voiced his concerns, 'This throne has become too hard to sit on, it needs to be upholstered.'

The third time he went to the theatre, the man selling tickets smiled at him, and he met Yusra.

He closed his eyes, enjoying the sounds, since he had memorised all the words. He was enchanted by the play and would say the actors' lines before they did.

She suddenly asked him if he liked the play, and he smiled at her and told her that he found it very entertaining, especially the ending.

'Entertaining?' She found that hard to believe. She was alone, too, and there was an empty seat between them.

As soon as they went out to the street, she asked him to light her cigarette. They walked side by side, silent. The evening seemed inviting. They headed to the corniche across from the American Embassy. She smoked as he tagged along. There were only a few corn-on-the-cob vendors, holding on to the hope that more customers would show up. She was thin and smoked passionately, with a vengeance. She'd be beautiful if only she took care of herself.

Perhaps she needed some time to get the echo of the king's final scream out of her system, as he died and the world before him faded into darkness.

She tossed her cigarette butt into the water and lifted her hair behind her head with both hands, as if she was shaking off of her body, or rather her heart, the image of the king holding a staff that looked more like a child's rattle.

'*Who* are you?'

Her question was dramatic, comic. It made him laugh as if it were another line from the play. They walked around for over two hours. They weren't in a hurry to part ways.

Her name was Yusra. She was born in Abidjan, and she lived with her parents reluctantly. She had a lot of friends, but she went to the theatre alone. He told her he lived in a flat nearby and had plenty of room for friends. They leaned on a rail, turning their backs to the sea. They heard the sound of a deep explosion. It came from the direction of the airport, she thought.

'They only strike from the air, the cowards . . . '

She speculated that it was an Israeli raid.

They went back to the death of the king, and she said she didn't believe in God and that happiness was *here*—to be or not to be.

They headed in the direction of his flat. He avoided walking with her by the target area, where they would be within full view of the Ain Mreiseh young men who assembled day and night in front of the orange juice shop. He invited her to come up.

'Tomorrow,' she said.

He gathered up his courage all at once and said, 'You can come live with me.'

She kissed him goodbye on the cheek.

4

She didn't lie, Yusra Maktabi.

Shortly after noon, there she stood at the door of the flat, panting and holding her belongings: long, dark-coloured dresses, since she didn't approve of women wearing trousers as a matter of principle. She also brought her records and books on chemistry and Marxism. She flung everything onto the living-room floor and collapsed, exhausted, after being forced to take the stairs because of a lift malfunction.

'I'm here!'

Mindlessly, she stretched out on the couch, as she raised one of her legs and then bent it in front of her, revealing her thighs all the way up to her underwear. She talked without a care in the world about how she couldn't stand living in her parents' home any more—about her mother, her mother's friends, and her brother, an up-and-coming lawyer. She didn't care for social climbers.

She liked the house that overlooked Beirut's now defunct lighthouse and the American University of Beirut. She went out on the porch, raised her arms towards the sky, and then turned around, happy, celebrating her new living arrangement.

'I should learn how to dance,' she said.

Nizam volunteered to sleep in the living room, but she refused and said she'd rather they share the big bed, if he didn't mind. Things moved faster than Nizam anticipated. They didn't sleep until three in the morning, after making love for a long time and smoking cigarettes. She recalled her disappointment with a young man from the town of Nabatiyyeh who reeked of tobacco, or so she imagined. He took pride in the fact that his parents made a living planting tobacco and stringing it out in the sun to dry. She loved his proletarian story and fell in love with him, but she said she later realized that she had fallen in love with his life story, not with him. She fled from him and his stupidity and loutishness. She fled from the smell of sweat, as he never found his way to a bathtub.

'I always borrow other people's lives . . . ' she said.

Nizam smiled without understanding what she meant.

Walking the streets of Beirut, Yusra fancied herself as the heroine from *Stolen Kisses* walking the streets of Paris. She was constantly making up all sorts of fantasies.

But she had come to Nizam of her own free will, and now she was at peace.

She slept comfortably at first, but half an hour later he was awakened by the sound of her gasping. She cried and complained in agony, 'That's the way I am. I don't know what to do with my happiness, so I cry.'

He wrapped her in his arms and soothed her with his words, so she dozed off for a little while. But when he tried to withdraw his hand from behind her head, she held on to it. She relaxed but would let out a gasp from time to time while he remained wide awake until the morning.

Yusra Maktabi walked into his life and planted herself there. They hung out at the flat for three whole days, and he would only slip out once a day to get some groceries. They played 'Battleship' on a piece of paper and made love in every part of the house. Every time Yusra's gaze would fall on the picture of one of Olga's white Russian relatives wearing a fur hat or frowning—frowning either because they had to pose in front of the photographer or just because they were Russian—like the officer in his military uniform with all the medals, she felt as if he were looking at her and she'd turn the picture around so that it faced the wall. Sometimes, she'd realize how strange the whole thing was and would turn to Nizam and ask, 'What are we doing here?' in the same feigned dramatic, funny accent. She would look at him and re-examine the picture before asking him, all over again, about the name of the woman who owned the flat. She concocted stories about why she and Nizam were in the Russian woman's flat, standing in front of pictures of her family and St George.

They spent hours in bed, with Nizam reading Jurji Zaydan's *Fatat al-Qairawan*, as she listened to John Coltrane, poring over the organic chemistry formulas she was studying in college.

They would soon go back to hugging one another tenderly, and her whole life would resurface before her. She dumped it all on Nizam, and he endured. Sometimes, she'd catch herself going on and on, and would pause to ask Nizam about his childhood, but he would dodge her questions and stick to generalities, so she'd resume her own story. He suggested they work together on a huge crossword puzzle, in an attempt to distract her from her life story that was filled with deep crevices, just like Hawra's mountainous road.

On the fourth day, he felt restless, so he opened the door and walked outside. He had missed Burj Square, so he went up to Zahrat al-Shamal where Raffoul met him with open arms—which was not like him—and told him that he'd been absent for far too long. He wasn't talking about himself, of course, but rather about all the things that had been sent to him from Hawra and that Raffoul had stacked up for him in one of the corners of the lobby. He apologized again for giving some of the stuff to Yasmeen. 'The poor woman,' he said. 'She's got a little daughter. Her husband died and left her all alone . . . ' It was as if Raffoul was supporting them himself, or that's what he liked to say all the time.

There was also a message from Hawra, or rather from Touma, hoping that Nizam would visit his father Mahmoud al-Alami and check on him because Mahmoud had had a heart problem. He had returned from Homs to Tripoli and wasn't taking good care of his health.

Nizam stayed out until evening. He entered the movie theatre twice but ended up leaving at the beginning of the film both times. He enjoyed the previews more than the films themselves. He soon got bored and went back out in the dark. He wandered about aimlessly before heading to the airport. There was a huge billboard across the road that read, 'Weapons make a man look good.'

He sat for two hours at the airport coffee shop in front of the window overlooking the runway. He never got tired of watching the planes take off and land; it was like watching a burning fire or running water.

He came back to the flat. Yusra sensed his desire to get away. 'I am heavy, so heavy,' she said.

He consoled her, and she promised herself not to lose him.

She could not bear any more losses.

She invited some friends to dinner, for his sake, so he willingly agreed. He shopped for the party at nearby shops. She made them some quick Italian dishes. He stood at the door greeting everyone. The flat filled up with people—guests of both genders.

The young women were like Yusra—not tall and not beautiful enough to be satisfied with their beauty.

There was Dima. She was round—not shy about her plump figure. She laughed from the bottom of her heart, laughed a lot. She gave the impression of being trustworthy but didn't allow anyone to lean on her. She, too, was a liberated woman.

And there was Huda. The prettiest thing about her was her puffy cheeks like two perfect apples. She would become infatuated with Nizam for a brief time, steal some glances of him only to back off in deference to the feisty Yusra.

And there was Furat. He was tall and dark with a thin mustache. He seemed a bit strange. He had an Iraqi accent and spoke a form of Arabic that was much older sounding than the Arabic all the others spoke. He was over thirty.

The young men were nice. They shook your hand, looked you straight in the eye for a long time and didn't give more than their first names when they introduced themselves.

There was Alaa. He was young, composed, quiet, determined. He wore thick glasses.

And Ramon—their authoritative resource and eloquent speaker. The only one among them who didn't smoke. He said he'd been suffering from asthma since childhood.

Vasco was disabled. He arrived in his wheelchair. Another young man with big muscles helped him out of the car, wheeled him into the lift, and watched over him through the night. He had a tattoo on his arm and always kept his shirt sleeves rolled up to let it show. Vasco was blond with green eyes.

Maurice. Heavy set. He brought along his flute in its expensive case with the red velvet lining. He only played it if the atmosphere was conducive to listening, so he said.

They brought bottles of wine with them and drank a lot. Debated a lot, too. They spoke French flavoured with simple Arabic. They switched rather abruptly from books they'd read and films they'd seen to the belt of poverty that had started encircling the capital Beirut from several directions. Ramon pulled out a paper napkin from his pocket, drew a circle on it and started labelling it. He placed the Kurds and Arab al-Maslakh—The Slaughterhouse Arabs—to the north in the Karantina area.

The displaced Shiites fleeing the Israeli raids that destroyed their houses and burned their fields on a daily basis he placed in the southern Dahiyeh suburb. On the east side was the industrial city—the mechanics and printing shop workers who never let a day go by without going on strike for some reason or another. Also in that area were those he called 'the Christian poor' with no further explanation, in addition to the various Palestinian refugee camps scattered around different parts. The Palestinian refugee camps were the tip of the spear. They appeared to be pleased and excited about this poverty belt.

'But there's nothing along the seacoast . . . ' Nizam said.

No one commented.

Whispering, he asked Yusra about the full name of one of her friends after he'd made a very confident interjection laying out a logical argument about how the bourgeoisie was responsible for all our ills. She told Nizam she didn't know and didn't want to know. He didn't believe her, so she explained to him, after he insisted, that one should not get to know the full names of comrades who preferred to keep it to themselves.

5

The comrades!

Nizam loved those guys, and just like that, the flat in Ras Beirut transformed into the headquarters of the Farajallah al-Helou cell, a branch of the Communist Action Organization in Lebanon. The cell took its name in honour of the communist rebel leader who refused to betray his comrades even under torture. In the end, the Syrian Intelligence 'melted him', as people put it, in a barrel of acid, which occurred alongside other events during the 1958 Revolution.

The invitation to dinner had been tantamount to a meet-and-greet party after which Yusra asked Nizam for permission to invite the comrades back to the flat for a meeting. They were the very same devourers of seafood pasta and guzzlers of French wine from before, with the addition of one or two others. This time their demeanour was more serious and organized. Thrilled to have so many guests, Nizam volunteered to serve them. He made them coffee two or three times while they were immersed in discussions. He'd found it difficult living alone before Yusra Maktabi came along, and after she came, they lived alone together—him and Yusra Maktabi. He was attached to her, never left her side, but he was never satisfied just being with her alone. He showed the comrades such a warm welcome and so much affection that afterwards they never hesitated to hold a meeting at his place at whatever time they decided, without asking him or even informing him first. They had no qualms about entering the flat unannounced, especially since he had made extra keys that he would give to anyone who said he'd come by and hadn't found Nizam at home.

He never turned away anyone whose relationship with his parents had soured because they wanted him to grow up to be a surgeon, for example, but who then chose to major in psychology or sociology, causing a big rift between them after which he left home and didn't know where to turn.

Nizam never tired of people. One time he cackled proudly as he counted the number of people who had a key to Olga Filipovna's flat—seventeen at the very least. From time to time, Olga sent him strange letters with postage stamps from Cyprus or Greece in which she told him about developments—or setbacks, rather—in her relationship with James Coburn and the possibility of her imminent return to Beirut. On the back of a post card of the Statue of Liberty she wrote: He loves me, but he is in high demand. Women invade our room at the hotel and snatch him away from me!

The flat in Ras Beirut filled up with people. Even Nizam now rang the doorbell a long time before using his own key to open the door, in order to give whomever was inside a chance to gather themselves. It was his new friends inside—the comrades Yusra brought over and some others that Yusra's friends brought who hadn't known her personally when they timidly entered the flat for the first time. Nizam adopted them all, greeted them all with a smile. One day he was surprised to find a young man he hadn't seen before making love with one of Dima's friends on the living room sofa, before noon, right beneath the picture of the Grand Duke Nicholas Nikolaevich. They were only half-naked, having been in such a passionate rush. The strangest thing about it was that they didn't stop their climactic crescendo of panting and moaning even after turning to look at Nizam and confirming his presence there as he stood in the wide-open doorway not knowing what to do. That was the way he was. He made others feel that what was his was theirs, and even more than that, he smiled at them, to their faces, so they wouldn't feel embarrassed. Seventeen, in addition to many other passers-by who came to meetings and smoked hundreds of cigarettes. The young men among them put salt in their beer while the young women always carried condoms in their purses—just in case. They stated publicly that God did not exist and was merely an invention created by the powerful to pacify the weak as they wallowed in their misery. Once in a while, they would mistake the flat and knock at the door of some other flat in the building, but it wouldn't take long for someone such as the wife of Mamoun al-Itani—who owned the fabric shop on al-Maarad Street and lived on the third floor—to notice their baggy shirts and the dirty hair dangling across their foreheads to surmise, before they even asked, that it was Nizam's flat they were looking for.

'It's up on the roof! The roof!' she'd tell them somewhat contemptuously before hurrying to lock the door before something of theirs could leak into her flat.

Their demeanour changed the moment they sat down to a meeting. They addressed each other as comrades and called Yusra 'Meera'—her 'nom de guerre' as they said. In the beginning, Comrade Ramon objected to letting Nizam sit in on their meetings on account of the titles of the novels Nizam left around the house that suggested how weak his level of revolutionary awareness was, as did some of the strange ideas he came up with sometimes.

But they quickly became enamored of his good character and started frequenting his flat—which was perfect for their meetings—after Yusra made him promise to keep their secrets safe. After that, they never commenced a meeting without making sure he was seated among them, right next to Yusra, who hugged him and clung to him and sometimes caressed his face to clarify to the others—the female comrades especially—that he was hers.

Nizam had no idea how to participate in the discussion. The flow
of conversation was a stormy current he was unable to swim in.
He was like a deaf man at a noisy wedding celebration in the beginning. People's war, class betrayal, the Fourth International, the
Fourth International and a half. They had heated disputes over
Leon Trotsky but were united in glorifying Ho Chi Minh. Nizam
emptied the ashtrays four or five times over the course of the
evening because Yusra would be busy remembering a quotation by
Rosa Luxemburg. Vasco, meanwhile, was too busy writing everything down in his personal notebook to have much time to speak,
except one time when he made a lengthy criticism of the Fatah
Movement for requiring its cadres to read Hitler's *Mein Kampf,*
which he considered shameful and unacceptable. He spouted off
the entire diatribe in French, with a perfect native accent. He never
missed a meeting and stayed until the very end, even when the discussions continued into the wee hours of morning. His assistant
stayed by his side and sometimes picked him up and carried him
to the bathroom so he could relieve himself. Vasco would ask the
comrades to stop until he came back so he wouldn't miss any of
the conversation about a plan to block the road to the airport, for
example, as part of the demonstration scheduled for the next day,
since the road to the Beirut airport was the main artery for the
comprador service sector, as they called it. By the time Vasco
returned to the mire of disputes at around one o'clock in the morning, fatigue would have started to creep into his assistant's eyes and
his head would roll forward onto his chest while his body remained
upright in the bamboo chair. The conversation would start to
digress sharply in response to Vasco's comments about the working
class and where their priorities lay in relation to country and religion and also their condition as downtrodden labourers. In turn,
Nizam would get sleepy despite Yusra's caresses as she attempted
to keep him tuned into the conversation. Addressing Yusra, they

would say that they should get going as it was time for bed, and so Nizam would open his eyes and beg them with all sincerity to stay and continue. He was sleeping happily while they talked, but after a little while he noticed the light from the lamp was hitting him in the eye, disrupting his snoozing, so he covered his face with a copy of *al-Hurriyya*—'Freedom' magazine, which was their organization's mouthpiece and whose caption in big letters asked a difficult question: 'How do we transform feudal demands into a revolutionary movement that can stand up to the ruling class?'

Nizam would lie back a little, and Yusra would curl up in his lap. Dima or Huda would cast disapproving glances at her that masked their envy of her for enjoying the good graces of this easy-going, cheerful, handsome, well-built and gracious young man, while the pages of the magazine rose and fell as he breathed. Whenever he heard the chairs moving as the meeting came to a close with the reading of the minutes and the agenda for the next meeting, he would open his eyes in a fright and plead with them to stay longer. But soon he would realize the naivete of requesting that their meeting turn into nothing more than an opportunity to keep him company, and so he would offer them one last drink or cup of coffee to refresh them.

All of that was an attempt to avoid being alone—that is, being alone with Yusra. Yusra started noticing this. If he asked her, 'What shall we do tonight?' First, she'd say, 'Don't worry,' to reassure him that they would be in the company of others and wouldn't just spend the time staring at each other.

It confused her how he could love the comrades so much while simultaneously not caring about the things they discussed. She'd ask him to take a nom de guerre, but he wouldn't pay her any heed.

'You're the only one of us without a name . . . I'm going to find a name for you from a Dostoevsky novel. Something close to the names of your Russian friends . . . ' she'd say while pointing to the pictures of Olga's relatives.

She liked to find counterparts for people she loved in movies she'd seen or novels she'd read.

'I'm just so comfortable with you,' she would tell him repeatedly.

What she really meant was that she found comfort in the fact that he never got tired of listening to her as she recounted the hardships of her life to him.

He remedied his solitude by spending time with Yusra, and he remedied his feelings of loneliness with her by surrounding himself with a big crowd whose clamour overflowed to the outside.

During one of their nightly gatherings, when debate had been whittled down to just two or three diehard philosophy enthusiasts, some of the comrades—particularly those who were exhausted by all the abstract ideas—ended up singing at the top of their lungs out on the balcony in order to silence the experts on dialectical materialism. Vasco then requested a moment of silence so he could recite a poem in French. Nizam thought for a moment that Vasco had written the poem himself because of the way Vasco had gazed at the dark horizon over the sea as he recited the entire poem from memory, his eyes lightly closed.

'Narrow are our boats. Narrow are our beds. Never-ending are the waters. Vast is our empire in pleasure rooms behind closed doors . . . '

Soon after, pandemonium broke loose with winking and cheering and screaming, all of which Nizam indulged in, until a frowning first sergeant from the Internal Security Forces—who had a thick southern accent and was accompanied by a younger officer—came knocking at the door. One of the comrades had been carrying a hunk of hashish in his pocket, so he got scared and passed it stealthily to one of the young women who then tucked it safely inside her bra.

The officers had shown up in response to a noise complaint that al-Itani's wife had called in herself, claiming that the commotion from the roof had become intolerable, that the singing was preventing the neighbourhood kids from getting any sleep, and that there were ill residents who had the right to get some rest. The first sergeant demanded to see the identity cards of the male comrades only, stacked them together in his hand, and started lecturing the comrades and warning them not to bother people again, all the while shooting puzzled looks at the women and Vasco and checking out the pictures on the walls. Then he started reading the names of the young men out loud before handing back their IDs; he yelled the names at the top of his voice as if he were a court reporter. He was nosy and had a comment for every name.

'Hussein Ismael Maallawi!' he yelled.

Comrade Ramon reached out to take back his ID. He seemed annoyed that his real name had been spoken out loud. A womanly giggle drew attention to the possibility that Hussein was hiding behind a Christian name, before the sergeant asked him with a hint of reprimand, 'You're from Hasbayya, right?' The sergeant himself was from the Druze community in Hasbayya, as evidenced by the way he pronounced the letter *qaf* fully. Perhaps he disapproved of people from his own area bothering the neighbours, especially since he had respectable friends from the Maallawi family.

'Joseph Emil al-Farneeni!'

Vasco raised his hand like an elementary school student; as his assistant reached to grab the ID for him, the snake tattoo on his arm became visible. Her eyes almost popping out of her head, Dima couldn't restrain herself from asking, 'Vasco! You're from

the al-Farneeni family?' It was as if this was the greatest discovery
of her life.

The sergeant continued to show off his geographical
knowledge.

'Are you from Achrafiyeh?' he asked.

'I'm from Beirut.'

Vasco's answer was patriotic, dry.

'My mother is a Farneeni,' Dima said, laughing. 'How come I
didn't know you from before?'

As if wanting to silence her, the sergeant moved on, 'Alexi
Baida!'

That was Maurice, the flute player.

The sergeant stared at Maurice, inspecting him from head to
toe, up and down, before examining his ID a few times, front and
back. He couldn't believe what he was reading. He put all
the remaining IDs in his back pocket. Puzzled, as if this whole
thing was some kind of an error, he whispered to Maurice, 'Are
you Israeli?'

The comrades had known that Maurice was Jewish but hadn't
seen any reason for telling Nizam about it.

'I'm Lebanese, Jewish by birth and an anti-Zionist.'

The first sergeant didn't seem to understand what Maurice
meant by that answer, so he wanted to confirm. 'It says here that
you're Israeli', he said.

'It's the religion that's Israeli, not the nationality', Maurice
clarified. He seemed to have done this many times before.

The sergeant continued, 'But you speak Arabic very well.'

'I speak Arabic because I'm Lebanese.'

To clarify things further, Maurice asked the first sergeant,
'What is written on your ID in the spot for religion?'

'*Durzi*,' the sergeant replied.

'Well, I'm *Israeli* . . . '

Maurice continued, 'I was born in 1947 in the area of Zuqaq al-Blat, registry number 53.'

Full stop.

Things were getting too complicated for the sergeant, so he asked a general question, 'And what are you all doing here?'

'Singing,' the comrades said in unison. An honest, deceitful chorus.

The sergeant resumed reading the names. It seemed like he was now having fun discovering their identities.

'Chamoun Yuhanna Rikho,' he said condescendingly. He could smell the fear of the weak just by looking at their names. 'Where are you from, Rikho?'

Comrade Furat answered him, with the tone of a guilty man and an Iraqi accent, telling him that he was originally from the city of Mosul, from the area of 'the two rivers, the Tigris and the Euphrates'. He said he resided near the National Museum across from the Palace of Justice, as if mentioning these landmarks might secure him some amnesty.

The sergeant grabbed Nizam's ID and looked at it closely. He didn't read his name out loud. His eyes widened, as he made one discovery after another.

'And what's *your* religion?' he asked Nizam.

When Yusra intervened, protesting why Nizam's religion was relevant at all, the sergeant told her that it was the first time he'd ever seen an ID with the spot for religion left blank.

'Here, take a look. Your friend has no religion.'

Nizam winked at the comrades, promising them more drama.

The sergeant shrugged his shoulders, gesturing that he didn't care, before moving on to comrade Alaa, the only one whose real name the sergeant hadn't publicly announced out loud. Attempting a dialect that he thought only people from Tyre spoke, he asked Alaa, 'Are you from Tyre?'

Alaa nodded positively in response to the sergeant's question.

'Any relation to Colonel Fawaz?' he asked just for the sake of asking a question.

'My dad . . . '

He didn't believe him.

'Colonel Ali Fawaz?'

'Yes, he's my dad,' he said, raising his voice a little.

The sergeant wondered what to do with the remaining IDs in his hands. He was so nervous, he almost rendered the military salute to Colonel Fawaz's son before leaving, now that he had enabled the members of the Farajallah al-Helou cell to find out, for the first time ever, that the only son of the Commander of Beirut's Internal Security Forces—the man who gave orders to douse protestors with fire hoses or fire shots in the air, if necessary, in order to forcefully disperse them—was in fact one of them. The comrades felt safe and betrayed at the same time.

6

They tried not to say anything that would embarrass Maurice, but they didn't let Nizam off the hook. They asked to see his ID, but he playfully evaded their demands. When they kept at it, he confirmed that at that moment in time he himself didn't know whether he was Muslim or Christian, which piqued their curiosity even more.

'You're making fun of us . . . ' they said.

He smiled slyly and told them that he was born in Tripoli, across from the seaport, and that he learnt the Arabic and French alphabets by reading the names of the ships as they approached the dock. He and his friends would wait for the ships on their balconies, so they could compete at reading their names out loud—*Olympia*, *Bint Iskindiriyya*, and *Marseille*. Sometimes, one of Nizam's relatives would take the kids aboard the ship, where the captain would hand them presents, as they stood mesmerised by the sailors' uniforms.

'OK, get to the point . . . ' someone said.

But comrade Furat was of a different opinion. 'That sounds so poetic. Go on, go on . . . '

He got to the part about Hawra and how he lived with a Christian family in the mountains because his father went to jail after being charged with planning a military coup before moving to Homs in Syria, but the comrades curled their lips, unconvinced. He talked about memorizing the entire Quran at al-Bahr Mosque and about Sheikh Sameeh al-Shaarani who loved him and preferred him to his friends because he was the first to finish any surah that the Sheikh started reciting . . .

He would digress again, get to another chapter in his life, and drown there. He neither satisfied their curiosity nor knew how to tell his life story well.

They took him back to the very beginning by asking a straightforward question:

'So, are you officially Muslim or Christian?'

He said he was still Muslim and didn't want to convert because he didn't want his first mother to start crying all over again after she had cried for so long, thanks to his father's actions. He would have almost digressed again, telling stories about Mahmoud al-Alami and all his sagas, had the comrades not raised their voices in protest. So, he backtracked and told them that he was still officially Muslim according to the personal status records and that one of his aunts occasionally checks—through an acquaintance of hers who works at the Personal Status Department—if her nephew is still a Sunni Muslim.

Just as his story seemed over and done with, Nizam smiled and winked at comrade Furat. He added, 'My second mother has . . . '

'Second mother?' someone interrupted.

'Yes, Rakheema,' Nizam said.

'Rakheema?'

He explained that Rakheema had a certificate that said he was a Maronite Christian.

The comrades howled, accusing him of messing with them, so he swore that he was baptised as a Christian on a rainy day, and that thanks to the rain, and the excessive amount of water that the priest had poured over his head, he caught a cold that lasted for over a week. In brief, he said he was now pleased with where things stood.

'That's it?'

'Yes, that's it,' he said smiling.

This meant that his second father—who was skilful at everything that he did—was the one who most likely erased the reference to religion on Nizam's ID. Nizam didn't even attempt to get another ID because he loved his picture on that first one.

They were having so much fun quizzing him, so they asked him if he believed in God.

He didn't know for sure. He told them how one of his friends was the only one from his family who survived after the family's car had plunged into the valley on the mountainous road between Tripoli and Hawra. The boy had clung to a tree, while his parents and sister tumbled to the bottom of the valley and died upon impact. He was left all alone in this world. Whenever the priest asked the students in religion class to have faith in God, that friend would say, 'If God truly exists and is capable of everything, why would he have this pressing need for me to believe in him?' The comrades liked the Hawra boy's answer, since it provided them with yet another creative justification for their atheism. Nizam went on to explain that while his second father didn't trust the clergy, he did believe in God, thanks to the juniper trees that covered the highest mountains and that wouldn't germinate were it not for the fieldfare birds who carried their seeds.

They curled their lips, wondering what to make of him, and they spent the entire night discussing his life story and its implications. Nizam became their plaything for days. They told their friends about Nizam's story. Some considered him a product of the sectarian system while others considered him a role model that every Lebanese citizen could emulate, once Lebanon entered the initial stage of transcending all religions, without necessarily denying their existence, on its way to building a secular society that was based on the idea of 'pure citizenship' that was dear to Vasco's heart.

They trusted him more after hearing his story. He was easy-going, helpful, and discreet, so they included him in their meetings with the factory workers from the Red Shoe store who were at risk of losing their jobs. He joined their march under the pouring rain, as he—and Yusra, of course—huddled under the same umbrella. They walked to the United Nations headquarters in celebration of the victory of the Front for the Liberation of the Western Sahara and Wadi al-Dhahab. Laughing, he joined them as they called for the death of King Hassan II of Morocco. Nizam was among the first who were doused by the high-pressure hoses that Beirut's fire department used to disperse the protestors as they clung to one another. He was the last to budge from the middle of the street where the protestors had lain, and he almost choked in the pool of water he sat in all by himself.

He also didn't run away when shots were fired from American M-16s in the Barbir area. When the police blocked the road to stop the protestors at the front of the march, Nizam led Yusra and the female comrades and Vasco into a side street and then came back with Furat, Ramon, and Maurice, to stand in the middle of the street and wait for the firehoses to hit them. But the fire trucks didn't show up. There was just pandemonium and shouting, and then suddenly, a tear gas grenade went off. It caused some of the protestors' eyes to tear up, but they didn't disperse. A protestor threw a Molotov cocktail at the police in retaliation, and a small fire broke out, followed by the sounds of small explosions over the protesters' heads. Nizam could see the blood flowing. The crowd ran for cover down the side streets amid yelling and screaming and chanting. That's when the casualties on the ground became visible.

'We're pulling them out of here,' Nizam said after he caught his breath and the shooting had stopped, per the orders of the officers on the other side.

'Let's take them to Dar al-Ifta, the Islamic Educational Institute,' someone suggested.

'Allahu Akbar!' another yelled.

Many others repeated after him. The chanting spread like wildfire.

The other slogans died out. 'Allahu Akbar' was also broadcast from the minaret of the neighbouring mosque. Many, including Nizam, volunteered to carry the dead. He, too, felt invincible. He said, 'Allahu Akbar', as he dragged a dead man by the shoulder towards one of the cars. Giving orders from one of the back streets, Furat asked Nizam to move out of the line of fire. They loaded three of the dead into three different cars and headed to the Grand Mufti of the republic so he could see with his own eyes what was happening to the sons of Beirut. They unloaded the bodies into the garden of the House of the Fatwa. Yelling and chanting 'Allahu Akbar', they lifted the bodies of the dead over their heads. Two of the dead men were skinny and easy to carry, while the third was fat, so the men carrying him had to put him down more than once in order to take a break. When the Mufti finally went out on the balcony of the institute and started preaching and asking them to show some respect for the dead first, they interrupted him yelling that they were martyrs. He agreed that they were martyrs and asked them to put them down and honour them by burying them, and he placed the responsibility for what happened on the government. When they went through the pockets of the dead, they discovered that the fat man was a Christian from a village in the Western Beqaa District. They handed the dead to the Red Cross medics before dispersing, each to his own home.

Yusra started calling him 'Gavroche' between greeting him with two kisses and telling everyone who hadn't been at the demonstration about all his amazing deeds.

He got excited and started walking at the front of the demonstrations. They'd write fiery rhyming slogans on slips of paper for him to shout out for the crowd to repeat. One time he carried Yusra up on his shoulders as she waved her fist in the air, and the next day their picture appeared on the front page of *Al-Muharrir* newspaper under the headline, 'Rowdy Demonstration in Support of Tobacco Farmers and Gandour Biscuit Factory Workers'. A copy of the paper made its way to Hawra with a young man who, upon seeing the picture on a copy that an itinerant newspaper vendor was waving about in his hand, bought one and brought it with him to Tripoli and then up to Hawra where it made the rounds among Touma and Rakheema's friends and relatives. They shook their heads in dismay, saying, 'A wolf cub can never be tamed!' as they pointed at the Palestinian keffiyeh Yusra had wrapped around her neck in the picture, affirming once again that Nizam was going to rob Touma of every last ounce of health and wealth he still had.

For Touma, selling property was the worst thing a person could do. If someone had asked him during the prime of his youth whether he wanted to sell the tiniest piece of land he owned, he would take it as a personal affront and would tell whoever made such an offer that he was prepared to buy everything that man owned, just name the price. After Touma got married and was subsequently unable to have children, any suggestion of that type produced a harsh response from him, one that might have even included an attack on the person's honour. As a result, people hungry to buy up property stayed away from him so as not to be pummeled by his insults. Whenever Touma was short on cash, he refused to let those people—the ones he so harshly rebuked—see him broken. He would rather borrow money and take a low-interest loan. There were three loan sharks who coordinated with each other and who didn't make him put up property as collateral; they lent him money solely on the basis of trust. Sometimes, he would 'roll over' a loan, as they say in debt lingo, or extend the repayment period, in other words. That was how Touma put off having to drink from the bitter cup of selling property. He put up with visits from the loan sharks who insinuated and warned that he might become incapable of paying his debts if he continued to send money to Nizam. He was always doing that in the form of new bills with consecutive serial numbers that he always seemed to know how to get and send to Beirut. He kept only what he needed to buy his diabetes medication. The rest Nizam would spend on the comrades for the most part, as the comrades were always broke. They scorned money and only had enough in their pockets to cover transportation or buy their French cigarettes with the dark-brown tobacco. They considered it beneath them to ask their parents for an allowance even though some of them came from rich families.

They did as they pleased. They made fun of girls who were still virgins, and none of the female comrades dared claimed to be a virgin for fear of being mocked. They justified stealing certain amenities that didn't fulfil any real need and permitted themselves to steal books from bookshops but not from university libraries. Some of them were pros at it. On clear days they'd wear trench coats with big inner pockets. The comrades would request a specific book, and they would promise to get it for them in twenty-four hours on condition it was some piece of Marxist literature or Guevara's biography or *The Long March* of Mao Tse-tung or Louis Althusser's *Ideological State Apparatuses*. If someone asked them to steal *Don Quixote* or a popular novel by Françoise Sagan such as

Bonjour Tristesse, they considered it to be petty theft, which they rejected and flat out refused to do. And Nizam liked nothing more than historical stories—*Abu Muslim al-Khurasani* or *The Queen's Necklace*. He was forever entertained by endless stories about castles under siege, poison being slipped into goblets, and relatives getting thrown into dungeons. He'd buy them from pavement vendors in Burj Square. He loved their colourful covers. He did notice, however, that those books didn't raise his status in the eyes of the comrades, so he tucked them under his mattress to hide them from their sight. Nizam became a delegate for their rowdy non-political projects. The girls loved him, and Yusra had him besieged to the point that he forgot all about Hawra and forgot his parents living between Homs and Mina. That is, until the news about his father reached him.

Raffoul relayed the news to him via a taxi driver coming from Tripoli, who transmitted it orally to the Manara pharmacy. That was the agreement Nizam had with Raffoul for emergencies. The owner of the pharmacy would send his young assistant to the concierge of Nizam's building who would tell Nizam whatever Raffoul wanted to let him know. The task was urgent and difficult for the latter—the concierge, that is—who hesitated and then made up his mind to do it. He rang the doorbell and with-out going inside informed Nizam that he must go to the North immediately, because his father was in critical condition . . .

'Which father?' Nizam asked without hesitation.

Thinking that Nizam didn't believe him, the concierge insisted the matter was serious and offered his help. He thanked him and headed to the pharmacy where he didn't get a clear answer, so he rushed to Burj Square and from there to Tripoli where the burial rites would be taking place after the afternoon prayers because it so happened that a short while back, Mahmoud al-Alami had come back from Homs to the house in Mina. He had come back to die.

Nizam arrived late. He stood before the death notice taped to the main door to the building. He tried to catch his breath before going inside to his mother and brothers. He read the death notice and didn't find his name listed among the sons of the deceased which mentioned only Bilal and Khaled. It was also the first time he noticed that girls' names were omitted from death notices. They had substituted Maysaloun with her husband, the deceased's son-in-law, Mustapha Hijazi. Nizam would have put Maysaloun at the very top if they had asked him to make a list of the al-Alami family. She lived in Beirut, but he hadn't met up with her yet. He would look her up as soon as he got back. As soon as he calmed down.

The concierge's son approached him. Nizam had known him as a child. They used to sit him half-naked at the entrance to the building. He didn't know Nizam. When he saw Nizam reading the death notice, he told him that they had gone to the mosque to pray. Nizam asked him how Mahmoud al-Alami died. He told him how Mahmoud had started experiencing a sharp pain in his chest, so he consulted a doctor who prescribed some medicine. He seemed to be improving but then that morning they found him dead. They found him on the balcony. Nizam asked him about the children of the deceased. He looked inquisitively at Nizam, then looked again at the death notice before answering him in a neutral tone, as if he understood his intention, 'His oldest son became a Christian, so he's not listed with the others.' Then he added that there were only women inside the house.

Nizam looked at the death notice again. He wouldn't go up to the house. He continued on to al-Bahr Mosque. He stood at a distance, near the post office where the smell of the fish market and sounds of the public auction reached him. It appeared that there had been strong winds the night before, causing a spike in prices. It was a sparse turnout at the mosque courtyard. Muflih al-Haj Hassan was there in his keffiyeh and agal and abaya robe along with Sheikh Bassim al-Khatib and some others. They started going inside for prayers. He spotted Bilal and Khaled from a distance. Two tall young men, one of them wearing glasses. He didn't know which one was Bilal and which one was Khaled.

They went in to pray, leaving Mahmoud all alone. They left him by himself outside in the courtyard, laid out on the stone table in his white shroud, in the shade of the lofty quinine tree. All alone before the blue of the sea.

Nizam watched from a distance. He had no place among them. He felt a lump in his throat but shrugged his shoulders. They didn't acknowledge him. They didn't want him. He might as well leave. He waited for a taxi to take him to the Beirut-bound bus stop. The two lines of poetry about seeing 'the dog rise to power' had been removed. No one sat near him. There were only a few passengers. As they passed the salt mine pools on the coastal highway, he checked to see if there were any signs left of the traffic cop. The dead motorcyclist. All he saw was the blue of the same sky reflected on the surface of the water in the square salt mine pools.

7

He went back to Yusra and the whirlwind of the comrades.
They brought him along to Tel al-Zaatar Palestinian refugee camp.
They let him join their secret program—what they called a 'crash
course in how to bear arms'. While at the camp, he was not allowed
to reveal his real name, 'for security purposes', as they whispered
among themselves. This time he was forced to choose a name,
if only for this occasion.

'Call me Nano.'

In their haste, they agreed to it, despite thinking it sounded
more like some sort of 'bourgeois' pet name.

And just like that, like all the nuns who'd taught him at
al-Mahabba school in Hawra and all the students there as well,
and like the public souq ladies on al-Mutanabbi Street, those purist
Marxist–Leninist comrades from the Farajallah al-Helou cell
started calling him 'Nano' from time to time—something between
a nickname and a nom de guerre.

At the camp—where some barefooted and nearly naked kids
followed after him down alleyways that were filled with dirty water,
pictures of martyrs, and party slogans—no one asked him his
name. It was quite the spectacle to see them in their uniforms, a
mixed group of men and women, being led to an open area by a
captain from the Popular Democratic Front for the Liberation of
Palestine. They stood around him in a semi-circle while he taught
them how to dismantle a Kalashnikov rifle one piece at a time and
then asked them one by one to reassemble it. After that, they
proceeded to shooting practice, where they aimed at a dummy of

an Israeli soldier made of plywood. Nizam won the admiration of the comrades with his consistently accurate shooting. The sun started to go down over the tin shacks. They had made it through a long day, subsisting on some sandwiches that had spoiled after sitting out in the sun and serving as landing pads for the flies, while they waited for everyone to finish reassembling the Kalashnikov rifle. They left to the sound of a woman ululating and another screaming; the women had gotten news that a young member of their family had been martyred in a Fedayeen operation in the Jordan valley.

The attack had destroyed an Israeli tank, forcing the enemy to call up its air force.

The comrades spent the rest of the night humbly listening to Maurice, the son of the manager of the bank located near the Al-Omari Grand Mosque, as he played some pieces by Mendelsohn and Mozart for them on his flute in his parents' living room. He stood in the middle of the spacious room, and they sat cross-legged on the carpet in a circle around him. They wouldn't sit on the sofas. No one dared even a whisper. Rather than sipping the glasses of licorice juice with crushed ice or rose julep with pine nuts that they had been served, which they had difficulty setting down between their legs, and to avoid making any sounds that might spoil Maurice's harmonious playing, they sufficed to drink up the silence between his tender musical phrases and clap only sparingly when he reached the end. With no idea when he should clap, Nizam was forced to imitate the others and refrain from initiating the clapping no matter what.

In the blink of an eye, an entire year passed during which Nizam didn't go up to Hawra except on New Year's Day—when all children remember their parents. Touma and Rakheema found him to be infectiously joyful and radiant. They were pleased with him and were convinced more and more that life was moving forward and all that mattered was that he remained in good health. One other time, despite Yusra's pestering, he didn't dare drop in on them when early that spring he joined the cell comrades on an organized excursion that took them to the Cedar Forest. They made fun of how small the famous forest was in contrast to all the hype over it. One of the comrades even lit up a cigarette while sitting on a branch of the Lamartine cedar when the forest guards weren't looking. But Touma and Rakheema started to worry and decided one day to go to Beirut to check his place of residence. Raffoul had instructed them to tell the taxi to let them off in Manara. They got lost there in the maze of buildings. Sometimes they'd ask about Nizam Abu-Shaheen and other times Nizam al-Alami, but they never found him. They returned to Hawra full of despair, despite being relieved that the neighbourhood seemed nice.

It was a year during which, on two occasions, Nizam woke up to the actual reason for being there in the capital and re-registered in the school of law. He lasted a whole hour that seemed to him an eternity, trying to listen to a lecture on contract and obligation laws. He compiled lectures on general constitutional law and bought reference manuals about Lebanese political institutions and personal status laws. He put them all in the corner of his bedroom along with a stack of new notebooks all ready for taking notes in. He piled up all the difficulty in one place, next to his head, within his reach if he was lying on his bed, as though confining it all to a tight space would make the task easier. But then he would bump into the books and scatter them everywhere when he'd wake up at dawn and try to sneak out to the balcony without waking Yusra. He didn't want her to ruin it for him with her garrulous talk—his desire to silently take in the incandescent horizon over the sea and the glimmer of the light upon the layer of snow that still remained on the high peaks of Mount Sannine. He'd trip over the books and never once crack one open to read it. There was always some pressing appointment to distract him, such as a visit he had put off too long to Maysaloun after finally finding out where she lived with much difficulty.

At the entrance to the building, in the Tariq al-Jdeideh area, he saw a huge picture of the leader of al-Tanzim al-Shaabi, the Popular Organization, talking on the phone—a big black phone attached to a cord. He was smiling in the picture as though pleased with whatever the person on the other end of the line was saying. There was a caption that simply read, 'Brother Issam'. When she opened the door, he didn't recognize her. She looked into his eyes and waited, smiling. She'd cut her hair short and had put on some weight. She hugged him tight to her chest. She could feel his arms wrapped around her.

'Sister!' he cried, straight from his heart.

Maysaloun, his ally.

They sat together on the same chair, hand in hand. She spoke sweetly to him and patted him with her hand. He filled her in about how life was going for him in Beirut, and she told him how she had gotten married, but that they were holding off on having children until they could move to a larger flat. She didn't get up to make coffee for him because she didn't want to waste a single moment away from him. He told her how he had gone to his father Mahmoud's funeral but didn't enter the house or go close to the mosque. She told him she'd gotten in an argument with her brothers over omitting Nizam's name from the death notice.

'Khaled is stubborn.'

She laughed, remembering how she had removed Nizam's face from all the family photos. She hadn't done it out of hatred for him, but rather to make it easier to free him from the al-Alami family. She had wanted for him what she thought he wanted for himself, but now she didn't know anything any more.

Maysaloun asked him for his address.

She would soon visit him in Manara, where the comrades were discussing the matter of expanding the cell's ranks to include some newcomers from the French Lycée who had been influenced by a teacher who'd taken part in the Paris student revolution of 1968. They frequented the Hamra Street cafés where they carried on their discussions in loud voices with no concern for a young couple who might be in the middle of an intimate conversation or a poet sitting alone trying to extract a prose poem from amid the clamour of the city. They would charge out at night to the souqs, always spurred on by some idea Nizam had come up with to have fun. They'd go out at dawn for ashtalieh with honey, or they'd plan a trip to the south to help build shelters to protect refugees from Israeli attacks. The folks there would stop them and tell them to leave because the quadrangular foundation holes, dug by the guys coming from Beirut, looked just like graves. The comrades would forbid each other from listening to Umm Kulthoum songs. Some of them went secretly to the annual Dalida concert and took group trips to the temples of Baalbek to see Joan Baez in concert. They'd stand on their chairs cheering when the long-haired musician started singing, 'We Shall Overcome'. Whispers would start circulating among them about sending booby-trapped packages to the American Embassy, and they talked about money that had started coming from Libya and Iraq in support of the 'Nationalist Movement'—as they started calling it. Things went along in this way, until Yusra Maktabi decided to fire an 8-caliber semi-automatic Makarov pistol at Nizam, hitting St George on his Roman helmet instead.

Yusra had been spending some time away in the impoverished al-Nabaa neighbourhood where she'd recently started organizing a discussion group on women's rights. She would invite some of the neighbourhood's female residents who managed to steal themselves away before their husbands came back from work, tired and hungry. The discussions progressed to explore issues including the importance of women demanding their rights and asking that men do their share of the housework if the women worked outside the home. One of the women laughed, as she imagined her husband Abu Hussein doing the laundry or hanging it with clothespins out on the balcony for all the neighbours to see. Yusra refused to give in to the prevailing cultural norms and went too far in her fight for equality, to the extent that she once suggested that a woman not stay in missionary position during sexual intercourse but rather switch positions with the man so she's not on the bottom the entire time. In response, one woman burst out laughing while two others withdrew altogether, so Yusra ended the meeting and returned to Manara.

She didn't find Nizam or anyone else at the flat that day, but she smelled something fishy—a trace of something in the air that she didn't like. She accused him of cheating on her, and when he denied it, she said that her heart never deceived her. She kept quiet as he went on denying it. Two days later, she left the flat to attend a practicum at the university, since she now risked losing the entire academic year at the College of Sciences and being prohibited from taking the final exam. She was almost halfway there when something flashed in her mind, so she turned back and used her key to enter the flat without ringing the doorbell. She smelled the aroma of freshly brewed coffee. She tiptoed to the kitchen where she found Nizam standing behind a beautiful barefooted brunette she had never seen before. He was hugging the woman as they stood in front of the stove making Turkish coffee and giggling as they got it to foam at the top. Yusra let out a scream and retreated towards the living room. Nizam assured the girl that everything was fine before running after Yusra, but he soon realized that she had already taken the Makarov out of her purse.

'Even you?' she yelled, pointing the gun at him.

She had insisted on getting a gun after the political office advised that the security situation that year necessitated that comrades carry personal weapons for self-defence and that they could get them from Fatah's Lebanese military office in the Palestinian refugee camps of Sabra and Shatila through someone called 'Abu Khaled Athena', whose nom de guerre paid tribute to one of the operations he had led in the Greek capital and that targeted the offices of El Al Israeli Airlines.

Almost exploding with anger, Yusra said that she loved him but that he was a cheat. Stuttering, she unleashed all sorts of accusations against Nizam, calling him a petit bourgeoisie who saw a woman as nothing but a body that provided him with pleasure. She said that all men were cut out from the same cloth.

Nizam thought that now that she had spilled her guts, she wouldn't do anything else, but she soon started all over again. She seemed incapable of controlling her feelings of bitterness which were doubled by the fact that the female stranger stood there as both the witness and the cause of her repeated defeat. Waving the gun around, she uttered incoherent phrases and hurled random accusations and epithets. She desperately tried to come up with just the right zinger that would express all her anger that she could hurl at Nizam's head, but it was in vain. So she closed her eyes and pointed the gun at Nizam. He jumped automatically in the direction of the balcony door as she fired two bullets with her eyes still closed—despite the Palestinian trainer's warning that a shooter should never close her eyes under any circumstances and that closing your eyes might cost you your life. Add to all this the fact that a Makarov was not known for its precision since it sometimes spit out numerous bullets all at once.

One of the bullets went missing. Nizam looked for it later but couldn't find a trace, which meant that it may have exited through the balcony door.

The second bullet hit St George, Olga's saint.

When Yusra opened her eyes, she seemed horrified by what she'd done. It was as if she was awakened by the two explosions—as if it was someone else who had just fired the gun. Her feelings regarding the magnitude of what she'd done were stronger than Nizam's feelings about being shot at. For him, the shooting seemed merely a conclusion to Yusra's harsh words. He shifted his attention to the other woman and called out to her that everything was all right. Yusra put the gun back in her purse, gathered her strength, and sat up straight on the couch as if ready to be reprimanded and punished. Nizam approached her and took the gun out of her purse. The atmosphere became less tense, so the brunette came out to the living room and looked around, assessing the damage. She was a Jordanian student at the American University of Beirut, and if her parents were to find out what happened, her father would have put her on the first plane back to Amman. She was looking for the flat of her American professor, Mr Parker, so he could help her with picking her courses, but she had knocked on Nizam's door by mistake. So Nizam had invited her in for some coffee, which she insisted on preparing and he insisted on helping her with, and that was all there was to it.

Yusra remained quiet until the Jordanian woman, who was so happy to get out of that mess safely, left the flat. Then she went to the bedroom. She gathered her long dresses, books, jazz albums and French love songs, picked them up, and left the flat—tormented by her delusions. Before shutting the door to the flat behind her, she apologized for what she had done, glanced at the icon, and whispered to Nizam in a serious tone—as if in compensation for what had happened—that she had a classmate named Janan Salem who was an artist and an expert in art restoration.

Shooting him with yet another arrow on her way out, she added, 'Don't forget to hit on her too . . .'

The only thing that Olga had advised him to take care of was the icon that her mother had carried on her arduous travels. Ali Soueidan had also advised him to take care of the icon, calling it 'priceless', and Nizam had always made sure to warn the comrades not to mess with it. At first, Nizam was certain of the comrades' disdain for money, but he later realized that it was the type of collective virtue that didn't prohibit individual acts of embezzlement. He had discovered that many things, which had no revolutionary benefit whatsoever, were missing from the flat. A couple of straw hats decorated with colourful ribbons, an umbrella, and an ebony pencil-holder, in the shape of an elephant with a raised trunk and carved back, also went missing. He even lost the samovar for over a week, only for it to reappear one day in its usual place. He became certain that the samovar was not made of real silver as someone must have initially told the comrades. Maybe whoever had run off with the samovar had shown it to an expert who confirmed that it didn't even contain any silver, so the comrade put it back where it belonged.

St George had remained hanging in his place, looking out at the sea.

Nizam ignored the gunshot at the beginning, until everyone else started noticing it. Any comment about the hole in the St George icon became an opportunity to talk about Yusra who was now absent from the group's meetings and who seemed to be acting strangely, not calling the comrades and cutting conversations short whenever she ran into them. She came back to the flat only once in order to return Nizam's pocket watch that she had borrowed—the same watch that he dropped at the salt mine as he rushed towards the dead policeman. It had stopped working, but he had gotten it fixed, or rather the watch repairman in Burj Square said he'd fixed it. Touma had told Nizam the day he'd given him the watch that it was a gift Touma's uncle had given him on the day he returned from Brazil. It was the same uncle who had left Touma a big inheritance. Yusra told him that she'd thrown the watch on the floor in her fit of anger, so the glass broke but it was still working. She said she'd avenged herself, one way or another, against anything that reminded her of him, but that she was sorry for everything she'd done to him. She was so sweet that Nizam found himself consoling her, even reassuring her that everything was fine. But she blamed herself, speculating that whatever sickness was in her was incurable. She handed him the key to his flat and gave him three kisses on the cheeks upon leaving. She also asked him if he'd been to her friend's place to get the icon repaired. She said she wanted to clear her conscience, fix what she'd ruined. So she gave him her friend's address, 'Lebanon Street, above the flower shop', and passionately said goodbye as if it was their last farewell.

Fearing Olga's sudden return, Nizam carefully wrapped the icon and carried it, bulky as it was, under his arm. Awkwardly, he got into a taxi whose driver inundated him with all sorts of news without giving any specifics. He said that unidentified corpses were being discovered, tossed here or there, and that the prices of eggs and meat were on the rise.

'It's always the poor who suffer!' he added.

He dropped him off on Lebanon Street, and Nizam paid him double the regular fare.

And so, just like that, he showed up at her studio without an appointment.

A tall blonde, she had her hair up in a ponytail and wore dainty oval-shaped glasses. She was pretty, and she knew it.

8

Janan Salem.

She stood amid unframed oil paintings, canvases, finished and unfinished drawings that were strewn all over the room—some were hanging, some lying on the floor, and some propped up against the wall or lifted onto chairs. The paintings had similar colours and were large or medium-sized. They were spread out in a way that allowed the onlooker to see them all at the same time. It seemed as if she was painting one scene that was divided up across numerous paintings. The room was flooded with daylight that surged through a wide glass panel in the wall. Large plants in clay pots stood in a row. Her workshop looked out onto the blind sides of two taller buildings that overlooked the street from the opposite side, concealing Janan from any view—except for her paintings.

She looked at him without paying much attention. She was wearing an artist's apron stained with different colours, and a necklace with a medium-sized gold cross was dangling from her neck.

'Yusra Maktabi, your classmate from Collège Louise Wegmann, sent me to you.'

'You know Yusra Maktabi?' she smiled.

'I have a painting that I'd like to get restored.'

She gestured to him to sit on the one couch in the room, a loveseat, before raising her finger to indicate that he wouldn't be waiting for too long. She stayed focused, determined to finish what she had started. It was as if he had come upon her in the midst of a celebration she needed to conclude, in the midst of a sentence she wanted to finish.

She worked on all the paintings at the same time. She made a brush stroke on one of them, before taking a step back. There were small cuts on her arm all the way from her wrist up, which she kept covered under a baggy shirt. She then changed the brush, contemplated it, and dipped it in paint before moving to another painting, to which she added a small detail that was barely noticeable.

An angry sky appeared in all the paintings, a sky the colour of clouds. The colours in all the paintings were similar and dark. Dark forest green coupled with a gloomy grey. Grey in all its shades, in all its possibilities. But, here and there, once or twice at most, dark-bright red appeared in very small amounts in each of the paintings, like in the fine lines of a wooden window, its small panels now cracked. Or a window with a hanging dahlia, with dead colours, on the balcony of an old house. Or a stain, the colour of blood, on the pavement of a pavement drawn with utmost precision, including the parts that the feet of pedestrians had long worn out. A puddle created by a stream of droplets leaking from a punctured exterior plumbing pipe that had the same colour as the building and that extended all the way down the building's facade. Blood dripped from houses and overflowed from their pores. Water skins so full they were about to burst. The streets were jammed with cars whose paint had faded. There were other empty structures, sketched with utmost precision. The storefronts, doors, street corners, and Beirut's streets themselves—everything looked gloomy and well-defined. But the bodies of pedestrians were sunken, their faces mysterious. They looked more like shadows than actual bodies. Janan purposely intended not to finish drawing anything that walked on two legs, anything human.

She barely added anything to her paintings during those few minutes she'd requested from her unexpected visitor, before giving him her undivided attention. Perhaps she just needed to pass her brush here and there to touch up some details that she'd added before Nizam entered her studio.

Nizam didn't sit down. He remained standing, holding the icon under his arm, as he watched the artist. She exuded a charm he couldn't resist. She was confident, standing upright, content. She tossed her brush and looked at him. Her eyes were so unusual.

He unwrapped the white paper from the icon, propped it against the wall, and turned it around so she could see it. Stunned, she gravitated towards it. She moved closer to touch it. He studied her delicate hands which looked clean despite all the colours and oils. She touched the hole in St George's head, which was at the same level as his ear. She felt it with her fingers with such familiarity as if merely confirming something she already knew. She had the demeanour of a doctor examining a dislocated shoulder or an inflamed appendix.

Her hands, her long proportional fingers—everything that she did and was—the colour of her skin, her apron, the colour of the sky appearing through the glass panel behind her, her one couch with its old, worn out black leather—everything was perfect and created the complete picture of who she was.

She took down one of the paintings that was sitting on top of her easel and put the icon of St George in its place. She backed away from the icon, stepping in Nizam's direction, so she could take a good look at it.

Feeling sorry about the saint's injury, she said, 'Too bad.'

She almost brushed up against Nizam, standing with her back turned to him, as if she'd forgotten he was even there. She didn't pay any attention to him. Without looking at Nizam, she asked him how the hole in St George's head came about. He said it was from a gunshot. She didn't react or seem surprised.

'It was an 8-caliber semi-automatic Makarov pistol,' he said, as if telling her the type of weapon might help her better treat the injury.

He told her that the owner of the icon was away in Los Angeles, that she might come back soon, and that he had to fix the damage. As much as possible anyway. He went into too much detail as usual.

She looked him in the eye for the first time.

Her eyes were two different colours.

He walked under her spell for a long time before finding a taxi to take him back home. He had written her phone number on his hand. Fearing that it might get erased, he borrowed a pen that the driver had been using to solve crossword puzzles while sitting in traffic and wrote it on the back of his ID.

He was smitten by her like he'd never been smitten before.

He woke up the next morning. It was as if her presence never left him even while he was sleeping.

He didn't get lonely spending the night alone in bed, though he tossed and turned for a while as he replayed in his head all sorts of scenarios—all of which ended with her surrendering to him as she sighed, her eyes pleading. There she was amid her paintings, dark streets and glass panel that overlooked the smooth walls of buildings. In all the scenarios in which he won her over, she was wearing her necklace with the gold cross; her soft skin and warm hugs made up for the paint stains all over her apron. Her apron had the same colours as those in her paintings. It was dark, but it was splattered with red spots. It looked like just another one of her paintings, which all resembled each other. As soon as Nizam would get to the end of the story that he was telling himself—or the various scenarios in which he imagined himself seducing her with one move or another—he would go all the way back to the beginning and relive his desire and pleasure in winning her over.

Standing in front of the mirror the next morning, he felt for the first time that he should take better care of himself, maybe change his hairstyle. He looked at his fingers and his nails. Somehow, she had uncovered for him all his shortcomings, despite having barely paid him any attention. She'd barely seen him. All of a sudden, Janan had given him a special set of eyes through which he now saw his own appearance. He showered twice that day, even though he wasn't expecting to see her, and he bought three different types of cologne. Yusra and the female comrades prohibited colognes and perfumes. They flung themselves at him just as he was. Actually, the comrades forced him to have what they considered a total disregard for appearances. He gave away to the building concierge some clothes that no longer suited his new look. He asked about her right and left until Dima finally led him to a friend of hers at the Art Institute who told him that Janan was well-known there because she left school before getting her art diploma. She had been at the top of the class but was constantly arguing with the instructors. One day she just took off and never came back.

This information only made her more enchanting. Nizam started counting the days until the week that she'd asked for to work on St George came to an end. The comrades had also started missing St George. When they asked Nizam about him, he answered in the plural, laughing, 'We are fixing him . . . '

He went back to her studio on foot. The appointment was at 11. His heart started pounding the closer he got to Lebanon Street. He was dressed in what he thought were his nicest clothes—the ones most likely to catch her eye.

She didn't notice, or maybe she pretended not to care when she opened the door and gave him that expected look, along with a couple of soft-spoken words, 'Oh, it's you?'

She had taken care of her appearance, too. She was wearing a silk scarf around her neck that matched the two colours of her eyes. She had undoubtedly gone to some trouble to find a scarf that combined both the brown and blue of her eyes.

She kept her words to a minimum. She'd exerted her very best efforts to restore the icon but couldn't do more because the bullet hole was too wide. St George's helmet had gotten back some of its sheen. She didn't go into detail about it. In any case, he wasn't listening and wasn't looking at the saint's head, either. He just watched every move of her hands.

She stopped talking, so he offered to pay her for what she'd done. Maybe he could make a chink in the wall of her indifference. She refused. She seemed set on ending the conversation and blocking every attempt he made. She asked him to just write down his name and address—for her records, she claimed. He complimented her studio, not knowing what else to try. He'd never felt such strong feelings before or had such a lack of imagination. Perhaps Nizam al-Alami, who'd never in his life exerted the slightest effort to attract women, was experiencing for the first time what they call 'true love'. He tried asking about the recurring theme of her paintings, but she wasn't responsive. He seemed pushy, like he was pestering someone he didn't know well. In the end, he told her how pretty her dress was. She slammed the conversation shut with a smile.

He wrapped the icon back up in the white paper. He apologized for 'taking her time', and she smiled. He lingered a bit, but nothing happened, as if she'd stopped breathing. She watched him tape the paper over the icon. She wanted to see the whole matter come to an end, so he would leave, and she could get back to some other work he'd stopped her from doing. She was addicted to what she did. Her paintings, her colours, the houses, and the streets gobbled her up.

He picked up the icon and headed to the door. She stood there, not moving an inch. He reached the door, opened it, and left. As he went down the stairs, he heard her shut the door, making every effort not to make the slightest bit of noise. He walked slowly. He was defeated, just like the first and last time his father Mahmoud al-Alami slapped him in the face the day he came back from the ice-cream vendor in Mina with more ice cream on his face and clothes than he'd gotten into his mouth.

He returned to the house in Manara carrying the bandaged St George under his arm and a gaping hole in his heart—a hole whose pain he'd never experienced before.

The comrades noticed it over the next few days. They thought his sitting off on his own in silence had to do with what Yusra had done, but he claimed to be worried about his father's diabetes— the father he still had in Hawra. He was enchanted by Lebanon Street. Janan occupied his immediate surroundings, his vitality, and he no longer felt the need for the comrades to fill it night and day. He didn't dare even imagine those scenarios of her surrendering to him but rather reverted to merely designing solid ploys and pretexts for knocking on her studio door once again. He wouldn't know what to say on the phone if he called her at her parents'. If she had let him pay her, he would have gone back to her with some other painting, that he would have destroyed with his own hands, just so she could restore it.

He went back to the mirror and took a long look at himself. Maybe he wasn't from her world.

One morning, in the middle of the week, the building concierge called to him as he stormed out the door. The postman had put a letter in his mailbox. Nizam thought it must be for Olga or from Olga, so he continued in his rush out to the street. But something—a ray of hope that just might seal that hole in his heart—led him back to the mailbox.

'Nizam al-Alami, such-and-such a building, such-and-such a street, Manara, Beirut . . . ' Word for word, the address he had given her.

He got flustered opening it, finally arriving at one single sentence written in beautiful handwriting—an artist's handwriting: 'For five days I worked on St George. Shouldn't you take me to dinner for my troubles?'

No name, no signature.

If Nizam could reflect on his past feelings, he would discover that Janan's renewed invitation resembled the second time that Touma opened the garden gate for him. The gate to heaven is opened twice.

He left the mailbox open, carried the letter, open, to the lift where he read it ten times in a matter of seconds, all the way to the flat where he scrambled opening the door, to the bathroom nervously, to the bedroom closet, to the mirror at length, to the cologne, to Lebanon Street. She had been expecting him. They laughed out loud as a new flame was ignited in Nizam's life.

9

She joined him that evening at the Flying Cucotte, the same restaurant where Brigitte Bardot had dined the week before at the invitation of the President of the Republic's son. Janan had agreed to leave the house, which was very unlike her. She usually avoided crowds and commotion. At a loss as to how to make her happy that evening, Nizam tried to create a cheerful and friendly atmosphere, clowning around and making her laugh at stories about Hawra and its mischievous inhabitants. He exchanged pleasantries with a young couple seated at the next table who were having dinner together too and invited them to join them for coffee. He had an insatiable appetite for company. She kept quiet and was polite, but after a while she seemed a little nervous, as if she was in a hurry to get back, so he took her to the studio where some calmness was restored to her face after she'd stood for a few minutes in front of the painting resting on her easel. She added a little something to its sky before politely bidding him goodbye. He was afraid to try to kiss her.

He grew attached to her, and as a result, his tolerance for others increased, as did his propensity to spend money. She had an open invitation from him to go out any time, but she preferred to stay in her studio, so every day he invented a new reason for her to love him. She became his oasis, which he journeyed to every day. She didn't have a phone. Her parents owned the building where her studio was and lived in the flat above it. She said she couldn't stand telephones and the way the shock of the outside world would suddenly ring and jolt her from whatever she was immersed in.

'If you miss me, then come see me . . . '

Getting to her wasn't always easy.

'I like knowing that you roam the area outside my studio before coming up. If you'd just go around once or twice, from behind the volleyball court down to the library and then come back around from the direction of the insurance company . . . '

He fell for her in one crashing fall.

He would circle around the neighbourhood the way she wanted before entering the building. He went around two or three times and was greeted by a hunched over Jesuit monk who was exiting through the back door of the Oriental Studies Institute. When he passed by the second time, a city sanitation worker gave him a strange look. Nizam was very disciplined about doing the things Janan liked him to do and never cut corners, as though she was watching him, and seeing him do these things made her happy.

Finally, he would make his way late at night to Ras Beirut, eagerly for the most part, filled to the brim with Janan. The comrades told him that Jonathan and Barbara Parker, the professors who lived on the second floor of the building and who'd been enticed by all the hullabaloo up in the roof flat, had now become regulars. They would join in as soon as they finished their teaching duties for the day. Living in Beirut without any children, they always showed up with those wide American grins of theirs. They were grateful for having been welcomed, even by people who considered them without a doubt to be spies working for the CIA. They accepted everything that was offered to them and never got tired of meeting people and handing out their publications to them, even the ones who unequivocally declared their atheism. They clarified that they weren't Jehovah's Witnesses, but Quakers; they respected all religions and creeds and believed all were equal.

They also told him that his sister Maysaloun had stopped by with her husband, Mustapha Hijazi.

They remembered his name because when he came in, he shook hands with everyone and dragged out each handshake, introducing himself repeatedly with full confidence.

They really liked his sister's name, as if it were a carefully chosen nom de guerre. They envied it, themselves so sick and tired of the names their parents had given them at birth.

They were surprised to see her. 'You have a sister?'

'And two brothers that I can't tell apart . . . '

He started liking everything Janan liked. He went with her on Sundays to Orthodox Divine Liturgy services with their never-ending kneeling and standing segments, plus the few rare moments of sitting. Janan kept her eyes closed throughout the Holy Oblation as though she was seeing something others didn't see. He helped her mix paint colours with patience and precision. He tried his hand at putting a few brush strokes of his own. He learnt how to stretch the canvas for her and always volunteered to go to the bookshop to buy sketchbooks or tubes of paint. She asked specifically for black and white, from which she would extract grey, her only colour.

He was dedicated to her, and she started expecting him every day. He'd made meeting her into a ritual. He'd leave the house at nine in the morning, so he could enter her world early in the day, something for which he would have cleared his schedule to be able to do, so he could be with her. He crossed Beirut from west to east, walking opposite to the direction of the line of demonstrations. He whistled and smiled to the passers-by on their way to work as he made his way to happiness. He never avoided the morning hustle and bustle of the souqs, and he never arrived at her door without a bouquet of flowers or box of sweets in hand. He'd tiptoe in so as not to muddle her concentration. She'd smile from the corner of her mouth the moment she saw him come in filled with awe. She pretended to stay focused for a little while in front of the painting propped up on her easel while he stood ready and waiting for her to put down her brush and rush to him. He'd pick her up and twirl her around as she held tightly to him. Every morning was a new discovery. He had become her need, and she had become his daily celebration. They would agree to go on Sunday to the Long Beach swimming pool or on Thursday to Hamra Street, so she could pick out some new clothes for him. They'd plan longer trips so one could introduce the other to friends. 'You'll like this guy', he'd say to her. 'You'll like this girl', she'd say to him. But they never kept any of their promises. They didn't need anyone else. They spent the entire day on the leather loveseat, or in close proximity to it. They conversed calmly together. She told him that she sometimes restored paintings at churches. They would set up metal staging for her, and she'd climb up to the ceiling where she'd spend days all by herself returning the lustre to the saints' faces that the passing of time had erased. She didn't explore his world, didn't ask about his roots or his background. He didn't bring her to the flat in Manara. He told her about the keys he'd handed out to friends, and the idea frightened her. She asked him just once or twice about his acquaintance with Yusra Maktabi, her classmate at the German school who turned her nose up at everything ever since she was little and whom she hadn't seen since they'd finished school. He didn't tell her that she was the one who'd fired a gun at him and ended up hitting St George instead.

One day he arrived at the studio and she was nowhere to be found.

He'd brought her a red heart-shaped cake stuffed with almonds and sugar; he'd asked the seller to write her name on it with frosting.

He didn't go up to her parents' flat to ask about her.

She disappeared for days that tortured Nizam, and then she reappeared—wilted and emaciated, so he took her out for a stroll in the neighbourhood, like a convalescent being taken outside for some sunshine. She didn't explain her absence, and he didn't ask her about it. They chatted and laughed together, which helped her regain some of her lustre.

And that's how Nizam entered Janan's labyrinth. She would disappear, usually for a couple of days, but occasionally for an entire week. All of a sudden, she'd warn him that it would be better if they didn't meet up. She'd withdraw into herself, and so he too would retreat into himself at the Ras Beirut flat. His days were suspended in time. She'd stay away from him, so he would try to write to her. She asked him to, saying that words were the key to her heart. A beautiful phrase that suited her mood—that was something she would succumb to. He would seize the opportunity in the empty flat to lie down on the bed, searching for the right words. But the only thing he came up with were quotes from the French teacher up in Hawra. He'd laugh at them, laugh at himself, and decide he was no good at writing. He became even more certain of that when he read and reread—never seeming to tire of it—the succinct notes she sent to his mailbox at the Manara flat during her first absences. Slips of paper or the backs of pictures on which was written some statement whose creativeness he could never succeed at imitating.

'I return to the eyes of passers-by, to the purple flowers of the streets. I am a fish out of your water. Don't stay away too long.'

She'd go through periods of intense activity, a torrent of creative productivity, that lasted four or five days. She painted all day and for hours into the night. She couldn't get enough, never got bored. Her parents would worry about her. Her mother would go down to check on her and find her in the middle of her paintings, so she would leave her to her own devices, even if the excessive fervor didn't set her mind at ease. Janan would invite him to stay with her. She'd stand there with the brush in her hand until the crack of dawn sometimes, painting, or rather adding those never-ending little touches. Then she'd turn around and say to him all of a sudden, 'Something somewhere between my body and my soul considers you special. Your burden on me is light and heavy at the same time.'

She compared him to a parachute and said that she felt she could throw herself from a high place, if he was with her. If she was certain that he loved her, she would land without getting hurt, because she would grab onto him.

She'd paint. They'd eat. They'd love one another passionately. And then, all of a sudden, everything would come to a halt. Life stopped. She'd be filled with the urge to withdraw all over again. If he insisted on staying, the time would pass, white and dry, practically dead silent. None of his attempts got him anywhere.

So Nizam withdrew. He left the comrades on their own and went to visit Maysaloun again. This time, she told him he needed to go see Khaled and Bilal in Tripoli about something pertaining to his father's death.

'The inheritance?' he laughed.

'Why not? You are just as much a son of Mahmoud al-Alami as they are. Don't make it easy for them.'

'This is your house, Nizam,' she said before he left, with tenderness in her eyes. 'Come back any time you wish.'

He went back to Lebanon Street, circled around the neighbour-hood, and entered the building. He found the door to Janan's studio open, but Janan was not inside. She would go up to her parents' flat sometimes to shower or eat. He found solace in her paintings, in her colourful drawing books and picture books with all the amazing colours, as he waited calmly. Once, around noon, he heard her voice—not a pained voice, but the angry kind that spills out what's in a person's heart. She was shouting at a woman. She was refusing to eat lunch. She couldn't bear her parents.

'Especially you . . . ' she was saying to her mother.

He didn't wait for her to come down but decided instead to leave her the bouquet of roses he'd bought at the shop in front of the building from the mute flower seller with the big smile. He put the flowers on the black leather sofa and left, baffled.

His feelings of powerlessness grew stronger. His only option was to wait for her to return to normal and to cling to him once again.

'I want you here . . . '

Standing behind her, armed and ready. Silent, not talking to her, and not caressing her. For two hours. Three hours. Behaving himself, content, because she would sense his nervousness if he lost his patience or felt the need to leave.

'You are painting with me. I lose my concentration the moment you start getting restless.'

Something started to change in her paintings. The bright red that she once used sparingly to draw attention to certain details was now occupying more space, reaching one of the layers of the horizon, covering a bigger portion of a wall or a window. As for the people, the lost passers-by, they remained just as obscure, with the details of their faces and bodies wiped out. No males, no females, just humanoid shapes on two legs.

One day she was going to put all those similar paintings of hers on display in an exhibition: *The Arrested City*.

They weren't always reverent or focused before her paintings. They had fun on days when she was happy, satisfied with her colours and details. The black leather couch became their playground, as they fought with numerous pillows and sometimes with their hands. Their embraces became more passionate, their kisses more intense, and they prevented any noises they made from reaching the other flat by playing loud music that she liked. She played with all her heart, like a child. He kissed every part of her body. He kissed her fingers like one would kiss a baby's. They would laugh and laugh, fall on the couch, and then roll onto the floor. Then they'd stop suddenly, out of breath, panting. They would cool off from their intense feelings for a few minutes before resuming their foreplay. They raced each other across the room as they competed at collecting the largest number of beads from a rosary that had fallen apart. They crawled and snatched the little glass beads from each other's hands, their bodies plastered to one another. Then they'd calm down and lie on their backs. He asked her repeatedly about the cuts on one of her arms, but she wouldn't answer. She'd caress him instead, putting an end to his questions. He would take off his jacket and lean over her. He would start by undoing the top button of her shirt, gently, as she closed her eyes. She liked that he had never loved anyone before the way he loved her. They wouldn't go on that way for very long. She would stop, her rhythm broken. She would say she had imagined things would happen differently, and her mood would shift. She would straighten out her clothes and sit upright. She'd regain her composure and insist that they stop. Nizam didn't know how to act in a way that suited her mood. He had to exert new efforts and come up with creative ways to seduce and corner her, with the hope that she'd surrender the next time around.

In an attempt to get her out of her playground, he took her with him to the North one day, when she was feeling optimistic. He took her to his parents. She'd been to the North only once on a school trip to the Cedars, and her only memory from the trip was the heavy rain pouring over the windshield of the bus. She didn't ask him much, and he didn't tell her much. She just wanted him, the way he was when he had arrived to her studio carrying St George under his arm. He took her to the house in Mina. They didn't go up to the third floor, didn't knock on the door. He didn't even know who would open the door for them. Janan looked around her, surprised. He showed her where his father Mahmoud was buried across from Rabbit Island—where they had laid him out all alone in the courtyard of al-Bahr mosque, while everybody else was busy praying inside, as Nizam stood alone and watched him from a distance, not daring to get closer to him to say goodbye. She said she wanted to go inside a mosque if only once in her life.

'They'll think we're tourists,' he said. 'Come on.'

He was blond, and she was blonde with coloured eyes. He took off his shoes. He showed her where they used to sit in a circle around Sheikh Sameeh al-Shaarani and told her about the time he'd let the green cicada fly loose over peoples' heads. She asked him to pray, but they didn't remain standing for long, instead fleeing the stares that some worshippers cast their way. They walked on the boardwalk. The waves were high, and Janan went into a trance, contemplating the turbulent horizon. They walked back in the direction of the house and then sat down at the small café across from it, where they could see anyone entering or exiting the building. The fat owner of the café with the furrowed brow didn't recognize Nizam. They called him Castro. He had rented the space where Pâtisserie Moderne had been and was content using the espresso machine, serving tea and refreshments.

He remained single, and according to neighbourhood gossip, it was because he had fallen in love once in his life—with Maysaloun al-Alami—but he didn't know how to express his love for her, so she slipped from his hands.

Suddenly, his mother Sabah appeared—all alone like a grimacing tree. She took a look at the road and then started walking. She was wearing a black dress and a white scarf as she was still mourning Mahmoud. Feeling playful again, Janan insisted that they follow her. They paid the bill and left. Sabah passed in front of the fishery where tired fishermen who'd come back from work sat in a row, their eyes fixed at the horizon, as they puffed on *arguileh* and exhaled smoke. Sabah tiptoed carefully to make sure that nothing of the debris on the seashore would get stuck to her shoes. She cast a fleeting, disdainful glance inside. She kept walking, taking small footsteps. He whispered to Janan that she must be going to the seamstress to confer about dress alterations, since she wasn't carrying any fabric in her hands. Janan encouraged him to go up to her, but he didn't have the courage. She would have approached her herself if he hadn't grabbed her arm forcefully.

They didn't wait for her to come down from the seamstress' and headed to Hawra instead. The valleys parallel to the road were no longer terrifying. Janan had borrowed her mother's car.

'She's a good driver, but you have to stay alert because she's not good with directions,' her mother had secretly warned Nizam.

Going to Tripoli was easy since no one knew him there, but in Hawra, everybody was on the lookout for him.

They got there around sunset, the night shielding them from prying eyes. Rakheema saw him first.

'My mother,' he said, introducing her to Janan. Janan didn't bombard him with questions. She was slowly discovering his life, discovering his family, and she was enjoying it.

Rakheema cried. She cried because he had called her 'my mother' and because she missed him. Because he came to them and because he would soon be going back and because he had become a man who now showed up with a woman on his arm.

Touma was still working in the orchard.

'As much as he can,' Rakheema explained.

They went to him. Touma was with a labourer who was helping him out. The orchard was a daily battle, and he was sick.

When he saw them come in, he smiled and quickly dismissed the worker by paying him and showing him to the door. It was as if they had caught him in an undesirable situation. He was happy to see Nizam, but since he wasn't the kissing type, he just held Nizam's hand and kept it in his for a long time. Janan stumbled on one of the molehills that filled the orchard and that Touma had stopped trying to fight like he used to in the past.

'The house is a more fitting place for your friend,' Touma said.

Nizam tried to catch a firefly that zipped by on their way out of the orchard. He clasped his hand shut behind it, thinking all over again that he had caught it. But when he opened his hand, there was nothing there. Touma laughed and tried to catch one in turn, succeeding on the third try. He gave it to Nizam, who then gave it to Janan, but it got away from her.

'City girl . . .'

They all laughed.

They showed her the pictures of Nizam that were hanging all over the walls, even in the kitchen where Rakheema spent a lot of time. Their house was an exhibition of him—Nizam getting into trouble with the girls from the nuns' school, surrounded by Mademoiselle Laure and Sister Francesca, Nizam sitting in the folds of the mulberry tree and refusing to come down before having his fill, and then a picture of the three of them together before he got on the bus to Beirut for the first time.

After she had seen Sabah from the back and met Rakheema face-to-face, Janan returned the favour. Her parents threw a dinner in Nizam's honour at their house, and her father offered him a cigar with cognac after dinner. They talked politics. Her father was in charge of all the ceremonies at the Ministry of Foreign Affairs, and he knew all about protocol and good etiquette. He stressed the importance of defending Lebanon and drawing the line when it came to the creation of a Fedayeen state. Nizam thought of the comrades from the Farajallah al-Helou cell, but he didn't raise any objections. Janan's father reiterated his fear of repercussions from the hostage-taking operation that had occurred before noon that day at the British Bank on al-Masaref Street. The kidnappers had shot one of the bank employees who tried to escape, and he fell to the ground, wounded, at the front door. The Maghaweer special forces from the Lebanese army intervened and arrested the kidnappers. It turned out that they were 'radical socialists', as the news channel had referred to them, and among them was a girl whose identity was as yet unknown.

Janan's parents had a very amicable relationship with their daughter, standing at her beck and call and doing everything they could to ensure that she was at ease. It was as if they felt some kind of guilt towards her and were constantly trying to make up for it by paying her too much attention and giving her the liberty of living by herself and choosing her own friends. They welcomed him with so much kindness to please her, since what made her happy made them happy too. She was independent, yet her parents—or her entire family rather—watched over her. Janan was like milk being warmed on a stove, as Rakheema would say about people with unpredictable reactions. She could boil over the moment they turned their back.

Nizam's life shifted to Lebanon Street, on the other side of Beirut, so whenever he sneaked off to Manara, he felt as if he was coming from enemy territory. He gave the friends excuses for his absence, but they didn't believe him and had the feeling that he was drowning in some adventure. He would show up sometime around midnight, after a long work session in Janan's studio, and they'd make room for him to sit among them, but he didn't really listen to their discussions. A little while later he would apologize and go out on the balcony. They said he was in love.

The next morning, Yusra reappeared.

The initials Y. M. were mentioned in connection to the perpetrators of a crime reported in the newspaper *An-Nahar*. The reporter indicated that those who attacked the British Bank distributed a printed statement when they came in, and some of the people who fled brought the statement outside with them. It was a statement attacking the banking system and global capitalism, signed by the Organization of Arab Socialists . . . and one of the witnesses said that there were four of them and that there was a girl with them. They had terrified the bank customers and employees by pointing their Kalashnikovs at their chests and barking out orders at them.

In the morning, comrade Furat arrived at the flat, disturbed.

'It was Yusra, the girl at the bank . . . ' he said.

'Yusra?'

Furat was worried more than anybody because he feared that if his name ever came up in the investigation, he would be deported back to Iraq.

'I won't go back to Mosul no matter what,' he said. 'They'll kill me if I go back there!'

The comrades arrived, one after the other. They were on edge, worried about what Yusra might confess.

But it seemed like she was being stubborn, maintaining absolute silence. The only problem she'd run into was when the investigator started chastising and reprimanding her for what she'd done, especially considering she came from a 'reputable family'. He tried flattering her as he asked her about the motives for the operation and about who had led them astray. She sat there, silent and pensive—until she finally mumbled something that the investigator didn't catch.

When he asked her to raise her voice, she muttered, '*Dog Day Afternoon . . .*'

She was referring to the film starring Al Pacino, who robs a bank with one of his friends. She had seen the film at the El-Dorado movie theatre a few days before. As soon as she'd uttered the name of the film in English, the investigator— who didn't know any English—slapped her in the face because he thought that she was calling him a dog and ordered the guards to take her back to solitary confinement.

She had gotten entangled with those young men, thinking that it was a fresh start. They believed in revolutionary action and scathingly criticized those armchair revolutionaries who couldn't even speak Arabic that well. They hadn't told her anything and just asked her to tag along with them that morning on an 'exploratory mission', as they had called it. But as soon as they entered the British Bank, they brandished their weapons. She had merely been dragged into it with them, so she wasn't going to be of much use to the investigation. She wasn't going to snitch on any Farajallah al-Helou members or anyone who frequented the flat in Manara.

10

The Manara flat was in complete disarray.

The small flat with the spacious balcony had been transformed into a boat weighed down by a heavy load—bustling with activity, its door was always open during the day, its lamp lit at night. Whoever got hungry bought food and drink. Only Vasco paid the electric or water bills if the collector happened to come by while he was there. No one cleaned, and no one complained.

Nizam had saved a black-and-white photograph from the flat's busy days in which the young men appeared with their long, ugly sideburns and mandatory thick moustaches—the markers of revolutionary brooding. It was a group picture of all the guests who had been staying at the flat-turned-hostel, with the exception of Yusra Maktabi. It was said that her father wouldn't stop talking about how he spent his lifetime working hard in Africa only to end up with a daughter in prison on a robbery charge. But her parents gave her a lot of money, most of which she distributed among fellow prisoners, and they also brought her hot food, which she shared with other inmates. Her mother was terrified at the thought of her daughter catching a disease of some sort.

Yusra Maktabi vanished, and Maysaloun appeared.

She too remembered Nizam's birthday.

Nizam himself didn't remember. It was Rakheema who reminded him.

She sent from Hawra to Zahrat al-Shamal what she referred to as 'a little something to eat' that was actually enough to feed twenty people. Two big pots of grape leaves stuffed with rice and topped with exquisite fawaregh that were filled with rice, pine nuts, and ground meat—alongside peeled garlic and mint that she put in a separate bag. She must have worked on the meal for over two days. She sent along a note, written in her shaky hand, saying that Touma was 'tired'. What it meant was that Touma was getting sicker and that he'd become 'prickly', because his diabetes made him irritable. She wished Nizam a long life, a hundred years of happiness, and she added that all he had to do was warm up the grape leaves on low heat before digging into them with delight.

Maysaloun showed up unannounced. She came in with her husband, carrying a cake. Nizam got a little nervous but then surrendered to her presence. Her husband shook hands with everybody, remembering some of the faces. In the picture, Mustapha Hijazi seemed lost in the clamour of the residents of Olga's flat. He stood in the back row, with the old folks—the American professor and his wife. He wasn't standing next to Maysaloun when the picture was taken because she must have been preoccupied with Nizam since arriving there. Mustapha looked on, uncomfortable. He seemed unsure about why he was there among those people who stood in two or three rows like students at a graduation ceremony. He was more concerned with trying to understand the reason behind their gathering and friendship than actually looking into the camera lens.

Rakheema was present among them, thanks to the food her hands had prepared. With Dima's help, Maysaloun put out everything that had arrived from Hawra on a table they took out to the balcony. Maysaloun had explored the fridge and cupboards and their contents on her second visit to the flat and was now acting like she was the lady of the house.

They invited one another to start eating and pounced on the ruby-red quince jam and grapes swimming in sweetened water, which they licked off their fingers. They let out shouts of approval with every discovery they made. They asked about each dish and how to make it, but there was no one who could answer their questions. There wasn't much left after they were done. Nizam was delighted to see that the handiwork of a woman from Hawra—those pickled red and green tomatoes soaked in vinegar, salt and oil—could so impress these Beirutis. They also impressed Maurice, who arrived late, carrying his flute in its expensive case and wearing a strange black hat. In front of the camera, Maurice held on to his hat and flute. Maurice loved the bitter orange slices dipped in sugar, and he'd close his eyes for a long time so he could truly relish their flavour.

Jonathan Parker and his wife Barbara also ate gluttonously and asked in their broken Arabic about the secrets behind Rakheema's cooking. Their curiosity was boundless. They even wanted Maysaloun to list every single ingredient in the ready-made cake that she'd bought at the shop. They asked Vasco about his religion in the same matter-of-fact manner that they asked about his name. They wanted to hear from all those in attendance why they didn't consider Lebanon a democratic country. Jonathan took out his small notebook and starting jotting down some notes. After learning that Maurice was Jewish, they tried earnestly to get his opinion regarding the decision to partition Palestine in 1948, but they didn't know exactly—thanks to the back-and-forth switching between Arabic and French—the reason behind the celebration that they had joined in the flat, until comrade Furat planted some candles in the cake and lit them. Everybody asked Nizam to blow out the candles as they sang for him and showered him with kisses. Nizam leaned over so Vasco could give him a kiss too. The neighbours went out on their balconies to follow the festivities, this time without expressing any annoyance.

Then, it was picture time. They first made room for Vasco and his wheelchair by putting him in the centre and gathering around him. Comrade Furat stood off to the side. He didn't want to appear in the photograph, but they had insisted. He could never get rid of his Iraqi fears. He'd portrayed Mosul to the comrades as a damp prison that men were transported to at dawn. He was worried that the photograph would serve as material evidence, irrefutable testimony, of his presence in Beirut. But he finally succumbed to everybody's wishes and stood in a spot where he thought the camera wouldn't capture him, but it did capture him looking like he was trying to get away.

It took several calls and appeals to get all of them out on the balcony. The picture was Vasco's idea. He had brought a camera and a tripod with him that his assistant, who took most of the pictures, had set up. Comrades Dima and Huda were smiling in the direction of the cameraman as if they were watching something entertaining happening in front of them. The camera flash flickered in their faces several times before they dispersed and went back to eating grape leaves and drinking.

It started getting late. Maurice stepped into the middle of the room and slowly began taking his flute out of its case, alerting the comrades he was going to play. They were surprised, because usually they had to beg him to play. Here he was, tonight, deciding to do it of his own accord. They formed a circle around him and listened as usual in such complete silence that the sounds of the city found their way to their ears. They clapped for him when he finished, and so he smiled, removed his hat, and took a long bow before them with the hat in one hand and the flute in the other. The short applause that had followed Maurice's performance did not warrant so much gratitude or for him to bow so low he nearly touched the floor.

They ate everything and drank everything, especially the vodka, but their eagerness waned as they listened to Maurice's flute. They drooped back in their seats. Maysaloun cleared the table and started washing the dishes. Seeing that they were about to break it up and head out, Nizam suggested they go for a night-time stroll. The weather was nice, even if a little on the chilly side. They would see a flicker of light from time to time in the horizon over the sea. Spring was still just beginning, and the night was still young. They all helped Vasco out with his wheelchair and took the lift down in shifts. A complete night-time chorus. They headed without any clear plan towards the sleepless streets of Ras Beirut. Nizam was the most excited of everyone. They comprised a full chorus with a range of styles in their repertoire. They went up Phoenicia Street while transitioning from 'Old-time Lovers' with its tender French arrangement and throaty existential sufferings into the military rhythm of 'The Red Flag' with its decisive victory cry in revolutionary Italian. The marchers didn't last long up on the pavement before meandering into the middle of the street. The cars slowed down behind them and waited for them to open up some space, so they could pass by and beep their horns to them in salute.

The Parkers were a little late catching up with the procession, because they had been hesitant to join in at first. They said that getting to bed early was a part of their daily regimen. They had intended to say goodnight at the lift and go down to their flat, but everyone insisted they join the chorus. Maybe they felt they were a bit too old for the others, but they smiled sympathetically as they followed them past the cabaret entrances with their voices raised in song, increasing the volume every time people looked at them. The dissonance was amplified due to the wine's effect on their voices, so the people entering the Kit Kat would smile, and the doormen in their folkloric outfits would swarm them, as each one tried to draw the group into his own nightclub.

They took turns pushing Vasco's wheelchair. Comrade Dima remembered all the songs. She had all the pop tunes memorised and would sing out the first verse in the approximate tune, and then the others would join in and excitedly drown her out, each one singing the rest of the words however he or she pleased. The rest chimed in little by little. Comrade Furat started singing a Baghdadi song that the others sang along with as best they could. Maysaloun stayed close to her husband so he wouldn't feel out of place. She didn't feel out of place because Nizam was her brother. She was surprised by Mustapha who joined in, gradually adding his voice to the chorus, up until he took advantage of a silent pause and in a strong and melodious voice belted out, 'Oh you, travelling in the land of the Nile, I have a lover in Egypt . . . ' The chorus repeated the refrain while he made his voice doubly melodious and raised it louder and louder. Vasco headed the parade, which sometimes drew in passers-by who caught the night-time singing bug and marched with them for a few hundred metres before parting ways, their faces filled with a joy they'd never known before.

Nizam was the one to keep the beat. He walked backwards at the front with his hand raised, remembering and imitating the funeral dirge conductor in Hawra. Nizam and his friends had so often mocked him for the way he waved his baton with exaggerated movements in front of the trumpet and cymbal players and the way he stood on his tiptoes because he was so short. They would laugh whenever he took a break from his frantic arm waving while the lead trumpet player performed the death dirge solo. That was how Nizam found himself, walking on tiptoes—though he wasn't lacking in height—and waving his hands to the beat of a song he might have been hearing for the first time. He was the first to laugh at this performance of his. He led the group through the hotel district. They passed in front of the entrance to the Phoenicia Hotel, which was crowded with guests and partygoers, while some members of the group took heart in the face of scrutinizing stares. They showed their solidarity by singing along with raised voices. The comrades felt that by repeating those revolutionary songs, with their voices raised tirelessly, they were standing up to those people with the special privileges, like the women in their fur coats getting out of Jaguars, accompanying their husbands or their lovers—something comrade Furat enjoyed emphasizing—as they smoked their fat cigars dressed in fancy suits with matching pocket squares and neckties. They headed in the direction of the shopping district, where their voices got lost in the streets that were closed for the night. They came back around from the direction of the sea. They reached the Abdel Nasser statue, much to the surprise of some youths from the quarter loitering at the street corner late at night. They started joking back and forth, making fun of them, shouting their usual epithets, giving them dirty looks, and inviting them tfor sugar cane juice. At the cross-walk, they were joined by some people coming out of the Beirut Theatre who had just seen the play *Mr Puntila and His Man Matti*, while tracer bullets embroidered the city sky without making any sound—bullets no one asked about or cared where they'd been shot from or why.

They continued like vagabonds towards Avenue des Français, and from there they travelled along the Corniche where they were met with applause by some night-time pedestrians leaning on the railing. They sang and sang until the refreshing night-time air wiped out the effects of the red wine and vodka from their heads and until their voices and their legs got tired. They turned back towards Manara and from there they started heading in separate directions, each to his own house, as they sang out their finale—a song Dima suggested by singing the opening line—'We all live in a yellow submarine'. They chimed in, blaring the song into the dark Beirut streets.

PART THREE

Are You Ahmad?

1

Palm Sunday.

He was on his way back from Lebanon Street.

Janan was complaining again. She'd lost her desire to paint. She said it with a sigh, as if she could see her desire walking off into the distance.

He suggested a leisurely activity for Sunday. He'd take her to the church procession. New clothes, candles. She flat-out refused.

The children's eyes troubled her, whether they cried or laughed.

'I'm going to tear up my paintings,' she suddenly said, agitated. 'I don't want to see anyone.'

'Anyone' meant him—Nizam.

She stood firmly, put her foot down, and withdrew.

She went up to her parents' flat and locked herself in her bedroom, not opening the door even for her mother. She buried her head in her pillow. Wouldn't read. Wouldn't talk. Wouldn't shower.

She had opened the door of the studio and left.

Her purse lay tossed aside, wide open. She'd forgotten it on the sofa in the heat of her frustration.

Nizam didn't try to resist his desire to snoop:

Red lipstick.

Tweezers.

A round hand mirror.

A small drawing pad: pavements, houses, cars. Pencil sketches. Drafts for her paintings.

Hurtful expressions here and there about the sea, life, waiting.

No mention of him.

Two photographs: Janan in colour and another girl from another time, the time of sepia.

On the back of the photo: 'My grandmother before her marriage, before her madness.'

Janan was a replica of her. The only thing he would ask her later on was whether her grandmother's eyes were two different colours.

He walked to the door, paused, and then walked back to the purse. He took her picture and left, heading back to Manara.

As soon as he got on the pavement, he realized he might be the only one out there just walking along.

Three men standing on the street corner were whispering about something, most likely something serious. One of them was pointing with his hand insistently in the direction of the south.

As Nizam got closer to the Oriental Studies Institute, he saw a man dressed in civilian clothes carrying a machine gun. He was regulating traffic, calling on drivers to move along while he concerned himself with pedestrians.

'Where to?' he asked Nizam.

Nizam waved his hand in a vague direction. 'Manara . . . '

'Don't go there!' the armed man warned.

Nizam asked why.

There were thirty dead in Ain al-Remmaneh.

Nizam whistled in shock and didn't understand at first why the armed man didn't want him to go to Manara. The man was much more familiar with what was happening, and the fact that he had gone out into the street carrying weapons over his regular clothes—his Sunday clothes—was a good indication of the seriousness of the situation.

Nizam stood indecisively.

He wouldn't go back to Janan, his personal war.

He picked up his pace and headed towards Burj Square.

A light breeze wafted through the square, scattering plastic bags of various colours, newspapers that had fallen from the hands of hasty readers, and used facial tissues.

Cars sped past quickly. The movie theatres interrupted the films that were playing, and the few moviegoers came out from the dark theatres into the daylight, frowning as they tried to figure out what was going on.

Raffoul was sitting on top of his desk, supervising the small crowd that had gathered in the lobby of Zahrat al-Shamal. He delegated various tasks to them. The door was wide open as usual. The people, who had been talking, suddenly fell silent when Nizam appeared at the door of the lobby.

'Even *you* are here?' Raffoul called to him as if to admonish him for the additional care he would have to provide now that Nizam had come to him for refuge, which, added to the needs of all the others, would push him beyond his abilities.

Raffoul was very busy. He was getting his day of revenge, revenge on those stupefied people in the hotel lobby, some standing, some sitting. Hawra and its neighbouring villages' native sons—the Christians of the northern mountain. They'd come to him for refuge the moment the news spread.

They had no idea how to get themselves back to their distant homes. There were men and some women, some had their children with them too. They'd been brought there by various job opportunities or for visits to the capital. Now they were confused as to which direction to go after the streets had emptied. They were left all alone in the middle of the street, no place to call home, no address they felt comfortable heading for other than Zahrat al-Shamal.

A man and his wife were whispering to each other while eying Nizam who was noticing how much the people from Hawra resembled one another. Their resemblance was almost scandalous in the capital, so far from their hometown. Something about the nose, the shape of the head, the way they looked at you. That gaze. Eyes popped open at the sight of anything different. In a perpetual state of shock like Moussa had been.

Nizam's entrance through the door of Zahrat al-Shamal on that particular Sunday was something that made them widen their eyes. They resumed talking in his presence, even though they remained cautious with their words. They didn't trust him, even if some of them had heard whispers about him being baptised secretly in Maydoun. They would rather he'd stayed true to his first religion.

Raffoul seemed happy seeing the fear drawn on their faces. If he had wanted to settle accounts, then he would have left them to manage on their own. For over two years he had been warning them to be careful whenever they came down from their town and wandered through the capital. He made it clear to them that the situation had soured, but none of them listened or heeded any advice. They didn't pay any attention to his fears and acted as if he was the paranoid one. Now all his suspicions were confirmed.

'A hundred dead . . . ' they said.

'Between the young men from Ain al-Remmaneh and the Palestinians.'

They opened fire on the church, on Palm Sunday. The new church. St Michael's. One of the young men was exiting through the church door, crossing himself with holy water when they shot him.

Raffoul said all this matter-of-factly as he looked towards the door through which Ibrahim al-Simsmani entered.

Abu Ali arrived in a hurry. The incident had propelled him, too, to Burj Square.

Raffoul winked at them so they would watch their words even more. Maybe he'd also given them a wink when Nizam had arrived.

'Where are you coming from, Abu Ali?' Raffoul asked, purposely revealing his name from the outset.

Al-Simsmani had something to say—something had happened in front of him, and he could still see it. His eyes said it all.

They were at the horse race when a hail of bullets descended on them during the fourth lap, just as the horses were turning the 'Corner of the Roses'. An armed man—who was said to be Palestinian—came from the direction of the Military Court and fired an RPG towards the horses and the jockeys, wounding Amir al-Layl, Prince of the Night, before taking off.

'Amir al-Layl?'

Raffoul knew him. He'd sometimes bet on him with Abu Ali.

Amir al-Layl was worth the price of a four-story building. Blood gushed from his stomach, and he dove to the ground in a cloud of dust. People didn't understand what had happened. The jockeys pulled on the reins with all their might before throwing themselves off the horses' backs in order to escape, every man for himself, which caused the horses to go berserk as chaos ensued and bullets poured down on them from the direction of Horsh Beirut . . .

Abu Ali had arrived on foot. He'd come down Damascus Road. People were running away to their homes, and the streets were now empty.

The folks waiting in the lobby of the hotel didn't say anything in response. They were feeling more and more overwhelmed by the day's events.

Al-Simsmani went out to the balcony after giving his report. When one of the children tried to follow him out on the balcony, his father forbade him as if the bullets were still raining down outside. Abu Ali looked around in all directions and came back to say that things had calmed down. It was as if the scene outside confirmed what he was saying.

'It's just a dark cloud,' he said. 'It'll pass.'

Those waiting for taxis to take them to the north—now that all the buses had fled Burj Square—felt reassured.

Abu Ali went out to the balcony again since he couldn't find a place to sit down, and Nizam followed him outside. Now the people from Hawra could speak more freely with Raffoul.

Some of the pedestrians who were in a rush were still weaving their way through Burj Square, trying to find the shortest path to safety. The place looked different, empty without cars. The four figures of the Martyrs' Statue now had the empty square all to themselves—the woman standing and holding the torch and her friend and the two men rolling on the ground. They were left all alone looking in the direction of the life-sized model of Anita Ekberg towering over the Rivoli Cinema.

Al-Simsmani went back in. 'They're working things out,' he assured everyone. 'Don't worry.'

'We're not worried,' someone said as if sensing some kind of a challenge in Abu Ali's reassurance.

Abu Ali al-Simsmani didn't care for trouble, didn't wish for any problems.

Raffoul winked at them again, this time cautioning them not to be fooled by Abu Ali's optimism, maybe because Abu Ali had no idea what was happening, or maybe because he was just a 'Metuali', as Raffoul had always referred to him when he was not there.

Raffoul described the incident again, filling in more details. Things were more serious than they could have imagined—a whole bus was headed to Tel al-Zaatar refugee camp, and no one had gotten out of it alive.

'The dead are still sitting in their seats, even at this very moment,' he said. 'No one has been able to get close enough to pull them out.'

He stressed the words 'even at this very moment' with utter confidence as he lowered his head, imitating the way a dead man would look sitting lifelessly in his seat. As he described the situation, there was a tone of admiration in his voice for the speed and precision of those who had opened fire on the bus passengers and didn't give them any opportunity to get up from their seats and use the weapons that—according to him—filled the bus.

'It's a tug of war,' Raffoul concluded, sighing.

He hired taxis to transport the village folks to their distant villages and wouldn't leave them in the hands of the drivers before confirming their identity. He didn't want to send them off with any Muslim drivers since they had to go through a Christian area. He tried to arrange their travel before nightfall. The road map was crystal clear in his mind, and all he had to do was drill it into the heads of the drivers.

'Don't take them through Tripoli,' he said. 'Take a right and head north at Chekka . . . '

He didn't bid them farewell. He just asked them to tell Touma and Rakheema that they had seen Nizam and that he was doing fine so they wouldn't worry about him . . .

Always alert, he didn't forget anything. His request was met with some muttering. On their way back, shortly after feeling relieved for getting out of the circle of danger that was surrounding the city, they started talking about Nizam as they chatted with one another.

Raffoul, the only person who still maintained his composure, took care of all necessary duties that day, as if he had been training for that moment for a long time.

He turned to Abu Ali and suggested that he go down to his village in the south, if only for a couple of days, until the situation cleared up. The latter protested with a hand gesture and went to his room without shutting the door behind him.

Raffoul's recipe for Nizam was simple.

'Go straight home,' he said. 'Don't slow down for anything on the way there.'

Expecting the worst, he added, 'In any case, don't wander around too much. If you find a shop open on the way, be sure to stock up for a few days.'

The servers in white aprons were closing up Jumhuriyya Café. Every time they carried a table from the pavement into the restaurant, they'd pause, taking a long look at the square that they'd never seen so empty before. Everything that could close up was now closed, and everything that needed to be transported away was transported—in anticipation of the imminent tidal wave that would be arriving from Ain al-Remmaneh where the dead, who had been sitting in their bus seats, had fallen. It was a wave that had sent pedestrians fleeing to their homes, emptying the streets that awaited it. A wave that was soon arriving and that Nizam beat to Manara. The taxi driver who took him there told him that bullets and explosions were now being heard on Damascus Road.

'Oh Beirut, what a loss!' he addressed the city, mourning it.

'They burned you,' he said, without naming names.

'May you all burn in hell,' he threatened them.

Heartbroken, he wouldn't accept the fare from Nizam.

The concierge at Nizam's building insisted that there were many casualties, but that the radio station was being tight-lipped about the exact number so people wouldn't panic. It had also interrupted its classical music program in order to broadcast breaking news about the Council of Ministers' emergency meeting.

The sun was setting in the sea as the sound of intermittent gunfire could be heard from hard-to-determine places.

He didn't find anyone at the flat.

'No one came by to see you,' the concierge told Nizam, almost sarcastically.

He wasn't afraid of staying by himself.

He sat out on the balcony. The news had not reached the girl on the fourth floor whose opera singing rehearsals reverberated freely at the beginning of the night. No one chastised her. Even the bullets whizzed by, parallel to her voice. Drops of water started to fall down, one at a time, the last of winter's stubborn attempts.

His hair got wet at first, but he didn't take shelter. He didn't even put his hand over his head to check how wet it was. Accustomed to putting up with water, he opened his mouth and stuck his tongue out to catch a droplet that rolled down his cheek as another trickled on his nose.

He wished the rain would hit him harder.

2

It was Jonathan and Barbara who went up to his flat with the tally on Tuesday morning. They were shocked. It was as if they had been fooled about Beirut, as if someone had made them a promise that was later broken—given them goods that they soon discovered were damaged.

Jonathan had jotted down in his notebook what he'd heard on the BBC: 156 people dead—127 men and 29 women, and 291 people wounded. Losses were estimated at about four million Lebanese liras, with 1,400 homes hit or destroyed. He showed Nizam the page so he could see for himself.

The station had not counted Comrade Furat among the dead or injured since the media was not counting displaced migrants yet.

Chamoun Rikho would have been among the first, most likely.

He lived near the office of one of the Christian militias in the National Museum area. He lived where he was supposed to live, in the Syriac neighbourhood. When he was on his way out to buy coffee on Wednesday morning, the office guards made comments within his earshot about not wanting to see any 'strangers' in their neighbourhood. They didn't address him directly, but one of them sounded the accusation out loud at that exact moment when no one but Chamoun happened to be on the pavement. The armed man added that there were 'spies among us'. The guards were Syriacs too, and Chamoun's own cousin was one of them.

Chamoun always made light of his situation. He'd say that all the Eastern Christians put together didn't amount to anything worth mentioning in the bigger scale of things. So one could only imagine the even sadder status of the Syriacs—or rather the Catholic Syriacs to whom he belonged and who were a minority themselves within the larger Syriac community. He joked about what he would do if those Catholic Syriacs—who couldn't even fill up their one church in Beirut for Mass on Christmas Eve— disowned him.

After he'd bought the coffee, he checked his pocket to ensure that his wallet and cash were still there. Then he turned his back and walked away. He wasn't going back to his parents' home in the Syriac neighbourhood, and he wasn't going back to Mosul. He continued on his way to Manara, to Nizam's flat. They drank coffee together during the break that followed the first round of fighting. Then Rikho moved permanently to al-Ahyaa al-Wataniyyah, the Arab nationalist neighbourhoods.

The ceasefire lasted for a while, and the comrades trickled in one after the other. Nizam bought food that was easy to prepare. He clung to those who showed up, made them coffee, poured them whiskey, and invited them to sleep over if they stayed late, giving up his bed and sleeping on the floor whenever space was tight. But they didn't stay very long. Dima came over without her parents knowing. They were insisting that she go to Paris and con- tinue her studies there since she could stay with one of her uncles for a little while, but she refused. Hussein Maallawi, Comrade Ramon, was busy preparing for a training course in Havana after his relationship with the political attaché at the Cuban embassy in Beirut became much closer. Vasco was living in East Beirut since he insisted on staying at his parents' home for reasons that most likely pertained to his inability to use the bathroom and take care of his daily needs by himself. He would come to Manara in the morning. His assistant would roll his wheelchair out on the balcony where he'd take a look at the city, inhale deeply, and say,

'There is some kind of poison in the air . . . ', as if quoting a character from some movie. Nizam asked about them, one by one.
There was no news of Maurice, so Nizam volunteered to visit him.
He went down to Wadi Abu-Jamil, where an old woman eyed his
every move. He knocked at the door, waited, and then wrote on
the wall, 'Nizam came by to see you, but you weren't home . . . '

Jonathan and Barbara received instructions from the American
embassy telling them to exercise caution and avoid wandering
around, which prompted Chamoun Rikho to expect the worst
since he was making arrangements to stay in one of the Palestinian
camps. Nizam gave everyone a copy of the photo from his birthday. He discovered that St George appeared in all the pictures,
hanging above their heads on the wall of the living room—busy
planting his spear in the mouth of the dragon. Nizam laughed
about the way they stood in that photograph, but the others didn't
laugh. They felt as if eons had passed since that night.

Nizam was bombarded with advice from all over the place.

Rakheema had gotten worried upon learning that the flat that
she and Touma had looked for but didn't find in Beirut was located
in a Muslim neighbourhood. She remembered that Nizam was
baptised, but she forgot that he was Muslim.

'He should come up to Hawra until God eases the situation!'
she told the Hawra driver, hoping he could convince him of that
if he ran into him in Beirut.

Janan wanted him in Achrafiyeh with her. Her mother had
answered the phone and was so happy to hear his voice. She had
insisted on calling for Janan so she could talk to him. Janan had
emerged from her depression.

'Come on over,' she said. 'Don't worry. My father knows a lot
of people around here.'

People with influence lived on the other side of the capital.

Maysaloun came alone. She invited Nizam to her home in Corniche al-Mazraa where they 'had protection', she said half-seriously, half-jokingly. The office of al-Tanzim al-Shaabi was in the same building where she lived. She'd come to check on him and let him know that their brothers were insisting on meeting with him.

'They may be young, but they've got strong personalities . . . ' she said, nodding her head admiringly yet cautiously. 'Especially Khaled.'

Nizam finally made up his mind. He headed to Mina by bus. He couldn't find a sea-view seat. He arrived a little before noon.

The third time was a charm. He was going inside.

Sabah opened the door. She hesitated for a split second, gasped, and put her hand on her chest as if she'd lost her breath.

'Long time, no see . . . '

Mahmoud al-Alami's death had left its mark on her face, but she was still elegant and well-groomed.

They stood facing one another as she retreated inside while he stood, frozen, at the door. He didn't greet her with a handshake, and she didn't give him a hug. She said she needed to sit down.

The furniture was different, the colours now dingy and dull. He couldn't bring himself to sit down and relax. The curtains had become darker too. He only remembered the house bright and sunny. Sabah sat down and looked at him, studying his tall stature and his eyes, as he stood there.

Quranic verses, written in calligraphy, hung on the wall.

'What happened to your wedding picture?'

There used to be a picture of Sabah and Mahmoud going down the stairs of the Colorado Theatre a few days after they had gotten married. They had just come out of a Farid al-Atrash concert and were laughing so hard, like the world wasn't big enough for the two of them.

'Khaled took down all the pictures,' she said in a tone of resignation. 'They're teaching him all sorts of stuff.'

She'd stopped visiting Nizam in Hawra and didn't follow him to Beirut because she thought he didn't want her, didn't want *them*.

'Maysaloun let me know that you're doing OK.'

Feeling bashful, he kept quiet. He wasn't going to open his heart and tell her that he'd come to Mina twice, that he got all the way to the door of the building but didn't go up the stairs.

Sabah wouldn't turn her gaze away from him. Since the day he'd turned down the rice pudding with honey and stopped doing homework—rejecting any type of consolation here in Mina, except for the promise of going up to the folks in Hawra—she no longer knew what to do with her arms, how to stop herself from hugging him every time she ran into him or he approached her. He had dug a hole between them. She cried only after he'd left. As soon as he headed back to Beirut, she went to her room and buried her face in her pillow. It was just like it used to be when she'd take out her handkerchief and wipe her eyes—as Bilal laid his head in her lap—in the back seat of the taxi, after cutting her visit to Hawra short because Nizam had run away from her. Nizam would pretend he had a play date with his friends, and just like that, he would leave her with Touma and Rakheema, as Bilal ran around between them, oblivious.

He asked about Khaled and Bilal. It was almost noon, so they'd be home soon. They had started working together at the travel agency just a couple of months earlier.

'Just like their father,' she said, choking up.

She recognized the sound of their footsteps coming up the stairs. She told Nizam to open the door for them, so he could surprise them in person.

They embraced each other as best they could, like men who didn't have past accounts to settle. One was cold; the other was slightly warmer. First, Nizam asked which of them was Khaled and which Bilal. The warmer, smiling, clean-shaven one said he was Bilal. The bearded one, Khaled, asked how the highway from Beirut to Tripoli was. 'I hear they've been putting up makeshift checkpoints from time to time.'

Bilal smiled as though to indicate he understood what his brother intended by asking the question, or perhaps because he was one of those people who smiled in response to anything anyone said in their presence. Nizam said he hadn't heard of such checkpoints or run into any on the way.

'There's also news,' Khaled clarified, 'that your friends have been putting up checkpoints at the Cedars Highway exit.'

'My friends?' Nizam asked, smiling with surprise.

'They're trying to kidnap Muslims . . . '

Khaled was baiting him with words. Maysaloun knew him well.

Changing the subject, Bilal asked Nizam about conditions in Beirut while Sabah got up to prepare lunch. Khaled muttered 'Bismillah' signalling he was about to delve into the heart of the matter. Nizam peered outside through the opening between the curtains hanging over the window. Khaled began with a long elucidation about the necessity of executing the inheritance, insisting on abiding by the stipulations imposed by Sharia Law.

'You mean you want to give Maysaloun half the share of a son?' Nizam asked, intentionally interrupting him.

Khaled's words were loaded like a weapon. Too heavy for Nizam. He was besieging him. Khaled responded by saying it was not his own volition; rather, he was merely operating according to the Holy Verse. Khaled was constantly quoting verses in Nizam's presence. Perhaps on purpose or perhaps out of habit.

Nizam was concise with his words, straightforward. He asked about the value of his father's inheritance, since he was under the impression that his financial circumstances were not good. This prompted Khaled to rattle off a noble Hadith which says that justice and law are to be applied across the board.

Nizam was confused. He made an appeal to Bilal who was content to just keep smiling.

It was no use.

Nizam persisted, so they told him.

They told him that the inheritance included the house in Mina and an orange orchard that Sabah inherited in Homs whose value was going up as a result of the new construction in the area. Additionally, Muflih al-Haj Hassan had come back to see them two days after the burial and asked to speak in private with his friend's widow. He handed Sabah an envelope with a large sum of money inside it and blurted, 'Mahmoud is entitled to this . . . '

He refused to clarify why or how. He could have chosen not to show up or give them any money at all. He assured Sabah the money was due payment for her husband's hard work and not a handout from anyone. He advised her to deposit it in the bank and use it to take care of herself.

Mahmoud had worn them out while he was alive. Now he was paying them back.

Sabah came to their rescue and called them to the table.

Khaled ate in silence, ate well.

'They told us you were getting married,' Bilal said.

'To a Christian girl,' asserted Khaled. He stopped eating when he spoke.

Nizam laughed. 'Who told you that?'

'No one. I assumed as much. As they say, "If you live among a people long enough . . . " '

By 'a people' he meant Christians.

Maybe Castro or the concierge's son had told them that Nizam had come to Mina with a young woman.

'They told me she was beautiful, like you . . . ' Sabah said, not taking her eyes off Nizam. She was trying to find an inroad. He smiled, taking pleasure in hearing Janan's praises, but he didn't respond.

They resumed their story after lunch. Khaled resumed his attack. 'There is a problem . . . If you are no longer Muslim, then how can you inherit from your father?'

Nizam's answer was ready, cutting into his heart. 'It was all of you who decided I was no longer a Muslim, the day of my father's death notice.'

Things heated up.

'Did Maysaloun tell you that?'

'No. I saw the notice with my own eyes. I was standing right here, while all of you were saying the prayers at al-Bahr Mosque . . . '

Sabah choked. Bilal softened.

Khaled set things straight. 'Then are you still Muslim? Should we include your name with ours?'

Nizam began to get agitated. His blood was boiling. He raised his voice.

Yusra Maktabi had shot a gun at him, and he didn't get mad. He had managed to carry the demonstration casualties to Dar al-Ifta without losing his composure. But Khaled threw him off balance. In a loud, sharp tone, Nizam asked, 'What would make you feel better? For me to be Muslim or Christian?'

He felt Khaled preferred him not to be Muslim to make it easier to cut him out of the inheritance, the value of which he still didn't know. He didn't want to know. Khaled was pushing him to admit he'd changed his religion, thereby betraying them and betraying his birthright. And betraying his two paternal aunts Najeeha and Zayneddar and his grandfather Haj Yasser al-Alami. He wanted to make Nizam understand that cutting him off from his father's inheritance was rightful legal punishment to him, especially since in the end he was going to inherit from other people.

The bewildered Sabah—the tormented one among them—came straight out with it, even if it seemed as a mere gesture of support. 'Yes, Touma and Rakheema are rich, but Nizam is your brother.'

The scene had come full circle. Nizam couldn't bear any more.

They must have found out he had been baptised, and if he said he was still Muslim according to the Personal Status Registry, then Khaled would say that what mattered was not what was written in the register, but what was in the heart and soul. If a person was Muslim, he was Muslim without any outward sign.

Khaled said they wanted to give him his share of his father's inheritance, but only in accordance with the law of God and his Messenger. 'In accordance with the law of God' meant Khaled would raise the case in the religious court.

Nizam stood up as if about to leave and then dropped his final declaration on them.

'I don't want a single piaster of my father's inheritance. He kissed me once or twice in his lifetime. I won't take payment for that. I already told Maysaloun that in Beirut . . . '

Dejected, he squeezed his eyes shut in anguish. He added that Touma and Rakheema were burying him with money; they didn't have anyone else besides him. He wouldn't tell Khaled if he was

Muslim or Christian; he was free to be whatever he was. He wanted nothing from them except the right to come back to this house someday. He might never come back, but he wanted to feel he could pass by, even spend the night there someday. 'I don't know . . . '

Bilal shouted out, welcoming the idea. Before leaving, Nizam asked to go out on the balcony overlooking the port. His mother and Bilal joined him. Khaled picked up a book and started reading it or pretended to read it. Nizam stood gazing out at the sea. The small boats decorated with ribbons and colours that ferried families out on excursions to the little islands during holidays were still there, and a massive freighter ship carrying used Mercedes was unloading its shipment onto the dock. The ship was named 'Excelsior'. Bilal informed him that numerous ships had started unloading their cargo in the port of Tripoli following the incidents that had taken place in Beirut and rumours about the militias robbing the cargo containers there.

Sabah said goodbye to him at the door while getting ready to cry. Bilal said goodbye smiling. Bilal didn't smile; he had a smiling face.

Nizam returned to Beirut exhausted. He hadn't continued on to Hawra. He couldn't bear two visits on one trip. He grumbled to Maysaloun that he was finished with Tripoli. He was resolute and sad.

3

Nizam withdrew to Janan, showered her with gifts. He bought her things that could speak to her for him. She liked scarves and rings and necklaces, but he liked buying her shoes and lingerie. He slipped into women's boutiques and cowered at the mocking glares that came his way. He didn't know how to talk to the saleswomen. He would pay whatever price they asked without trying to bargain—anything to curtail the torture of standing there amid the mannequins in their panties and bras and the supple ladies' display legs in their silk stockings. Janan made fun of his taste. Black spike heels and red bras—hooker apparel, she'd say and laugh. She wouldn't wear them, but she would keep them as a memento from him. He also tried books and records—the Beatles, Miles Davis.

Then he remembered the parrot.

She didn't like the usual things. So be it.

He would bring her the parrot that had frightened him the day he arrived in Beirut. Wasn't it for sale just like all the other caged birds on display? If he were to buy her a pair of lovebirds, she would laugh at him. He knew her. No gift could speak for him better than a parrot. Maybe he'd be lucky enough to teach it a few phrases that would make her smile.

He woke up early and headed downtown.

The shops had all reopened for business as usual, even if a little late. The shop owners wanted to be sure the day was off to a safe start.

The bird shop owner, elegantly dressed in bowtie and all, was outside the shop hanging the birdcages up himself. The parrot was one of them. Nizam cast him the endearing look of an old friend.

The man brushed the little bit of dirt off his summer suit in a show of frustration. He cursed the birds whenever they shook their feathers briskly inside their cages and sent some of the debris flying his way.

He was talking to himself.

Nizam greeted him as he entered and so he continued his conversation with Nizam.

He was grumbling about having to work with his hands.

And about Ahmad, the boy who had worked for him for years. He'd raised him so well that he'd become a bigger expert on birds than him. The day before, a group of young militia men had stopped in to ask if he had someone working for him by the name of Ahmad. When he asked them how they knew that, they said that they heard the parrot calling his name every day as they made their rounds. They wanted to ask Ahmad a few questions as part of their efforts to maintain 'security in the area'. Ahmad was fifteen years old. He would teach the parrot to say his name, and whenever a customer came and bought the parrot, he would teach the next parrot to say his name, too. Ahmad had arrived a few moments earlier that morning to help the owner open up the shop, but he told Ahmad he must leave right away and never come back again. They might take him away and never bring him back. Kill him and toss him aside. Ahmad stroked the parrot's beak with his index finger, bidding him farewell, and went home. He would never return.

Nizam asked how much for the parrot, having decided he should bargain over the prices of things he wanted to buy. He haggled every time, but he always ended up paying the seller's asking price. The man looked at him, but before he could answer, they heard some commotion outside—the sound of people yelling and a scuffle of footsteps. Nizam started to go outside, but the bird shop owner held him back for his safety.

A tall young man with a dark complexion was rushing by on the pavement outside the shop. He was terrified, and kept turning to look behind him as he ran. Two armed men were chasing after him and ordering him to come back. He didn't heed them. He was alarmed beyond description. Nizam poked his head outside despite the shopkeeper's warnings not to go out. One of the armed men stopped. He aimed his rifle at the runaway and fired. The young man walked a few steps with his back arched before stumbling and falling to the ground. The two armed men took off in the same direction they had come from.

The young man's arm had reached the ground ahead of his face, so his arm was hiding his face, like a child covering his eyes while his friends hurried to hide from him, or as though he was displeased with the scene around him and wanted to cover his eyes. No blood flowed from him; he was just resting there in front of the Armenian Church.

The birds went crazy. All the fear felt by the passers-by and the shop owners had been transferred to them. They started flapping their wings inside their cages as if trying to escape. They didn't chirp. They didn't prattle when the bullets were fired but rather all tried to escape in one go, and when they failed, they calmed down, and a heavy silence prevailed. Cars stopped passing by in the street, and any pedestrians who hadn't run off were now standing in fear, waiting to see what would happen. A priest came out from the church, locked the door behind him with the key, and went on his way uphill without turning to look in the direction of the fallen young man who was still lying there with his arm over his face.

The bird shop owner resumed his speech. 'It was inevitable. They just had to kill someone. Now they've finally done it. In the end they'll destroy the country . . . '

Nizam remained standing in the doorway watching the scene unfold. An elderly man with a slightly hunched back approached the dead man lying on the ground and threw a white cloth over him. The man wanted to conceal the corpse from the eyes of passers-by before the Red Cross arrived, but the piece of cloth was too small and only covered his torso. His head and legs remained exposed.

The birds went back to hopping around and flapping their wings as usual. The seller was saying that the armed men had been on alert for days with their weapons practically in plain view. They said they were protecting the area from an imminent attack— a surprise attack that the Palestinians and the al-Tanzim al-Shaabi were preparing for. They claimed the goal of their mission was to make sure there were no infiltrators.

The police Jeep arrived quickly. The lieutenant got out and started giving commands to his men. They were wearing metal helmets. They stood in a circle around the dead man until the ambulance arrived.

The elegantly dressed bird seller was lamenting the loss of business, but he wouldn't give Nizam any discount on the parrot. He would have told him his whole life story, cursing the hour in which he'd decided to return from Africa, if not for the fact that Nizam paid him what he asked, thanked him, picked up the green and red bird in its cage, and walked off in the direction of the dead man lying on the ground. One of the policemen signalled for him to step back, causing the parrot to screech as though he wanted to wake up the dead man lying on the ground. The policemen gathered around the corpse smiled in spite of themselves. The lieutenant leaned over the body and started searching the dead man's pockets. He didn't find an ID or anything indicating the man's name. The only thing in his pocket was a passport photo of himself that would end up in the next day's newspaper for his family to identify.

Nizam stood nearby, holding the parrot in its cage. Two newspaper photographers showed up before the ambulance. They hurriedly kneeled on the ground in front of the corpse and aimed their camera lenses at the dead body. The police officers struck a pose as the flashes went off, and the photographers captured in one shot the dead man, the church, the police officers, and a middle-aged man who out of curiosity had taken advantage of the opportunity while the officers were preoccupied with the photographers to come close to the scene and turn his face towards the cameras as if he, too, were posing for a commemorative photo.

There were hushed rumours that the dead man was Palestinian—an officer in the al-Saaiqa Organization who had been spying in the area. Someone claimed to know who he was and said that he was a Syrian or maybe a Kurd who worked in the vegetable market.

The photographers stood back up. One of them noticed Nizam holding a parrot, so he took a picture of him and then asked him to stand next to the dead man. The picture of Nizam posing next to the dead man—with a caged parrot in hand—didn't appear in any of the newspapers. Maybe the journalist had gotten distracted by the ambulance that arrived on the scene, its sirens blaring, and had turned his camera away from Nizam in order to get a shot of the ambulance—forgetting about him. Or, maybe, whoever was in charge of selecting the photographs for the paper wasn't in the mood for irony, given all the horrific tragedies that had occurred that day. Two paramedics lifted the dead young man onto a stretcher. He'd been lying, as if asleep, in a pool of his own blood. They strapped him in and loaded him up into the ambulance that took off at full speed, blowing its horn at the highest volume possible, even though the man had long been dead. In turn, the officers left the scene. There was nothing left for prying eyes to see, except for the bloodstain that would soon be wiped away by the feet of pedestrians, since no one volunteered to clean it up.

The shopowners started closing their doors and heading home. Their day was over before it even began.

Nizam stood for a moment as if smelling the breeze. He remembered Raffoul and all the advice he'd given him, but he didn't change his plans. He headed in the direction of Lebanon Street, still carrying Janan's present in his hand. The pedestrians, who by now had received the news about what happened after they'd heard the gunshots, looked around worried. But when they saw the parrot in Nizam's hand, their faces lit up for a second.

Suddenly, without making the slightest movement with his wings—out of annoyance or boredom—the colourful bird blurted out a single question, 'Are you Ahmad?' in the face of a man who was rushing by. When the man turned around and saw the source of the sound and the bird's handler, a look of confusion and surprise appeared on his face. After Nizam had crossed a short distance, the parrot repeated his question in a clear and perfectly audible voice. While it was not the same parrot that Nizam had seen when he'd first arrived in Beirut, the way he'd asked the question was exactly the same. Little Ahmad must have also taught this parrot to talk before running away. The parrot asked the question in an insistent tone, a tone that awaited an answer from pedestrians who hadn't yet heard about the dead man in Dabbas Square. The bird started blurting out the question non-stop and in all directions as if he was having a fit. The teachers leaving Ahliyyeh Orthodox School turned to look at him, entertained. Their look of entertainment was immediately followed by one of puzzlement at the possibility of an Ahmad being present among them during such troubled times—as the sound of gunshots from downtown Beirut reverberated through the streets.

Nizam took longer steps as he headed down Lebanon Street. He was now running in an attempt to shush the parrot, but his efforts were in vain. By the time Nizam had arrived at the entrance to Janan's building, he'd taken off his jacket and thrown it over the cage in order to make it a little darker inside, hoping the parrot would stop calling out to pedestrians. But the parrot started flapping his wings relentlessly. Nizam arrived with the parrot at the studio where Janan had sought refuge from the phone at her parents' house, which hadn't stopped ringing, as she said. Friends and family believed that her father must have some information about what was happening since he worked for the Ministry of Foreign Affairs. They would ask him questions, but before he could even respond, they'd say that the tunnels that Palestinians had dug—which extended all the way from Tel al-Zaatar camp to other areas—had been discovered. They said that some people—and don't you start asking who these people were—discovered these tunnels after hearing underground noises, deep roars, especially at night when the city was silent.

Janan ran off to the studio where Nizam found her. She was so happy to see the parrot. Clapping her hands, she welcomed the bird and started playing with him.

'Murky swamps are made up of the flowers of the deep. The mermaid's head is cut off,' she told the parrot. 'I'm searching for the rose that can't prick me . . . '

As she fluctuated between sarcasm and heartache, Janan seemed to be performing a theatrical role that she'd memorised by heart.

Nizam looked at her, astonished.

Her mother came down to warn her against leaving the house because the situation had exploded in a very bad way. Janan didn't listen. They didn't tell her much because she couldn't handle much.

Nizam wasn't going to be able to return to Manara. He was going to spend the night at the Lebanon Street studio.

Janan asked Nizam to take care of the parrot before leaving and going up to her parents' flat later that night. She loved the parrot and believed they'd be having conversations for a long time to come.

Nizam fell asleep amid her paintings, which teemed with dark colours, although the glare of the deep red paint would sometimes shimmer in the light that seeped from the outside into the studio at night. Janan wanted Nizam close to her but concealed from her. She left him her paintings.

Besieging him with her words, she said, 'The most valuable things in the world for me are you and my paintings. Here you are, asleep together.'

She liked to see him with her paintings when she woke up in the morning, so she'd come down to the studio with some coffee for him. He'd cover the parrot with his jacket and lie down without taking off his clothes, not even his shoes.

News of the war would reach Janan's parents' flat and then descend upon the couple in the studio in a watered-down version. Her mother would go downstairs with the news, and Janan wouldn't ask for any details. Rather, she'd put on her apron and get started on selecting her brushes. She'd walk away, attending to her paintings, giving her mother—who stood near the door—an opportunity to fill Nizam in on the details.

'They're kidnapping Christians,' she said. 'Blindfolding them before taking them to the Bashoura Cemetery and killing them there . . .'

Whispering, they agreed to spare Janan such news.

He spent three nights in the studio, inside a bubble guarded by Janan's parents. He got used to the strong smell of paint and loved it, just as he loved the smell of the sea and the fish in Mina.

On the fourth day, her mother came in smiling and announced that a ceasefire had been reached.

'You're not leaving!' Janan yelled at him.

She took off her apron and threw her brush on the floor in surrender.

He held her, his arms wrapped around her head, for a long time.

'I'll be back soon,' he said, pulling her close to his chest.

While Nizam had been staying in the studio on Lebanon Street, Chamoun Rikho was staying in the Manara flat. Chamoun slept in the children's bedroom for one night before moving into the master bedroom with the double bed. He'd finally gone into one of the Palestinian camps where they had given him a small office to work and sleep in. He almost died of boredom, so he'd go out every day and didn't hesitate to spend the night out whenever he could. The whispering Iraqi spent his time explaining to the American couple what was happing in Beirut, which made them ask even more questions.

They asked him about Maurice.

Alexi Bayda.

Alexi had vanished—along with his kindness, his music, and his family.

His father had demanded his severance pay from the owners of the bank where he worked as a manager. The neighbours had found the door to their house open, and so they went inside, only to find the flat completely empty of furniture. They had secretly sold the furniture to some loyal friends and left. It was said that they were worried about Maurice staying in Beirut, so they'd shipped him off to Amsterdam first, during the first ceasefire. Chamoun Rikho was convinced that Alexi had known all along about what was going to happen and that his showing up at the Manara flat and playing the flute for a long time that night—without anyone begging him to do so—was his idea of a farewell party.

Later, it was said that the Baydas' final stop was Tel Aviv, where the family found a move-in ready house waiting for them.

The comrades forgot Maurice. Life went back to normal again, so Nizam returned to Manara.

Vasco had beaten him to the flat. He'd felt imprisoned on the eastern side of the city. Handicapped from head to toe, he had not befriended anyone or gone out in the neighbourhood. He listened to the successive newscasts and insisted on moving to the west side of town no matter how tense the situation became. Whenever the news anchor would announce that all the crossings had been closed or that the roads were not accessible, he'd call one of the comrades on the other side and ask if they needed anything. If the comrades ran out of fuel, he'd come loaded with gallons of gas or a stash of bread that he carried in the trunk of his car, so he could spare them from standing in grueling lines at the bakeries. He knew which roads to take and had become an expert at identifying crossings that remained open for cars.

4

Olga Filipovna came back without warning, without sending any kind of message.

She landed at Beirut Airport sometime between the second and third round of fighting and came banging on the door of the flat with the ring on her finger.

'I lost my key,' she said as she came in.

'I changed the lock because half of Beirut had the key to your house,' Nizam responded without hesitation, as if he'd been expecting her to question him about the key for a long time.

Three years ago, they had chatted for a few minutes before she disappeared. Nizam had pieced her story together based on what she'd left behind—pictures, clothes, some books. Her story had many gaps, gaps that he sometimes filled in with his own desire for her, with the postcards she sent from one place or another, with what Cyril had told him about her at the public souq, and with the tales that Ali Soueidan had spun about her and her husband. The husband whom he had never met but whose traces he'd seen.

They laughed and hugged each other tightly, cheek to cheek. Nizam remembered the taste of the kiss they'd shared in the wobbly lift the day she advised him to escape from Beirut. His passion for her body remained deferred, ever-present in her things, in her clothes, in his ability to easily imagine her in her most intimate moments, in the beddings he slept in, and in the dresses and shoes she'd left behind.

When he tried asking her why she came back, she placed her hand on his mouth.

'I'll tell you everything later,' she said. 'Right now, I'm hungry . . . I didn't like the food on the plane.'

She ate quickly as if she was in transit and would soon be resuming her trip.

'The icon is still in its place . . . ' she said as she glanced at St George. 'It's guarding me.'

She sounded unconvinced when she said it this time around.

She remembered her mother. Pausing for a moment, she added, 'I love my mother, but only from a distance.'

Then she started wandering around the house, talking to some of her relatives in the photographs.

Delighted at the reunion, she said with a smile, 'Sergai . . . '

She wiped the dust off Sergai's photograph before moving on to her aunt's picture, which she held and kissed.

She was happy, emotional. She kissed Nizam on his cheek and then swiftly wiped off the spot where she'd kissed him with her hand. She kissed him the way a friend or an older sister would. She came back to the living room and checked on the Grand Duke, but she couldn't find the picture of her maternal grandmother.

'She was right here,' she said. 'They named me after her . . . '

She was almost in tears over real or affected anguish. She went into the bedroom, counted her dresses, and yelled as she asked about the fate of her red dress. He'd lent it to Yusra, who must have forgotten to return it the day she returned the pocket watch.

Olga returned to St George. She came closer. She, too, put her hand on his white, steel helmet and then asked Nizam the question he'd been dreading ever since she'd set foot in the flat.

'What happened to him?' she asked, soothing the icon as if it were a wounded child.

'I'll tell you what happened, if you tell me why you came back . . . '

'I told you I'd be back for my mother's sake. Her health has deteriorated . . . she sent me a letter asking me to come see her before she dies.'

She retreated and then approached the icon again. She asked the question again, so he told her that he had been standing near the small sofa, right there, when a bullet zipped by, a few centimetres away from his ear.

'A bullet?'

He told her it could have been worse, and that he had become a member of a group that idolized Lenin.

It was as if he'd stung her twice in one go.

She told him random details about her long absence, but she didn't mention anything about James Coburn or Los Angeles. Perhaps Moussa, the man who'd told stories about Nizam in Hawra, including the one about him hanging out with actresses—since Moussa believed that any woman James Coburn slept with must be an actress—was right after all. He was right since it would have been impossible for the skinny actor to be in two places at the same time, on the screen in Hawra's small movie theatre, skilfully fighting the bad Mexican guys who attacked the poor farmers' village with his knife, while also being in bed with Olga Filipovna at some fancy American hotel.

She sat down beside him and asked if he'd be OK with her spending the night in the flat since she was tired and preferred to go to her mother's in the morning. He smiled and offered her her conjugal bed, but she said she preferred to sleep in the other room. When he objected, she made it very clear that the two of them weren't going to sleep together.

Chamoun Rikho found her there the next morning. They were both still asleep when he opened the door without making a sound and sat down in the living room to wait for Nizam to wake up. Suddenly, there she was. She slept naked, so before coming out from the bedroom she grabbed the white bedsheet she'd been using as a blanket during the night. She reached the living room before managing to wrap the sheet around her beautiful white body and unexpectedly ran into Chamoun, who was enjoying a cigarette while reading with an equal dose of elation in a soft but audible voice a poem by Badr Shakir al-Sayyab in which he sings the praises of his beloved Iraq. Terrified, Olga wrapped the sheet around herself and sniffed the air.

'So you're a fan of Leon Trotsky and you smoke hashish before the sun comes up?'

Chamoun couldn't bear the two insults together. Captivated by her exposed charms, he replied, 'I'm not a fan of Trotsky . . . '

He meant that he supported establishing socialism in one country.

She concurred with him, saying, 'Trotsky killed half my family!'

Chamoun couldn't understand how Leon Trotsky could still have people who carried personal grudges against him living in Ras Beirut, where his books were readily available in bad Arabic translation as though hailing from a distant past that no longer had any connection to actual living people.

The next day Olga moved to Jounieh to check on her mother's health and started dividing her time between her mother's house and the flat in Manara. She preferred to sleep in Manara and spend part of the day with her mother. Her mother was rich and stingy.

Olga insisted she give her enough money to rent a small car—
a Mini Cooper—that she could use to come visit her.

They asked Nizam about Olga while she was out and couldn't
believe he wasn't sleeping in the same bed with her at night . . .
The comrades hadn't been envious of him about Yusra, but Olga
was a different story. A prize that was probably more appropriate
for them to win, considering they were far superior to him in intelligence and culture—if not so much in the way of good looks.
Olga was more than ten years older than Nizam, so he didn't
consider his spending the night in the same flat with her to be a
betrayal of Janan. He mentioned to Janan in passing that
the owner of the flat had come back, without going into details.
He was afraid of hurting her.

Olga made him feel as though the light touches and quick
caresses were simply part of her regular body language and not
actions that carried the familiar implications between a man and
a woman. In other words, if she held his hand for a long time and
caressed his fingers, it didn't necessarily mean he should wrap his
arms around her or slip his hands inside the various openings in
her dress.

On one night when there were Israeli airstrikes in the direction
of al-Madinah al-Riyadiyya (Citée Sportive), Chamoun Rikho was
forced to spend the night at the flat because he couldn't be certain
he could return safely to the camp, despite the Fatah Movement
ID card he carried, with the rank of lieutenant, under a fake
Muslim name—authorised with the signature of Abu Jihad himself. Unruly faction members came out in large numbers at night.

They gave Chamoun the children's bedroom, so Olga was
forced to move into Nizam's room. She placed a big pillow between
them, turned her back to him, and fell asleep after a short while.
Nizam couldn't sleep. He got up and went to the kitchen, went to
the balcony, came back, tossed and turned. At dawn he bumped

against her naked body. His thigh against hers, his hand on her chest. She nearly surrendered to him, still asleep. She woke up all of a sudden and kissed him on his ear as compensation. Laughing, she told him he couldn't be trusted. She rushed to the bathroom, showered, and came back. He told her not to worry because he was planning to marry a girlfriend of his who lived on the other side of the capital, but she didn't say anything in response.

Olga was entertained by the comrades. Nizam would come into the flat and find her with Vasco and his assistant who always stood beside him since he didn't like to sit down. Vasco kept coming to the flat, just as he had during peaceful times. He kept Olga company. She'd put her hand on his shoulder—same old antics. Quick intimacy. She told him the story of the St George icon, explain to him while looking at Nizam that it was antique and rare. Vasco said he'd seen it before in one of the churches. He asked if she was interested in selling it. Vasco was an expert and lover of carpets, which perhaps qualified him as having some expertise on Orthodox icons. That was in addition to his extensive reading of German philosophy and his nearly finished translation of *The Critique of Pure Reason* by Immanuel Kant.

5

Nizam went with Olga to Jounieh Saturday morning in the red and white Mini Cooper. She'd barely finished introducing him when her mother launched her assault.

'You just can't get your fill of handsome young men, can you, Olga?' she shouted, having grown very hard of hearing.

Olga responded full force despite her mother's age.

'Like mother like daughter!'

Olga could see that her mother was in good health. She'd claimed she was dying so Olga would come see her. She preferred not to stay overnight at her mother's because they would spend the time quarrelling over every little thing.

Her mother invited them to stay for lunch but apologized for having to leave for an hour to go to Mass.

They decided not to wait for her and headed back to Beirut. The streets that time of the morning were jam-packed with pedestrians and cars, so Nizam signalled for her to take the coastal road towards the port. That's when they suddenly found themselves stuck at a makeshift checkpoint.

Until that time, Nizam had never shown his ID to anyone, except the police sergeant who'd barged in on them at the flat in Manara. Touma had procured the ID for him from the Sérail in Tripoli. Touma was always telling the story to his friends, claiming it was the Civil Registry Officer who entered all the personal data information into the application, based on what Touma told him in Nizam's absence, but Nizam's ID didn't reflect what he'd said. Touma also tried to get the employee to leave the part about religious affiliation blank, but he insisted on following the rules. And so, Touma resorted to erasing the phrase 'Sunni Muslim', which the registrar had entered under 'Religion', himself. Nizam remembered seeing the phrase on his ID at one time, but then noticed it was gone, with some evidence of tearing where the paper had been rubbed with an eraser. Nizam had passed through numerous armed checkpoints before, and every time it was the same. The soldier or policeman or armed militia man who was in charge of checking the IDs of all the car passengers, waiting for him to signal and peer through the window at each one's face, would get to Nizam, take a quick glance, and look away. Generally, the guards at checkpoints were comfortable with Nizam's appearance. None of them ever asked to see his ID.

The gunman at Marfa Street who now had his ID wasn't looking at people's faces. He was looking all about, preoccupied and nervous about what was going on around him, worried there might be some threat to his own safety. No actual checkpoint had been set up. Gunmen appeared from side streets or nearby buildings and pounced on the cars. Just like that, the place was suddenly swarming with them. They were dressed in civilian clothes with belts of ammunition strapped around their waists, some with hand grenades or revolvers too, in addition to automatic rifles. They spread out. Some performed patrol while others pounded on cars signalling the drivers to stop.

'IDs. Hurry up!' the gunman shouted at the passengers, without looking at them.

The young man who'd given them the order was agitated, flustered, afraid. He frightened them. Olga winked at Nizam and handed the young gunman her ID. He glanced at it, then leaned in to get a good look at its owner. The Mini Cooper was low to the ground, and he was tall. It was hot, and Olga was wearing a lightweight dress that showed her shoulders and a bit of her back and chest. His stare lingered. Then he glanced over at Nizam. He liked Olga. All men liked Olga.

Nizam felt that older men did not see him as an obstacle when they were hitting on Olga. He seemed young and nice, which made them assume he was a relative of hers, worst-case scenario. He did not provide her with sufficient protection against those with sudden desires. Their hungry eyes gobbled her up while flitting past him in contrast, merely to ascertain what his relation to her might be.

Cars were lining up behind them. The gunman returned her ID, bidding her farewell with a piercing stare. He was about to wave her along when he remembered Nizam.

'You. Give me your ID.'

He started looking around again, troubled. He was quick to lose his patience.

Nizam heard the first round of gunfire from somewhere nearby. A grey-haired man in the car that was stopped behind them stepped out of his car. The gunman yelled at him to stop and get back in his car. The man obeyed.

Nizam could see that the armed man was Christian by the cross dangling from his neck as he inspected IDs. He was holding Nizam's ID and still hadn't taken a look at it, due to his preoccupation with the situation developing around him in the street. Nizam reached out to take it back. Only then did the gunman lean in to take a look at him. As usual, he did not find anything in Nizam's appearance to cause concern. He had the ID in his hand but wasn't reading it, as if he'd really been taken by Olga and didn't want to let them go into that sea of cars and was searching for some pretext to keep them there. They heard some more gunfire from behind the customs building. The popping sound of the exploding ammunition was somewhat muffled: bullets hitting their target, not fired into the air. Dozens of cars were backed up in line, waiting for the gunmen's decisions.

No one dared speak or get out of their car as the gunmen hopped between the cars, barking out orders, and calling to each other by their first names, more like neighbourhood buddies than members of a political party.

Rather than reading the ID, the gunman asked Nizam for his name. His eyes were darting about incessantly. The name Nizam didn't faze him. Just as he was reaching to hand back the ID and reluctantly let them go, he caught sight of Nizam's father's name on the ID.

'Mahmoud!' he suddenly shouted, as if finding what he'd been searching for. 'Get out!'

Olga said his name was Nizam, not Mahmoud. He looked at the ID to check and then ordered him again to get out of the car. Nizam got out, and the gunman signalled for Olga to move along. Flustered, she tried to shift the gears, but the motor stalled. He shouted at her to get going. The sound of gunfire in the nearby streets was accompanied by distant shouting, like someone pleading or protesting. Traffic was jammed, so one of them fired his machine gun into the air while his buddies screamed at drivers to get moving. The gunfire subsided. The gunman who ordered Nizam to get out of the car spoke to one of his buddies.

'George. Take him . . . '

George was holding some black cloth sacks. He quickly put one over Nizam's head and started nudging him along with his hand. Most likely he was taking him to where the voices and sounds of gunfire were coming from. George was a gigantic, heavy-set man with a beard, but he was not one of the killers. His job was to hand people over to his comrades hiding behind the building.

He ordered Nizam to walk. Nizam wasn't sure where to plant his feet on that crumbling pavement. He could hear Olga's voice in the distance, from where she'd driven ahead. She was saying that he wasn't a Muslim, that he was innocent. She added in Nizam's direction that she was waiting for him up the road a little way and told him not to be afraid. She was forced to move forward quickly beneath a flood of shouting from the gunmen. Nizam held his composure and kept silent for a few stumbling steps, the bag over his head having turned him into a blind man. They were getting closer to the customs building. His escort had his hands on his shoulders, guiding him in the right direction. As long as Olga was driving parallel to them and he could hear her telling him not to be afraid, that they would let him go, he felt he could still hang on. But when one of the gunmen yelled at Olga to shut up and drive away, and they nearly reached the source of the gunfire, Nizam broke down.

He came to a complete stop, unable to move his feet forward any longer. George shouted at him. Nizam reached in his direction, searching for him, groping from his darkness. He suddenly blurted to George that he was Maronite. A Christian, like him. He pleaded for him to believe him. True, he'd been born a Muslim, but his grandmother on his mother's side was a Christian from Syria, and he had become a Christian. Nizam was speaking loudly enough for his escort to hear. He tried to remove the bag from his face, but the gunman prevented him. He was speaking quickly and nervously. True his father was called Mahmoud, but he didn't grow up with him or any of his father's family. They never asked about him, and he never asked about them.

The gunman grabbed him using the hand that wasn't holding his machine gun and shoved him forward, forcing him to keep walking. Nizam took one or two steps with a great deal of difficulty. He remembered his ID and begged him to look at it to see there was no religion listed on it. The gunman took the card, looked at it quickly, and put it in his pocket. The sound of machine guns being fired increased. The man told Nizam to be quiet, but he didn't obey. Instead he told him how he'd been baptised in a church up in the mountains near Hawra.

'You know Hawra?' the gunman interrupted.

Nizam continued his story, about the priest pouring water over his head, how he was twenty-one years old at the time. The gunman was still pushing him, but Nizam felt he was slowing down a bit. Nizam was blabbering on, saying anything that came to mind. He told him the woman driving the car was a Christian. He was planning to marry Janan Salem, whose father was in charge of protocol at the Lebanese Ministry of Foreign Affairs, he said, waving his hand in the general direction of where he guessed the ministry was located. He told him to check her phone number, which was written on the back of his ID. Nizam didn't stop at just talking; he slid his hand inside his shirt, wanting to pull out the little pendant Rakheema had given him before he set out for Beirut—the one of the Immaculate Conception. He felt around with his trembling hand, being careful not to pull out by mistake the Ayat al-Kursi pendant with its Quranic verse. The Ayat al-Kursi was square, with sharp edges. The Immaculate Conception was oval. There was the blue bead, too. He fished for the Immaculate Conception and pulled it out from his shirt. He yanked it from his neck, breaking the chain, and started kissing it like a lunatic. He practically started gnawing on it with his teeth. He gave it to the gunman, who slipped it into his pocket with the ID.

His escort stopped pushing him, giving him a little rest, but Nizam didn't stop talking. They were definitely getting close to the customs building. Nizam started reciting the Our Father and the Hail Mary. He didn't say the whole prayer, just the opening line of the first one and the opening line of the second one, to prove he knew them. He felt compelled to heap on proof, so he moved on to, 'We believe in one God, the Father Almighty, Maker of

Heaven and Earth . . . ' He said all his friends were Christian and that he'd gone to a school run by Lazarite Nuns. He started rattling off the nuns' names—Sister Basile, Sister Francesca, Mademoiselle Laure. He no longer felt the gunman's hand on his shoulder pushing him forward. Encouraged by this, Nizam put forth his biggest piece of proof: he started chanting funerary prayers in Syriac. He intoned them the way he'd heard them, in a loud voice, amid the intermittent gunfire and commands barked at drivers and their passengers in the line of cars.

'Choboho el morio kolkhon aame w el etran besme tobe w rih mdoran nasimo nehwen . . . '

George shouted at him to stop, but his tone was much softer this time. Suddenly, he removed the bag from Nizam's head and looked him in the face.

'It seems you are a Christian. Get out of here,' he ordered and then added, 'And don't come this way ever again.'

Nizam reached for George's face, to kiss him, but George barred him with his shoulder. Nizam grabbed his right hand, brought it to his mouth to kiss it, but George wrestled it away. He yelled at Nizam to get going and warned him not to run.

The situation and manliness and death all made kissing out of the question.

Olga had been watching them from the distance. She saw Nizam try to kiss the fat gunman's hand. George turned to head back to where his buddies were making many other passengers get out of their cars. If they happened to find one they were looking for, they'd turn him over to him. Nizam was left all alone there on the pavement. He didn't run. He walked quickly, barely looking right or left, expecting a bullet any moment. As he passed in front of the customs building, he heard voices and clamour and a shower of gunfire. He trembled with fear. He felt there was nothing left of himself, except for his head and his two eyes nailed to Olga's car parked waiting for him. She opened the door for him, and he staggered into the car. He sat down, drew in a deep breath. He said the man who let him go was called George.

'Bless his namesake!' Olga cried. Nizam rested his head on his knees and sank into utter silence, as if he'd said everything he had to say to that burly gunman, in one go. Olga asked Nizam if he'd seen what was going on behind the customs building, but he didn't answer. He had seen, but he didn't tell her. He'd seen them piling the corpses on top of each other. Lots of men and some women too. There was a young man among them wearing military garb. They would bring the detainees over, with a bag over the head, to another man who would shoot them—perhaps the shooter didn't want to see his victims' faces. Then they'd remove the bag from the dead person's head and toss him aside.

6

He had no idea how they made it back to the Manara flat. As soon
as they stepped inside, Olga headed to the icon of St George, knelt
in front of it, and planted a long, reverent kiss in the painting's
lower right corner, near the dragon's protruding claws. Then she
muttered short prayers in Russian as she made the sign of the cross.
Exhausted, Nizam flopped down on the sofa. Olga took her shoes
off, sat next to him, and interlaced her fingers with his. Some of
the explosions were close and others deep. Rounds of gunfire filled
the air, and it sounded like they were coming from all four directions. There was a knock at the door. They didn't budge. They
heard the American professor and his wife chattering before they
finally left.

After the Americans left, Olga tiptoed to the door and bolted it
from inside, in case someone who had a key to the flat decided to
drop by. Nizam was drained, dazed. The explosions increased, and
so did the ambulance sirens. They didn't exchange a word, and not
once did she look at him with pity. She didn't try to console or
distract him. She didn't make him coffee or offer him a cigarette
or a glass of water. She didn't even light a cigarette for herself. She
bent down in front of him, crouched on one knee, and slowly took
his shoes and socks off. She asked him to stand up. As he surrendered, she took off his belt and started emptying the cash and
documents out of his pockets and setting them on the table. She
continued to remove his clothes, and he helped her a little. She
threw a big towel on his shoulder and directed him to the bathroom. She turned the water on, felt it with her hand, and waited

for it to get a little warmer before pushing him under the shower. He caught his breath and then stood in surrender under the water for a few minutes. He came out of the bathroom before drying off completely. He had on a white abaya that he rarely wore. He found Olga sitting on the bed, her legs criss-crossed in front of her. She'd wrapped her body with the bedsheet, leaving her right breast and white thigh exposed. She was looking at him with deliberate seduction. The explosions sounded close, as if they were going off at the end of the street. He smiled with difficulty as he attempted to get up on the bed, while she leaned her body backwards, pretending to get away from him. He hesitated before catching on to her game. He closed his eyes and threw himself on the bed, trying to catch her, so she scratched him a little bit with her nails in order to keep him away from her. When he retreated, she got up on her knees and wrapped the bedsheet around her as much as possible. When she approached him, he paused so he could allow her to take the lead. She brushed his cheek with hers, whispered in his ear, and stuck her tongue inside, caressing him, before retreating again. The buzzing of bullets filled the neighbourhood, and the sound of people screaming out warnings was heard in the street. He grabbed the white bedsheet and tried to pull it towards him. She would either be fully exposed, or she'd have to cover herself with the bedsheet—which would then force her to get close to him. She allowed both things to happen as she snuggled against him and let the bedsheet drop loose onto the bed. He lifted her a little as he knelt, and she tightly wrapped her arms around him. Then he gently laid her back down on the bed. By then, the sounds of gunfire and sirens had become intermittent and were no longer reaching them with the same force. She pulled him towards herself. His erection was so strong it surprised him. She felt it and laughed with delight, proud of her success. As he was trying to take the abaya off his head, while still kneeling over her, someone attempted unsuccessfully to open the door with his key. Olga threw her hands up in the air, disappointed. The visitor knocked at the door and called for Nizam twice. It was comrade Alaa. He lived nearby, and he had come by to fish for news. The abaya remained stuck on Nizam's head, as he stood there, panting. He remained motionless, so that the man standing at the door wouldn't detect that the two of them were home. Olga held her index finger in front of her mouth, warning Nizam not to make the slightest move. Perhaps Alaa had waited for a little while in front of the closed door and then left. They heard the sound of his footsteps as he went down the stairs. They waited for a few seconds before Nizam finally tossed the abaya all the way across the room. The fear of being interrupted made his erection stronger. As he leaned over Olga once again, the Ayat al-Kursi pendant and the blue evil eye bead dangling from his neck, she playfully took the Ayat al-Kursi in her mouth and then let it go. She bit on the blue bead then wrapped her arms around his neck with determination, clinging to him. She raised her thighs and opened them to receive him, and he entered her while kissing her on the mouth, his eyes shut. The commotion in the street grew louder, and they heard the sounds of militiamen divvying up their patrolling and searching respon-sibilities, as they were most likely setting up a makeshift checkpoint in the middle of the road. Nizam's thrusts were fast and tense at first, so she asked him to slow down as she smiled and wrapped her legs around his back. She tried to control the rhythm of his thrusts as much as possible, but he unwrapped her arms from his neck and put them behind her head. She didn't give up and started to raise and lower her pelvis to make sure he didn't lose his way. A loud explosion went off nearby, shattering the windows. Nizam paused, as he listened attentively to what was happening outside. He was distracted. She worried about him stopping, so she held him by the shoulders and got him off of her, as she got on top. She opened her legs so he could enter her again, but they stumbled with the bedsheet that had gotten all tangled up beneath them. Frustrated, Nizam pulled the bedsheet and tossed it far away, where it landed next to the abaya, making more room on the bed. Olga knelt over Nizam. She tried to pull her hair away from her face by putting it in a ponytail. Meanwhile, Nizam doubled his efforts at entering her as she swayed on top of him, their panting growing stronger. She steadied her arms on his shoulders and pressed her cheek to his, so he would not lose focus. Her body rose and fell. He bit her neck, and she licked his eyes. He sucked on her nipples, and she moaned as he continued to enter her, without calling a truce. He waited for her to reach orgasm and restrained himself until she collapsed on top of him, her head on his chest after screaming with pleasure as they climaxed together—or maybe she was just pretending. Then she turned on her back, and they rested in silence as she laid her head on his arm. His eyes teared up as the sounds of war nearby filled the room.

Now that Nizam had relaxed, the day's exhaustion caught up with him. Olga moved her head from his arm and dozed off next to him.

They did not receive anyone the next day and left the door locked from the inside. They went out on the balcony. Thick, black smoke rose from the port's warehouses.

Around ten o'clock in the morning, Jonathan and Barbara Parker knocked at the door again. When they didn't get a response, they started addressing the people inside with a loud voice. They assumed that Nizam was in there listening to them. Maybe the concierge had told them that Olga and Nizam had gone inside and that he had not seen them leave the building, or maybe they just wanted to put their words out there in the universe. Barbara said that they'd come by the night before to say goodbye to the group but didn't find anyone. They wanted to let them know that they were leaving with heavy hearts, worried about what might happen. She used the expression 'we are sorry,' as if she were paying her condolences for the loss of a dear friend. They had packed their bags because a diplomatic vehicle was coming at noon to pick them up and take them to the new embassy headquarters, where a helicopter would later transport them with other Americans to Cyprus. They would catch a flight from Cyprus to their hometown in Delaware. Barbara was talking nonstop, without expecting an answer, as if she were leaving a message on someone's answering machine. Some echo accompanied her voice, as it reached the inside of the flat, mixed in with the sound of the old lift every time it stopped on one of the floors. Olga was trying to control herself from laughing, but Nizam couldn't help but smile. It was the first time he'd smiled since the day before. Barbara promised that they'd be back in Beirut as soon as things calmed down, but her tone didn't seem very confident. She stopped talking for a little while.

Then, as if the couple had been deliberating in hushed whispers, they said at the same time, 'We'll never forget Beirut. We'll never forget you.'

They ended with the word 'bye', which they carried with them as they went down the stairs for the last time.

He spent the day silent. Olga did all the talking. She told him her stories—stories about how her mother had gotten married twice and about how there had been dozens of lovers between the time Olga's father had died and when she married her second husband. The woman didn't quit until only a few years ago. Olga made him laugh with the story about her husband, or rather her marriage. She had met her husband at a time when he was repressing his real desires, and she fell in love with him. Handsome and elegant, he played bridge at the St George Hotel, and half of Beirut's women fantasized about him, but everyone ultimately discovered his tendencies.

'Everyone but Olga . . . ' she said.

A month after they got married, he went back to his old ways, back to his friends. He'd just take off and leave her all by herself. Men would hit on her, and she would fight them off. He brought some of his buddies over to the house. She found him in her bed with Ali Soueidan, naked as the day they were born. He brought Ali Soueidan in off the street—poor and destitute. He cleaned him up, gave him money, and taught him how to be fashionable. Olga told Nizam about Cyril too—the other nutcase. Her husband used to go after Cyril while Cyril in turn chased after her. He tried to get her on the cast of the Casino du Liban stage show, but the casino fired him after one of the girls died of an overdose, which they accused him of causing. Olga's life story was never-ending, and she narrated it with an air of contentment, as if it was all just a matter of destiny. Nizam's one request to Olga was not to sell St George. He didn't caution her not to tell anyone what happened to him near the customs building; he knew she would keep that secret between them. At around midnight, Olga headed to sleep in the children's bedroom, but Nizam blocked her path and insisted that she take the master bedroom. Sensing that was what he really wanted, she accepted. He moved his things into the other bedroom and spent the night in peace. The next morning, he made coffee and brought it to her room. He called to her sweetly to wake her up. He didn't approach her, didn't touch her. Even those ambiguous caresses between them stopped.

They spent an entire week locked up inside the flat. Olga went out to get coffee, cigarettes and fast food. She asked the concierge to tell anyone who came looking for them that they weren't home. The concierge smiled in agreement, letting his imagination run wild. He didn't notice Nizam slip out of the building one morning when the sounds of gunfire had gone silent and the streets became calm, when Arab and foreign mediators arrived in Beirut. Nizam had gone out to the balcony, looked out in the direction of the port, and for the first time ever from such a distance, spotted the customs building. He didn't wake Olga, but he left her a short note. 'I'll be back soon. Don't worry about me.'

He stopped at the building entrance, turned left and started walking with brisk, confident steps. As he passed the St George Hotel, heading towards the port, he increased the speed and confidence of his steps. He mustered up his strength—physically and emotionally. He didn't want to listen to the voice telling him to stop, turn around, and go back home. When he saw some navy officers on the other side of the street in the midst of their morning running drills, he started to run as fast as he could, surpassing the average speed maintained by the best long-distance racers. Pedestrians gave him glances showing their skepticism of any scene or action that might signal a resumption of the tensions and tragedies of recent days. He slowed down just as runners do after crossing the finish line. He stood in place, panting and catching his breath, waiting. He looked around in all directions and then started tracking the cars that were passing by peacefully on that clear, sunny morning. He tried to imagine the passengers' intended destinations. Some labourers packed into a little truck joking around. A man driving a fancy car waving his hand around and arguing with his wife seated beside him. A young man on a bicycle, dripping with sweat. They passed by, filled with the concerns of their everyday lives. He sat down on the curb. He scrutinised the few pedestrians. He stood up and slowly walked those few metres he'd walked with the black bag over his head and then went back to the spot where they made him get out of Olga's car. He went back and forth numerous times. He counted the steps. Then he sat back down and waited. He waited, but no one bothered him. He didn't draw anyone's attention. Passers-by didn't even give him a strange look. He didn't know how long he had been sitting there waiting before he remembered the customs building. He started walking towards it, trailing the employees on their way to their offices. The employees entered the building and disappeared inside it. They passed by the spot where they had been dumping the bodies. Nizam stood there a long time. No one objected. The place was clean. No traces, no smell.

As though nothing, nothing at all had happened on that cursed Saturday.

He returned to the flat slowly at noon. He informed the concierge that they had come back to the flat. He ate, drank, and gave a kiss to Chamoun Rikho who had come over with some big news. He was distraught, saying that everyone on both sides of the battle was mimicking the other. Beirut was no longer bearable. He was afraid he might be forced to immigrate to Sweden where some of his Syriac relatives had gone ahead of him.

'I'll travel the whole world trying to flee, and I'm not even thirty. From Bartella, between Ninevah and Erbil, to Mosul, to Damascus, to Zahle, to Beirut, and the journey continues . . . '

Olga found Chamoun Rikho charming. Whenever she would ask about him by his full name, she'd pronounce the 'r' as 'gh', like a Parisian 'r', and then with the 'kh' right after it—it ended up sounding completely obscured—'Ghikho.'

Olga saw a bit of herself in him. She'd started out in St Petersburg and still didn't know where her journey would end.

Chamoun ended up his talk about the open possibilities of his migrations by telling them about Yusra Maktabi getting out of prison.

'She escaped?'

'They set her free,' Chamoun said mockingly.

A group of armed men set her free—some previously unknown organization. They attacked the women's prison the same Saturday when people were being murdered on the basis of their IDs. It seemed they had been determined to do it. They were just waiting for the new round of violence to erupt so they could carry out their plan. The battalion of policemen guarding the prison surrendered to them without a fight. The young officer was native to the area and wanted to avoid bloodshed. When he called headquarters, they told him to act prudently. So he decided to open the doors and let everyone out. That was the only women's prison in Lebanon. When they reached the courtyard outside, they separated them—Muslim women over here and Christian women over there. Yusra protested in a feeble voice, so one of the armed men asked her what her name was. 'Yusra Maktabi' she said, so he told her to go join the Muslim women, and she obeyed. The Muslim women were immediately released while it was decided that the Christian women would be detained for their own safety. After a day or two, the situation would settle down and they could be sent to the eastern side of the capital. One of the women said that her house was in Msaytbeh and she didn't want to go to Achrafiyeh, because she didn't know anyone there. In fact, half of the Christian women lived on the western side. The armed men were at a loss as to what to do with them, so their leader claimed falsely that an emergency situation required his presence at the demarcation line, and they turned around and left.

Yusra's family was waiting for her out in the car. They shoved her into the back seat as her brother, the lawyer, sped them away. Just like that, Yusra Maktabi disappeared for good. It was said she married some rich guy who took her away to Canada and that when she gave birth to a son, she insisted on naming him Nizam. Her husband agreed without asking too many questions.

'And what about you? Where will you go?'

The question Olga hadn't asked Nizam that entire week—she now surprised him with it in front of Chamoun. 'I'll go to Hawra . . . ' he answered without hesitation.

It was the first time Olga heard of this 'Hawgha', which she said pronouncing the 'r' like a 'gh' again.

He told them about the smell of the soil and the angry skies at the end of September, for a brief period that was just long enough to shoo the frightened strangers away. Then the weather would return to being clear and fresh and the native inhabitants of the town could enjoy it all by themselves, amid the autumn colours when the grapes became as sweet as honey and the slow thrushes passed in rows across the sky overhead, flying faster and separating whenever some young men loitering along the path would take aim at them in a series of shots from their hunting rifles, even though they knew their meat wasn't edible.

'And mulberry season just started there now . . . ' he added.

7

The usual sounds from the vegetable market had all died down—defeat was evident throughout Burj Square. There was life, but reluctantly. The broken glass hadn't been replaced, and the debris from the selective fires that reached some shops while leaving others unscathed hadn't been cleaned up. Jumhuriyya Café was not open for business. The chairs were still stacked up on the tables. The Hawra taxi was parked in its usual place. He found Shaytan sitting there alone with Raffoul. The two of them were lost in thought. The owner of Zahrat al-Shamal seemed less confident about his predictions now. His eloquent talk waned, and his moments of silence grew longer.

Nizam asked the driver to hold the two front seats for him. Suddenly waking up, Raffoul asked disapprovingly, 'Are you heading up to Hawra?'

With his grimacing expression, he tried to dissuade Nizam from taking the trip. Raffoul didn't say anything further, as though he'd started to surrender to the situation and was going to just let things take their course. Nizam waited with them while the car filled up with passengers.

Nowadays Shaytan only came to the capital once or twice a week, when it was necessary. His trips were scarce and gloomy. But at least the journey was no longer monotonous. Armed checkpoints broke up the distance—the permanent ones as well as the surprise ones that people said Palestinians and leftist militias would sometimes set up all of a sudden. Shaytan had never run into any of those, but he heard they sometimes kidnapped people crossing their checkpoints and then disappeared. It was a smooth trip; they made it through the checkpoints near the Casino du Liban and at the exit for the Cedars without any problem. In fact, the armed guard at the Cedars checkpoint knew the driver and the passengers and started joking around with them, calling them by their first names.

The passengers didn't spark up conversation with Nizam, and he had no desire to talk either. They didn't even speak among themselves, perhaps to avoid saying something he shouldn't hear.

Nizam's presence at the door surprised both of them, as always. Touma looked tired and emaciated with sunken eyes. 'Living on insulin', as he said. Rakheema held Nizam in a long embrace. He wilted in her arms. He was transported back in time—Rakheema's scent, her constant worrying about him, her kitchen, and those polka-dotted dresses of hers never failed. He drew in a deep breath. She felt his sadness and asked if he was all right. He assured her he was fine, but she was unconvinced. Everything was the same as ever, just as he had experienced it from the beginning. Everything was in its place. Not one piece of furniture would be moved from its position until after the two of them had died.

Rakheema asked if what people were saying was true, that parents in Beirut were sending their children off to school in the morning with their names and addresses hung around their necks for fear of some sudden attack that might cause them to be separated and get lost. They had no idea what sort of advice to give Nizam, so they stuck to cautious generalities. In any case, they didn't know where it would be better for him to live.

'Stay where you are and leave it in God's hands.'

'And listen to the radio before you leave the house,' Touma added.

They didn't dare try to persuade him in one direction or another for fear of causing him harm with the wrong advice. They let him do as he wished so they wouldn't have to suffer the subsequent guilt they would feel and which they could not possibly bear.

As he went out the door, Rakheema whispered to Touma, 'The boy doesn't look right to me . . . ' She wasn't sure why, but he didn't seem like himself. 'He's down,' said Rakheema, pronouncing it in her local accent.

Nizam walked through the orchard. It seemed small to him, quiet. Rex had died a long time ago. He and Touma fixed up the shack. They carried a mattress out to it.

'Stay with us,' Rakheema begged in a hushed voice as she piled on some heavy blankets.

Nizam would sleep by himself. Touma would not be able to bear the cold outside.

Nizam stretched his legs and clasped his hands behind his head. He searched for Ursa Major and Ursa Minor. He flipped through the possibilities of his life in his mind as he listened at length to the night-time being penetrated by the sounds of frogs croaking and what was left of the sounds of the far-off town. Starting tomorrow morning, he would take up the pickaxe and work the soil, turning it over before watering it. He'd put on the rubber boots Touma always wore when watering the fields, and maybe one day if he got a little fat, he would keep his trousers up with a pair of suspenders just like Touma did. He didn't own a wristwatch, but the pocket watch would do fine. He'd pull it out ceremoniously whenever the church bells rang to make sure the procession was starting at the right time. He'd befriend the trees once again, making his tour around them with the clippers in his hand. He'd sit on the ground without worrying if his clothes got dirty. He'd put on clean ones before heading out to the Palace Hotel to meet up with a calm and composed friend who would play backgammon with him out on the patio, and they'd keep score on the edge of the table with a piece of chalk. And during the long days of winter, he'd sit beside Touma and Rakheema next to the sobia heater reading historical stories. There were still lots of them. Maybe he would tell them the story of the fall of Granada if they wished to hear it, though Touma would likely nod off before he reached the end. But before all of that, he'd go to Beirut. He'd go one last time, and to ensure his return, he would ask the taxi driver to stay with him during his farewell tour. He'd have him take him first to Manara to say goodbye to Olga and reassure her that she had a home in the high elevations of North Lebanon that she could come to whenever she liked. He wouldn't take any of his clothes or belongings back with him from the flat. Throughout his stay in Beirut, he never bought any furniture of his own. He stayed at Zahrat al-Shamal, lived among Olga's things and her family pictures and her saints, slept in Janan's studio in his clothes. He would stop in at Lebanon Street and tell Janan about his plans to settle down in Hawra, hoping she would understand his wishes, and he'd ask her to give him one of her paintings which he'd hang in his room and wouldn't tire his mind looking at too much. He just wanted it as a souvenir. His last stop in Beirut would be to the toy shop to buy a ship he'd seen in the shop window, complete with its big white sails and its high masts and all the little sailors spread out on the deck. He'd buy one with little pieces, thousands of pieces. He'd choose the biggest model and take his time building it. He'd work on it at a table out on the porch, glueing the pieces of wood together, painting it. It would take him over a year before he could finally write a name on its front side. He liked women's names for ships. And he'd put a flag up on its big mast.

He pulled the blankets over himself and fell asleep.

Rakheema went out to check on him with the first rays of sunshine after he'd been covered in the dew of a new morning.

The next day, he didn't do any work in the garden and didn't go very far.

The house he'd spent successive summers in with his family had been abandoned.

'No one even inquired about the rent,' Touma explained.

The hotels were empty. Their owners hadn't even hired workers to tidy them up in preparation for the summer season. The brother of the Mufti of Tripoli sold the house that he had bought—sold it dirt cheap; he went through a Christian broker whose family had fled Tripoli without being able to take even their clothes along with them. The homes of Muslim vacationers who had left some furniture behind over the winter were burglarised.

He entered his parents' rental home by himself, wandered around the rooms, and threw himself onto the bed that he used to sleep in. He stumbled on the little British Airways model aeroplane, lifted it up and waved it around as if it were soaring over the skies of the room, before landing it again on the bed next to him.

The days passed. Some nights, he'd sleep early, and other nights, sleep would flee from his eyes. He'd lie awake, waiting for dawn to rise from behind the tall mountains, before dozing off in a morning nap from which Rakheema would then wake him, breakfast in hand.

One day, she came to his room and put the tray down on the floor, but she didn't leave the room. She seemed restless, as if she had something to say.

'Don't leave the house today,' she said. 'Don't wander around the village by yourself.'

He didn't understand.

'We don't want anyone saying anything rude to you . . . '

'Why would they do that?'

Rakheema sat down on the floor of the shack and said, 'Because they killed Aziz.'

Aziz Abu-Shaheen, the tailor.

He was killed in Tripoli. He had refused to leave the city, thinking that everybody loved him and that his clients couldn't do without him. But some men, who were not his clients, had come by and forced him to accompany them at gun point. It was said that one of them took two suits along with him that Aziz had made. He'd grabbed the first suit that was hanging on the wall and held the jacket up to his shoulders, while it was still on the wooden hanger; then, he'd checked the length of the trousers. He liked the suit and decided to take it. He also grabbed a second one that he didn't even try. The fishermen found Aziz near the Ras al-Sakhr area, where the waves had deposited him—he was all swollen. In one week, the sea had spit up over five bodies.

The body arrived around noon, delivered by the Red Cross. A big crowd had been waiting for it. People started shooting in the air—heavy shots were fired all at once from dozens of machine guns.

Touma joined them. Aziz was his cousin.

'Stay here with him,' Touma ordered Rakheema. 'You can go pay your respects at their house tomorrow.' He wanted her to stay at the house in order to guard Nizam.

The women's wailing grew louder and was soon drowned out by the sound of mournful dirges signalling for the funeral procession to set off. Rakheema made Nizam get up from his chair on the balcony and pushed him inside. She asked him to watch the funeral from behind the window that overlooked the main road. The owners of the shops, Nizam could see from where he was standing, lowered their steel doors halfway, which meant they would be raising them back up again after the procession had passed. Aziz was Hawra's first fallen martyr. The cross-bearer was followed by the leader of the procession, who appeared in semi-military clothing and waved his baton conducting the brass players and cymbalists. They were followed by a crowd that included members of the fraternity, who wore mourning sashes and carried a sympathy banner and the Immaculate Conception Flag, as well as young men in camouflage clothing, who proudly waved flags of their political parties—all of which included the Lebanese cedar in different shapes and colours. He recognized some of his old friends among them, many of whom volunteered to carry the casket. Crowded under the casket, they pushed and shoved their way amid screams warning them not to drop it. Funeral prayers were broadcast through amplifiers that Nizam could hear from inside the house. He also listened to the priest's sermon.

Touma and Rakheema felt anxious the entire next day. They emphasized to him that he should not leave the vicinity of the house or show his face among Hawra's people. He got tired of being in the orchard, so he headed back inside where he found them whispering. He stood at the door. They had not heard him come in. He stood there, motionless. In her trembling voice, Rakheema was trying to convince Touma of something.

'These hoodlums might hurt him,' she said. 'Yesterday, when news of Aziz arrived, they immediately remembered Nizam. They started threatening and chattering about not wanting any Muslims in Hawra any more. I will not sleep at night as long as he's still here. I will run and stand by the window anytime I hear footsteps outside.'

Touma said he was going to buy a gun the next day.

'Let them come any closer . . . ' he said. 'I'll be here waiting for them.'

'If anything happens to him, I'll die,' Rakheema sighed.

Nizam stepped back outside. He slid his hand over the wall where he used to draw the faces of his mother and her girlfriends from the morning gatherings before hitting them with his ball. He continued towards the gate of the orchard. He entered the orchard and started kicking the molehills that had now multiplied, one after the other, scattering the soil everywhere in his wake.

He went back inside and stood at the door of the living room where he'd gotten used to announcing his decisions.

Leaning on the side of the door, he said, 'I'm going back to Beirut tomorrow.'

They had still been negotiating with each other. They didn't object.

'As you wish.'

Touma gave him a big sum of money that would last him for a long time. Rakheema went to see the driver under the cover of darkness and negotiated with him at the door, out of the earshot of the driver's wife. She asked him to come by early the next morning and not bring along any other passengers.

Nizam sat next to the driver; they didn't exchange a word as they went down the narrow, winding road dotted with pine trees. It wasn't until they'd gotten to the coastal road that Nizam finally asked the driver why he'd quit singing traditional mawwal and zajal songs.

'Our hearts are broken . . . ' the driver said with a sigh.

Nizam asked him why they called him 'Shaytan, the Devil', and the driver told him about how he used to give his mother so much grief as a child because he was such a troublemaker. She would yell at him and call him 'ya shaytan, you little devil'.

The neighbours had picked up the nickname from his mother, and it had stuck with him ever since.

As they approached Beirut, the driver said, cutting to the chase, 'Listen, son. Touma Abu-Shaheen is a goner. It'll be over for him any day now. Rakheema won't be able to stand up to her husband's relatives or even her own.'

He didn't divulge anything else. After a pause, he added emphatically, 'I've warned you, and you're free to . . . '

Nizam thanked him and asked him to drop him off on Lebanon Street.

Before stepping out of the car, he said jokingly to the driver, 'No, I'm not free . . . '

Shaytan did not understand what he meant, and perhaps Nizam didn't mean anything by it.

8

Janan's mother's face lit up as though Nizam was exactly the person she had been waiting for.

'Look at her,' she said. 'She won't eat or drink or paint. All she wants is Nizam.'

Janan was sitting on the couch. She'd wrapped herself in a blanket that she pulled all the way up to her shoulders as if she'd come down with a bad cold in the middle of the summer. She just sat there, huddled for hours, as her mother said. She had hoisted the caged parrot onto a wooden pole. As soon as she saw Nizam, she ran to him and threw herself in his arms for a long time, closing her eyes. She didn't care that he felt embarrassed by the way she was acting right in front of her mother. She grabbed him by the hand and led him towards the couch where she asked him to sit down so she could get in his lap. She couldn't stop caressing his face and kissing him, as soon as her mother left the room. Smiling and satisfied, Janan's mother could now get back to her daily chores after being on alert and standing by her daughter all morning.

'Don't you ever leave me. Don't you ever leave me . . . where did you disappear to?' she said as she hit him on the shoulders. 'You said you'd be back, but you didn't come back.'

During his long absence, she had been asking the parrot about him.

His sudden return made her emotional, as if she'd lost all hope of seeing him again. She jumped up and down all around him; she didn't even notice the stillness that had overcome him. She offered him food and drink, but he declined.

'I lost your parents' phone number . . . ' he said. Then he quickly added, 'I had written it down on my ID case, but I lost it . . . I don't even have an ID now.'

Nizam didn't tell her that the huge armed man, George, had forgotten he still had it in his hand when he told him to run off. He probably noticed he still had it after Olga took off in her car and disappeared around the corner. Maybe he ended up tossing it on the pavement or sticking it into his pocket along with the pendant of the Immaculate Conception.

'So you've been going around without an ID?'

Nizam felt lighter ever since he realized that the militiaman never returned his ID. He didn't even want a new one. In any case, since the violent events had started, a group of armed men had attacked the Sérail in Tripoli, setting fire to the floor where the Personal Status Department was located. It was said that that department was the main target for sabotage and that all the personal records had been burnt.

'It's better this way . . . ' he said.

'Anyway, the hostilities are over,' he added, assuring Janan. 'It looks like they're going to work things out.'

He needed some sort of promise so he could face Beirut.

She laughed sarcastically.

Janan's parents invited Nizam to lunch, and she didn't give him a chance to decline. She was vivacious, happy, talking up a storm, eating, regaining her appetite, feeding Nizam with her hands. She told her father that Nizam had lost his ID and couldn't get a new one because the Sérail in Tripoli had been burnt down.

'They burned it down so they can grant Lebanese citizenship to anyone they want . . . '

That was Janan's father's final verdict, though he preferred not to name the culprits in front of Nizam. Moving on to practical matters, he asked Nizam if he had a passport picture. Nizam took out a photo that had been in his wallet ever since he had his picture taken in order to renew his enrollment application for law school. Janan's father was thinking of securing a political party ID for Nizam so he wouldn't be harassed whenever he came to the Christian area. Sometimes folks asked about the strangers in the neighbourhood, about people they didn't know. Janan's father had good connections with prominent higher-ups in some of the political parties.

'Janan loves you so much,' her mother said, as a way of explaining her husband's concern for him.

Janan's father asked Nizam if he would like to change his name. He was a bit surprised by the question, but just shrugged his shoulders with indifference.

'No,' Janan protested. 'His name is nice.'

Janan's father began saying his name out loud, 'Nizam al-Alami', as though to test out how it would sound to armed checkpoint guards when they read it. After pronouncing it with several different intonations, he stuck out his lower lip in frustration. The first name was unfamiliar and so was the family name. 'Nizam' wasn't a Christian name for sure, and 'al-Alami' wasn't either. There was the Maronite 'Alam' clan from the northern town of Darayya with other family members hailing from various villages in the Shouf District. And he also knew people from the 'Alaama' clan who were Druze—'a respectable family', as he said. He ended his survey with the famous judge Amin Allaam, who was most likely a Sunni Muslim from the city of Sidon. He suggested dropping the 'I' from the end of Nizam's last name and then said the two names out loud, 'Nizam Alam', but he didn't like that either.

'It seems a bit contrived,' he said. 'I'll take care of the matter of the ID tomorrow.'

He promised them that as the two of them headed down to the studio where Janan smothered Nizam with hot kisses intermittently throughout the afternoon, while the parrot let out crippling screeching sounds from time to time. It had forgotten how to talk after having lived for so long with the ever silent Janan, so it reverted to making those primal disconcerting sounds of the jungle.

Janan spent hours pinching Nizam, in disbelief that he was actually there, before asking him to take his position standing behind her like he used to. She made him hold up a book with lots of pictures in it while she regained her desire to paint. She leapt up all of a sudden as evening fell, put on her apron, and launched a mad attack on her brushes, her colours, and all the details in every direction. It appeared that the whole time when she had been sitting on the couch covered in blankets up to her shoulders, she had been contemplating her paintings. Throughout those long days of waiting for Nizam to come walking through her studio door, she had been planning everything she would add to her paintings in terms of brushstrokes and colours. All she'd needed was the burst of physical motivation to actually do it.

The night-time hours didn't cut into her enthusiasm at all. Rather, she continued to caress and dote on Nizam. The next day around noon, she went upstairs to her parents' flat and came back with some food and Nizam al-Alami's membership ID card for the Lebanese Front. Her father had chosen a name for him at the last second, as he told her, when the front representative started filling out the ID.

'Joseph Safi', Janan's father said.

The name—empty and transparent—just popped into his head. There was no spot to fill in the father's name on the ID. It was a small square card, laminated. Nizam shoved it into its little sleeve and slipped it into his back pocket. He barely looked at it and forgot all about it the moment he fastened the button of his pocket.

Janan bid him farewell that afternoon, after making sure he took down her parents' phone number again, and in return for which he gave her the number of the pharmacy where she could reach him if needed or leave a message for him with the pharmacist. He also promised her he would keep the time he would spend at the Manara flat to a minimum, just long enough to check on things, and then he'd come right back to her at the studio. She walked him to the door, chattering and laughing, half-sarcastic, half-earnest, singing songs with words she concocted herself.

'I love you when you come back to me happy, to throw yourself into my arms . . . '

Then, addressing the parrot from across the room, she said, 'He will stay with me forever. I'll learn to cook the best dishes for him and compete with Rakheema for his heart. The key to a man's heart is through his stomach . . . '

Then she started mimicking the high society ladies with their sophisticated voices and in an exceedingly put-on accent in French, she said, 'Mademoiselle Janan Salem?'

To which she answered for herself, also in French, 'No, no. I am Madame Alami.'

He struggled to keep hold of himself, hiding his sadness. He picked her up and spun her around until she got dizzy. He put her down and walked backwards towards the studio door with his finger pointing up in the air. He opened the door with his hand behind his back, without turning around, and went through the door repeating, 'I'll be back, I'll be back . . . '

9

Olga, he discovered, had been worried about him. Her mother was doing just fine, especially since her relationship with the priest was growing stronger. She was constantly criticizing Olga's behaviour—the way she dressed, the way she spent money. Ali Soueidan had shown up all of a sudden offering to be of service—just like that, without an ounce of shame. She didn't blow up in his face, though, because she was scared of him. She didn't trust anyone except those Bolsheviks, as she called Chamoun and Vasco. Vasco brought news about the east side of the city, about how they were preparing themselves for battle since there would be no solution without a winner and a loser. Nizam asked Olga what she was going to do, and she said she planned on leaving the country again. She didn't know where she would go. That had been at around noon. Vasco and his assistant had arrived, and Chamoun brought sandwiches for everyone. He went back to telling them about numerous rumours spreading about an attack on the area. They sent Vasco's assistant out for some soft drinks. They were sitting and eating when there was a knock at the door. They thought maybe Vasco's assistant had come back.

Four men barged in on them, just like that, out of the blue.

The oldest one in the group had a revolver at his waist and spoke on behalf of the others. Another had some sort of weapon in a leather case, which they suspected was a sniper rifle. He was holding it with both hands like some valuable possession that had been placed in his care. A third one, the second one's assistant, was holding a box that undoubtedly contained lethal ammunition.

They appeared to be a crew devoted to serving the sniper rifle; it was the only weapon they needed. The revolver that the man in charge had was merely to establish his authority. That man had a beard, didn't shake hands with anyone, and didn't introduce himself. Rather, he said that they had come by the day before and didn't find anyone at home, so they waited until today as a final deadline because they were determined to respect the privacy of homes and families.

If he hadn't found anyone at home this time, he was going to break the door down and enter.

That was what he didn't say as he surveyed the house, its contents, and the people inside it in one swooping glance: Nizam, Olga, Vasco and Chamoun Rikho. No doubt his idea of 'families' didn't exactly match up with the group he found in the living room—three men, one of them in a wheelchair, and a beautiful woman in skimpy clothes, the only one smoking when they'd come in, with a smear of red lipstick on the white filter of her cigarette. Olga chose a shade of red lipstick each day that matched her mood, and that day it leaned towards a blue hue.

As soon as they came in, the men occupied themselves with the military mission they'd come to carry out. They had been eyeing the balcony, and the one carrying the sniper rifle didn't hesitate to go outside and explore, followed by his two companions. They quickly removed the rifle from its leather case and began taking turns holding it and aiming it, focusing on a nearby residential building, on a ship in the sea close to shore, or on the heights of Mount Sannine, in an attempt to determine the range of the scope. It was a recent acquisition, and they were still familiarizing themselves with it. Their having gotten in the lift and out of it on the top floor of the building and entering into the flat and then going out onto the balcony caused them to lose their sense of direction. Their leader went out to them in his turn to assess the military situation. He discovered one of them holding the rifle and aiming it at the al-Hammam al-Askari (Bain Militaire), so he shouted at him that the enemy was on the exact opposite side. He smacked himself on the head showing his frustration with those men of his and their utter lack of sense.

The bearded one with the thick, dirty, unruly beard typical of revolutionaries, unlike Nizam's brother Khaled's beard—the Islamic type that's artfully drawn on and kept up impeccably on a daily basis—was more concerned about the situation indoors than getting military matters out on the balcony under control. Possibly to cover the backs of his fighters, and also because he felt that most likely the young man in the wheelchair and Nizam—the blond amateur—wouldn't be able to stop him from getting to Olga. Olga, who had caught the man's attention the moment she'd crossed her, revealing part of her thighs. The right leg over the left, and then the other way around out of nervousness. The bearded one started addressing Chamoun as his counterpart, as leader of the other side—of the flat dwellers, that is. He asked him, for example, about the number of rooms—a question he tried to attribute some military significance to. With a hand gesture, Chamoun appealed to Olga and Nizam, not because he didn't know the answer, but because he didn't want to impinge upon the authority of the flat owner and the tenant.

'Two bedrooms,' Nizam said in a dry tone.

The armed man looked over at him and asked his name somewhat impatiently, since Nizam answered a question that had been addressed to someone else. Chamoun butted in before Nizam had a chance to answer. 'Nizam Mahmoud al-Alami, owner of the flat.'

Mentioning Nizam's father's name was Chamoun's way of trying to strengthen their position. He was the only Muslim on their front. Then, for no apparent reason, Chamoun added, 'Nizam won first place in the shooting contest at the Democratic Front for the Liberation of Palestine in Tel al-Zaatar refugee camp . . . '

Nizam shrugged his shoulders sarcastically. The one with the beard held his annoyance with Nizam at bay, but he didn't back down.

'The building concierge says the owner of the flat is a Russian woman.'

Female. Foreign. Christian.

Chamoun corrected him this time, pointing to Olga. 'Russian origin, but Lebanese.'

He didn't mention she was married to a Lebanese, because that would open up the issue of what the three men were doing there with a married woman whose husband was away. Olga kept quiet and smoked her cigarette, while the rest of them had their heads down trying to come up with a way out of the mess they'd suddenly found themselves in. The heavy silence was broken by a knock at the door. The bearded one raised his revolver, cocked it, and aimed it at the door in a cinematic motion, causing the others to shout that the person at the door was one of them. They'd forgotten about Vasco's assistant, but now there he was, back at the flat with bottles of Coca Cola in hand. At least now they out- numbered them with this tall assistant with the tattoo and big muscles. He came in and didn't seem surprised by the armed men's presence. Maybe he thought they were friends of the cell. He never meddled in things that were outside the purview of his duties carrying Vasco and looking after him. He showed his physical strength in other situations; someone once said that he participated in body building competitions. The armed man inspected him for a long time, trying to assess the extent of the threat he posed. He read a gentle-heartedness in his eyes that didn't seem to fit his physical abilities, so he resumed asking questions that were more like accusations. He asked them if they knew an American couple who lived in the building. Olga burst out laughing, despite everything that was happening, or possibly because she was so nervous about what was happening. She suddenly imagined Barbara saying her farewell to Beirut while standing out in front of the flat door that had been shut in her face. Nizam cracked a smile in spite of himself. The bearded one furrowed his thick brows, so they told him that Jonathan and Barbara left for their country the month before.

'So it appears you know the Americans well . . . ' he said accusingly.

Vasco sneered at the bad joke, and Chamoun tried to level a political accusation against the United States for having stirred things up for Israel's sake. But the leader of the sniper rifle brigade altered his plan and decided to come take a closer look at the picture of the Grand Duke to find out who he was. Vasco continued, somewhat haughtily, that the man in the picture was a Russian who had died more than sixty years ago. He turned to Olga and smiled, obligingly for the first time and asked, 'Is he a relative of yours?'

While the other armed men were deliberating out on the balcony, the one in charge was inspecting Olga's relatives up close one by one, as if that might help him recognize some of them.

Not finding what he was after, he suddenly turned to Nizam and asked, 'Is your name Mahmoud?'

He, too, swallowed Nizam's first name.

He said he knew him and had seen him a few times around the neighbourhood. Nizam appeared to have recognized the faces of two of the armed men who were dressed in khakis and had quit shaving and combing their hair on a daily basis, as if the military missions they'd committed themselves to had caused all other daily duties to seem trivial. The two men belonged to the group of young men who gathered at the street corner in front of the juice shop, where the stack of sugar cane always stood.

The bearded man arrived at the icon of St George—which he'd saved until the end—and gave it a suspicious, inquisitive look. When he was done studying its details, he announced out of nowhere that they were fighting a national battle against reactionism and separatism and that it was the other side that wanted to turn this whole thing into a sectarian issue.

One of the armed men came back from the balcony pleased and announced that the location was suitable for them.

'We can control the Holiday Inn perfectly from here,' he said, as he took his turn looking at Olga's bare shoulders.

'I know, I know . . . ' the leader replied, almost sarcastically.

When Olga went into the bedroom, Chamoun tried telling them that the flat was the main meeting venue for the Farajallah al-Helou cell, but the leader didn't seem to have heard of that name before, so Chamoun got to the heart of the matter and told them that the owners of the flat were Arab nationalists like them, but the bearded man explained that they were just following orders from their leadership.

Vasco seized on the opportunity to try to understand what was going on.

'What leadership?' he asked. 'What organization do you belong to?'

'Brother Issam called me personally', came the ready answer.

It was the al-Tanzim al-Shaabi Organization.

'Brother Issam' himself must have called him, using the same black phone that he was holding in the picture of him that hung on the wall of the lobby in Maysaloun's building.

Their orders entailed retaliating against the impending attack on the area—the area that they were in charge of protecting with their own lives.

'Attack?' Chamoun asked and then started explaining that they were leaning towards de-escalation and dialogue.

'That's just newspaper talk,' the bearded man said sarcastically. He insisted that they were seeing with their own eyes what was happening on the ground. He invited his interlocutors to go with him out on the balcony so he could show them where the weapons were being transported and stationed in new locations.

'They reached the heart of our area' he said.

After settling on the location, the bearded man delegated responsibilities. Abbas, the man carrying the sniper rifle, would remain stationed on the balcony for now; they would switch daily, with Abu Yasser taking over Abbas' place, and so on and so forth. Before leaving with the others, he whispered something in Abbas' ear and then said to him in a loud voice, 'Don't you worry. These people are nice. They won't let you starve.'

He didn't forget to specify to the sniper his targets. 'Anything that moves in the Holiday Inn and the surrounding streets . . . '

He added, 'You should aim at the chest because the rifle might recoil in your hand.'

As a final gesture, meant to reassure the inhabitants of the flat, he promised to drop by in person from time to time. He said that without taking his eyes off Olga, who had come back to the living room after covering her shoulders with a light scarf. She didn't sit down though.

They were sitting quietly, except for Olga, who remained standing as she leaned against the door. When they did talk, they did so in a low voice. They couldn't see the man called Abbas from where they were sitting, and they couldn't tell if he had come closer in order to listen to what they were saying—since the military situation was completely calm. Vasco worried that this was all a pretext to occupy residential flats. Chamoun predicted that the stupid sniper would start shooting his marvellous gun, one bullet after another, likely without hitting anybody and that those on the opposite front would respond to him with machine guns or even a canon and perhaps hit their target. Chamoun's faith in the fighting effectiveness of the team he was rooting for was deteriorating day after day. Nizam didn't make any predictions. He was frowning a little bit, and he only spoke as needed. As the sun started to set, Vasco's assistant checked his watch every five minutes. Vasco had to go back to his house in Achrafiyeh. Times had changed and venturing out at night was not recommended even if the ceasefire was still in effect. That's the advice Vasco's parents had given his assistant after they had failed to stop Vasco from crossing to the other side of the capital. Chamoun promised that by morning, he would try to pull some strings with the Fatah Organization—with Abu Jihad himself—in order to keep these armed men away from the flat.

'You're going to do that personally too?' Nizam asked, not in the mood for sarcasm. The sniper appeared suddenly at the door of the balcony. They had not heard his footsteps. He stood there smiling, somewhat sheepishly, before asking where the bathroom was.

He was going to eat there and use the bathroom too!

The cold sea breeze must have struck him when he was outside, giving him stomach cramps, or maybe he got bored sitting all by himself and decided to approach the lit room. They pointed him to the bathroom inside, and he crossed between them with the sniper rifle—his treasure—in hand. He never parted with it. They stopped talking completely, as they listened to him trying to shut the pesky bathroom door behind him without much success, since they didn't hear the sound of the bolt. They did hear the sound of the butt of the rifle hitting the floor, as he likely set it in the corner behind the door so he could relieve himself. They didn't say anything because they assumed that he could still catch what they were saying. Then the slightest sounds, which allowed them to guess what he was doing, step by step, started to reach them. Chamoun Rikho felt somewhat embarrassed, so he decided to drown out the noise by asking them who wanted sugar in their coffee and who wanted it black, even though he knew exactly how they all liked their coffee. Abbas crowned his fairly long stay in the bathroom with a hard flush of the toilet. He then apologized for bothering them, as he said. He too stopped in front of the icon of St George, which he had finally discovered despite passing by it many times before. He stared at the pot of coffee from which they filled their cups. He was stalling. When they didn't invite him to join them, he went back out on the balcony.

Vasco and his assistant left before dark, with Vasco promising them on his way out to help them find a solution to the situation in the flat.

Chamoun stayed with them until late and offered to spend the night with them, but he looked anxious, so Nizam insisted that he leave.

Olga didn't feel safe spending the night alone, so they shared the big bed again. Nizam spent the night tossing and turning. It was hot, and they were forced to close the one window in the room since it overlooked the balcony on the side where the sniper was stationed. Olga was going to stay in the flat in spite of them. That was her decision, and Nizam was going to stay with her. He wouldn't leave her. He wanted to go back to Janan, but he wasn't going to abandon Olga. He was stuck there. Exhausted, he finally dozed off for a little bit before Olga woke him up as she started pulling back the sheet that she had tossed away earlier because of the heat. She covered her nakedness as she gestured for Nizam to look towards the window. When they had entered the bedroom, the darkness outside had prevented them from seeing what was happening out on the balcony, but a light that someone had turned on in a neighbouring building at some point during the night suddenly exposed to Olga—who also couldn't sleep—the shadow of the sniper behind the window. Leaning forward, the sniper put his hands around his eyes to avoid the light reflection, as he tried to see through the green curtains what was happening on top of the bed. Nizam whispered that the person standing outside couldn't see the inside of the room unless the light was on. In any case, Abbas wasn't going to see anything that would quench his thirst. Nizam was sleeping on his right side with his back to Olga. He had his knees folded in front of his stomach in a fetal position. During the early hours of dawn, the armed man kept going to the bathroom. He didn't stay there long, but he was making the same sounds from the night before. All the standing outside must have given him a serious case of diarrhoea.

In the morning, Abu Yasser, his replacement, took over the rifle and post. Nizam and Olga didn't open the bedroom door until Olga was done putting on her clothes and makeup. The living room had now become the outside of the house. It was a public street, a crossing for the militia of the al-Tanzim al-Shaabi Organization that led to the balcony overlooking the St George and Holiday Inn hotels. However, Abu Yasser didn't stay put behind his rifle for too long.

10

Around ten o'clock, Beirut exploded all at once. The factions had restrained themselves for three months—far more than they could bear—until finally all hell broke loose, and they started using the new weapons that they had acquired during that time.

At noon, Vasco and his assistant came upon one of the makeshift checkpoints that were suddenly set up by militias at all the hotspots and roads that connected the capital's two opposite sides. The warring parties had taken advantage of the long summer truce, studying the lay of the land so they could swoop down on it when the time came. They stopped Vasco and his assistant as they were crossing to the western side of the city by way of the National Museum Road as they usually did. They asked Vasco to step out of the car so they could search him, but he told them that he couldn't walk. They thought he was being defiant and screamed at him again, so he showed them his frail, bowed legs and the wheelchair in the backseat. The armed men studied the car—a new Peugeot 504 painted a unique colour. They asked the driver to sit in the back, and three of them squeezed into the car, which one of them started driving to an unknown destination. That his assistant kept repeating that Vasco was rooting for them against his own parents didn't deter them. They dropped Vasco off in an area close to Beirut International Airport—or rather they asked his assistant to remove him from the car and then continued on their way. They kidnapped his assistant, took the Peugeot 504 and his wheelchair. Vasco didn't make it in time to rescue Olga and Nizam, but rather remained where his assistant had sat him down on a short cement wall on the corner of one of the side roads—his legs flailing loosely, his brown shoes perfectly clean, never having touched the ground.

He didn't know what to do. A taxi driver went by and thought he might be waiting for someone to pick him up, so he honked at him and gestured with his hand—asking him if he needed a ride. Vasco just thanked him and waved him off. He stayed there for over three hours, in a state of utter disbelief about what was happening to him, as the echoes of explosions demolishing downtown Beirut reached him. No one came to his rescue, until he finally flagged down an ambulance that had lost its way. The ambulance driver and nurse transported him to the National Museum area, where they handed him over to Lajnat al-Irtibat al-Amniya, the Security Liaison Committee, which then took him to his parents' home. After that, none of his remaining comrades or friends ever heard any news about Joseph al-Farneeni again, although it was said that he had joined the other camp because his assistant disappeared and he couldn't find out anything about his whereabouts—despite all the petitions and despite the assistant's name appearing for years on the lists put forth by the committee investigating the fates of the kidnapped and the missing.

The seafront opened up too, and the Manara flat entered the battle through its wide-open door. As soon as the first few shots were fired, the new sniper realized that he was more exposed than necessary, so he demanded some sandbags that he could hide behind and asked for backup men with machine guns. Men in muddy boots passed through the flat, so Nizam and Olga rolled up the big rug and stashed it in the smaller bedroom. In her mind, Olga started keeping track of all the things she would regret losing if they were stolen so she could lock them up in the bedroom. Nizam worried about St George.

'I don't like the way they look at him . . . ' he told Olga. 'Every time one of them passes by, they stop in front of him.'

'Don't worry,' she assured him. 'They can't get to him.'

When the explosions drew closer, the fighters asked Olga and Nizam to go down to the bomb shelter. They refused. They weren't going to let them take over the flat and do as they please. The sound of explosions grew louder, and bullets hit the walls of the building. Nizam tried to convince Olga to go down to the shelter. She was scared and didn't want to leave him. She finally went down and joined some of the families who lived in the building— particularly Itani's wife who'd taken up residence in the shelter, with her children, half of her kitchenware, the transistor radio that she never turned off, and her bad manners. She wouldn't stop making accusations, right and left—including clear insinuations about the residents of the roof flat and how they and people like them were responsible for the outbreak of the war and for Beirut going up in flames. She went on about young men who weren't satisfied with anything and who preferred foreigners to their own fellow compatriots. She blamed them and those who 'took them in', as she said, while looking incessantly at Olga, who left the shelter and went upstairs even though the bombs were still pouring down and the roof was more exposed than any other floor.

The presence of armed men and their bullets caught the attention of the faction on the opposite side of the flat, so they started showering it with barrages of bullets from their own machine guns from time to time. In turn, the al-Tanzim al-Shaabi members withdrew inside, into the living room. Olga retreated into the kitchen and bedroom. Just like that, for no good reason, Nizam decided to remain seated in his place facing the balcony and refused to move to a safer spot. One of the snipers screamed at him and almost threatened him with his weapon. They couldn't live with the idea of retreating further than he did, when he was the defenceless one. As the buzzing of bullets drew closer, there were screams telling everybody to get out of the flat and at least head to the stairway. Meanwhile, one armed man stayed inside the flat, even though he was only two or three metres away from the door, in a spot that his manliness would not allow him to retreat from and where he could face off with the enemy. The night was also turbulent, as the armed men feared a nightly landing or a military siege of the area from the sea. They fired, by way of a warning, in the direction of the lights, but generally it was just some poor fishermen's boats. On calm nights, the armed men stationed on the balcony didn't have anything to keep them busy, except for Olga and Nizam, so they'd hunker down in the flat, seeking company. The bearded leader volunteered twice for the grueling night watch under the pretext that he wanted to give his men some rest. He would come by after making sure that Olga didn't have any company but Nizam. In any case, the two of them were now all alone. Even Chamoun hadn't come back since he was likely stuck somewhere inside the Burj al-Barajneh camp. Rather than monitoring the enemy's movements outside, the leader would spend the night hanging out with them in the living room, trying to figure out if they were a married couple, lovers or relatives— he needed something to work with. He didn't get a satisfying answer. He didn't get any answers. As soon as Olga would go into the bedroom, the bearded man would leap at Nizam and ask him if he needed any help, all the while winking at him. 'They told me you haven't been doing your duty . . . ' he said. He smiled as he spoke to ensure that this pestering of his came off as something in between seriousness and jest.

Nizam didn't know what to do with the man who asked for his permission to sleep in the living room. He neither approved nor denied the man's request, so the bearded man set down his rifle on the floor and lay on the couch with his military boots on. It was impossible for Olga to go out to the bathroom at night, as long as he was there—with his imposing stature and odour— blocking her way. Nizam joined Olga as the siege tightened over them. It occurred to him to hit the man on the head with the Samovar, for example, pick him up with that damn sniper rifle of his, and throw him and his rifle from the roof of the building onto the street, next to the juice shop that never closed its doors— come night or day or war.

The next afternoon, Nizam tried to take matters into his own hands. He asked Olga to stay in the bedroom until he returned home, and he advised her to dress conservatively. Then he went to his sister Maysaloun's house in Tariq al-Jdeideh. When he came back to Manara in the evening, he found the door to the flat open. There was no one in the living room. There was no one on the balcony. Sandbags and bullet casings and two empty whiskey bottles. The clashes had almost stopped, as downtown Beirut became the new frontline. They were gone. He turned around to find the bedroom window wide open. There was a heap on top of the bed, a curled-up body, crying.

'Olga!'

'It happened right in front of my aunt and grandma . . . ' she sobbed.

He jumped to her side from the window, held her close.

'Oh, Nizam, his smell . . . '

They had broken into the bedroom through the window. They broke the window after she slammed the door shut in their faces. The bearded one staggered, drunk; he was barely able to jump through the window with his two companions. He climbed into the bed without asking for permission as he accused her and Nizam of failing to provide even a crust of bread to the men who were putting their lives on the line in order to protect the area. He started crawling towards her and giving her pathetic looks of seduction. He was very aroused, and she escaped from him as she dashed towards the door. The two other men tried to stop her, but she made it out to the living room and from there to the balcony, where she screamed for help at the top of her lungs, but to no avail. They brought her back inside and threw her down onto the sofa. Their leader sauntered over to her and told one of the other two men to take off her underwear. He left the nightgown on, though, and slipped his hand beneath it. They were in in a state of frenzy as she tried to fight them off with her hands. She scratched them with her fingernails, clenched her thighs together, bit them. As she kicked and screamed, no matter which way she twisted and turned, her gaze kept falling upon the face of her paternal aunt in the picture on the wall across from her. She cried out for help, calling her aunt by name and also calling out to her grandmother. Then she began speaking in Russian. She begged the men in Russian to get off of her, to turn her aunt's face towards the wall at least, so her aunt couldn't see her. She swore at them in Russian while the leader taunted her, saying her boyfriend had run off and left her . . . She cried and laughed in Russian and said, 'Where did you go, Nizam, leaving me here all alone?'

They made fun of how she pronounced the 'r' as 'gh' when she said, 'leaving me, taghaktni'. The more she resisted, the more aroused they became. One of them grabbed her by her delicate wrists and held her down with both his hands while the other one worked on her lower body and managed to pull off her underwear. Then their leader threw himself on top of her. She nearly passed out from his smell. He pulled out his penis without taking off any clothing. The one holding down the lower part of her body forced her thighs apart with his hands and started licking her with his tongue. She screamed, bawling at the top of her lungs, 'I surrendered, Nizam . . . '

But the moment the leader's penis had brushed against the lower part of her stomach over her nightgown, he ejaculated in spite of himself.

She shed hot tears as she clung to Nizam's shoulders. 'He came on me, on my stomach . . . ' she said before running to the bathroom to throw up all over again.

'How did they leave?'

One of the militia men had come into the flat, stood in the doorway, and barked orders from Brother Issam that they were to vacate the flat immediately, so they gathered their equipment and left.

'Come here . . . '

As they walked past the icon, Olga cast a reproachful glance at St George.

Nizam took her to the bathroom, sat her down naked in the bathtub, and started scrubbing her back, stomach, shoulders and arms with a soapy loofah. He told her while she sobbed from time to time that he'd gone to see Maysaloun because in the lobby of the building where she lived there was a picture on the wall of Brother Issam talking on the phone and smiling. Maysaloun had welcomed him and called her husband who pulled some strings to get the men out of the flat. As Nizam doused Olga with more water and started scrubbing her again, giving her a deep cleansing, he told her about the Roxy Cinema that his father Mahmoud al-Alami had opened in Homs and about how much Maysaloun loved those movies and how his father had fallen in love with Gloria Swanson after seeing one of her films. Wanting to watch the film again outside the scheduled showtimes, his father closed the cinema doors and asked the projectionist to give him a private showing as he sat there all alone in the theatre. The projectionist, forgetting Nizam's father was there in the theatre, accidentally locked him inside. Then, combing her wet hair, Nizam suddenly started reciting lines from the tragicomic dialogues of the dying King. Olga began to calm down as Nizam dried her off and carried her to the bed where he very carefully lowered her like a precious possession while continuing to cradle her in his arms. He stroked her hair and told her about his father's attempts to smuggle hashish inside the film canisters, until she fell asleep on his arm, letting out gasps—reverberations from her long bout of weeping. He took a deep breath and lay down beside her, his energy depleted, his spirit empty.

She woke up early, clean. The memory of the day before came back to her like a heavy blow, but she overcame it and tiptoed to the bathroom. She returned to the bedroom and opened her red suitcase beside the bed where Nizam was still sleeping. She quietly packed her clothes into the bottom of the suitcase and then began her final tour of the Manara flat. She said goodbye to the things she would leave behind. She took down the picture of her aunt from the wall and placed it in the suitcase. She stopped in front of the picture of the Archduke but didn't pick it up. She shut the suitcase, sat on top of it, and lit a cigarette as she watched and waited for Nizam. He wasn't surprised to see her when he opened his eyes.

'I want to say goodbye . . . '

He started getting dressed. 'I'll go with you.'

'No, no,' she said, frightened. 'I can't take any more.'

He would leave, too, and go to Janan. He'd take Olga to Jounieh and then come back to Achrafiyeh . . .

Burj Square was in flames. The souqs had been destroyed and looted.

It was no longer possible to go there or pass through, even with the announcement of a new ceasefire and the formation of liaison committees. Moving from one side of the capital to the other had become a major undertaking that required time and effort. He gave her a year's rent in advance from the money that Touma had given him that was still in his pocket. No expenses during wartime.

They made it to her mother's house in Jounieh after some trouble at the crossings. Choking traffic in both directions. The ship to Cyprus would sail in the afternoon. No reservations. Whoever showed up could pay and get on board.

'I won't be coming back again after today, Mom . . . '

Without any real emotion in her voice, she said, 'I haven't had my fill of you, Olga . . . '

Her mother refused to join her on her travels. She was finished with such roving, tired of moving from one country to another, and from one man to another. They'd all died. Her house suited her just fine. She'd gotten used to it and could never get used to any other. She didn't have the strength to travel. She was going to die there with her cats, end of discussion. She assured Olga that she had made all the necessary preparations with the parish priest.

Olga did not want to leave before settling an old score with her mother. 'You're such a bitch, Mother. You married me off. You loved him because "he loved life" . . . ' she said sarcastically and in French, mimicking her mother's voice. 'And because he was handsome and rich and played bridge with you, to the point that your friends practically accused you of being the one in love with him.'

Her mother shut her up, suggesting Olga should stay there with her if she wanted to open up old books from the past. Olga paused before concluding, 'Mother, if this young man here, Nizam, comes by and asks you to give him everything that you want to leave behind in Lebanon, then give it to him. If only I weren't thirteen years older than him, I would have married him, borne his children, spent my life serving him and even brought young women to his bed . . . '

He stood at the port in Jounieh next to her mother; she too held his hand, just like Olga. As they watched Olga strain to drag her suitcases, her mother said that she'd never heard her daughter talk about a man the way she had talked about him. They stood waving to her. Entire families with all their children made their way aboard the ship. It was a short trip that they could spend up on deck. If Nizam ever managed to build his sailboat, he would name it Olga.

Nizam caught up with her and stopped her. He unbuttoned his shirt, removed the blue bead necklace from his neck and slipped it over her head. She tried to refuse, saying she was going to the land of safety and wouldn't need it there. He insisted and kissed her on the lips. She kissed him back and they embraced each other like that for a long time right in front of all the other passengers.

'The taste of your first kiss lasted a long time . . . '

'Nizam!' interrupted Dima. The shout had come from aboard the ship.

'Dima!'

The chubby, smiling comrade had yielded to her parents' pleas to go to France. She and Nizam communicated with each other with their hands. She asked him about their friends, which he responded to by shaking his head. She approached them. She'd found herself a travel companion; they would talk about Nizam all the way to Larnaca.

11

He went straight to Janan's. The taxi dropped him off at the top of the street. He ran down the hill and knocked at the door to her studio. No one. Her parents' door. No answer. He asked the flower vendor. She flung her arms open, looked up to the sky, and then pointed in a vague direction. They had left, and she didn't know when they would be back.

He would wait around in the neighbourhood, casing it the way Janan liked.

He started back up the hill and came upon Raffoul headed down the hill. He was walking slowly on the pavement towards the Oriental Studies Institute. He had a black leather hat on his head. He was wearing a tattered overcoat and carrying a pathetic pink umbrella in his hand. Out of boredom, he would bang its metal tip against the walls wherever a spot opened up. There was only a very light rain, so he wasn't using the umbrella for cover.

'What are you doing here?' he asked Nizam in surprise.

Clearly something had come loose inside Raffoul, like an alarm clock that still worked even though a piece had broken off inside it, and if you put it up to your ear and shook it you could hear it rattle around. He scrutinised people even more than before and rediscovered them, but he hadn't lost his ability to pinpoint the identities of everyone under the sun and in which neighbourhood of Beirut and its suburbs they belonged.

Nizam asked him how he was doing, and it brought tears to his eyes. He pulled out his white handkerchief and wiped his eyes from beneath his glasses before catching his breath and digging deep into his memory in order to tell Nizam that Touma and Rakheema had sent him something with the taxi driver two days before Beirut had gone up in flames.

'I forgot it down there . . . ' he said, pointing in the direction of Burj Square. Then he looked at Nizam before making up his mind, 'Come with me. You're one of my old customers . . . '

After a few minutes of walking in silence, they turned right, and there before them appeared the long, straight, narrow road that ran parallel to Burj Square. Nizam stopped where he was standing at the top of the hill to take in what had suddenly been exposed to him—crowds of people, vegetable carts, goods on display on cartops, and laundry hanging from clotheslines. Suddenly, Raffoul started cursing Hawra in the foulest terms.

'I don't have anyone up there any more . . . '

Nizam knew that road very well. He used to hike up it on his way to see Janan and always found it pretty much deserted except for some old folks or a student quickly making his way to the nearby law school.

Now it was flooded with people, with everyone Burj Square had spat out. It had sent them scurrying behind the demarcation lines, fleeing from the battles and the fires. They'd backed up only a few dozen metres from their original spots, but the trip had been harsh. Their faces looked tired, and their bodies seemed limp. They sat on low chairs in front of their goods, leaving the customers to freely touch the fabrics and handle the glassware and cheap jewellery. Some of them had written the name of the shop they'd left behind on a plank of wood or piece of cardboard, even though the sign was tacked up beside the tiny, semi-symbolic fraction of their goods that they had set up there on a table on the pavement—the few things they'd been able to grab before getting out. There were goods that in some cases really seemed to have been snatched up in a hurry and clearly weren't intended for display out on the street on top of a car, like bolts of English broadcloth of various colours or a female mannequin its owner had grabbed in his rush to get out—in favour of other items that were hard to gather up in such circumstances—and which he'd had difficulty setting   up naked amid the scattered merchandise. Some of the male shoppers carried rifles on their shoulders, perhaps as a precaution, considering the street's proximity to the demarcation line.

Nizam and Raffoul were walking along the street crowded with people who'd come there expecting to find a bargain, and with the few cars that ventured that way headed for nearby destinations on the same street or the side streets that branched off of it. There was no passage from there to any place except Burj Square and its burned-down souqs.

Raffoul knew exactly where he was headed. He cut a path through the crowd with his hand and umbrella so they could make their way to a side road to the left which they were guided to by a small sign planted in the middle of the street that read: 'Caution. Sniper'.

And another sign after that: 'Road closed. Mines.'

Raffoul didn't stop. Didn't read, didn't hesitate. Nizam kept pace with him until they reached the public souq. The houses appeared deserted and there was garbage in the middle of the street. After a few steps, some armed militia men positioned behind the corner of one of the old buildings stopped them. Raffoul and Nizam could make out some parts of Burj Square. They'd made it within a few metres of Zahrat al-Shamal. One of the armed men recognized Raffoul and rebuffed him with a sigh, 'How many times have we told you it's off limits! Off limits!' Then, pointing to Burj Square, he added, 'It's all destroyed. Where do you think you're going?'

Raffoul didn't answer.

They warned him that the entranceway to the hotel was directly in the line of fire. They would shoot him down like a bird. Nizam said that there was a ceasefire, to which the gunman mockingly responded, 'The ceasefire only exists in news reports . . . Last night they snuck up on us from the direction of Rivoli Cinema . . .'

Raffoul was standing there defeated, asking permission to enter Zahrat al-Shamal from men he'd never seen there before. He appealed to Nizam for help. He grabbed his arm and took him aside.

'I *have* to go up to the hotel. I left some valuable things there that I can't live without . . .' He was pleading in a hushed voice.

'Every day you come up with a new excuse!'

Nizam couldn't tolerate him being in such a state, so he whispered to Raffoul, 'Follow me. If they shout at us, don't look back, and don't say anything.'

They proceeded towards Burj Square. No one shouted at them. The armed men didn't stop them. One of the men said to his companion that he wasn't going to rescue them and wouldn't pull them out if they got killed or shot. Nizam walked in front while Raffoul walked directly behind him as if using him as a shield. A few steps and they found themselves looking onto Burj Square from the pavement in front of Jumhuriyya Café. Nizam froze in place. He was mesmerised by the destruction, the fallen trees, the bricks from buildings strewn about the square, the grey colour like something out of one of Janan's paintings, the two stray dogs roaming amid the rubble, the big holes and bullets in the bronze martyrs' statue, the piece of the Anita Eckberg model that had broken off despite the fact she was still looking southward. Complete calm after the storm. Raffoul nudged him to the right, towards the entrance to the hotel. He was in a hurry to get there.

They went inside. The smell of Zahrat al-Shamal had vanished beneath the dirt and the pebbles. They climbed the stairs cautiously. The lobby was now open to Burj Square. Half of its wall was demolished. The furniture was submerged in rubble. Bullet holes covered the walls that were still standing. Raffoul started hitting his umbrella against the chunks of cement that had flown off. He went up to the door of one of the inside rooms and called out, 'Yasmeen, Yasmeen . . . ' as though there was some depth behind the walls that his voice could reach. Nizam recalled having heard a lot about Yasmeen though he had never seen her.

Yasmeen was Raffoul's only woman. She cleaned the hotel, washed the sheets, and came to his bed. In front of everyone, he claimed she was ill, suggesting it was syphilis and that she might pass it on to anyone who was intimate with her. He pushed customers away from her, so he could keep her to himself. He loved her.

Or maybe she didn't exist. Maybe Raffoul had invented her, had created a family for himself out of her and her alleged daughter.

In the same tone, he called out to Abu Ali and asked Nizam to also call out and search for the two among the rubble.

'I'm pretty sure they're here,' he said. 'Look carefully.'

Nizam almost believed him and started searching, but as he went around the small hotel, he realized that there was no way that someone could be hiding—or lying dead.

Raffoul sat in his chair, not caring about the thick layer of dust. He went behind his desk.

'I was sitting right here . . . '

She had been with him there at the hotel, sweeping the floors, and he was waiting for her to finish as he ogled her 'voluptuous buttocks', as he said, smiling. They were not alone. Abu Ali was out on the balcony smoking a cigarette as he usually did. Every time the battles resumed, he'd head to Sidon and then continue on to his village close to Nabatieh. But as soon as a ceasefire would be announced, he'd return to Beirut since he didn't have anything to do in the village and no longer knew anybody there. But he hadn't been staying at Zahrat al-Shamal since he'd found a small hotel on the other side of town.

'It's safer for him there . . . '

Abu Ali would only visit Raffoul during the day. He'd spent five years at his hotel, so he would drop by to chat. Ever since the horse track went out of commission, Abu Ali went out of commission too. He had lit up a cigarette, annoying Raffoul with the smoke, before going out on the balcony to finish smoking it. He was about to go inside when they heard the first blast. Raffoul tried to imitate the sound of the explosion as he got up and then plopped into his chair again. The entire hotel had shaken, and all the glass had shattered. Bullets poured down on them, as if the fighters had been biding their time, waiting for the green light to start firing. The sudden explosion had propelled Abu Ali inside the hotel, and he had fallen flat on his face.

'The three of us huddled here in the corner.'

Raffoul said he was holding Yasmeen from behind. He winked at Nizam, flaunting his manhood. He even smiled, boastful. He had his arms wrapped around her, he said, gesturing and spreading his arms further apart as he tried to estimate the size of her behind. Minutes had passed before the shooting became intermittent. Al-Simsmani raised his head and tried to get up on his feet. A second explosion went off, and Raffoul's head hit the wall. He didn't know what had happened to him. He wasn't scared, but he looked at Yasmeen as if he couldn't recognize who she was. He didn't know why he started cursing her. His head was all messed up, as he said. He stood in the middle of the room—

not caring about the bullets raining down—and started accusing her of being in love with money and of sleeping with the highest bidder. He recounted everything he'd told her as he smacked himself on the face, sorry and remorseful. He'd told her that she was a greedy lowlife who was carrying every disease in the world and that she belonged in the back of the souq. She'd slapped him hard on the face and said she regretted ever having cared about him. The last thing he remembered was Abu Ali trying to grab him and get him down on the floor so he wouldn't get shot. He'd passed out after that, remaining in the hotel until the next day when some fighters, who were scouting for locations that overlooked the other side, found him. When they shook him, he moved. They gave him some water, and he got up on his feet. He asked about Yasmeen and Abu Ali, but the fighters mocked his questions and helped him out of the rubble.

'So what do you need now?'

'Help me find them . . . '

Nizam didn't believe Raffoul's story, but he helped him call out their names—exaggerating as he brought his hands together around his mouth like a trumpet, just to please him.

'Abu Ali . . . Yasmeen' he called out.

He'd pause to listen for an answer. He repeated the call after Raffoul. His voice was like an echo to Raffoul's tired voice. Nothing.

After they had exhausted their voices—and the entire place— Nizam grabbed the owner of Zahrat al-Shamal by the arm and escorted him down the dark stairway. The militiamen asked them sarcastically if they'd found their friends.

They went back the same way they'd come. The light rain had resumed, as Raffoul walked, despondent, having lost his ability to speak. Nizam was still holding his arm, in an attempt to console him, when he heard a faint voice calling out to him.

'Nano, Nano!'

A woman was calling to him stealthily, hoping that he was the only one who would hear her. He stopped and looked for the source of the sound coming from the direction of Nadia's house. The woman called to him again, sounding doubly insistent. There was no doubt that she was hiding behind the door. Nizam asked Raffoul to wait for him for a little bit, so the latter stood in the middle of the street, opened his dainty women's umbrella with difficulty, and held it over his head. Nizam quickly walked up the steps to the entranceway. The door was open, and the silent Greek woman led him to the living room that also served as the waiting area. She threw herself on him, hugging him enthusiastically, as if he were a relative of hers that had returned from his travels after a long absence. She said she missed him, and her tone was sincere. She spoke in Arabic with a rural accent. Cyril was right—she was not Greek.

She had seen Nizam walking with the owner of the hotel in the direction of Burj Square, so she waited for him, standing behind the window. She used to watch Raffoul pass by there every day, all by himself. Nizam remembered Raffoul, so he went outside to ask him to wait a bit longer, but it looked like Raffoul wasn't going to wait for him. He just kept going, all alone, with his women's umbrella amid the vendors and vegetable carts. Nizam called out to him from Nadia's porch, so he retraced his steps and stood facing him in the narrow street.

'They sent you an aeroplane . . . '

Nizam didn't understand what Raffoul had said and thought it was just another one of his senile comments, until the owner of Zahrat al-Shamal took the British Airways model aeroplane out of his coat pocket and started waving it around like someone waving a farewell handkerchief. He laughed, revealing the gap between his teeth.

'They also advised you not to go up to Hawra since the situation there hasn't changed . . . ' he said in a half-audible tone, as if talking to himself. He supplemented his comment by making gestures with his fingers that signified money and tried to explain to Nizam that sometimes he'd had to spend the money that Touma and Rakheema had sent for him, because the revenues from the hotel weren't enough.

Nizam didn't ask him where he was staying or how they'd meet again. At any rate, Raffoul seemed incapable of making any clear promises.

The Greek woman called out to Nizam again. He asked her if she was Lebanese. She told him that her parents had died when she was just a child, and that nobody took care of her, so she ran away from the orphanage to the clothing factory in Burj Hammoud before finally coming here. She asked him not to tell anyone that she was Lebanese since she was still pretending that she was Greek in front of the militiamen. They were attached to her, but she thought that if they found out that she was Lebanese like them, they would stop taking care of her. She was staying in Nadia's house, but she didn't know when the ceiling would collapse on them. She never said anything when she was around the militiamen, so they spoke freely because they assumed she couldn't understand anything. That's how she learnt before anyone else that they planned to raid Souq al-Sagha, the jewellery market, and then burn it down. She sat next to him on the couch that was upholstered in thick, colourful fabric and told him how Cyril had disappeared for a very long time before reappearing one day. He'd arrived, clean-shaven and tidy, but he hadn't found a cure for his wandering eye. He took out some money in front of the women, a stack of hundred lira bills—which he'd neatly arranged with the Baalbek Temple side facing up—before folding them slowly, just so he could show everybody that he no longer needed money.

The conversation was over after she'd told Nizam everything she knew. She didn't know much about him. She grabbed him by the hand and got up, hoping he'd come with her to the bedroom. He took some money out of his pocket and put it in her hand without counting it. He told her he was in a hurry and had to meet up with some people who were waiting for him.

He went back to Lebanon Street alone in the rain. The vendors at the makeshift market had started collecting their merchandise and running away.

As soon as Nizam arrived in front of the flower shop, the girl gestured to him, pointing him in the direction of the building's entrance. She motioned to him to keep walking, knowing how eager he was.

12

Janan's mother answered the door at the studio. She was pale and depressed.

'Where's Janan?' he asked, peeking inside.

Her mother's eyes teared up at the sight of his grief-stricken face.

'She asked for you every day, but we had no idea how to reach you.'

They had called the number he'd given them twenty times a day, but to no avail. The Battle of the Hotels had been taking place only a few metres away from the Manara Pharmacy. The owner of the pharmacy was very scared.

'Where is she?' Nizam asked. 'What's wrong with her?'

She was alive, at the hospital.

Nizam clasped her mother's hands, pleading for more information. She assured him again that her condition was not life threatening.

He listened to the rest of the story without budging.

Janan had slit her right wrist with a blade, with the Carter that she used for trimming any extra canvas fabric that she would stretch tightly over a wooden frame before beginning to sketch. Her mother found her just as she was about to take her last breath. Something had told her to get up and find her daughter. A voice had called out to her; she'd heard it with her own ears. She was in the building bomb shelter on a night of heavy shelling. Janan never went down with them, and they didn't worry about her too much since the flat was protected by the nearby buildings. Janan would say that she'd lose her mind downstairs and that she couldn't handle seeing people fearing for their lives, their children, and their belongings. Her mother had found her almost bleeding out, and she was turning cold. She would have been long dead if it weren't for her mother, who always kept a key to the studio with her. They worried about her behaviour and would insist every day that she sleep with them in the flat upstairs. They never left her by herself for long and would make up all sort of excuses to check up on her. Her mother would go down and offer her food and drink. She'd suggest they visit someone or go for a walk—anything— just to get her to the outside world. She was their only child, no brother or sister. She hadn't left the house for years, except with Nizam, and she no longer had any friends. Her mother was surprised that Nizam had made his way into her heart. They felt reassured whenever he was there. Janan changed in his presence and went back to being the daughter they once knew, laughing and playing. She would become approachable, before putting her guard up again and hiding out with her paintings, her tools, and that parrot of hers. She couldn't do without him. She said the parrot made her feel as if Nizam was there, and she'd wake him up if he fell asleep. The parrot didn't learn anything from her because she never spoke. She was going to take him with her. She insisted on having *him* too.

'Which hospital?'

The doctor had recommended that Janan be shielded from any emotional shocks. It was enough for her to have her mother and father with her. Her father was there and wouldn't leave her side for a second. Janan's mother didn't give him the name of the hospital. From the beginning, Nizam felt that he had arrived too late for something, since the decision had been made, and there was no need for him any more. He'd gotten used to that feeling lately—whatever happened had already happened.

Her mother talked about Janan's relationship with Nizam like a lost hope. She had straightened out the studio, gathered the paintings in the corner by the front door, put away the brushes and paints in cardboard boxes, and carried the parrot upstairs so she could feed him. She had collected Janan's art tools because the doctor had said that they would be of help with her treatment. Janan badly needed her tools. But the doctor preferred that they keep her away from her paintings or at least from the paintings she was in the midst of working on. If she insisted on painting again, it would have to be under the supervision of a doctor.

'A doctor!'

He had been treating her ever since they discovered that she'd been cutting her wrist 'for no reason', but they hadn't told him the story about her grandmother who had passed away under mysterious circumstances that were rarely discussed among the family. She had thrown herself off the roof of a building and landed on the pavement. Janan looked just like her; she was beautiful like her. When the latest round of fighting erupted, she started asking for Nizam and wanted him then, that very moment. She'd write him notes on scraps of paper—drafts of letters that couldn't reach him. Sentences in her own beautiful handwriting:

You are the sunshine of my life. You didn't say much, you didn't do much, but you lit up my barren land, which is good for nothing.

And this:

How can I imprison you? How can I surround you from the four directions? My colours are fading in your absence, and vile threatening creatures are advancing towards me at a rapid pace. There is no emergency exit.

She had written those notes the day before her attempted suicide. Janan would stand in front of her never-ending paintings, even when the explosions were rocking the entire neighbourhood. She would stand there with the brush in her hand, adding more and more—the grey was constant, and the blood red spread out or lightened, depending on the day and her mood. She just couldn't hold on. They rescued her on her last breath. She was lying on the sofa with her arm extended. Blood dripped from it onto the floor tiles as the parrot flapped its wings, letting out all sorts of sounds. They transported her to the hospital. They gave her blood in the ambulance. A brave paramedic from the Red Cross saved her life. That's what the doctors said when she arrived at the emergency room at the hospital. She would not be coming back to the studio any time soon.

He wanted to see her.

No one would be visiting her during the first stage except her parents. They planned to rent out her studio as a residential flat. Maybe they would give her back her art tools someday, if the doctor agreed. Maybe . . .

Janan's mother invited Nizam to spend the night there as he used to do sometimes. The crossings between the two sides of the city closed as soon as it got dark. She asked him to shut the door behind him on his way out in the morning.

He asked her to turn off the light for him.

He lay there stretched out on the sofa.

Indistinct sounds reached him.

He could hear the sound of footsteps from the floor above, a deep, uninterrupted rumble—little generators here and there on balconies—and an ambulance siren.

He got up, turned on the lights. He set up Janan's paintings, which her mother had nervously gathered up, without caring how they got knocked around, and placed in a pile near the door, as a first step towards banishing them and most likely getting rid of them altogether. He held them one by one. He lifted each one with both hands and raised it to eye level before choosing where to prop it up against one of the walls of the studio. He knew all their details. He lined them up in a semi-circle. He placed one of them up on the easel. He gently stroked the colours with his fingers. He completed the scene and then backed away. He turned the lights off and lay back down on the sofa, breathing in the colours' strong smell. He didn't catch a wink of sleep before the sun came up and light came creeping in early through the wide glass panel. Janan's paintings emerged gradually from the darknes of the night. Their features and colours began to intermingle, appearing before the eyes of Nizam, who was exhausted after a long day, much like Burj Square and the colours of the surrounding streets as he had seen them during his day trip with Raffoul.

Just before dawn, he fell asleep. He rolled over on the sofa and nearly fell onto the floor. He saw the blood-red colour flowing from cracks in the walls of the houses, from crevices in the windows, onto the middle of the streets. It emerged from the rain pipes that were visible down the sides of the buildings and from the flowerpots that Janan could not imagine any balcony being without. The stream of red widened, inundated the pavements and immersed the cars, like a heavy downpour during a rainstorm. An inexhaustible outpour flowed in the painting and began spilling onto the floor of the main room of the workshop where Nizam was standing like someone bracing himself to face the incoming surge. The colour of blood was rising from the bottom of the painting to the top of it, submerging the distant multi-storey building before inundating a little ficus tree or the streetlight in the foreground of the scene. In the studio where Nizam was holding up as best he could, the level of the blood-red colour began to rise little by little as if it were filling a smooth page too, in only two dimensions, covering Nizam's legs up to his knees. Stricken with fear and the desire to flee, Nizam, began to enter—from where he was standing in the middle of the studio—into the humanoid shapes with the obscure features that Janan had distributed here and there in the streets and at the entrances to buildings. He entered the empty outlines like a child who, having found the suitable wooden shape, places it into the spot designated for it, completing the scene. Nizam entered the empty shapes and gave them a face—his face—and a body, believing that he could hide inside them this way from the torrential flow that followed him wherever he went, reaching his torso and rising up to his shoulders, the red of the blood nearly reaching his mouth, drowning him, choking him. He woke up in a fright, propelled outside the studio.

He left the paintings standing upright and left. He shut the door behind him slowly as he breathed in the outside air. He made sure the door was shut well and went down the stairs slowly, on tiptoes. He didn't want to wake anyone up. He just wanted to get away. His face was exhausted from lack of sleep. The flower vendor hadn't opened her shop yet. He headed up Lebanon Street without looking around. He traversed the small streets of Achrafiyeh taking the shortest path he knew to the National Museum area—the pedestrian crossing between the two Beiruts. Anyone who saw Nizam al-Alami going on his way on that morning—with his back straight and his eyes wide-open, walking along the pavement on the right side of the street across from the military courthouse and the temporary Parliament headquarters, which people generally took to get to the western sector of the capital, whereas those crossing to the eastern side preferred the pavement on the other side near Qasr al-Snobar, the official residence of the French ambassador, and the horse racing track—anyone who saw him would not need to delve deeply into physiognomy to realize that this young man with the blond hair and blue eyes and beautiful face had his mind set on some grave matter.

PART FOUR

Firefly

1

The concierge was sitting on his chair in the building reception area waiting for Nizam to arrive.

'Your sister came to see you . . . '

She was worried about him. She would be back around noon. She didn't want him to stay there. She wouldn't have peace of mind until she saw him, until she held him in her own arms.

'One of your friends also came by.'

The friend with the soft voice. He had come by and left a letter for him.

'There's no avoiding the cold of Stockholm, no matter how long I put it off. 'Till we meet again someday, dearest Nizam. I envy your patience, your smile, and your love of life.'

It was signed: 'Chamoun Rikho, exile of all homelands, orphan of all friends.'

Nizam folded the letter. He slid it into the envelope and handed it back to the concierge as though it had been addressed to him.

The concierge took the letter absentmindedly; he, too, was bewildered.

His face spoke of other things that he was trying to figure out how to tell Nizam.

Nizam started for the lift, so the concierge tagged along.

He swore to God and the Prophet Muhammad that he'd tried to drive them away.

Nizam didn't ask who 'they' were.

'The very same men!'

They had come back in a small truck, the day before, early that night. One of them pointed the Kalashnikov at his chest.

'Thugs!'

Nizam opened the door of the flat. The concierge followed him inside with apprehension.

They'd filled up the truck and left.

They'd taken the pictures but left St George.

The concierge presumed they wouldn't dare steal him. Muslims believe in him; they call him 'Al-Khidr'. They were probably afraid some harm would befall them if they messed with St George.

Nizam took one last look at the face of the boy saint wearing the Roman helmet that had been punctured by the bullet from the Makarov. St George didn't seem capable of hurting anyone.

They toured through the flat, the concierge taking stock of the things they'd left behind.

There was a pair of woman's sandals with a narrow high heel tossed in the middle of the bedroom. They'd taken the double bed. When they had lifted it up, the sandals happened to be there underneath. Olga must have shoved them under the bed at one time and forgotten about them.

The concierge found the samovar.

'They left this too!'

'Take it . . . ' said Nizam. Then, a little while later he added, 'Take everything they left behind.'

'What should I do with St George?'

'Don't worry about him. He'll look after himself . . . '

When he saw Nizam going out through the flat door and heading for the lift, the concierge asked, 'And what about you? What will you do?'

He walked. He wandered about, pale.

He passed in front of the theatre. He saw that the door was wide open, so he went inside.

Posters for the play *The Cherry Orchard* were still hanging on the bulletin board. It had played for three nights before the infamous Palm Sunday explosion, before all the actors scattered back to their own neighbourhoods.

He could hear some sounds behind the curtains. He sat down in the dark. The seat was plush—thick red velvet. His body relaxed. He settled down. He let go, worn out and empty, but he didn't fall asleep. His day—his waking hours—weren't over yet.

The music started soft and sweet, emerging from the darkness and rising little by little as a steady circle of light appeared on the stage. Suddenly, the mime—with his face painted bright white—entered on tiptoe with his arms stretched wide. He scurried over to stand in the middle of the circle of light that had been drawn for him.

He smiled to the audience, not noticing Nizam was there. He was performing to an empty auditorium, but he acted as though he was being watched by a large crowd. He stands on one leg, stretches his hand up high, twirls around like a ballerina, and then sits down. He sits on the air, on a bench, possibly a wooden bench. He whistles out of boredom. He greets the pedestrians strolling through the public garden with an exaggerated bow of his head. He looks at his left wrist. He is waiting for someone he's made an appointment with. He bounces his knee. He loses his patience, and then his face reveals a wide smile. His beloved has arrived.

He makes some room for her beside him on the bench. He coaxes her, talks to her, caresses her gently. He passes his hand behind her shoulders and welcomes her arm, which he wraps around his neck. He kisses her, lips against lips, a long and excessively passionate kiss to the accompaniment of the music. He moves his hands around behind her back. He pays no heed to the strolling pedestrians. Lovers are entitled to their freedom in public parks. The embrace continues, along with the sighs and smiles of joy and hand gestures. The music stops all of a sudden, and so the loiterer in the park falls off the bench onto the wooden stage floor. The dust flies up and he finds himself all alone, hugging himself, his arms wrapped around his own shoulders. He begs the audience to pity him, to console him. His eyes well up with tears. His act comes to an end as the music stops, to be followed by the gradual vanishing of the circle of light surrounding him; the clown enters final darkness, and Nizam gives him a round of applause.

He practiced there every day. He even came amid the bombing sometimes. He didn't know when he would perform his pantomime act or even if the Beirut Theatre would ever reopen its doors to audiences.

He walked out with Nizam and asked him where he lived.

'I used to live there!' he said, pointing to the west.

Starting to feel cold, he smiled to the actor and went on his way.

Nizam walked, searching for the sun. He found it nearby, up on a wide pavement.

He stopped and looked up into the sky, bathing his face in the light. He steadied his gaze on the sun's disc, staring until he was forced to shut his eyes as the particles of light continued to flicker for a long time against the darkness of his eyelids.

He repeated the challenge until he couldn't see any more. Light exploded in his eyes, but he felt warm. He felt the desire to lie down and curl up right there on the ground out of weariness. He settled for sitting down on the doorstep of a restaurant that had shut down; its menu was still posted on the front door. He shut his eyes for a long time, buried his face in his hands in order to retrieve some blackness so he could resume looking at the sky.

He didn't hear the voice calling him, shouting at him from the other side of the street.

The guard at the entrance to the unfinished high-rise building had started surveilling Nizam the moment he stepped onto the pavement. The guard observed every move from where he was sitting, on top of a rusty barrel with his weapon propped up against the wall beside him. He amused himself with the passers-by, hit on a young woman crossing all alone, frowned in the faces of the busybodies. He knew everyone who entered the building and everyone who exited it. He was bored.

Nizam, who was peering at the sun with full force, happened to also be staring with the same persistence—without knowing it—at the headquarters of Harakat al-Afwaj al-Wataniyya—the 'National Regiments Movement'. The Movement had taken over the building and turned it into its headquarters. They planted their flag up on top of the thirtieth floor. The giant crane was still towering in the sky next to it. They plastered their slogans and pictures of their fallen warriors all over the concrete walls. The hero of the Battle of the Souqs. The martyr of the Battle of the Hotels. Young men with moustaches. Piercing stares. Determined.

The guard whistled to a colleague of his who was standing nearby. He pointed out Nizam who was busy burning his eyes in the April sunlight. The armed man started to cross the street. A passing car stopped to make way for him.

'What are you doing here?' he asked Nizam sharply.

'Getting some sun,' answered Nizam, looking in the direction of the source of the voice without seeing its owner because of his continued sun blindness. He tried again to look at the sun if only for one second, to prove what he'd said.

Then the inevitable happened. The militiaman thought he was mocking him.

'What are you looking at?' he asked, twice as sharply.

'The sun.'

That tipped the scales with the Afwaj Wataniyya gunman.

He pointed his rifle at Nizam and told him to get up and come with him.

Nizam did as he was told. He walked in front of the armed man without hesitation. The little grains of light still flickered in his eyes. He walked, avoiding the patches of shadow cast by the buildings, trying to stay under the sunlight.

At the door to the building, the militiaman pointed to Nizam's head and then motioned with his hand as if he was shaking a rattle. He was trying to convey to the guard sitting on the barrel that the young man walking in front of him was not quite right.

'What's your name?' the guard asked with contempt.

It appeared as if Nizam didn't hear.

He repeated the question, agitated.

No answer.

He asked him what he was looking at.

'The sun,' answered Nizam.

The militiaman repeated his previous gesture to the guard, letting him know the man wasn't normal. The guard assured him that they would 'sun him' in their own way.

'Where did you come from?'

'The theatre,' he answered directly. 'Over there.'

'Give me your ID,' he said, trying to catch him off guard.

He didn't move and didn't answer.

They both tried to figure out how to deal with him.

'Where do you reside?'

'I don't reside any more . . . '

They both laughed and then continued on.

'Were you spying on us?'

'On you?'

His innocence confused them.

'Where are you from?'

Silence.

They deliberated about him close enough for Nizam to hear.

The armed man who had brought him over wanted to let him go; he couldn't really find any cause for concern. But the guard worried that Nizam's innocence was all an act and wanted to investigate him.

'Take him to Abu Jaafar . . . '

The armed man grumbled. Abu Jaafar was on the tenth floor.

The armed man suggested again that they let Nizam go.

No lift. Just a big hole in the midst of construction where the lift was going to be.

He grabbed Nizam by the arm and headed with him towards the stairs. All the tasks had been falling on him. He was fed up.

They ran into some militia members and some civilians whose voices reverberated as they came down the stairs. As they went up, Nizam walked in front as if he was the one who was eager to get there. The armed man would stop him every three flights of stairs so that he could catch his breath. Determined, Nizam climbed up the stairs, pushing his body to the limit.

The armed man sat him down on a chair next to him. They waited for Abu Jaafar for half an hour as they sat across from a wooden door that had the sentence 'Please don't throw toilet paper into the toilet' scribbled on it.

The armed man asked Nizam—nicely—about his name again. It was as if Nizam couldn't hear him.

'They're going to make you talk,' he said, feeling sorry for him.

Abu Jaafar was sitting behind a desk that looked like the kind found in government offices. A pile of papers sat in front of him, and he had a pen in his hand. He had fat fingers, so the thin pen kept slipping out of his hand.

The armed man told Abu Jaafar that they started suspecting Nizam when they saw him roaming around the headquarters and looking right and left. Abu Jaafar didn't raise his head to look up from his papers until the armed man mentioned that the detainee refused to divulge his identity. It was as if everything else that had been said—before this one detail—was normal and not worth knocking at his door for.

He looked at Nizam. He noticed the exhaustion written all over his face and eyes. He asked him if he was from the neighbour-hood, but Nizam didn't budge. When Abu Jaafar asked Nizam if he was deaf or mute, the armed man said that the young man could speak, but that he would answer only some of their questions while refusing to answer others. To prove his point, he asked Nizam about his name, and Nizam didn't answer. He then asked him what he was doing across from the headquarters, to which Nizam replied automatically, 'I was looking at the sun.'

Abu Jaafar stood up behind his desk and then approached Nizam. He was going to devote some time to dealing with this weirdo.

He asked Nizam again about his name, as if giving him one last chance.

When Nizam didn't answer, Abu Jaafar slapped him on the face.

He had slapped Nizam with his heavy hand with such force that he was propelled towards the wall and would have fallen to the ground if he hadn't regained his composure and managed, with some difficulty, to get back on his feet.

He had not warned him. He hadn't gotten angry. He hadn't lifted his arm up in preparation for the slap. He'd swiftly drawn his hand and slapped him. He was a pro.

Abu Jaafar had bet on the impact of the shock to do the trick.

Nizam remained silent. He didn't even raise his hand to his left cheek to feel the spot where it hurt.

Abu Jaafar liked to hit the iron while it was still hot. He quickly dealt Nizam a second slap, but Nizam was a little readier for it this time. It shook him a little, but it didn't make him lose his balance.

The armed man tried nicely to convince Nizam to cooperate, but he didn't respond.

Abu Jaafar dismissed the man who had accompanied Nizam to the tenth floor after he inquired again about the reason for detaining the suspect. It was as if Abu Jaafar had not been listening the first time around. He called two of his assistants.

'Search him,' he said, resorting to preliminary measures first.

He had initially hesitated about searching Nizam since he was only wearing a shirt and trousers. He couldn't be hiding any weapons.

He repeated his orders, 'Take everything out of his pockets.'

The pocket watch—Touma's watch. It had stopped again.

Money. A big wad of cash—what was left of the money that
Touma had given him the last time they'd met. New bills that had
gotten a little wrinkled. Abu Jaafar stared at the money, flipping
the bills between his fingers, as if trying to guess how much
was there.

A small leather wallet in his back pocket.

Abu Jaafar gestured to his assistant to hand it to him quickly.

He took out the photograph of the woman first.

'Who's this?'

'Janan Salem.'

'Nice to meet her,' he said. 'Who is she?'

Nizam elaborated, 'Her eyes are different colours. One eye is
blue, and the other is chestnut brown. If you look closely, you can
tell there's a difference even in this black-and-white photo . . . '

Nizam was making Abu Jaafar lose his temper and become
more curious. He resumed looking through the small wallet.

He took out the small plastic ID. He saw the cedar symbol of
the Lebanese Front. He knew that cedar very well. He shook his
head for a long time and then pushed his chair back. He crossed
one leg over the other. It didn't take that Abu Jaafar very long to
get what he wanted.

He stood up and approached Nizam as he waved the ID in
front of his face, threatening.

'Joseph Safi, huh?'

Nizam had stuck the ID Janan's father had given him in his
wallet and forgotten all about it. It had gone into a black hole.
He missed Janan and would contemplate her picture sometimes—
that look of hers, how perfect she was, her beauty. His uncontrol-
lable desire for her came down to her perfectly harmonious
features. He'd get his fill of her picture and then put it back in his
wallet. Not once did he notice the ID in there.

'Search him again.'

The tender young man who stood in front of them in surrender and who was obstinate only with his responses— maybe he was a drug addict who came from a rich family in the neighbourhood and had gotten lost, or maybe he was a patron of the nearby bars who had been out all night—was transformed in the blink of an eye, after the discovery of what Abu Jaafar thought was his true identity, into a serious threat that should not be taken lightly.

Like reverberating echoes, a series of orders poured over Nizam. He had to raise his arms, spread his legs apart, turn his face towards the wall, and undo his belt all at once.

Nizam had become a legitimate enemy, and nothing was off-limits. Nizam's sitting on the pavement and looking at the barren building where the Afwaj Wataniyya were stationed, his insistence on staying mum about his identity, and his naïve proclamations had acquired new, interconnected meanings.

Following a long-established signal from Abu Jaafar, the assistants blindfolded Nizam, tied his hands behind his back, and took him to another room. Before identifying Nizam, they had been at loss as to how to deal with him, but now they were able to treat him as they had treated all the others from the opposite side who had fallen prey in their hands.

They took him up two flights of stairs, pushing him as he stumbled on the untiled steps. He fell twice since he couldn't see where to put his feet. Exhausted, he let his body relax, saving his remaining energy for the next imminent confrontation.

He wouldn't see Abu-Nar, Father of Fire, with his own eyes. They were just trying to scare the blindfolded Nizam by repeating Abu-Nar's name.

'He was gathering information about the headquarters. He has a Lebanese Front ID . . . '

298 | JABBOUR DOUAIHY

That was the report that the militiaman who brought Nizam into the new room had given. He handed the ID that they'd found on Nizam to Abu-Nar and dumped Nizam as someone would discard a bag of trash, by the tips of his fingers, while trying not to look at the spot where it landed.

Abu-Nar's tone of voice was a lot less brutal than his nickname suggested.

They made Nizam stand up on his feet,

They forbade him from sitting,

He couldn't stop panting.

Abu-Nar addressed Nizam by the name 'Joseph Safi', and Nizam didn't correct him.

He promised Nizam that he would teach those who had sent him to spy a lesson they'd never forget.

He threatened to throw him from all the way up there—or even from the thirtieth floor—if he refused to talk.

They had thrown others before him.

One of the men struck Nizam on the shoulders with the butt of his rifle without asking him anything. Nizam didn't see it coming. He fell to the floor.

They got him to stand up again. They tightened his blindfold.

Blood streamed from his forehead. He turned white.

They bombarded him:

His real name?

His age?

His hometown?

His address?

The names of the party leaders in charge of him?

The type of weapon he had?

His father's name?

Every question came with a punch.

Every question came with a curse.

He was an easy but elusive target.

He was so exhausted he could no longer talk.

He did say—whispering so quietly that they had to stop yelling so they could hear him—that he had two fathers, so they mocked him. Then he said he had two mothers, so they beat him.

They beat him because they felt helpless, because they couldn't get one meaningful word out of him.

Then Abu-Nar beat him.

He hit him on the head with his gun.

As Nizam collapsed, he waved his hands trying to find something to hold on to. They stepped away from him. They didn't support him.

He fell, but he didn't scream.

He hit the ground.

Motionless.

2

Maysaloun and Mustapha went back to the Manara neighbour-hood. The concierge at Nizam's building pointed them downhill in the direction of the theatre, and the mime showed them where Nizam had sat on the pavement. They crossed the street to the Afwaj Wataniyya building, where the guard exchanged some words with those on the top floors via intercom and then gestured to his colleague to escort the couple upstairs. Another sad and brutal trip to the tenth floor.

'I'm looking for my brother. His name is Nizam al-Alami.'

'We don't have anyone by that name.'

After Maysaloun insisted and described Nizam to them in detail, they brought her the ID.

'This *is* his picture,' she said. 'But that's not his name.'

'How's that possible?'

'His name is Nizam al-Alami,' she said. 'I'm his sister, Maysaloun, and this is my husband, Mustapha Hijazi. And my brother's name is Bilal, after the prophet's muezzin. My other brother is Khaled . . . '

The man left, sullen. He came back, sullen.

'Your brother didn't help us out . . . '

She became emotional. She feared the worst.

'Where is he?' she asked. 'I want to see him.'

'You can't see him now . . . We're in a state of war,' the man said. 'We found a Lebanese Front ID on him. He was spying on the headquarters.'

She mocked them for making that accusation. She sensed the tragedy.

'Her brother is a Muslim?' One of the militiamen whispered to Mustapha in disbelief.

A higher-up wearing a tie showed up, accompanied by two bodyguards in military clothing.

'Al-Awad bi-Salamitkun . . . Sorry for your loss' he said.

Maysaloun screamed for help. Mustapha grabbed hold of her. They didn't hear the man as he went on defending his group's behaviour. Collapsing, she sat down. She had been scared since the morning. She smacked herself on the head, cried, and asked out loud about how she was going to tell her mother, what she was going to say to Rakheema and Touma and her aunt Najeeha. She lauded Nizam's eyes, his hair, his politeness, and his generosity, and then she demanded to see him. They tried to dissuade her, but she insisted.

The room's cement walls were unpainted, and there was a gap in one of the walls but no window—just a blue plastic sheet that served as a curtain to keep the light out. They had covered Nizam in a green wool blanket, likely confiscated from one of the army barracks that had fallen into the hands of the militias. They had made some room for him by moving some things to one end of the table—loose, blank papers torn out of notebooks, pens for jotting down the confessions of those they brought into this dreadful room for questioning, small, round coffee cups—some of which had been overturned upon being moved aside, causing some of their sticky black contents to drip onto the table—and cigarette butts that had been stubbed out into tissues. There was a discarded pair of shoes with socks stuffed inside them in the corner.

Mustapha grabbed Maysaloun as he tried to stop her from seeing Nizam, but she pulled the blanket off him and looked upon his face. Her heart broke.

'They beat you, abibi, my darling!'

She bent over him, kissed his forehead, unbuttoned his shirt, and touched the chain that was still around his neck.

She yanked it and started to wail repeatedly, 'They searched him. Why didn't they find Ayat al-Kursi?'

Mustapha approached Nizam, grabbed his right hand, and raised his index finger. He hesitated a little before pointing Nizam's finger in the direction where he assumed the qibla was. He closed his eyes and whispered to himself, 'Ashhadu alla ilaha illAllah wa ashhadu anna Muhammadan rasul Allah.'

Maysaloun noticed what he was doing and tried to stop him.

'What are you doing?' she said. 'You're a religious expert now?'

She collapsed on top of Nizam, caressing his face and hair, as Mustapha tried to pull her away from him.

She cried until she finally surrendered. Mustapha walked her out of the room.

He tried to be practical.

'We'll bury him here in Beirut,' he said. 'In Bashoura Cemetery, on the Hijazis' burial grounds.'

'No . . . ' she yelled.

She didn't want to bury him with the Hijazis. He had nothing to do with Bashoura. And why Beirut? What did he reap from Beirut?

'We'll take him to the North . . . '

She hesitated a little before making up her mind about something. Addressing Mustapha, she added, 'I'll take him myself. It's not your business. Tomorrow morning.'

They transported him to the nearest hospital and ordered a casket. Early the next morning, a long black car, with the words 'Organization for Honoring the Dead, An Affiliation of the Islamic Charity Association, Registration No. K/121' written on it, showed up.

No one knew exactly who had called for the hearse.

Maysaloun spent the night perched on one of the emergency room beds since the nurses had insisted that she lie down.

The driver of the hearse wouldn't go north. His religious affiliation was marked in capital letters. He was worried about putting himself in danger since he would have to pass through a large Christian area. Just two days before, they had found a corpse that had been thrown off a bridge on the coastal road.

Mustapha Hijazi offered the driver some money, but he declined apologetically. He couldn't violate the organization's guidelines.

The hospital owned only one emergency vehicle that it couldn't do without. The only alternative was to hire a regular cab—with a cargo carrier—whose driver would be willing to make the trip by crossing to East Beirut and from there on to Tripoli, and then come back the same way. They finally found a driver, who asked for an inflated fee in compensation for all the dangers involved.

Back in Mina, in the eyes of the city's residents, that Monday morning seemed strange and depressing, as it was enveloped by something that looked like fog but that didn't really have a name. Even the older folks had not witnessed anything like it before except once maybe, during the Palestinian Nakba that had prompted thousands of refugees to flood the city. The fog that assailed the city swiftly—as if discovering it for the first time—came in scattered, lost white puffs that explored the town before surrounding the buildings and ficus trees planted all along the pavements.

Despite the weather, Castro noticed early and unusual activity in the direction of the al-Alami household.

They had nicknamed him Castro because his eldest brother had immigrated to Cuba and remained there, as he was content living with less and had adapted to the Socialist regime. Castro—for no reason other than family solidarity—became a supporter of the small island that stood its ground in the face of the Americans. During his free time, Castro volunteered at the Volunteer Emergency Services, where he sometimes worked at the office answering the phone or drove one of the three ambulances that the Kingdom of Saudi Arabia had donated to the organization. He had courageously transported the wounded from areas that witnessed heavy bombings and clashes.

Castro would open the café by himself early in the morning before the young man who worked for him arrived. He would drink espresso with no sugar, smoke, cough in order to get the gunk out of his chest from the previous night's smoking, read the paper, call for the shoeshine boy, receive his first customers, and follow the activity on the street outside.

Maysaloun was gone. Castro hadn't been able to stop her from leaving, but he would still be on alert every time he'd catch a glimpse of her returning to her family's home for a visit during one truce or another in Beirut, whenever the roads were manageable. One time she came by herself. Castro felt encouraged, continued to watch her comings and goings diligently, and then waved at her from across the street. She dropped by his café. As she stood by the door of the café, his heart started to beat faster, and she noticed the sparkle in his eyes when he invited her inside for a cup of coffee. She made him nervous, and he liked her sad-looking face. She asked him how he was doing and why he didn't have a wife yet. He stuttered and didn't know how to talk to her and get her to stay longer. He just settled for smiling and being a good host. It always went like that. Every time he tried to flirt with her, he'd end up sticking to small talk. She sipped her coffee quickly and left, but some of his past infatuation with her still hung in the air between them.

During Maysaloun's semi-permanent absence, Castro paid close attention to the al-Alamis. He monitored them without meaning to, just because they were her family and warmed his heart with their daily activities that he'd gotten used to watching. The twins were finally going to the travel agency—leaving in the morning and returning at noon—and, around ten, Sabah would go out for a visit or a walk. He even followed the comings and goings of the girl they had hired to help Sabah.

Najeeha, Mahmoud al-Alami's sister, was the first one who showed up in black clothes on that foggy day. She was emotional, and she looked like she was about to start beating her chest with her hand. A little while later, she was followed by Maysaloun's other aunt, Zayneddar, who also looked troubled. He knew the sisters, but he hadn't seen them in a long time. Initially, he thought that the issue had to do with Sabah, who had been taken a few days earlier to the Islamic Hospital and was still there.

Sabah had fallen down as she was going down the last three steps leading to the main street, right before she'd reached the pavement planted with the tedious ficus trees. It was hard for her—as a woman who was always mindful of the way she sat and in control of her gait—to admit that her fall wasn't just a slip that could happen to anyone. Her body had gotten away from her, finally avenging its long history of compliance. That was probably the hardest part for her.

Castro was the first one to reach her. They transported her to the hospital, where the young doctor who treated her insisted that she tripped because her pelvis had broken, causing her to fall down, and not the other way around.

'It's osteoporosis, Madame.'

He recommended that she remain immobile, and he was going to wait for a few days before deciding whether she needed surgery.

She started feeling some pain while she was lying on the bed, with Bilal keeping her company and not leaving her side. She talked and talked. At one point, she ran out of things to say and just yelled, 'I want Nizam.'

Her loud tone of voice coincided with a bout of sharp pain.

She adjusted the way she was sitting, asked for a glass of water, and demanded that her eldest son be brought to her—wherever he was. She had fallen down and then woke up with Nizam on her mind. She talked to distract herself from the pain, recalling her entire life in front of Bilal—what she owed others and what was owed to her. Mahmoud never even let her breathe, and the whole idea about spending the summers in Hawra was something Mahmoud had planned in order to keep them away for three months so he could be left to his own devices, unsupervised. She did not say that she wanted to see Nizam before she died, but rather that she had something very important to tell him.

That Monday morning—which had been deserted by the seagulls who had escaped the small clouds that the wind scattered in all directions—Bilal was at a loss about how he was going to show up at the hospital, as he usually did every morning, and tell his mother Sabah the news. The young maid beat him to it. She arrived at the hospital, on foot, after she had been surprised by the morning visitors with sad faces. She didn't know what to do, so she rushed to her boss to tell her that her two sisters-in-law had arrived at the house dressed in black, along with some neighbours, and that Khaled and Bilal had not gone to the travel agency.

'Nizam is dead?' Sabah yelled in the face of the young maid who didn't know about Nizam, except for what Sabah had mentioned about him from time to time. She didn't know how to respond, or how to deny that, but Sabah was certain. Nizam had been haunting her for days, ever since the day she fell down.

Her heart burned, and she wanted to leave. She veered her body towards the edge of the bed—as pain and terror dug into her face—and with some difficulty managed to get up on her bare feet. She tried to pick up one of the ironed dresses that had been flung across the chair next to the bed, in preparation for an emergency or a sudden departure from the hospital. She leaned on the maid and tried to walk; she didn't want to stay at the hospital. Sabah took one step at a time, with the help of the maid who had no idea how she had caused so much chaos. The pain was intolerable, and Sabah felt her soul leave her body every time her feet touched the floor. She resisted, but the pain rose to her heart and she fell flat on her face, passing out on the floor. The maid screamed. The nurses rushed to Sabah, trying to revive her and return her to the bed, as blood streamed down her face. She broke her nose and upper teeth . . . They returned her to the bed, gathered around her, hooked her up to an IV, and gave her a sedative and some sleep medication before stitching her face as she went in and out of consciousness, crying out of pain—crying because of Nizam's death. She remembered that hot night, their very first night in Hawra. In between two bouts of pain, she spoke to the maid, who'd started crying without knowing exactly what was going on.

'It's as if Nizam is sitting right in front of me now . . . ' she said.

She made whistling sounds more than talked, her mouth aching. She blamed herself, saying she should have paid attention to Nizam's question.

'I just didn't know how to answer him,' she said. 'But I should have been more careful.'

She raised the arm without the IV towards the sky. 'Where is he?' she asked, hallucinating. 'He said he was walking on Port Said Street and people were laughing at him, and that I, his own mother, wasn't helping him . . . '

She wept silently. She resisted the medication that the nurses had injected into the IV, until sleep finally overpowered her. She lay down with her mouth open and dreamt that she was sitting in a movie theatre in Homs, with Mahmoud and the children— including Nizam—and watching the film *Blood and Sand*. Suddenly, she saw Nizam wearing a bullfighter's outfit, embellished with brightly coloured buttons, and a black hat. She saw him starring in the role of Tyrone Power, as he stood with his sword in hand in front of a raging bull. But instead of facing the imminent danger about to befall him, Nizam turned to give her the exact same look. He took off his hat and threw it behind him, smiling boastfully. The hat flew in the air, amid the applause, and landed in Sabah's hands. She screamed from the bottom of her heart, but her voice was muffled because the bull had dug its horns into the sand and charged towards the fighter.

Sabah woke up one more time before the nurse doubled up her sleep medication, causing her to drift into a deep sleep.

Around ten o'clock, Sheikh Ibrahim Hamza arrived. He extracted his large body from the front seat of the car, got up to his feet, huffing and puffing, and made it to the al-Alamis' flat, nearly dead. Castro was now certain that the situation involved death, so he left the café and crossed the street in order to join those headed to the al-Alamis' flat.

Najeeha and Zayneddar were in the living room with three other women from the building who had come to offer consolation and satisfy their curiosity. The women knew some of the chapters from Nizam's story. They looked at his aunts whose sadness was transformed to anger as soon as they'd heard the news. They held an old, unspoken grudge that absolved their own brother of any guilt while placing the blame on everybody else around him. Zayneddar shook her head, muttered under her breath, delegated responsibilities. Najeeha—who wouldn't stop crying—sat on the edge of her seat, her body upright, as if she was ready to leave her brother's house at any moment in protest of anything that she didn't approve of. Bilal told her that he wasn't going to tell his mother now since she was bound to a hospital bed and couldn't even move. Najeeha didn't agree with him, but she just shrugged her shoulders. If he had asked for her opinion, she would have advised him to tell his mother. It wasn't right for a mother to remain ignorant of her son's death. She whispered to Zayneddar that she wanted Sabah to shed tears of blood because of what she had done. They knew that Sabah had broken her hip, but they didn't visit her at the hospital. Something had broken between them a long time ago.

A handful of men gathered around the brothers in the living room where Castro had followed Sheikh Ibrahim Hamza. Castro shook the brothers' hands firmly, thinking that he was offering his condolences for the death of their mother. He sat next to a man who talked in a hushed voice about the strange fog that had forced the drivers passing through Mina to turn their headlights on.

Khaled was nervous. Silent, he rested his head in his hand. For one rare moment, he seemed hesitant and unsure of his feelings. He thought about all the things that he should do, but he had not been able to make any decisions since the phone rang at five in the morning. He had quickly gotten out of his bed to hear his brother-in-law Mustapha from Beirut say to him without any introductions, 'Sorry for your loss.'

Nizam's death was the last thing he had expected.

Mustapha only said that Nizam had died suddenly. An unexpected accident.

Khaled put on his clothes quickly, woke up Bilal, and told him the news. Bilal asked for details, pondered sadly, and waited for his brother to tell him what needed to be done, but Khaled couldn't take any action. He called his two aunts and decided to let things take their natural course and just let everybody behave as they saw fit. He sent after Sheikh Ibrahim Hamza—who was older than him and had more experience—since he consulted and listened to his advice on worldly and religious matters from time to time and had already discussed the subject of Nizam with him at length.

Sheikh Ibrahim started talking in a loud voice, trying to control a situation that he knew was difficult. When he asked about the body, Bilal told him that their brother-in-law and sister Maysaloun were transporting him from Beirut and that they probably wouldn't be running late since they had set out early.

The conversation caught Castro's attention. 'Who died?' he asked his neighbour.

'Their older brother . . . '

The man tried to say more, but he could not think of anything appropriate to add.

Sheikh Ibrahim said it was too late to print a death notice, without clarifying why it was too late.

He switched to generalizations—war-related incidents and the fall of innocent victims. He was not capable of anything except taking refuge in Quranic verses and proverbs that he would weave into an eloquent sermon that left his listeners shaking their heads in awe. With some difficulty, he got up again so he could take Khaled and Bilal aside in one of the interior rooms. He asked them what they wanted him to do; Bilal responded by saying that the Sheikh knew best. Sheikh Ibrahim sighed and said that never in his life had he faced such a situation. He did remember an occasion at the Great Mosque when Sheikh Muhammad al-Masri refused to pray over a French woman—who was married to a local doctor from the town—in front of the French authorities. She died in a traffic accident and Sheikh Muhammad knew she had not proclaimed her conversion to Islam.

He didn't commit himself to anything. 'We'll see. We'll pray over who's present . . . '

In Beirut, Mustapha used Nizam's money to pay the hospital bill plus a tip for the paramedics. Then they set about the task of lifting the casket. The driver, who was advanced in years, lacked the physical strength, and Mustapha lacked the experience of securing caskets on the tops of American model taxis. They made use of numerous ropes and a nurse who volunteered to do the tying and tightening, and an excessive amount of talking, too. He was the same nurse who had volunteered the day before to wash the corpse with warm water and wrap it in a shroud without asking anyone's permission, because he had seen that Nizam was circumcised. And he had heard the sister weeping and lamenting her brother's bad luck and how they killed him because they thought he was a Christian. Maysaloun took a seat in the old white Pontiac beside the driver, who was casting strange glances at her after discovering she was the dead man's sister. He prayed for God's help and glorified Him using all of the al-asmaa al-husna—99 names of Allah—that he had memorised before starting up the car amid the popping sounds of its older model engine. Mustapha— driven by his arrogance and his manhood—tried to get into the car with Maysaloun in order to join her on the journey, so she reiterated her refusal. Sitting in the car, she looked at her husband for a long time as it set out slowly to make sure the cargo was securely tied, while he stood at the front door of the

Emergency Department not knowing what to do. Her eyes, reddened from tears, were fixed on his eyes, but there was no word or motion of her hand to say goodbye. He walked in a stupor behind the car, his hand raised in the direction of his wife whom he'd let go just like that, all by herself, on a mission that the least one could say was a man's job.

The streets were empty, but the driver was forced to pull over a short while after taking off. That was at the last Wataniyya checkpoint before crossing to the other side. The armed man, who was wearing an American cowboy hat with pride, initiated a quick dialogue with Maysaloun.

'What do you have with you?'

'As you can see.'

'Who is he?'

'My brother . . . '

'I wasn't asking about the driver.'

'Yes, I know. He's my brother.'

Dubious silence. The armed man looked at the colourful dress she was wearing, which she hadn't thought to change, and then asked one last question.

'Where are you going?'

'To the North . . . '

After that, the armed man opened the back door of the car and stepped up to eye-level with the casket. He didn't open it but started pounding on it with his hand trying to determine the nature of its contents by listening to the echo produced by banging on the wood. He hit once and then a second time to be sure. He asked for their ID's and the car papers. He asked about hospital documents or a death certificate or something of that nature. He read everything, inspected everything, and let them go, unsatisfied.

They stopped the next time after several minutes, at the first Christian checkpoint on the other side. The men conducting the search insisted on opening the casket to make sure it didn't contain weapons or explosives, complaining as they searched that the week before some weapons had been smuggled inside a casket—one just like this one—weapons and possibly drugs, too, to the Palestinian Fedayeen in the Tel al-Zaatar camp. That smuggling operation had succeeded, and they were not about to be fooled a second time. They untied the ropes. One of them climbed up to the roof of the car to inspect what was inside, but no sooner did he open the lid a little than he averted his eyes and put the lid back on slowly. They tied it back up the way it was before, urging Maysaloun to try to understand their actions.

The driver surrendered his soul to its creator more than ten times and recited the Fatiha in a whisper at every checkpoint they stopped at and every time he heard the siren of an ambulance speeding by or came upon a military vehicle of one of the militias out on patrol. After pulling over with his cargo to a desolate spot on the side of the road—because he couldn't hold himself any longer thanks to the enlarged prostate he had been complaining of for some time now—he started grumbling about being hungry. He hadn't 'wet his whistle' since morning, but he was also apprehensive about stopping at any of the sandwich shops in those areas. He preferred to keep driving, so he pulled out a couple of sandwiches and an apple that he had brought on the long trip, just in case.

They were able to breeze through a checkpoint halfway between Beirut and Tripoli. The men on duty made the sign of the cross over their chests out of respect as they looked on sympathetically at the Pontiac. On its own like that—with no other car behind it or in front of it—it formed a very strange funeral procession. An onlooker might have assumed it was an empty casket tied on top of the car that was being delivered to the customer who ordered it. It would be hard to believe that the family of the deceased were the only ones with him, unaccompanied by a single friend, unconsoled by a single neighbour. Maysaloun wept again and again, and showed signs of fatigue, as the Pontiac slowly made its way and they finally reached the Cedars exit leading to the mountain towns. There, Maysaloun asked the driver to pull over to the right for a moment. He thought she might be feeling carsick on account of her distraught condition, but in reality, she was torn between which route to take her precious cargo. In the end, she gave up and opted for the coastal road leading straight to Tripoli.

Maysaloun arrived, and Nizam's corpse arrived, too.

Khaled looked through the window and spotted the casket tied up on top of the Pontiac, which was parked in front of the building entrance with its driver out of the car, ready and waiting. He called to his friend Sheikh Ibrahim to come look out the window. He promised he would summon those in charge of burying the dead to perform the necessary duties and said that it was unacceptable for him to be left like that out on the street.

Khaled and Bilal went out to their big sister. She embraced them at the door where they were waiting for her, and then she continued to the women's section. She asked about her mother. They told her about her broken pelvis.

'Don't tell her about Nizam,' she said. 'I will tell her myself.'

'The maid already told her . . .'

She didn't hear the rest of what was said. She was hugging Aunt Zayneddar, who was filled with sympathy for Maysaloun for having brought Nizam all the way from Beirut all by herself. Maysaloun saved Aunt Najeeha for last. She lay her head on her shoulder and then opened her hand in which she still held the gold chain that she had been holding onto since the moment she removed it from her brother's neck. She gave it to her aunt as she said, 'This is from Nizam!'

Najeeha examined it. She recognized it.

'Ayat al-Kursi . . . '

She burst into tears.

'Take it, Auntiy' Maysaloun added. 'It didn't do him any good . . . '

Sheikh Ibrahim Hamza dispelled the confusion that Maysaloun had created, challenging her from the men's section where her voice had reached him. He chided the woman, with the authority of a religious expert, quickly rattling off—like some school lesson he knew by heart: 'Every soul must taste death. This is the will of almighty God, and it is not our place to question divine providence.' Then he added, but in a different tone because what he was about to say was merely a theological judgement, that it was not desirable for a man to wear gold on his neck or wrist or fingers, and that these were fads that had nothing to do with Islam. Then he added that he would not face off with a *female*. And he did not hold himself back from saying, so as not to hurt his friend Khaled or add to the difficulties he was facing, that it was impossible for the 'Nasrani' (Christian) to seek protection through the verses of the Noble Quran. In all probability, Sheikh Ibrahim Hamza intentionally stirred up that dispute, finding it an excellent opportunity to excuse himself from having to pray over the person who was repeatedly declared by his brother Khaled to be a 'Nasrani'.

Maysaloun gave the sheikh a way out. 'I did not ask your opinion, and I am not interested in it, either. This is my brother, and no one has any say in that . . . '

Her voice emerged like a wail, like a slap, from where she was sitting—in her purple dress and with her head uncovered—between her two aunts who had had enough time to dress in black and put white scarfs on their heads. She could not see Sheikh Ibrahim, and he could not see her. Between the two rooms was a half wall and a wide sliding door that was open. Sheikh Ibrahim got up with the same difficulty as before and headed towards the door to leave, full of gloom. Castro got worked up in support of Maysaloun and started saying things directed at Sheikh Ibrahim. He was trying to defend her while also possibly hoping she would hear his voice, but Khaled firmly cut him off out of respect for his friend, whom he apologetically escorted outside. Castro thought it best to back down, but Maysaloun had heard his voice and gotten up from her seat to make sure it was him.

Sheikh Ibrahim withdrew, leaving Khaled and Bilal to deal with their problem. Meanwhile, the driver of the Pontiac waited for orders as he responded to questions from numerous curious bystanders about the identity of the deceased and the reason for his death at age twenty-three—according to the calculations of one of the neighbours who remembered how happy Mahmoud al-Alami had been the day Nizam was born.

They were not used to seeing a dead man tied on top of a car, so they started offering to help get him down and carry him into the house or the mosque. The driver listened to all their advice while thinking about what was in store for him on his return trip to Beirut all by himself.

It was nearing time for noon prayers, so Khaled pondered silently one last time and then whispered to Bilal.

'We will pray over him here, at al-Bahr Mosque . . .' he said.

'Who will pray over him?' Bilal asked.

'I will . . .' Khaled said.

Bilal recalled their quarrel over the inheritance. Khaled looked at his wristwatch and said, 'It's almost time for the noon prayers. We won't be late. "To honour the dead is to bury them . . . " '

Then he added, 'How can we leave him on top of the car like this?'

He then asked Maysaloun in a loud voice if they had shrouded him. Her answer came in the same manner as her last utterance. Sharp, in the same tone as her battle with Sheikh Ibrahim.

'They killed him, and we washed him and wrapped him in a shroud . . . '

Khaled stood up, as did Bilal, and so Castro and the others followed them. The women remained seated.

The Beiruti driver never would have imagined that the half dozen men who came out from the building constituted the entire funeral procession had they not stopped beside the car so that Bilal could ask him to drive ahead of them slowly. The scantiness of the procession became obvious when they stepped onto the wide pavement, even though a passer-by headed for the fish market and two young men who frequented Castro's café were quickly added into the fold, out of curiosity. The 'procession' marching behind the son of Mahmoud Yasser al-Alami got mixed in with pedestrians strolling along the sea road. They became interspersed with them, especially since Khaled was walking quickly by himself ahead of everyone. He wanted to be done with a spectacle he did not want for himself or his family. Meanwhile the morning fog dissipated, and flocks of seagulls went back to sketching little circles in the sky overhead. The crews of anchored ships leaned on the handrails, watching the city's movements. Fishing boats were scattered here and there out to sea.

Maysaloun whispered something to the concierge's son, who then ran up behind the men. Castro—the overweight smoker—flanked the rear.

'Maysaloun wants to talk to you . . . '

'Now?'

'Yes, now. She told me not to come back without you . . . '

It was the first time Maysaloun ever requested something from Castro. His love for her was still concealed, waiting expectantly with him in the little café across from the entrance to the building where the al-Alami family lived.

He went to her without hesitation.

It was a short distance to reach the mosque. Everyone in attendance, except Khaled and Bilal, helped lower the casket from the car. They carried it from all sides and set it down where Mahmoud al-Alami had been shrouded. One of them suggested taking the body out of the casket, but Khaled refused. They were satisfied with lifting the lid off and then turning Nizam's head towards the qibla as they were accustomed to doing.

The driver did not take part in the prayers. He wasn't waiting for orders from anyone after Maysaloun disappeared. He gathered up the ropes and put them in the trunk. He repeated the Bismillah once more and took off for Beirut with the hope of eventually making it safely to his distant home.

Maysaloun rushed towards Castro when she saw him standing at the door, panting, too, from climbing the stairs.

He felt her presence. His heart trembled once again.

He offered his condolences. She thanked him.

'Are you still in the Volunteer Emergency Services?'

He was excited to be teaming up with her on whatever it was she wanted.

'Could you bring a vehicle? Drive it yourself?'

He didn't ask why. He only asked where she wanted it.

'We will take Nizam for a drive—just you and me, by ourselves . . . '

He didn't like what she was saying and didn't like her tone. He was worried about her. He opened his hands and said, 'As you wish . . . '

She asked him to hurry and pick up the casket after they finished praying over him.

'And if you can, before they pray over him . . . '

His concern for her grew. He didn't know her well in any case. Since he'd met her, they hadn't exchanged but a few words. Maybe she was always like that.

He gave in to his emotions and his solidarity with her. He asked her where they were going to bury him.

'They think he's a Christian . . . '

'Is he a Christian?'

'I don't know what he is. He's my brother . . . I will take him off their hands.'

Castro hesitated. He didn't exactly understand what she was calling on him to do.

'If you love me, hurry up, because they are going to finish the prayers quickly. They're besides themselves trying to be rid of him . . . '

She had resorted to pulling out the big guns.

'If you love me . . . '

She knew he loved her to the extent that he would not refuse any request from her.

Was it because of those glances he cast at her from his café or because he got flustered whenever he spoke to her on those rare occasions?

For so long, Castro believed that his attachment to Maysaloun al-Alami was a condition he lived in all by himself with no partner, one of his few passions that had turned hopeless the day she met that Beiruti with the old-fashioned accent, despite being a university graduate, and he asked for her hand in marriage, something no one opposed because there wasn't anyone in the al-Alami household to oppose—or accept—the proposal.

'Hurry, Castro . . . '. She even tossed him a flirtatious smile.

He would not escape from her.

He looked at his watch.

'Meet me in fifteen minutes behind the café, at the top of Port Said Street . . . '

She put her hand on his hand and squeezed it. 'I'll head down the pavement on the right side of the street.'

He took off as quickly as he could. He set up his plan as he went down the stairs with a nimbleness he was not known for. He advised his assistant to close the café at 8 p.m. and go home if he was late getting back. He headed for the Volunteer Emergency Services Center next to the municipality building. He told the man sitting behind the desk that he needed to take a relative to the hospital. They owed him a lot. He had been an unpaid volunteer; even when the battles were raging, he wasn't deterred. He took the keys to the ambulance from the desk drawer, started the motor but didn't turn on the siren. He didn't want to draw attention. Five minutes and he was pulling up beside al-Bahr Mosque, where there was no trace of a hearse or any other ambulance.

Khaled and Bilal were improvising in Sheikh Ibrahim's absence. Castro stopped the ambulance where he usually saw the hearses parked—at the spot closest to where the deceased was shrouded and prayed over—and sat waiting behind the wheel.

It appeared to anyone watching the scene of the prayers for the dead, which Khaled al-Alami was leading on his own with one row or half a row of worshippers behind him, that someone had made burial arrangements and had sent the ambulance to transport the body, especially since the cemetery where the al-Alami family members were buried was much too far to reach on foot.

3

Castro got out of the ambulance. The funeral prayers came in quick succession, as if they were a heavy burden the worshippers wanted to be rid of. If Castro hadn't heard the prayers dozens of times before, he would not have understood a thing. They sped through asking God to spread open the deceased's grave and fill it with light, make it into a garden, wash it with water and snow and hail, and cleanse him of sins just as the white robe is cleansed of stains . . .

When they reached the final prayer, 'Give him in exchange a family better than his family and a home better than his home,' Castro opened the rear door of the ambulance in preparation for receiving the deceased.

One of the worshippers closed the casket. They lifted it up and loaded it into the ambulance. One of the young café customers tried to get in the ambulance next to Castro. He was looking forward to driving through the streets, turning on the sirens and playing Quranic verses on the loudspeaker, but Castro pulled the door shut from inside and motioned to him that he wanted to drive alone. He took off without giving a signal. They would assume he was taking the casket to the cemetery and that anyone who wished to follow him could do so in their own cars. He headed out in the direction of the cemetery, watching in the rear-view mirror as the worshippers parted ways and Khaled and Bilal gestured to him to wait. Once they disappeared from view in the mirror, he turned around, taking a left behind the fish shop. He headed down the street where the municipality was located, and from there to the bottom of Port Said Street. That way he would be facing Maysaloun directly.

Maysaloun pretended she needed to go into the bedroom to rest a little and to find a black dress in her mother's closet to wear, but she only went as far as the bathroom. She looked at her face in the mirror and searched for some dark glasses. She found a pair in one of the drawers. She went into the kitchen where she found the maid trying to attend to all the women's demands. She stopped her and urged her to go to the hospital and tell her mother that it was Nizam who wished for that. She didn't trust the maid. She wanted her to memorise the message by heart.

'Repeat it. What will you say to her?'

The maid repeated, 'Mother, Nizam is the one who wished for that from beginning to end. Don't put the responsibility on yourself. Maysaloun will take care of him because she has known his desires since he was little.'

She made her repeat it twice. She did not let her finish making the coffee. She turned the burner off and insisted on watching her go out the door. She told her to also tell her mother that she would come back to see her soon. Today or tomorrow at the latest.

Maysaloun gulped down a lot of water and then slipped out too. She put on the sunglasses and walked off without looking back. Castro saw her from a distance walking briskly down the opposite pavement. He turned the car around and pulled up in front of her. She looked around and then climbed into the seat beside him. She thanked him and urged him to drive out of the city heading south.

'I will explain on the way . . . '

He took off, but she didn't explain anything.

He obeyed her, even though he had grown extremely anxious about the mission she was undertaking.

They exited the city. She told him to take the mountain road.

He should have warned her about the dangers of that road, but he didn't want to appear more cautious than she was, so he drove the Volunteer Emergency Services ambulance without asking more questions.

Never had Castro been awarded a chance to be alone with Maysaloun—until now, with her brother escorting them, stretched out in his casket.

It wasn't until after Nizam had left for his new parents for good that Castro opened the café. He'd heard parts of the story and might have seen Nizam once. He was with a pretty, young woman who had strange looks and strange eyes. They appeared to be completely smitten with each other. He would kiss her hand, and she would kiss his. They drank coffee, spoke together in whispers, and left.

Castro amassed the courage to ask some pertinent questions.

'How did your brother die?'

'He didn't die. They killed him . . . '

He asked her why she had brought him to Mina and why she was now taking him somewhere else.

She told him what her mother had told her about how Nizam had not asked for any part of his father's inheritance and how he relinquished everything to his two brothers. His only request was to retain the right to come visit the house, and so she had brought him for one final trip. He loved to sit on the balcony of their house at night, in the exact spot where his father's heart had stopped beating, not long after his return from Homs when he had been cleared of all the smuggling and conspiracy charges that had been brought against him. She said that her father Mahmoud al-Alami had gotten what he'd wished for too—for the least expense possible—ever since his doctor started raising his glasses above his eyes to examine the lines of his electrocardiogram, after which he would curl his lips and then look out the clinic window, gazing into the distance.

Maysaloun imagined how a sudden bout of sharp pain might have wakened him out of his slumber. No doubt he knew it would be the last, owing to how long he had expected its coming, having asked those who had survived it about the precise location of the source of the pain. He'd sat up straight with his hand on his chest. Perhaps he called to his wife and sons, but his voice had been too faint to wake them up. They didn't discover him until it was already too late, at a quarter to seven when they got up to go to work, awakened by a ship blaring its horn as it prepared to set sail.

She went on and on describing her father's death, driving her pain away with words. Having gotten tired from all the emotion, she rested her face on her hand and looked outside through her dark sunglasses at the village perched at the top of the hill, huddled with its red tiled rooftops, the dome of the church peering from the distance.

Castro drove cautiously at a speed befitting his special cargo. He prolonged being close to her as she gazed at the bottomless valley with its waterfall cascading all the way down to the electric power plant at the base, which Nizam used to like looking at in fear. He would inch his little head up to the window in the new Citroën. On the first trips, the two of them would sit by themselves in the back seat, one on each side. At the beginning of the trip he would insist on sitting on the left—the Qadisha Valley side. He would gesture to Maysaloun to keep quiet and slowly lower the window without the knowledge of his parents who were lost in thought preparing for their first summer vacation. From time to time, his mother would pause from thinking about the houses and getting them in order and counting which of her girlfriends would be spending the summer with her, to take in the view of the mountains and gasp in astonishment at how close they were to the sky, as she would say. Mahmoud would praise the powerful Citroën's ability to traverse the high roads, not regretting for a moment buying it new. Nizam would roll the window down, just halfway, because he was afraid to lower it more than that. He would raise himself up bit by bit to steal a view down into the valley, endeavouring to challenge the deep slopes that were garbed in oak and cypress trees or had been leveled into terraces bordered by white stones. He would immediately get dizzy from fear and excitement, causing him to back away and throw himself into Maysaloun's lap. She would wrap her arms around her frightened brother and hug him to her chest. She would rock him to ease his worries, whisper in his ear, and calm him down, but he refused to open his eyes, as though he had seen something he shouldn't have, or as if he wanted to preserve the view of the holy valley that had stunned him. He wouldn't open his eyes even a crack, fearing some other view might erase it, until he got tired of squeezing his eyes shut and would prop his hands on the leather seat and pull himself gradually to his place beside the window like someone approaching an area of imminent danger. He was drawn to the view of the valley. He'd raise his head up again, take a quick look, get scared and throw himself into her arms all over again . . .

She fell asleep, dozed off for several minutes. Her body went limp after a day of confrontation that wasn't over yet. But then she woke up. She wasn't going to abandon Nizam midway. She sat up straight, wiped her eyes, reached back to touch the wood, to caress it. She turned around and sat up on her knees, trying to reach the casket so she could kiss it. Ever since he was little, she had strived to abide by his wishes, which she always knew and which, if asked, he himself wouldn't know how to describe.

Turned around in the seat that way, she was nearly touching Castro. He lit one cigarette after another, contemplating what he was doing—taking a dead man for a drive. He didn't know if the young woman sitting beside him was of sound mind. He was apprehensive about what was going to happen back in Mina, how they were going to accuse the two of them of stealing Nizam. They clearly saw him take him away. They would have followed him to the cemetery and found no one there. He thought about how he was going to face them the next day when he came in the morning to open the café.

Suddenly the steering wheel felt heavy between his hands, and he started hearing a strange sound. He was pretty sure he had a flat tire. He pulled over to the right and pounded on the steering wheel in frustration.

She tried to help him change the tire. She stood out on the road beside him. There were no cars passing by at that time of day. He had trouble finding the jack. It was the first time this had ever happened to him in the ambulance. He panted as he unscrewed the bolts of the flat tire and nearly passed out from exhaustion as he exerted great effort to put on the spare. He was forced to sit down on the edge of the brook to rest . . . He didn't like the mountains. He never came to these villages unless he had to, like when he would join his mother on a visit to see his aunt who spent two weeks at the Palace Hotel every year, never missing a summer. He would spend the time looking at the clock and watching his mother and his aunt as they took turns puffing on a shared arguileh while catching up on each other's news, complaining of their latest aches and pains, and expressing their delight at the vast view stretched out before them.

Time did not pass there. Hawra slept during the winter season. Some of the townspeople left for Beirut for work or school, and it was said that many of the town's young men took up arms and joined the ranks of the various militias to go fight in the capital. A sufficient number of them who were not suited for street war remained in town to set up a permanent checkpoint at the town's entrance. They took shifts manning it, and no strangers to the area were allowed to enter except in rare cases.

'Volunteer Emergency Services . . .' The short-statured young man read the name out loud. When he asked Castro about his intended destination, he turned him over to Maysaloun, bearer of the secret.

'Hawra . . .' Maysaloun answered in an abrupt manner that did not please the armed guard.

Not much transpired during his shift from noon to eight o'clock at night. He pointed to the back of the ambulance. 'Who do you have with you? A patient?' he asked as if joking with them.

'The son of Touma Abu-Shaheen . . .' answered Maysaloun with the same abruptness.

He pondered a moment and then remembered.

'The Muslim?' he asked. 'Where is he? What's wrong with him?'

She peered into his eyes without saying anything.

The ambulance's tinted windows made it hard to see inside. The young man drew closer and saw the casket. 'We used to call him Nano at school. The teacher adored him . . .'

He was unmoved and unsympathetic, as though death was man's true destiny, as they said in those parts. As if Nizam's return to Hawra—in a casket—was inevitable, fully expected from the start.

He pointed out his colleague on the other side of the road who was stopping the cars exiting the town. 'He is one of Rakheema's relatives.' Then he added, raising his voice, 'It's your cousin . . .'

He didn't quite understand, so he repeated to him that the deceased was Abu Shaheen's son.

'How did he die?'

His question didn't reach anyone, because the armed guard had already motioned for Castro to go through.

The ambulance made its way through the main street of the town, passing the few shops displaying the white blocks of hard goat cheese whose production had started early that year in huge vats out front for passers-by to see. Some old-timers were playing cards at the café. Shaytan was sitting off to the side, watching them and scoffing at their ever-increasing mistakes. They told him to come on over, put some money on the table, and play with them if he was such an expert. He laughed.

He caught sight of Maysaloun.

Her sad face appeared suddenly in the ambulance that was slowly passing by. She had her hand on her cheek as she looked out from behind the car window.

He recognized her despite the dark glasses.

Touma and Rakheema had continued to send Shaytan to the al-Alamis' house in Mina until the war broke out and the residents of Hawra got cut off from Tripoli. Maysaloun used to answer the door when he came, and the moment she'd see him she would sarcastically shout into the house in a tone mimicking the cries of travelling vendors, 'Cherries and plums and farm fresh eggs . . . made by Rakheema.'

He never knew if it made her happy or upset to see him.

He got up from his chair. The card players who were immersed in their game felt that he left abruptly, as if he had suddenly remembered something he had to do, but they didn't stop their game to ask him what was going on. He got in his car, cranked the engine—which cooperated with him by sheer coincidence on the first try—and followed the ambulance. His intuition turned out to be right when he saw the ambulance turn the corner downhill, so he kept following it.

Maybe Touma's health had taken a turn for the worse and now they had to take him to the hospital.

Touma's eyesight had been deteriorating; he had been eating sweets behind Rakheema's back. He would ask Shaytan to buy him some maamoul cookies stuffed with walnuts every time he went down to Beirut.

Shaytan would drop by their house before heading to Beirut, and they'd ask him every time to bring news of Nizam. They would plead with him to look for Nizam, promising to pay him whatever he wanted in return.

On his way out, Touma would wink at him and raise his index finger in the air, gesturing that he wanted one dozen of the maamoul cookies.

He would come back with the cookies, but he never found Nizam.

He didn't like that the al-Alami daughter was tagging along in the ambulance.

He came up behind the ambulance on its way downhill, forming a funeral procession for Nizam.

Castro and Maysaloun stopped in front of the Abu-Shaheens'. Shaytan parked behind them and waited.

There was no one outside. There was no one on the road.

They didn't get out of the car. Castro wanted to know what was going on.

'Did you tell them?'

'No . . .'

Nizam had died without telling her either.

Touma Abu-Shaheen was sitting down, snoring—it was the snore of a light nap. In the afternoons, he would settle for a cup of tea, to which he added a little bit of sugar behind Rakheema's back. His head was bent slightly forward as he listened to al-Ahzab chapter, recited by Sheikh Abd al-Basit Abd al-Samad on the Cairo Channel. He'd taken his medicine and dozed off in the chair.

Touma had retreated inside his house, leaving his enemies to win the battle day after day. The mountain apple tree had withered. Touma hadn't made scarecrows this year, and hail pellets—the late-coming punishment at the beginning of April—had wiped out the almond blossoms. Even the sandalwood worms had nested in the big pine trees on the east side of the orchard, but there was no one to shoot them.

Touma would spend only a couple of hours outside, after lunch. He would turn on his radio and take a seat. And when his arguileh—as Rakheema referred to his snoring—would start, Rakheema would gently nudge him on the shoulders, not to wake him up but to get him to adjust his position so the snoring would stop. More often than not, though, only the tune would change.

Rakheema moved towards the window that overlooked the valley, where the pale daylight still came through. She put on her apron over her light blue dress, and then put on her glasses, her hands trembling, as she challenged herself to mend some clothes or sort out the red beans and pluck the mint leaves in preparation for the next day's dinner. She'd take a break from time to time, sigh, and look at Touma whose head had drooped onto his chest, so that some of his drool trickled down his chin. Theirs was a famous love story once upon a time.

She, too, was about to doze off with Touma's socks in her hands. Sleep could be contagious in the semi-darkness and silence. She heard the rumbling of car engines, specifically an old engine—the sound of the Mercedes taxi. They weren't expecting anyone since no one visited them. She got up from her chair and woke Touma up before looking outside. Startled, he opened his eyes, wiped the drool off his chin, and asked her as he usually did if he was snoring.

'We have visitors', she said. 'Let's go see . . . '

He stood up on his feet slowly, since he'd get dizzy every time he got up and needed a moment to find his balance.

He headed outside before Rakheema.

He might be sick, but he was the man of the house.

He gestured to her from behind his back to hold on, to wait for him inside. There was no need for both of them to appear at the door.

Every visit was a confrontation, with strangers and relatives alike.

The sunlight was still strong outside.

The first thing Touma saw was Castro opening the rear door of the ambulance. He was getting ready to make a delivery.

Touma called out to him, explaining that the clinic was not in the neighbourhood and that it was at the nunnery on the other side of town.

Castro didn't want to hear it. He kept on doing what he was doing, as he opened the other side of the double-door. The casket, which had been lifted onto the stretcher, became visible from the back.

Touma didn't see the casket as he walked to the front of the ambulance.

Maysaloun didn't move, hoping to delay looking into the couple's eyes.

She hadn't even seen her own mother yet.

When Touma approached the window, Maysaloun rolled the glass down. He started telling her what he'd told Castro—that they were in the wrong place and the clinic was far from here . . . They were now face-to-face. She took off her glasses, and he suddenly recognized her. He was tongue-tied.

Rakheema's curiosity was piqued since she hadn't heard any response to Touma's explanations to Castro. She took a quick look out the door but didn't find Touma. She checked what she was wearing, took off her house apron, went out and stood on the porch.

Shaytan was leaning on the door of his car, waiting to see what was about to happen.

He saw Rakheema.

Castro was standing next to the open door, as he persevered at his new job as driver.

Maysaloun grabbed Touma's hands, which he had rested on the passenger door.

Her eyes were red.

Shaytan realized that the whole picture would become clear in Rakheema's mind before it did for the poor-sighted Touma. For one moment, he thought about taking a few steps forward in order to stand between Rakheema and the ambulance— shielding the casket with his body from her view.

Rakheema's eyes darted around as she opened her mouth, thinking.

As the sun was about to set, its light became golden and was reflected through one of the glass windows of the summer head- quarters of the Maronite Patriarchate on the edge of the valley— it was reflected in the eyes of the owner of the Mina café, who had to close them as he stood firm.

No one budged. No one spoke.

The sound of the water from the irrigation canal that ran near Touma's orchard could be heard.

Maysaloun wept calmly.

Touma put his hand on her head, consoling her.

He still didn't know why she was crying. He tried asking her gently.

Rakheema saw Shaytan.

He had not gone down to Beirut. He was standing in front of their house, but he wasn't coming in.

She saw Castro standing, waiting. She didn't know him.

She saw the casket with its glossy light-brown wood.

Her heart dropped.

She turned her head in all directions pleading for help.

She saw one of the villagers in khaki clothes—farm clothes—with a shovel on his shoulders approaching the ambulance, his eyes filled with questions.

One of the neighbours headed towards the ambulance, his wife tagging behind him. They seemed certain that something serious was going on.

They were almost running.

The man who was on his way back from watering his land took off the cork hat that protected him from the sun.

He held the hat in his left hand. He made the sign of the cross with his right.

Touma backed away to give Maysaloun some room to open the door and step out of the car.

Rakheema saw Maysaloun.

She saw her face.

She saw the casket.

She saw an angel with red cheeks flapping his wings on the ceiling of the church on the Feast of the Assumption.

She tried to hold on to the door with her left hand.

Her knees buckled. Her hand slid down the side of the door. She dropped to the ground, her eyes empty.

Her sky-blue dress spread around her. For someone looking from above, she looked like a big, artificial rose that had suddenly opened up in the bright light of sunset.

Shaytan—who had been getting ready to rescue her the moment her eyes had started darting back and forth—rushed to her side.

Touma turned and found her huddled on the porch. He looked around. From where he was standing at Maysaloun's door, he couldn't see the casket.

He walked towards Rakheema. Maysaloun followed him. The villager returning from his land got to Touma, and he and the other man grabbed him by the arms. Two or three steps later, they started to drag Touma as the top of his shoes dug two furrows in the dirt.

The rest happened at night.

Between Touma and Rakheema and Maysaloun and Castro.

Feeling unwanted, the town's residents had left, and the news spread. When others showed up in the evening and knocked at the door, they heard Touma's voice from inside telling them that they didn't need any help or consolation from anybody. They didn't open the door, not even to Father Gabriel who was able to confirm that Nizam had been baptised at the hands of Maydoun's parish priest. They kept the door locked in the face of all visitors. Touma even pointed his shotgun—the one he used to shoot and destroy the moles with—in the face of someone who had insisted on knocking at the door repeatedly and didn't comply with the orders Touma had barked out from the inside.

Some nosy people who had been eavesdropping heard Touma's moaning.

'Rakheema, how did we end up with him?' he asked. 'Our life was simple. Either I was going to die before you, or you were going to die before me, and that would be it . . . '

People stayed away from them, and the stories abounded.

It was said that his sister had brought him to Touma and Rakheema so they could say their final goodbyes before burying him, that he was shrouded from head to toe in the Islamic tradition, and that his two aunts had insisted on burying him with his family at the cemetery in Tripoli. The two armed men at the checkpoint said that they had seen an ambulance leaving Hawra at ten o'clock at night and that his sister was resting her head on the arm of the driver, who was driving with one hand, his other arm wrapped around her. Rakheema's relative at the checkpoint insisted that he saw the casket in the back of the vehicle—going back with the two of them to where it had come from.

Others insist—and they are probably right—that they buried him there in the orchard and that Touma, despite his age and illness, dug a big hole for Nizam with his own hands, but that Rakheema couldn't help him lower Nizam' body into it. He accomplished the mission all by himself, almost passing out several times from exhaustion, until he finally covered the body with earth and smoothed the surface over. It was said that that was the condition that Nizam's sister had put on Touma and Rakheema—that they could bury him at their place as long as they followed the proper Islamic customs, burying him without putting any grave marker, a cross, or any other sign. Only they would know where he was and wouldn't tell anyone else. The proof that

Nizam is buried here in the orchard is the renewed care with which Touma tended to the trees and flowers, as he pruned and sprayed and watered them. He wouldn't let anyone enter the orchard except for one labourer at a time—a stranger from outside the village who would occasionally help him keep the orchard suitable for Nizam's stay in it. People say that Rakheema is no longer of sound mind, for she still prepares provisions for Nizam—saying that he likes *this* or he doesn't like *that*—and that she puts them all together to send to Beirut at times and to Tripoli at others. They say that Touma spends his free time listening to the Quran, that he won't stop eating maamoul, and that when his stash runs out, he shovels sugar into his mouth. One of the boys who has tried to catch a glimpse of the goings-on at the orchard says that there's a small space between the mulberry tree and the luxuriant damask roses where lost fireflies gather in swarms as if getting together for a rendezvous on hot summer nights.